# SONGS OF WATER

Print ISBN:979-8-9877779-0-9

 ePub ISBN: 979-8-9877779-1-6

contact: writefullyyoursperformance@gmail.com

# SONGS OF WATER

*A SOUTHERN NOVEL OF MOSAIC MYTHS AND MEMORIES*

JOVELYN D. RICHARDS

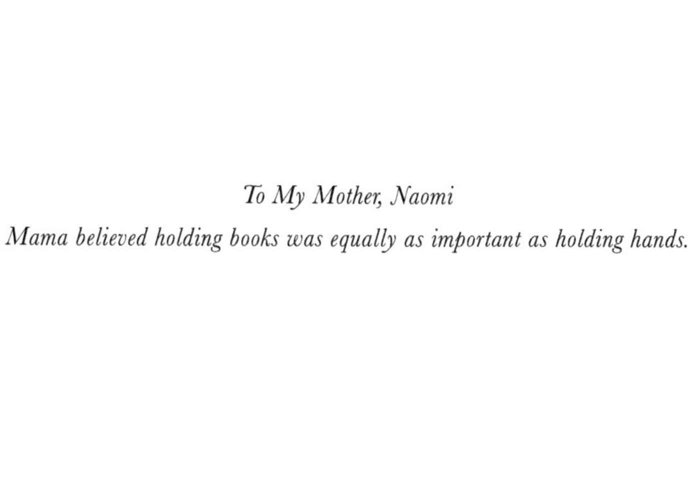

*To My Mother, Naomi*
*Mama believed holding books was equally as important as holding hands.*

*Yesterday at dawn,*
*A calling within us was rising*
*By dusk, we smelt fresh rain arriving.*
*Accordingly, we stuck out our tongues.*
*Eager to taste the joyful tears of God's Universe*

# O N E

In 1870 Sister Elizabeth sat statue-like in the Negro section of the steam train, praying on her rosary. A small boy watched and counted under his breath each time a bead passed through her narrow fingers. He wondered what the funny-looking lady was whispering to herself. She was dressed in black and white layers, from her head to her shoes. In the center, embroidered on her uniform, was a cross. A peculiar stiff covering with wings and a small opening revealing her pale face engulfed her head, which sparked his imagination. It appeared to the child like a giant bird had swallowed her. He leaned forward just a bit, not to be noticed to see what she was whispering. Was she praying for someone to free her from the bird? He put his hands together and prayed for her to be freed.

He liked the funny-looking lady the moment she stumbled into him. When Sister Elizabeth entered the train, she accidentally bumped into an old man and the boy. She said, "Please forgive me," first to the man and then to him before his mother helped her settle. No grown-up ever asked for his forgiveness. Did only people living in birds talk like that to children?

He was smart enough to know better than to ask his mama or daddy about grown folks' business. It was his second time on the train. The first was to visit his grandmother in Ohio, and now he was going home to Springfield, Arkansas. He wondered how folks could be so mean with a town named Springfield that others spoke anxiously about leaving. He could count to twenty and back again.

At one of the stops, the train conductor walked with authority to the section where Negroes sat mixed among the cargo and large crates of piglets on the floor covered in hay. He stopped and inspected the area; his face turned bright red when he spotted the nun. The conductor scrutinized her as closely as he felt was appropriate; he was mortified by the misstep of her being seated here among Negroes. As head conductor, he could be fired for this violation.

He cleared his throat and contemplated if this was one of those religious abolitionists that intruded on the South to rebuild and teach Negro children and poor whites. Had she willfully found her way to the cargo section? Either way, he had to right this oversight. "Sister, I apologize for the mistake. This is the cart for supplies and Negroes. Please come with me." He reached his arm out to lift her off the hay. "We are in the last hour of daylight and about to reach bad weather; I must get you settled in."

Her fingers became motionless. Sister Elizabeth turned in the direction of his voice with her head tilted slightly. The Negro boy was not as anxious as his mother and father at the interaction of the white man and the funny-dressed woman. But he stopped counting. He was curious why the woman was not looking directly at the conductor.

"Oh no, I'm fine, sir. I'm very comfortable right here." Her tone was firm. The conductor sharply withdrew his hand. The child thought she did not sound like any grown-up he'd heard before, black or white. Her firmness did not hide the music of those few words. He said them in his head, letting the words bounce. *Oh no, I'm fine, sir.*

He felt his mother's body shift ever so slightly, tightening up. His father took his hand and reached across to his wife with his other hand. The boy sat between them. The others in the colored section, as did his mother, father, and the boy, dropped their heads. And like the others, the family watched from their side vision.

They knew what the white man did not. The funny-dressed woman was a Negro. In the moments that passed, the conductor stood fidgeting with his pocket watch, looking at the time, and grunting his displeasure. Sister Elizabeth went back to her rosary, this time above a whisper. "Hail Mary full of Grace, the Lord is with thee. Blessed are thou among women…"

The boy listened intently to the song-like words while she finished, and then she began another. "Our Father who art in Heaven…"

The conductor stood defiantly against her prayers and interrupted her using his full authority. "Ma'am, I can't let a white woman of any religious understanding sit with Negroes. His breathing was heavy, "and certainly Negro men. It's dangerous for you and against the law. Ma'am, you have crossed the last northern Stateline." The conductor lifted his chin and pulled his shoulders back with pride. "You good Sister is in the South!" The air was immediately charged with anxiety. The Negroe's collective breathing was not heard in the utter silence following his words. The little boy felt the message tucked into the squeeze of his father's palm. It hurt, but he made no sound. The silence stretched on until the train's rumbling made itself apparent.

Finally, Sister Elizabeth spoke. "Sir, whatever lines I cross, I am a Negro."

The conductor's head snapped back indignantly. "Whatcha say?" He cupped his hand over his ear.

"I am a Negro," she repeated. The conductor's body jolted forward, eyeballing her face as if he would a shop window of unusual goods. For a moment, he was distracted by her odd, distant stare. *A Negro! Impossible.* He watched her dark pupils move back and forth within her slow, blinking eyes. *Something's wrong with her.* He turned his attention to the bowed heads of the passengers and took in the different ways their faces reflected their Negroid colors. Autumn, he thought. They were a variety of Midwestern autumns He was witnessing all hues of color upon their bowed faces, something he'd never noticed. One after the other, he gazed upon in the fading light of day, occasionally back to Sister Elizabeth. Shocked! The conductor immediately chastised himself for comparing Negroes to something as lovely as his favorite season. He looked back at the strange woman and lifted his right hand. He wanted to compare the flesh of her face to his own. The conductor found no satisfaction in her declaration of being a Negro or the intense pressure of confusion that was turning into a headache.

He abruptly turned and left, loudly cursing with every step. The rosary beads in Sister Elizabeth's fingers began to move. The little boy smiled and started counting again under his breath, "One, two, three, four."

Hours later, they arrived in Springfield. The white passengers were escorted from the train. Finally, the cargo door swung open. It was another conductor who came to the rear cargo area and pulled back the side door so the Negroes could climb down into a dark, wet night. The new conductor guided the funny-dressed woman to the covered platform out of the rain. He left her there. He was the one who had taken her ticket and watched how she went stumbling among the quiet voices of the Negroe's to the back cart. He also knew she was a Negro.

"You'se got somebody picking you up, ma'am?" the mother of the boy who had come to the platform's edge asked. Her voice was kind and warm. Sister Elizabeth did not know if her ride would come, given that she was three days off her journey. The heavy rain hitting the roof of the platform worried her.

"I think someone will come gather me—a man named Hargrove. I'll ask to go inside the station if no one comes soon. Thank you." Her words were polite, but her tone was concerned. She knelt to be closer to the woman. "Take your family home. I'll be fine."

"Yes, ma'am, I'm glad you'se understand." The woman reached out her hand, taking hold of Sister Elizabeth. "You'se best heed what dat conductor say to you'se. Now he knows you'se a Negro ain't gone matter if you'se a servant of God. You'se say Mr. Hargrove is coming for you. We know of him. He'll do right by you." She kissed the back of Sister's hand.  Not recollecting affection for years, the gesture startled Sister Elizabeth; she reluctantly pulled her hand back. "May I give your little boy something?"  But she was already going under the layers of outer clothing into the deep pockets. She pulled out a small, wrapped box of assorted candies and held it out. "It's different, sweets. What's his name?"

"Named after his daddy, Samuel, we call him little Sam."

"Good name, from the Old Testament, Samuel was a great man of faith, seems fitting.

I felt that in your child.  Tell little Sam I enjoyed his company and hope he enjoys the candy,"

"I'se thank you'se for my child. Well, I'se best git along now." With that, the woman turned and walked toward the moon, sitting over the mountain. She turned once over her shoulder. "You'se be careful, ma'am, dere's a lot of awful mean folks down here,"

"God bless us all," Sister Elizabeth replied.  She raised her hand and kissed the exact place the woman's soft lips touched.

She stood listening to the rain and the last wagons pulling away. "Jesus, you have brought me this far on my journey; keep me the rest of my way so that I might find the woman Evening."  What would she do if no one came to fetch her? Taking the train back to Ohio was her only choice. The thought of a solution was easy enough but did not comfort her. She did not want to fail her mission. Sister Elizabeth had not been outside the convent since being brought there as a young child. She knew nothing of the world outside the walls of the church grounds, indeed, the south. What Sister Elizabeth heard in the conductor's tone and voice concerned her, but what she felt in the Negros energy when the conductor entered was more worrisome.

Hargrove arrived just a few moments later to a lone figure standing on the platform. His anger had kept him company most of the way, the weather was God-awful. His knees agreed. The nun woman was three days late. Each night, he had come to the station to wait for her. He was past anticipation—he was frustrated.

Sister Elizabeth stood alone under the gas lamps on the platform. Hargrove was taken aback. Whatever she wore was bellowing wide as a ship sail, and next to her was a suitcase more suited for a child. From the station window, he saw Guston Matthews, who ran the station, and his attendants staring at her from the lit window. When they spotted his buggy, they quickly moved away. Hargrove was glad they had been decent enough to keep the lamps lit outside the station, knowing how inconsiderate they could be. But why was she outside on a night like this and not in the station keeping warm?

*So, this is what a nun looks like,* he thought. Not much of her face was visible, but from what he could see, she was nearly as pale as the moonlight. He pulled the buggy close to the station and rushed to the platform.

"I suspect by your clothing, you'se, Sister Elizabeth. You finally got here!"

Sister Elizabeth listened to the harshness of his tone. She thought *he must be an honest man not to hide his frustration.* "And you would be Mr. Hargrove, correct?" Hargrove wondered at the odd way she held her head tilted up away from his direction as if she were pushing her chin up towards the moonlight. *Bet that neck thing she got on hurt,* he figured.

"Yep, but no time for formalities in this weather." He took her elbow in a gentlemanly fashion. I'm here to fetch you up." He scooped up her suitcase. "Unfortunately, you got to ride beside me in my two-seated buggy." It was the largest of Hargrove's buggies with a customized heavier folding top; despite its size, it had sped.

"It'll suit me just fine; thank you for coming." Hargrove held tighter to her arm, keeping her from slipping and moving too far away from him; it seemed she was pulling in the other direction towards the horses. "You'se alright, Sister Elizabeth?" She didn't answer. He softened his grip, thinking if nuns married Jesus, his touch might be offensive. *If I had my carriage and the weather acted right, we wouldn't be fighting to go a few feet she could manage.*

"Wheels on both my carriages broke this week would have been more comfortable for this ride. I have been here every night to fetch you in one or the other."

"I'm so very sorry. I had no way of contacting you." The wind was slapping and drowning out her words. "Something happened…be…and delayed…my eyes."

Hargrove was being as careful as possible when hoisting up her, and it didn't help that she seemed to resist his assistance. Was she mad seeing it was a two-seater buggy? "Well, my carriages were fine. Then, suddenly, this morning, both broke down. Give me no other choice but my buggy." Once seated, he handed Sister Elizabeth a large cotton-oiled garment to help repel any rain through the top and another blanket over her head. He placed the suitcase behind his seat and hoisted himself up.

Hargrove got settled and turned his frustration away from Sister Elizabeth's delay to the weather. He chastised the weather under his breath as they began the journey to Culver Tusk. They were driving straight into the wind. It would be a long while before they reached the turn, and then the wind and rain would push against the back seat. Hargrove wondered if his carriages had broken on their own or if someone had done the deed out of spite. The mayor, or at least his office, was aware of the telegram. Hargrove had felt uneasy reading the last sentence, something ominous in the words, "They know about the message the nun is bringing, but I know more." It was signed by a clerk named Jed. Had "they" been responsible for his carriages? He finally spoke, making sure she heard nothing but kindness in his voice. "You'se sure you, comfortable?

"Yes, sir. This is a beautiful part of the country. I can feel the grass, the flowers, the trees, the dirt…Even the rain feels different in this part of the country. It's beautiful."

"Beautiful, what can you'se see in the dark about beauty?" he asked. "I can barely see the horses pulling us."

"The story of belonging tells me it's beautiful, even in darkness." Hargrove didn't know; besides, he was listening to try and figure out the speed they were traveling by the wind's sound. Rain wouldn't let him. The steady clopping of his horses told him they were at a safe pace, given the weather they were traveling in. The horses were neighing, letting each other know what was next. Hargrove went back to his conversation.

"That right."

"All living things have energy that helps shape themselves in your imagination. Plant life energy is a thousand times smaller than dust particles. Most folks only see plant life for its beauty or usefulness with their eyes. People can be spiritually shortsighted." She laughed. "I made myself laugh shortsighted."

"How so?"

"I'm blind."

"Whatcha means, blind?"

"My eyesight is gone." She quickly added before he could ask another question, "Shadows or shapes on good days."

"Well, that doesn't make sense." Hargrove figured she was trying to say something to keep company or make light of being in the dark and pouring rain.

"I can feel, see, and hear nature's beauty, which gives me another kind of sight. I see and feel what most people can't see in darkness."

"Feel… see?"

"Yes. How a flower feels, or the rain, people, feelings tell me how it looks spiritually. Different than its physical appearance."

"Hmmm." was the most Hargrove could answer.

"What do you think the horses talk about in the dark? What's in front of them beneath them? They feel and listen for direction and trust nature more than your hands on the reigns."

Hargrove did not say to her what he was thinking. She sounded as wild-minded as the women of Culver Tusk. "*Ya'll get along just fine*," he thought.

"Like now you think I'm being whimsical, Mr. Hargrove; your lips are tight. Am I right?"

Hargrove relaxed his mouth. He wondered if she sensed he was looking in her direction. "You didn't get on the buggy like you blind. You barely let me help you! You'se lying to me?" Then he caught himself and added, "I'm sorry; I can't believe that came out of my mouth. Ain't no need to doubt you; I sound like my Lena; she doesn't take kindly to dishonesty. Sister Elizabeth, I don't know where my manners are; this situation got my mind confused."

He got frank with her. "You'se the first nun I met. The telegram said you a Negro, but looking at you, I'se can't tell. Now you tell me you are blind. Telegram says you are coming to see Evening about her father, a woman you have never met! I'm struggling with what you might know about Evening's father! News of what kind? That got you traveling without sight from up North to the South, of all places, makes no sense to me." He thought, *"You'se got the same senses as the horses?* Hargrove wondered why he reacted harshly. Since she hadn't responded, and out of his discomfort with her silence, Hargrove asked another question despite feeling uneasy: "You'se come in the world blind?"

"No. No…I was about two, maybe three, but I did come into the world a Negro, even if my skin doesn't reveal it. I can assure you I am. In the first years of my life, I could see. Those images fade each year. But come to me in my dreams, shattered and scattered, in grace I attempt

to gather. To this day, remembering the last thing I remember has become a daily chore I can't recall with clarity.

Like life, it all fades away. I woke up, and my sight was gone." She smiled at her own words, which made her heart warm. She repeated them, "Remembering the last thing I remembered."

Hargrove heard her but knew she was talking to herself. "That sounds like words of philosophy. Like something God might ask you. What is the last thing you remember about your life, and you're just sorting through memories because it all fades so quickly?" Hargrove was confident he'd be able to offer his one memory with certainty. He woke up and went to bed with the same memory. It always left him with one question: Why? Maybe God had an answer.

*Something tells me this man knows something more than other men, even the priest I've encountered. I wonder what?* she questioned. *He has a good soul, yet his soul conflicts with this life; Sister Elizabeth had attended many sick and dying men of influence,* including those within the church. Each had an impenetrable wall within which they could not access. Sister Elizabeth didn't bother Hargrove with her curiosity for his words. "My Lena," he mentioned. She felt his longing in her name as sure as the rain falling on her face. She let it be. Sister Elizabeth took her thoughts to what Hargrove knew of Evening's father. Sister Elizabeth hoped it was less of a heartbreaking story than what she knew. The urge to ask Hargrove details of Evening tore at her, and she denied her urge. She could not explain to this man, nor herself, the desperate yearning her soul cried to find out as much she could of this woman Evening from the woman herself.

"My mother did not know when I lost my sight. It bothered her, I imagine, till the day she died. Mother said I was always a quiet baby. I started walking fine, playing, and learning to eat by myself.

"One day, Mother said she noticed that if I got ahold of something, I wouldn't let it go. Mother said I sat for hours touching whatever I had got hold of. Moving it around in my hands, smelling and kissing whatever it was: a plate, cup, shoe, blanket. It kept me busy."

"Kissing on a shoe didn't seem odd to your folks?"

"You ever work in the field from dawn to dusk, Mr. Hargrove? A baby playing with a shoe ain't gon' worry you. Besides, I wouldn't be surprised if they only had one shoe and were waiting for another to make a match, seeing nobody asked for it back." She laughed. "One shoe might as well be a toy until da other show up."

"I can hear a mixture of accents in your voice when you speak about your family. Born in the South, huh? Otherwise, you sound northern?"

"Yes, sir, and you're right. On rare occasions, I speak of my family; my heart finds a home in their speech, so I reckon you'se hear me right," she teased. "I notice you've mixed your you with you'se at times. Why's that?" That gave Hargrove a hearty laugh while he considered his answer. "I never noticed, but I guess my formal education and private tutors sneak in and disrupt my Southern nature."

Sister Elizabeth took a liking to Hargrove. "I was born in the South and have never been back until now." He closed his eyes briefly to see if he could sense Sister Elizabeth's feelings. He couldn't.

The rain slowed to a drizzle, making their challenging journey less distracting. Hargrove wanted to concentrate on Sister Elizabeth's story, not rain. Rain, he thought, I can get any time. "What let on to them something was wrong?"

"Mother said. I started eating with my hands, not walking as much, getting the food all over my face in my hair. She was expecting another baby. My grandmother said I was trying to crawl back inside my mother's womb to show my feeling of losing my spot as a baby. Funny how I remember their conversations almost word for word."

Hargrove looked up into the dark sky, opened his mouth, and let the rain in before continuing. The rain was cold and sweet, soothing to his tongue. "And then what?" His body had weakened when the image of a small child with her hair and face covered with food came into his mind and weakened even more, imagining a child wanting to go back into her mother's womb for safety. Sister Elizabeth fought to ask him what had taken him from the conversation. What memory weakened his voice? Her service to God did not allow anyone to be a stranger to her, and she wanted to ask him but knew sometimes silence was the answer.

She continued. "Mother started feeding me. When her breast milk came in, she let me suckle. The taste is still with me. That memory hasn't faded, thank God. You know breast milk is nothing like cow milk?" She felt Hargrove straighten in his seat and pull the reins. "I'm sorry; I didn't mean to embarrass you with such an intimate question." She rushed on. "My sister's name is Cassandra. We called her Casey. Since the time she was born, I was the only one who could hold her when she cried to make her stop. And Lord, she was a crier. My grandmother said over and over, 'She gon' have a beautiful voice for singing, but you'se gotta git ugly to sing.'"

"What does that mean?"

"It means you feel and express the world's pain in the songs, but you must tell the truth about the ugliness of that pain."

"Did she grow up and sing?"

"I don't know. They sent me to the convent orphanage—or the man who owned me did. My daddy was my daddy, but the plantation owner owned me." They listened to the rain talk and the horse's steps for a while. "Before they found out and I was sent away, I spent my days sitting on the floor holding my sister. I brought her great comfort; nobody else could."

Hargrove listened, thinking how comforting it must have been to Sister Elizabeth, much better than a shoe.

"How long before we get there, Mr. Hargrove?" Hargrove realized he should have asked if she used the outhouse at the station. He had no idea what he would do if she had to relieve herself; with the weather and the road so wet and she blind, he'd have to help her manage herself.

"Unfortunately, we'se still got a way to go. You'se all, right?"

"Yes, I'll be fine."

"Mother used to tell the story that I'd touch sister's face, play in her hair, kiss her, put her toes in my mouth—smelled her all day. I could tell them when she had to let go of her bowels. I'd call out, 'Sister boo-boo,' and sure enough, they put her on the pot, and she'd let go. Casey had no real need to wear rags between her legs."

Hargrove tilted his head back and laughed, enjoying the light snow mixed with rain that fell into his mouth. "I could see how that would comfort a baby, but how did they find out you lost sight?"

"Daddy made me a ball of inflated pig bladder he heated in the ashes. I sat and held on to it, like everything else, while Casey napped. One day, my daddy took the ball and threw it. Said, 'Go git the ball, baby.' Mother said, I stood up, and he repeated, 'Go git the ball, baby.' I turned around in circles like his words slapped me into a spin. I stopped spinning, tilted my head, and cried. It's right here.' Daddy's voice was firm; thinking back now, I imagine it was his disbelief. He repeated. Mother said I got stiff as a cypress tree until my father called me, 'Come here, daughter. There was more compassion in his words. I followed his voice; he moved, and I walked into the wall. He moved again; I went into the wall. My mother cried out to Jesus. My grandmother grabbed me. The grip of her hands on my shoulders warned me of my fate. Daddy took off and fetched the healer, Miss Lucy. She took me from my grandmother and laid me on the cot. I smelt herbs and sweet tobacco from her pipe. *Open you'se eyes wide, child.* She blew her pipe smoke in my eyes three times. Miss Lucy told my family, "This child is nearly blind to the world. This be best for now."

"Best for now… what does that mean?

"Miss Lucy said there was no way I could be useful in the field without my eyes. I'd never know the harness in the fields." Sister Elizabeth took a deep breath. "A ball, that's how they found out." Hargrove tried to picture what that must have been like: the chaos and pain of seeing your child walk into walls and find out she is blind.

"After that, I was seen as a burden to the man who owned us; he made that clear. Mother crying and praying over me, protecting me from everything familiar. Worse was, I couldn't hold my Casey anymore. She would be crying for me." Sister Elizabeth laughed, but Hargrove heard the grief. "If not for that ball, I might have gotten more time holding my sister. Casey seemed to look out for me when she was two years old. That wasn't right for either one of us. Confused the first love we knew for one another."

"Hmmm, she touched your face?"

"No." She smiled at the possibility of knowing the touch of her sister's hand on her face. "I guess because she could see my face."

"Ain't no reason not to touch it. I always believed faces you love should be touched." Hargrove heard the longing in his words. He was thinking affectionally of the negress Lena, safe for now living behind the walls of Culver Tusk plantation.

"You might be right; no one has touched my face lovely since my people." Sister Elizabeth sighed. They both went silent for a good while; the horses' hooves talked, and the night wind and rain. "A couple years go by, and Mother and Father were told I had to go to the convent for orphans up North. An unusual kindness is what I was told."

Indeed, it was unheard of, Hargrove thought, but he didn't want to add questions to the questionable events unfolding. Instead, he sought comfort in the rain on his face. He could appreciate it now, and she had been right; each raindrop did fall in its way, different.

"We almost to Culver Tusk. I won't be going in with you. The women are full of love and laughter." The lump that rose in Hargrove's throat didn't allow him to continue for the moment. If this woman could feel like she said, she'd feel how much he wanted to go in the house. Hargrove stared ahead; the lantern's light fell upon his horses' glistening backsides. He swallowed a lump of pain. "They'll make the introduction to Evening. The only way to get to Evening is through the women." Sister Elizabeth took a chance.

"Is the woman you speak affectionately of, Lena, there?" Her question caused him to shift abruptly, causing the seat beneath them both to move.

"How you know…"

"You mentioned her name briefly in our conversation."

"Yes, Lena, it's hard to explain, but you'll soon understand how that house is run. I've never seen anything like it before. Trust me when I say you'll be well cared for."

"Mr. Hargrove, I have a difficult question for you, if you don't mind."

Hargrove tightened his hands on the reins. It seemed only fair; whatever she might ask would be fine. "Ask me."

"I mentioned my father was my daddy, but the plantation owner owned me. "

"What part of the South?"

"Louisiana, born on the same plantation my mama and daddy were."

"Whatcha know about the South and the war? Hargrove tightened his grip, waiting for her to tell him she had been warned of the violence erupting against blacks, including the ones on his land. This was not the time, if any, to be traveling. Maybe they figured she passed for white and was safe. She'd deliver the message and get her back on the train. 'So, what do you know?"

"I know very little about the South after five years of age." Hargrove's heart sank. "The convent allowed messages from my family on my birthday until I turned twelve. Mother superior stopped all communication when my body started to change. The last message was my mother died the day before my birthday."

"That's an awful thing to do to a child."

"I can't speak to the awfulness of the circumstances that would settle your thoughts, Mr. Hargrove, but by then, I knew my life was devoted to Jesus. A part of that is giving up attachments. Mother Superior thought it was time to begin my journey of commitment; the church was my family. I cried over my mother and prayed for her soul to be at peace. I do not know anything about the rest of my family. They are always in my prayers. I confess I pray some miracle of God brings me news of Cassey. If I could touch her face, see how much she has changed." Sister Elizabeth broke with those words and cried with anguish. *My dear Casey.* Hargrove felt his own eyes burn with tears. How God, how! How can I drive this saintly woman into what might become a living hell? I got Lena and the others to protect from the Confederates. Hargrove tears streamed down into his beard.

Sister Elizabeth hadn't answered what she knew about the aftermath of the war. If she'd had said Negro's were freed with any level of foolish certainty, Hargrove might not be able to sit upright on the buggy but fall over onto the road leading to Culver Tusk. He certainly would not have time to educate her on the cost of freedom.

The urge to turn the buggy around threatened to overtake him. To hell with it! I should insist Sister Elizabeth tells me the news and take her away from the south. Whatever news she had for Evening, indeed, he could deliver. What kind of Mother Superior would let this woman travel this distance to the South without a companion's guide? Sister Elizabeth was blind in more ways than she could imagine. Hargrove tugged at the inside rein to prepare the horses for the turn. Sister Elizabeth said with determination as if she had read his thoughts.

"Mr. Hargrove, I don't know the South as you certainly do. What I can tell you is this. People who meet me see me as white, even the other sisters in my order. Only my superiors were aware; the white man who told me the stories of Evening's father thought I was white. Otherwise, he never would have spoken one word to me. I learned much about the South because of his blindness to my race." Hargrove redirected the horse back to their destiny.

"I learned riding on the train among Negroes and cargo; the conductor thought I was white until he knew otherwise. Both white men awakened something in me, crying out to be released, my identity. No matter the stories of the South, I will understand it, not what anyone perceives me to be, but from what I am, Mr. Hargrove, I am a Negro!"

Twice in one night, Sister Elizabeth could speak firmly about her identity. The temperature of her body rose abruptly, forcing her to pull apart the outer blankets. She welcomed the wet, cool air with a smile. She allowed the blanket to fall away, so there was nothing between herself and God's rain. "I will have it no other way!" Hargrove took a minute to let her words sit with him. "Your question for me, Sister Elizabeth?"

"Did you…your family own Negroes?" Hargrove had suspected that would be the question but was not prepared for the pain that contracted his heart. He felt as he always did around talk of slavery broken. "Yes. Including my Lena."

Hargrove turned the buggy down the final stretch of their journey. In the distance, he saw the lights of Culver Tusk. Hargrove stopped the buggy to light a third lantern on the carriage and add another cowbell to call out their arrival. All set, they started the final minutes on the road to Culver Tusk. If he'd known of Sister Elizabeth's blindness, Hargrove would've gone to Ohio and fetched this sweet soul. On the train, he'd have answered her question, "Did your family own slaves." The ride from Ohio to Springfield would have allowed him to go back over his family history, the years of lies, deception, and murder. He would try to explain why the Confederate families of Springfield were determined to kill five Negro women living in one of the wealthiest plantations of Springfield, Culver Tusk. Their freedom had led the Confederate families to believe they had been cursed with witchcraft. Hargrove had his own belief with roots in certainty. Hargrove knew he'd keep the five women safe, now six, with the arrival of Sister Elizabeth, seven with Evening. Or die trying.

# T W O

1863-Bailey, the taller of the two Negroes leading the horses, saw the beginning hue of the night rolling down the Ozark Mountains and wondered if the horses, like him, yearned to break away and run to receive the freedom in darkness. Bailey figured God came up with darkness so folks could listen to what their eyes couldn't tell them and trust their hearts to guide them. The world as he knew it disappeared into darkness when he closed his eyes at night.

The horse's thick mane brushed the backside of his swollen hand holding the harness. Bailey took that as a yes; the horse yearned for freedom. The overseer, Thomas, was seated atop the carriage, guiding the reins. He was alone in the cool air, with a rifle across his lap and a pistol in his shoulder holster. To Thomas, the sky offered nothing but the haunting uncertainty of darkness. As the long miles of their destination lessened, the overseer took up his rifle and shot into the air occasionally. It was the only form of communication he allowed the Negroes. They ran steadily on the road leading to Culver Tusk.

For the past two years, Thomas had been the primary overseer of Springfield's most extensive plantations: Grove, named after the deceased owner, and the more recently built Culver Tusk. The number of runaway Negroe's following the death of their original owner had brought Thomas to Grove Plantation to ensure the number of running decreased. There was no love lost between Thomas and the new owner, as their relationship was a contractual agreement that led back to England by Grove's widow. Now, it was coming to an end.

Thomas felt disdain toward men of wealth and power, even though he desired to be such a man. His boss was not a man of natural authority and leaned toward the pleasure that wealth offered. Thomas had decided those who inherited wealth might as well wear dusting powder and rouge on their faces. He amused himself thinking how many men of wealth, upon taking off their trousers, wore a hoop skirt or lace garments beneath them. His boss is often at the core of these self-indulging thoughts.

H.G., his boss, had only become the owner of the plantations following his older brother's supposed hunting accident. Thomas thought this twist of the truth was yet another allowance offered to the wealthy. He knew it was murder. What else do you call it when a son deliberately points a shotgun at his father and pulls the trigger? Thomas had never met the deceased but suspected, from the story, that he'd had more in common with H.G.'s brother, who reigned with a heavy hand over his plantation.

Thomas took a moment and fired it into the air. His eyebrows arched as he waited for the shot's sound to fade. The echo and the smell of gunpowder reached him within seconds of each other. He smiled with satisfaction and then returned to put his thoughts on his future.

He had asked his boss to forgo half his salary for land, and H.G. had agreed. At the end of the contract, Thomas would have ownership of twelve negroes and twenty acres of land on which he'd build his future in America. Thomas took immense pride in knowing he would be a landowner. He felt confident he'd one day be as rich as or more prosperous than H.G. He already knew the mistress he wanted to reign over his future plantation: Miss Sarah. He could only say Sarah's name in secrecy, for if Thomas's desire for Sarah was known, he could lose everything, maybe his life. Sarah was the true meaning of a southern bell: beautiful, trained with impeccable manners, daughter of wealth, submissive to her father's affection, and loyal to her family. Thomas had only spoken of Sarah briefly to his younger brother, Robert. "Robert Sarah is as beautiful as our Princess Alice back home." Sarah will be my wife.

Thomas spat thick, savory, spiced tobacco from his mouth into the night air. Sarah was the closest thing to desire; besides money, his heart had ever known. He felt his manhood awakened as her image gathered itself in his mind; her pouting, red-painted mouth took away any other thoughts. The first time Sarah had caught his eye, he noticed that while she blushed, despite her fine upbringing, she had not turned her head away in proper Southern fashion compared to other girls her age. He'd smiled hungrily and let his eyes linger on her. How could her father treat her like a small child when she was blossoming into a woman? At that moment, his intention was deliberate and precise, as he'd refused to let his eyes turn away, even when her blush covered her entire face, down to her bosom. Sarah, clearly embarrassed, could not resist his gaze. Like every woman in his presence, she, too, fell under the spell of his emerald eyes. Thomas remembered her fingers had fidgeted seductively with the lace of her dress. Sarah took a deep breath and slowly exhaled, her chest rising and falling. Thomas was sure it was deliberate. Ah, what a Southern tease. After that first encounter, he was sure she sought him out. Sarah would arrive in her carriage daily to the fields without cause, peeping from behind the curtains at him. On those occasions, Thomas would expertly guide his horse, prancingly circling the field workers, shouting commands, and showing off his authority. He'd end his presentation by riding a full gallop towards the carriage. Miss Sarah mimicked a diesel in distress, crying and quickly shutting the curtain. It was the confidence Thomas needed; Miss Sarah wanted him. However, Thomas knew he had one major problem getting to Miss Sarah.

Miss Sarah was her father's pride and joy, his most beloved treasure. H.G., Thomas's boss, was Sarah's father.

Thomas understood the risk of his desires. It would be hell if his desires became known to H.G. that a hired overseer had eyes on his precious Sarah. If he didn't have Thomas killed, he would have him deported back to England. H.G. could erase him as if he'd never existed in America. The early nightfall and cool air did nothing for the rise of Thomas's violent hatred for his employer. Equal to his lust for Sarah was his rage over being thought of as nothing but a keeper of Negroes, a servant himself.

Thomas rewarded himself with one last thought of Sarah's image before firing another warning shot. In his image, Sarah was naked, relieved of hoop skirts and corsets, dressed only with her desire for him. Her breasts were swollen, nipples ripe with tiny indentions like the flesh of a strawberry; his mind traveled down to the thick, soft, golden hair he dreamed of between her thighs. "Sarah," he inhaled the air as he would her body one day and mumbled, "She will be mine." Thomas spat again. "Even over your dead body, H.G." He smiled; H.G.'s dead body would please him just fine.

Over a year ago, H.G.'s response to Thomas's compliment of his daughter had solidified Thomas's hatred of H.G. Thomas had only stated what was obvious: "Miss Sarah is beyond beauty, Mr. H.G." He smiled, thinking his compliment would bring delight to his employer as her prideful father, Thomas he added, "Miss Sarah certainly makes the season flowers pale in comparison."

H.G.'s face quickly turned to stone; he walked to the window, looking at the vast, lush land before him. His silence was unnerving. Finally, he said, "If you are to continue as my overseer, Thomas, you will relinquish any thoughts or glances toward my daughter moving forward. If Miss Sarah enters a room, you'll leave immediately; if you see my daughter anywhere in the house or on my land, change direction!" Only then did H.G. turn toward his overseer, his top lip curled over barring teeth. Thomas felt the spit of H.G.'s words sprinkling on his face. "Not while I am alive will you ever be near my dear Sarah!"

Relinquish? Without a proper understanding of the word or even the ability to pronounce it, Thomas understood. He was not worthy enough to offer compliments or glance upon H. G.'s daughter. Thomas had mistakenly overestimated his position. He was a half-step above a Negro.

Animal, was that it? The word bounced in his head: relinquish. A man who leaned heavily toward violence, Thomas had to still his body with great inner strength while responding in a manner fit for the role of employee. He shoved his hands in his pockets. "Yes, sir, Mr. H.G., I'm sorry. No harm was meant or disrespect." Mentally, though, Thomas was imagining slamming his fist into H.G.'s face, knocking his front teeth out, and swelling the curled lip, drawing as much blood as possible from his boss' flared nostrils. The thought of breaking H.G.'s nose calmed his inner rage.

Thomas snapped the carriage straps, more eager to get to their destination. Even more so, he smiled as he envisioned H.G.'s ill fate on the road ahead.

In the carriage below, H.G. wondered why daylight had abruptly left, bypassing the glow of twilight and turning black. He leaned closer to the dimming carriage lamp and took out his gold-case pocket watch; the ornate hands read quarter past six.

"Thomas?" H.G. shouted through the partially opened window. He received no answer. H.G. waited pensively. No response. He went back to sifting through his thoughts. H.G. felt confident that Thomas would let him know if something was to be concerned about. After all, what was the alternative? H.G. inhaled deeply to smell any sign of rain, possibly a storm coming through, which would explain the sudden darkness in the sky. Nothing. He comforted himself with the movements of the horses under Bailey's command and the weight of his pistol by his side.

However, the Negroes, took the unexpected shift of the sky as God swinging his ax— striking day to night—as an omen. When told to stop at the watering hole, the shorter of the Negroes, Sam whispered it was an act of God warning that something terrible was going to happen. Bailey nodded in agreement. The men waited for their master to get out of the carriage. H. G. exited carefully, unlatched the lantern, handed it to Bailey, and walked them, along with the horses, to the watering hole.

At the watering hole, H.G. was busy pointing out to the servants the

Milky Way and did not notice, or was ignoring, their worried faces in the lantern's light. Negroes, he understood, were superstitious by nature. He lit his pipe from the lamp and took a moment to smoke. Thomas cautiously watched the Negroes from his seat.

His fingers were securely placed on the trigger of the rifle; Thomas had made it a point to cock it when they stopped. That sound alone was what he wanted them to hear. Satisfied, he watched H.G. complete his business.

They traveled on a night with minimal guidance from the pin-size stars, although one star, the North Star, was a particular distraction for Bailey and Sam. But for the lure of the North Star's promise of freedom, they remained steady in their course of servitude. The horses drank, and the journey continued.

Neither Bailey nor Sam wore shoes. Their feet made no noise to compete with the carriage wheels turning or the horses' high steps. Not even their paced breath on this long journey, with few breaks, brought forth sound. They navigated each complicated step and led the horses by the gentle commands of their soothing voices, which sounded to H.G., resting back on the passenger seat as, "Ha it ta, ta it ha." The call and response came first from a deep, barrel-like tone and was joined by the vibration of softer baritone notes: "Ha it ta, ta it ha." Neither Thomas nor H.G. knew that Bailey, who cared for the horses, had given them the names Ha and Ta. Most animals on the plantation were nameless, but Bailey believed that to be wrong. Bailey sang their names harmoniously with his running companions, Ha and Ta, and no one knew otherwise.

The horse runners ran steady despite the worry of an omen. "Ha, it ta, ta it ha." H.G., emotionally exhausted, dozed to the rhythm, awakened by an occasional bump, only to be lulled back into the light dream of slumber. "Ha, it ta, ta it ha."

It was a long route to his second home, a day-and-a-half journey that was neither easy nor safe. There had been talk of Union soldiers taking refuge in safe houses along the road.

Far off in the distance, kerosene lamps brightened the night, lamps belonging to the sparsely placed houses of both new settlers and squatters. At one point, the road descended quickly in a distinguished fashion; the horses managed the descent, but the wheels wobbling put the carriage at risk. Just as quickly, the leaning carriage rose at an angle safely. Each horse trusted the guidance of the servants. The road was called the devil's drop; it told H.G. they were nearing Culver Tusk. Bailey prayed as their feet and carriage rose and tilted backward; not for them, the horses knew how to manage the dip in the road. Bailey prayed for the unknown, for what was ahead of them in the dark; he knew it was nothing good. There had been something sinister in Thomas's response to H.G. before setting off. Brushing down the horses, Bailey listened discreetly to the two men. Thomas was visibly upset when H.G. suggested delaying going to Culver Tusk. Instead, he told Thomas he'd be going home to Grove. Thomas's body jerked, pacing back and forth like he was searching desperately for something he had lost. Thomas staggered his words, reminding H.G. of the urgently needed supplies, and emphasized the disappointment of Miss Eloise and the child. Inside, Bailey laughed at the hollow words. He thought H.G. surely would notice the overseer's desperate tone and the frantic look on his face. But H.G.'s face seemed peculiar, his eyes half closed, and his face frowned in distress. H.G. stared at the ground for a while before he agreed with Thomas. Thomas' erratic pacing stopped. If the stars had been brighter or the moon more generous, the road might have revealed what awaited H.G. less than a mile ahead. But the poised line of armed men was encased in darkness, revealing nothing to the approaching travelers.

The smell of the Mississippi River softened the scent of animal waste drifting from the remaining farms before the final bend in the road leading to Miss Eloise and her son. When the carriage leveled, H.G. sighed in relief.

It had been a long and heartbreaking trip. H.G. suffered something foreign to him: betrayal. No one had ever betrayed him, man or woman, in business or otherwise—except the defiant Eloise whom he'd forgiven. He squeezed his hands into fists and then relaxed. He willed himself to remember something good had come out of it. His heart was broken, but any news from Elosie's sisters would be good.

Her sisters were preparing to make the trip to America by next year. He had done his part to secure their passage. While God had the unfortunate task of taking their mother from the earth, releasing her of her painful illness, the sisters would bring happiness, which Eloise desperately desired. Only the war could delay their arrival, but he felt it would soon be over, so he prayed. H.G. kept Eloise's sisters' letters in a separate brown case, apart from the tainted legal documents. The legal documents represented hell on earth, but the letters in the box were a slice of heaven for Eloise.

H.G. was sickened by the forgery and vileness of the letters and deeds of land ownership, and the sales of the Negroes were deceptive and certainly under any circumstance not the legal intentions of H.G. but of his lawyer. There was a nervous energy in his thoughts on this matter. Just days ago, he had terminated his relationship, both business and personal, with his once best friend, whom he now referred to as Son of a Bitch! In hindsight, H.G. remembered the many warnings and advice of having his childhood friend act as his business associate and attorney. That move had become a conflict of interest, and now the price was being paid.

"Son of a Bitch is a liar and a thief," H.G. had come to utter of late to no one in particular, but often out loud. He mustered a smile, knowing what made them best friends for all those years. There wasn't one childhood memory of which neither was a significant part. This son of a bitch and H.G. had been in diapers together; hell, they gained their manhood mounting the same Negro during harvest time. But years of knowing someone had nothing to do with "knowing," H.G. realized after their last conversation. That day, the smoke of their cigars seemed to have their battle, puffing big rings that moved and overtaking most of the law office. The midday sun illuminated the hundreds of books and awards lining the walls as H.G. was offered a drink. His then-attorney, and now the Son of a Bitch, was a bit uneasy, carefully choosing his words. H.G. later chastised himself for failing to realize it was not a meeting meant merely for reminiscing. His frock coat unbuttoned, he loosened his tie and relit his cigar while waiting for his friend to speak. H.G. sat on the sofa.

"You'se remember when we were going off to college that last evening after the delightful farewell dinner at the Bonefins, H.G.? We were young men from the best families, and the world awaited us eagerly." It was not a question lacking an answer, H.G. noted, as his friend continued. "The women dining with us, bred to want nothing more than our asking their hand in marriage."

"Yes, indeed, and you went off to law school and I to school in England," H.G. added, waiting for his friend, whom he truly loved, drunk or not, to tell him why he had called him to town. Was he giving up his bachelorhood at last?

"H.G., if a man has the desire of one woman he must provide for, he is an honorable but poor soul, now…if a man has the desire of women of wealth, with lonely hearts, widows or even of more value women whose features couldn't attract a man condemned to death"—he laughed and took a long, deliberate moment to inhale his Figuardo cigar— "that man has great power; he holds the key to many political doors." H.G. pondered the thought and found it entertainingly accurate but still wondered why he had been summoned. Indeed, not for the delightful conversation of women's emotions, rich or unattractive.

His question was soon answered when his friend laid several unfamiliar claims, deeds, and other legal documents on the table before him. H.G. glanced down, semi-recognizing his signature next to the title of the Culver Tusk property. H.G. felt like he was looking at the fangs of a venomous snake. He felt the hairs on his neck rise as he threw back his drink in one gulp, ice and all. The servant quickly refilled it, even before the liquor burned the back of his throat. H.G. swallowed the liquid fire, reprimanding himself for signing the papers at some point in the past, for the signature before him appeared to be his own. His lawyer's voice interrupted H.G.'s internal dialogue.

"I told you I had one fear in life, you remember, H.G.?" He did not wait for a response, "That one fear," he pounded his fist against his chest. "Opening doors of opportunity and not having the guts to go forward can be a life of regret. You must walk over the threshold and enter with force!"

"Yes, yes, you did. Now tell me what door of opportunity awaits you that is worth more than our lifetime friendship. You seem to have no fear in this moment. Or are you so over the threshold you don't know how to turn back?"

In the following moments, H.G. listened intently, willing himself not to pick up the documents and throw them in the hearth, hoping this was a nightmare he'd soon wake from. The chiming of the grandfather clock struck the hour when H.G. resigned himself to the fact that, sadly, it was true. The haze of the liquor did nothing to dull the sick feeling in his body. He was heartbroken, and the stiff, smoke-filled air provided a welcome excuse for the tears that washed his eyes.

"I fear nothing now, H.G., not even death. Back then, in our youth, I feared that once one crossed the threshold of opportunity, the door closed, and only then the price of that opportunity had to be paid in full." H.G. held on to the last words paid in full and searched the man he'd trusted all his life. He saw nothing of the price being paid; he saw a man blowing smoke rings in his direction—the direction of the price being paid in his betrayal.

"And you think of this now for what point?" He felt warm sweat gathering quickly between his armpits. The hand holding his drink started to shake, and H.G. reached into his coat pocket and took out his handkerchief to wipe his forehead. His hands were nearly as pale as the white cloth.

"Trust is a fool's game you offer women when you can't offer love,

H.G., a game you've lost." The rings of smoke couldn't veil his lawyer's sharp, hardened eyes as he pointed to the signed sale deed of Culver Tusk. The once blue eyes of his childhood friend appeared grey. When H.G. wondered had his eye color changed?

"Business has no room for friendship-trust! I have added two other names in a partnership of Culver Tusk and the surrounding land that you intended to hand over to that Irish whore and bastard child!" Those words ignited a violent rage inside H.G. His heart started pounding with rapid speed, and he could feel his temples pulsating. He scanned the room desperately, looking for something unbreakable to break with his bare hands. His friend had broken what he thought unbreakable: their friendship. H. G.'s hand shook uncontrollably. He dropped the crystal glass he was holding; the sound of it shattering failed to satisfy his rage. The son of a bitch continued, "A whore, whose only offering is between her Irish thighs! which the governor passed on to you." H.G.'s mouth flung open; his muscles tightened at the vulgarity thrown at him. H.G. realized he didn't have the strength to break anything or defend the woman he loved; he didn't even have the strength to shut his gaping mouth.

In hindsight, in the comfort of his carriage and the soothing sounds of "Ha it Ta," H.G. wondered what he had been waiting for as he sat listening to the details of his lawyer's betrayal. He chastised his cowardice. "Why did I not stand up and beat him with my bare hands, turning my trembling fingers into weapons? I'm a coward and a fool," he declared. I do not possess the orientation of my brother, Grove would have ended this son of a bitch's life.

H.G. had been deceived because he trusted someone, he considered a friend and loved like a brother! My God, what is the world coming to? The war, now this? *The door of trust is not something to enter into business,* his lawyer pointed out. The statement's weight tore at H.G. what would his deceased brother do? Grove would have killed him damn the consequences. H.G. bit down on the inside of his mouth to stop the shaking of his lower jaw. Confused, sad, and wounded, he'd risen to leave; before reaching the door, a thought came to him as if Grove from the family graveyard tapped him on the shoulder to remind him of his family's power. He could hear Grove. *Laws are written for those that need to be contained, not for men of great wealth and power. We live outside of the law; lawyers do our bidding.*

With growing certainty the matter would be resolved, H.G. waved his former attorney's servant away and opened the wide oak door himself, turned, and called out, "You, son of a bitch, are the devil. But even the devil deserves a good dance partner; let's dance!" As soon as he released the words into the wading smoke-filled room, he knew it was a dance of death. The look on his once childhood friend was nearly unrecognizable. Was he willing to go so far as murder?

Now, here on this road, falling in and out of sleep, fighting not to become suspicious of his shadow, he wondered if the sky was falling upon him. This mayhem of war was more than H.G. cared to imagine the outcome; it was exhausting to consider anything but winning. He drifted off, wondering what Eloise and the boy might be doing.

It was well over a month since he had seen the redheaded Eloise, her delicate, fair skin and green eyes. Her quiet, soft beauty was starting to crack in appearance over time, like any delicate fine porcelain exposed to harsh circumstances. Madness combined with alcohol were Eloise's harsh circumstances.

They met years ago when H.G. was visiting upstate New York. Eloise had newly arrived from Ireland as a house servant to his friend, the governor. H. G. found her beauty unmatched, and her Irish accent amused him. Upon inquiry, he'd learned that an indentured servitude was the legal term of her contract. During his stay, their flirting bordered on obscenity. The governor suggested he might want to consider her for purchase. Consider, he did. The transaction was completed in no time.

"As a private tutor to my daughter, Sarah," he joked, laughing loudly. The room of politicians and investors raised their glasses and blew cigar smoke in amused agreement. "Tutor indeed." The governor laughed the loudest. "She'll teach you, H.G."

Eloise confessed in a delicate, nearly inaudible whisper when they were alone on the train back to his home, requiring him to lean forward, "I did not want to remain in the governor's house." She had touched his hand lightly. "I felt my true skills would go to waste." Her mouth came so close to his ear for a moment that he pondered if he had been kissed.

"Skills?" he inquired, both pleased and surprised.

Eloise turned away from his question to the train window. She asked, "Do you think there are more trees than people on earth?" It was a silly question, he thought and looked at the precipitous movement of the trees flashing by. H.G. knew the question did not require his response and returned her smile in their reflection. He had never thought the sound of a steam locomotive particularly pleasant, yet now, suddenly, it pleased him.

When they arrived at Culver Tusk, he revealed his reasons and tutoring was not one of them. H.G. had the house servants fill a hip bath, instructing them to bathe her despite her soft protest. H.G. enjoyed this ritual himself in his private chambers. Later, they feasted together in the formal dining room under the bronze chandelier.

After dinner, he escorted Eloise to the master bedroom and guided her to the four-poster bed. "My brother Grove had just completed most of the work before he…" This hesitation stirred his soul, and he wished he could mention the fact without stalling on the rumor of murder and, worse, the accused. He continued… "…died in a hunting accident." Her expression of compassion fortified him and made the memoryless melancholy.

"Where does your family live? Your daughter, Sarah, the girl I am to tutor? This is such a beautiful home. Fifteen rooms—what am I to do here?"

"Undress yourself for me." He surprised himself with his abruptness.

"Sir?" Her voice was more pleased than shocked.

"I said—"

She interrupted him by reaching up to unclasp the diamond hair clamp he'd given her, which bound her hair.

"I heard you, sir, but I did not hear you say, 'Please, Eloise.'" Her soft yet firm command poured softly from her red lips, shocking him. She tilted her face and waited. He watched her tongue part her lips and slowly wet the top lip, then the bottom, before speaking. "Say 'please,' H.G."

Astonished by her bold yet sweet request, his knees buckled. He sat on the edge of the bed, sensing he might fall otherwise. Never had a woman, and certainly not his wife, offered such a bold but sweet demand. H.G. did not have time to follow the path of his desires as it rushed in every direction in his body, scattering his senses with it.

Eloise stood before him, her green eyes tracing his face. *I know him, like most men, all too well*, she thought. She waited. "Please." H.G. heard the words, but his voice was unfamiliar to him. He had spoken a word long packed away since childhood. "Please" was not in his vocabulary as a wealthy man. He was, after all, H.G. He felt the sweat tickle his hairline, and his fingers trembled.

"P…lease." Her lips hinted at a smile, and he wanted more.

"Eloiseee, my dear Eloise, would you p…lease take—" A sudden rush of fear rose, mingling with his excitement, to unnerve him. He thought, *if this is how I feel with her fully clothed, what will happen to me when she is naked?* He did not care. "Please take off your clothes." He felt for the first time the purpose of language, where the soul rises out of the dark, begging to be heard. A delightful rush of dizziness came to him, tingling his brain. Could it be that, in her seductive, tender words, his heart squeezed with each letter? H.G. pushed away the confusion to avoid being distracted and watched this creature of lustful beauty before him.

With fingers that moved ever so slowly, the uncertainty and hesitancy of the wings of a tiny bird crossed his thoughts. He wondered for a moment if she might have changed her mind. No, she began to expertly untie and unhook herself as far as possible. She turned her back to him and lifted her hair. "Do it."

His fingers trembled, and he could not still them.

Eloise slowly arrived at the last garment, her underpants. H.G. had an instant reaction, noticing the seat of her panties was wet when she tossed them at his feet. His heart skipped. H.G. was introduced to a habit he'd acquire moving forward: sniffing Eloise's soiled underpants. Eloise crawled onto the bed, exposing everything about herself to him. She laid her body back on the pillows and asked for a drink. He complied, moving about, aware that he was serving her and the sincere joy he felt. The crystal decanter was not safe in his quivering hands. H.G. finally figured out that he could manage this simply by lifting the glass to the lip of the decanter and tilting it slightly. He handed Eloise the drink; she smiled at him. H.G. watched her momentarily, taking in her beauty, before pouring his drink and sitting on the chair facing the bed. And there Eloise lay before him; he choked on the first sip.

It might have well been the whole of the Mississippi River. He choked again, straining to breathe. Her actions left him breathless. Eloise was sitting propped on pillows, her thighs opening and closing much like an accordion and slower than a southern drawl.

He'd always been afraid to learn to swim. Now, drunk from lust and the burning pleasure rising from his groin to his throat, his emotions were drowning under her command. That afternoon, he knew he had become Eloise's devoted servant-lover. He felt ashamed that her bold, lustful beauty broke something in his manhood but more ashamed that he did not want to fix it. H.G. had no regrets about buying out her contract even when, over time, Eloise seemed distracted.

Their conversations were monotonous, and Eloise was lonely and bored. Since arriving at Culver Tusk, she began to barely notice as each season came, placed itself outside the expansive windows, and left for the next season to follow.

Eloise asked if he could take her occasionally to the social gatherings at Grove plantation, where his daughter Sarah lived. "And my wife and sister-in-law live," he always added, promising her a more adventurous social life, yet leaving for weeks to Grove.

H.G. would never know how long his promises could have satisfied their relationship or the money he gave her to send back to Ireland because there came the day when she defied him in the worst way and unequivocally their lives.

It was a brutal, hot day, even for Springfield. The house brought no relief; the curtains of the windows had no breeze to lift them. The servant Mary had stood fanning Eloise throughout the afternoon. The sweat ran from Mary's face steadily, the salt itching her face and neck and pouring down her body. The thought of wiping it away became a prayer as she lifted the banana leaf robotically. The air from the banana was not enough for Eloise.

Despite one of the house servants ' warnings, Eloise wanted to walk to the river to put her feet in the cool water. Startled, she asked sharply, "Why not?" The servant woman bowed her head as if anticipating a blow. "What's wrong? It's H.G. river and land; therefore, it's mine to walk!?" Eloise shouted. The servants did not tell her there was trouble on the plantation. It was not their place.

Angered by the mystery, Eloise was more determined. She left the house abruptly and walked down a path, approaching a small group of Negroes, their backs to her in a semicircle. Eloise stepped closer, following Thomas's voice, commanding them to stop their crying.

On the ground before them lay the body of a Negro man. He was dead. His flesh was torn apart so that bone was exposed. But still, the whip rose in the air one last time upon the man, as if it would matter to the lifeless body. It mattered to the people who had been forced to watch. H.G. stood off to the side of the group. He had not heard her coming until she screamed. "It's against God's law!" Eloise screamed. He had not expected her to walk upon the scene and was surprised when Eloise ran toward him. H.G. felt Thomas had carried the beating too far.

Thomas had warned him that something drastic had to happen when the search party found the fugitive slave. "Nigga run off three times, H.G., and come back this time to fetch his son. Foolish but daring thing to do."

H.G. did not respond. He was thinking, *Surely the slaves knew their treatment was far better under his care than when his brother Grove was alive.* "Whatcha waiting for, H.G.? Da darkies to return and take over?" Thomas stood, watching two of the slaves, upon his command, drag the lifeless body away. The unrest in the South and the last rebellion of the Negroes had caused many to become agitated, there was talk of Negroe's being asked to join the war.

H.G. knew Thomas was watching Eloise chastise him verbally, her red hair flying around her. Eloise's presence and defiant nature cost him respect. He knew well she was taking advantage of his affection and was ignoring his authority. How dare she think what worked in the bedroom would work on his land.

"You'se brought me as yah servant." she had shouted. H.G. was speechless and knew he was being seen as weak, allowing her to protest his authority.

Eloise was out of place, as no southern woman would have dared defy him. He glared at her, trying to convey a warning through his eyes. "Stop it!" He willed his tone and words to be as heavy as a door slamming the conversation shut.

H.G. waited for Eloise to silence herself. She went on at a higher volume and was full of rage. "How dare you allow this?"

In his peripheral vision, H.G. saw the Negroes' heads bent. But he knew they were listening to the conversation deep down in the marrow of their bones. They were making decisions that could be costly. The tears of some of the Negroe women dropped rapidly down their dark faces into the dirt at their feet. Thomas had forced the children who tried to hide behind the adults to watch the beating. "Git 'em from behind yawselves!"

he shouted. H.G. was sickened by Thomas' command but did not stop the children from being pulled to witness the deadly beating.

H.G. had watched, stunned, not at the beating but at the childlike features in their tiny faces being ripped apart by the terror of the whipping. The children reacted as if the sharpened blades of a cradle scythe had cut deep into the image of whatever childhood existed in their enslaved lives, mangling their emotions in its blades. They were all paralyzed under the threat of dying alongside the dead man, including the children.

Now, they witnessed their master and this woman's rage. Her screams were rising even louder as if their master had not spoken. "Thomas is a green-eyed beast and a devil." Eloise tossed a hardened look toward Thomas. H.G. reached out to take hold of her arm to drag her if need be, but she snatched it away with all her might. "Damn you. Damn him. Damn, America!"

H.G., stunned by Eloise's damning of him and America, swung his right hand over his left shoulder and brought the back of it down against her face with iron force. Her face and neck snapped backward. H. G.'s hand swooped up in the opposite direction and returned with even more determination, his palm striking her opposite cheek. When her neck snapped, her head fell backward, and the rest of her followed. She dropped. He left her on the ground and commanded the people back to the field.

He took moments to adjust to the burning in his swelling hand. Finally, filled with regret and anguish, he turned to Eloise. She had rolled onto her back. Her face was crooked as it started swelling, slanted to the right side, and tilted upward. Her hair, running loosely around her head in the dirt, was wet, stringy, and without any signs of the lush curls she had adorned upon their meeting. She looked dead. H.G. knelt, peering at her face. Eloise's breath was labored. Blood ran from her broken nose, pouring down the sides of her face into her ears. H.G. took his quivering fingers and gently lifted her right eyelid with his right thumb. The sudden thought of his hands harming her again was more than he could endure.

Through the slits of her rapidly swelling right eye, he saw a light flash momentarily, then disappear into the vacant space that would become permanent thereafter.

At first, he thought the sob that rose was Eloise crying out. It was indistinct, neither human nor beast. But his throat burned with an inaudible sound until it found its notes. "Noooo, Eloise!" It was his cry, attempting to call the light back. But the light did not reappear. Instead, the distraction of Thomas's groan of disgust from behind took over.

What little pleasure he found from witnessing H.G. finally chastise Eloise was being stolen. Before him was Eloise, lying on her back as if she had taken the place of Jesus on the cross, and H.G. replacing the Virgin Mary! Thomas felt the bile of soured food rise in his throat. He pushed past H.G., intentionally brushing up against him, thinking it might startle H.G. into his senses. No, the push only knocked H.G. onto his side into a fetal position, clawing at the air toward Eloise, clawing even when there was no more than the trail of dust left after her body was dragged away.

Thomas reached down and grabbed Eloise by her arm in one swoop. Half her body rested in the crook of his arm, limp as a wet rag, while the lower half dragged along the ground.

Speaking his mind, although he realized it would be lost on H.G., he uttered, "Don't be surprised if we'se got mo' slaves running after dis!" H.G. said nothing.

"She ain't weigh nothin'," Thomas noted, dragging her body. He glared back and cursed his employee. H.G. finally looked up and away from the ground in time to see Eloise tossed belly down over Thomas's horse.

Less than a week later, H.G. discovered Eloise was pregnant. She awaited their baby's arrival, staring into space or writing letters back home. No words of affection or touching her belly from H.G. brought the light back into her eyes. Eloise's labor was long and arduous. She left deep scratches and bite marks on the arms and hands of the attending Negroes.

In the wee hours, her son arrived and was quickly washed and placed in her waiting arms. H.G., sitting alone in the formal dining room, was summoned by Mary. He rushed up the stairs and threw open the door. Eloise beckoned him, and for the first time in months, Eloise spoke to him affectionately. "Peter. His name is Peter." It all seemed unreal now in the carriage ride to Culver Tusk.

Time had gone by, and much had changed. The wild, passionate woman he had brought to the South was gone despite being a mother whom the servants raised. Eloise lived to drink and suffered, as the doctor explained, from hallucinations and paranoia. And sadly, he admitted, it was getting worse. Her last letter delivered to him arrived at Grove's could have been written by headless chickens running without direction of sight. The handwriting went all over the pages. The content of the letters, for the most part, was filled with fears and accusations.

She wrote of her fear that the Negroes were going to do her harm. He knew this was not true and attributed such concerns to the doctor's diagnosis of a sickness involving her mental state.

Often, she wrote of awakening with bruises on her arms, and once a lump on her head, yet she had no memory of what had happened. "Sometimes the servants beat me, I believe, in my sleep, much like your overseer Thomas does to the Negroes." H.G. frowned at the allegations, knowing they were false. He had been with her on one of the occasions when she awakened with bruises and knew it was the result of her fighting when she drank. Stumbling through doors and slamming herself into walls, on the best of occasions and the worst, trying to toss herself over the balcony. He had instructed the white servants to tie her to her bed, if needed, and remove the straps before their son awakened. Peter grew into a bright boy who walked earlier than most. Each visit, the servants reported that more times than not, sadly, they'd had to restrain her. H.G. could not imagine Eloise losing her desire to live in a house filled with beauty and servants that would yield to her every thought if they knew them. How, he wondered, could Eloise put herself in harm's way with such an affectionate child as Peter? But then H.G. questioned. When had he seen his son Peter show affection toward his mother during recent visits? Only when the boy was with his Negro playmate did he seem happy or show affection.

H.G. turned his thoughts to legal documents that could substantially undermine his family's financial well-being. His signature surrendered half his property rights, including Negro servants, to the Bank of New York. Eloise's former employer was once on the Bank of New York board before becoming governor.

The world seemed to be falling into a dark hole, leaving him little light to see his way out. He wondered what Eloise was up to at this late hour. Had she gotten the message of his arrival and their monthly supplies?

# THREE

H.G.'s message and a wagon full of supplies had come just days before. Essie, the head servant and a robust woman from the south of England, was handed the message by her husband, George. She stood at the back entrance, nodding to discern the meaning of the letter. This was not to be a routine visit, she gathered. Mr. H.G. was promising to bring cheer to Miss Eloise and the boy. "Maybe a trip is being planned for them," Essie speculated out loud to George. Her husband smiled accordingly, understanding his wife's romantic nature. "Maybe." He patted her arm. "Maybe."

In preparation, each night, Essie instructed that all lanterns in the downstairs should be lit, along with the gas lights outside Culver Tusk. The servants were ready for action at a moment's notice. Yet the message of his upcoming arrival brought little relief to Mistress Eloise's agitated and brooding mood. Essie and George were praying that the bright lights and smells of baking for his arrival would bring a festive note to her spirits. Nothing! In the days of preparation, Essie had the servants lift Eloise's thin body from the soiled sheets after carefully removing her bound feet from the straps. Mistress Eloise wept in Essie's arms and promised to follow H.G.'s request and the doctor's order of no drinking and mixing her medicines, but by nightfall, the promise was broken, and her rages erupted.

Essie diluted the liquor two days before his arrival, hoping to get Eloise in half-reasonable shape.

Eloise had tried to get sober on her own but was not successful on the day of his expected return. H.G. would fuss at her drunken state, and she wanted to avoid that. The servants soaked the mistress's body in tea leaves to pull the smell from her skin. Then, they would refill the basin with flower petals to sweeten her skin. Overnight, Essie simmered the bones of a slaughtered cow, mixed with the bitterest of garden vegetables, which she insisted Eloise must drink. She gave the Negro servant Mary firm instructions. "Soak mistress feet in hot water and mustard seeds. See dat she drinks her broth down and then sleeps until supper." The pills Essie gave Mistress Eloise were from her supply and could bring a dead tree back to life. Essie herself knew the importance of being able to stand a whole night alert, as the devastation of religious persecution in her own life was never more than a shiver away. To think I escaped the burning in the village square to spend my days cooking over flames.

Eloise awakened from her nap feeling better than she had in months. In the past few days, Essie's remedies have been working. She even allowed Mary to open the window to let fresh air in and asked her to make tea. When she was finally alone without the eyes of the servant upon her, she quickly stole a long drink of brown liquor and downed her medicine. Mixing Essie's pills with the brown liquid proved a disaster.

Essie whispered a quick prayer of hope before opening the bedroom door, only to see Mistress Eloise stumbling around with an imbecilic look. Essie sighed and closed the door, and continued the evening's preparations. It was rather strange that nightfall had come much earlier than she remembered. Her husband, George, agreed.

Essie instructed Mary to go quickly and keep an eye on the mistress. "Make sure mistress doesn't stumble upon the poor child and suffocate him in her foul state." She laughed, immediately regretting having wasted her humor on Mary, who only replied, "Yes, ma'am."

Hours later, with fewer mishaps than expected, Eloise was upright and seemed steady enough. Mary watched her from the top of the stairs. Mary had washed and dressed Eloise in a dress H.G. had brought on his last trip, the rose-colored lace complementing her eyes. Eloise made her way to her son's room. Peter was lying back on his bed. Seeing her son's peaceful appearance, she began to cry and then sang an Irish lullaby.

Her crying no longer upset the little boy. Peter wished she had skipped that part of his good night and often turned his back to her tears, as he did that night. Her kisses tasted of bitter medicine and made his lips tingle.

Eloise looked down at his full red hair, peppered with blond hair, and his face turned into the pillow. He was already well into his rest.

*Whisht wee bairn as the river is slumberin' And all will be grand in the mornin' The echoes are callin' from the castle of Dromore So whisht and go to sleep How I wish to hear me own mammy's voice Whisht whisht wee bairn, good night Night, night, me child, dear da will be home soon."*

Eloise paused her singing momentarily, listening to what she had been waiting for. Her head turned sharply, coming to a stop over her right shoulder. In the far corner was her son's companion fanning the warm air with a banana leaf. "H.G., thank God you are home." Her voice lost the song's comforting notes and became anxious. Eloise rose quickly and stumbled back onto the bed. She sat briefly, letting the soft breeze of the fan settle her breath. She rose and carefully picked the lantern off the night table, leaving her resting child and his servant with only the pale light of the half-moon in the window.

Eloise's abrupt movement fully awakened the sleeping boy. He sat up in the bed, pushing the sheet away. He looked until his eyes adjusted to the dark. "Come, Peter, come. Sleep with me, Peter," he whispered, in case his mother might hear and come back with her madness. Although the fanning stopped, the other child did not move.

"Please, it's okay." He reached his arms out in the dark. The quiet footsteps of the boy comforted him. He reached down to help him into the bed. With ease, they wrapped their arms around each other, as familiar to one another as to themselves.

Peter tenderly brushed the boy's face as he settled beside him.

He loved his companion so much he renamed him Peter. Both Peters snuggled together, as Eloise's son was not truly worried his mother would come back. He knew she often fell asleep wherever she collapsed and left it to the servants to get her to bed. His mother never rose before his afternoon snack.

Miss Eloise was moving jaggedly but hurriedly down the narrow hallway. The light from the lantern threw her shadow, twice her size, against the wall. Mary was waiting on her knees and got up quickly upon seeing Miss Eloise. Mary was watching Miss Eloise's movements to determine her steadiness. Eloise's green-speckled eyes were bloodshot where they should have been white, and the lantern's light turned her skin pale. "Why were you kneeling on the floor? I told you I do not like that!"

"Yes, ma'am." Mary did not bother to tell her she had felt one of her spells coming, and the floor was the best thing for her. She glanced at her mistress, trying to see how she was this evening. Mary had heard horses on the road. She desperately hoped Master H.G. was coming, not for his arrival but for her Bailey, who often guided the horses.

"Mary?" Eloise's voice sounded nervous. "I think H.G. is home. How do I look?" *Terrible, Miss Eloise,* Mary thought secretly. *It be apparent to H.G. how you'se spent yo days and nights whilst he's away.*

"You'se look just fine, Miss Eloise. Should I run the brush in your hair and pin it up real nice for Mr. H.G." Eloise ignored the offer; her eyes glazed over. Mary wondered if Miss Eloise suffered dizzy spells as she suffered. Miss Eloise finally turned to Mary, the light illuminating her face. No, Mary thought she couldn't have the same spell no way she came back that quick. When Mary's spells came on, her body didn't belong to her. She was taken to places she'd never been behind a door, and she heard and saw things nobody else did. Things no longer of this world. No, Mary figured whatever Miss Eloise suffered didn't take her away. "Mary, have George begin heating water for the master's bath and pull the covers down on our bed."

Mary reached for the lantern on the staircase to avoid a mishap. "Hold on to da banister, Miss Eloise; I'se guide da light for you'se."

"Yes, it seems darker tonight. Even the lantern's glow is dim."

"Yes, ma'am, it 'tis, but we's got da downstairs lit best we's could. Outside, too, like you'se asked us."

"I asked?"

"Yes, ma'am."

Eloise moved hesitantly down the first step and turned back to Mary. "Make sure Essie has his supper ready. I'll be in the parlor."

"Yes, ma'am. Will you'se be eating as well?"

"Will I be eating?" It's a simple question that she should be able to answer. Had she eaten? Did she have dinner with Peter? She contemplated this momentarily but realized she did not know what the boy ate for dinner. Mary would know. He probably ate with Mary's child; *what was his name? Did he have a name?* she wondered. Although they played well together, Eloise didn't like it. Her son Peter was too attached and would cry when the Negro boy was absent. Even more so, Mary did not seem to like her, despite her obedience to Eloise's commands. This she had reported to H.G.

"It is not Mary's consideration that you need to worry about," H.G. told her when she complained. "And besides, when I am not around, you treat them as if they are equal to you. This confuses them and is dangerous."

"What do you mean?" She was already afraid and so far away from everyone, with only the white woman Essie and her husband, two white overseers, and the occasional visit from the devil Thomas. Eloise wondered how safe she and her child were if the Negroes were unhappy, not to mention the stories of the Indians. What about the road that leads to that house where an Indian woman lives? In many ways, Eloise had become more southern than foreign over the past few years, if her fears were any indication.

"You are safe. The servants in the house have been with me forever, and their families are on the other plantation. If any harm comes to you, they understand the consequences." He could not explain what the Negro families meant to one another, how the Negroes would give up their life for one another. In ways, he felt they acted more human than his own family. He thought back over the Negro whom Eloise witnessed being killed. He had run, found a path to freedom, and returned to get his family.

"They will protect you with their lives, if not for you, then for their own family." H.G. seemed confident in his words, but Eloise, bitten by loneliness and drowning in liquor, was moving closer to a world of delusions. She blamed the Negro playmate for taking away the affection of her only child.

Eloise made a note to speak again to H.G., who had insisted that the Negro boy become a playmate to their son. Her Peter was three when H.G. had presented the younger child to her. She had looked up one day from her needlepoint and, for a moment, thought it was her child holding his father's hand. Seeing the slightly darker color of his skin, Eloise quickly gathered her wits and set her needle point down, her eyes scrutinizing each detail of the small boy, which shocked her sensibilities. She wondered why she thought at first glance it was her own Peter.

"Who is that?" It was the light brown, curly hair and tan that distinguished the child and confirmed he was indeed a Negro. A thought tried to force itself inside her suspicious mind, and just as quickly, it left. "Who is that?" Her voice was more demanding as she saw the child had the same mouth and eyes as her son.

H.G. pushed the little boy toward the bedroom where Peter was playing. "Go," he told the child, who went quietly through the adjourning door to their son. Soon after, Eloise heard their squeals of laughter.

"He is the Negro Mary's boy. Let him play with our child during the day."

"Why? Peter plays well by himself. He has quite an imagination."

Eloise wondered if H.G. thought she was incompetent to care for her son or worse. But H.G. had reassured her. "Most of the plantation children have Negro servants that grow up to become their trusted servants." He lit his pipe and told her stories of his servant boy from childhood.

"I might have been starved for attention had I not had my Negress and her child." He smiled at the memory. "My brother Grove was older and more favored. All I had was my Negro servant." Eloise found his sentiment odd and confusing, seeing how the Negroes were treated. H.G. did not notice the frown on her face as he shared his story. "When my Negro servant passed away, I felt the pain as vivid as any pain, maybe more so than for my own family."

Suddenly, his jawline clamped shut, and the veins of his forehead pushed out. "Eloise, I lied when I said I lost my brother to a hunting accident. Some think his own flesh and blood murdered him." His face recoiled. "His son, my nephew Hargrove, over a Negro named Lena." Eloise gasped, and the air sucked into the back of her throat.

"It is rumored he murdered his father, my brother Grove." Eloise could not imagine the killing of one's father or mother and, therefore, could not find words to reconcile if this might be the case. She paused a moment and decided to ask another question. "Who is the woman, Lena?" Her question was met with silence. "I'm the only legal male bloodline left besides my nephew, and he disappeared soon after Grove's funeral."

Eloise broke under the weight of his story, collapsed, and sobbed at his feet, primarily for her nostalgic feeling at the word *family*. "There, there." He pulled her up. "I'm fine. I have our child Peter and my dear sweet daughter Sarah." He brought comfort to her with carefully chosen words. "Eloise, the point of this tragic story was to let you know Peter's value in owning this child. One day, the child will be Peter's first inherited property; there will be much more to his inheritance. I'm drawing up papers soon; no worries, my dear."

"Oh?" The word *inheritance* was most precious to her. "Oh…. Then, I will not be tossed aside in this America to starve to death? I could not go back home with a child in hand, poor and alone. The shame would be unbearable; I would rather die first."

"Eloise!" Surprised, he realized at the bottom of her pain was her fear of being discarded, as was the fate of most mistresses. Poor thing, he thought. "My dearest Eloise, this is a difficult time, as I cannot explain fully. With the war and all, but the war will not last long, and this matter will come to rest. And I assure you, you and your family will always be cared for. Tell me you believe me."

He held her tight, but nothing could stop her thoughts. *Our son, Peter, is not legitimate, and I am Irish. His bloodline is as tainted as his Negro playmate in America!*

"Mistress Eloise?" The sound of Mary's voice brought her back to H.G.'s arrival.

"What?"

"Will you'se be eating?"

Eloise, unsure of what to do under the watchful steady eyes of the Negro Mary, answered, "Yes, of course, I will be eating. Bring a brandy to the parlor for now!"

"Yes, ma'am."

But neither woman moved as the unexpected blast of a gunshot in the distance shook the front window below. Both women stood under their looming shadows in the light, eyes locked on one another, waiting. A moment later, two more shots rang out. The other servants' sudden burst of panicked voices carried throughout the house. Hurried footsteps below ran in their direction.

"Miss Eloise!" Essie shouted from below in the foyer. Essie and her husband, carrying rifles, appeared from around the corner at the staircase.

Eloise found her voice, and it trembled with anguish, stories of the war closing in. "Am I going to die?" She imagined soldiers marching into the house and beheading her, or worse, raping her and forcing her to witness the killing of her child. *Why have I come to this awful country?* She cried inside.

Mary grabbed the hand of her mistress, pulling her away from the stairs and toward the children's bedroom. "Please, Miss Eloise, go inside with da children." With urgency, she pushed as gently as the situation allowed the frantic Eloise into the bedroom, sat the lantern on the table, and closed the door.

In the dark, Mary, without the guidance of the lantern, fumbled along the wall with her hands. She returned to the top of the steps just as the sound of horses approached and the shouting of men. Mary stood still, feeling the tingling on her hairline, telling her a dizzy spell was on the way. "Let me make it down da stairs, Lord." Carefully, she made it step by step and gathered with the other servants in the front hall before she collapsed. Both the Negro servants and the white servants stood, jaws clenched, facing the front door. The white servants were armed. Ready for a burst of force to splinter the wooden door and the soldiers to march through, their imaginations ran rapidly with violent images. At that moment, none of them could fathom anything other than their deaths.

# F O U R

The first gunfire heard at the house, which had terrified Eloise and the servants, was the shot that killed H.G. The bullet blasted through his gold pocket watch, extinguishing his life within minutes.

Just before the shot reached Culver Tusk, the carriage had turned down the road, guided by a hint of moonlight. Thomas saw how near they were to Culver Tusk in the dim glow. A moment of dread seized hold, and he tightened his hands on the reins. He knew the plans might fail if H.G. made it to the house and inside. Thomas had to find a way to stall H.G.'s arrival.

"Stop the horses!" He called out. "Ha ta…"

The Negroes slowed the horses to a stop and waited to see what else the overseer wanted of them. Culver Tusk was so close there was no reason to take a rest. Bailey tried his hardest to listen to everything moving around them. The silence was unnatural; the darkness was charged. His horse Ta raised his head, stretched his neck, and snorted. Both men waited for Thomas to shoot in the air or to be given a command. Neither came.

Bailey brushed his hand across his horse's neck; her hair stood up. The horse sensed danger ahead. As he was accustomed to the horse, Bailey wanted to offer her soothing words, but he knew better. Besides, he'd be dishonest in comforting his horse; he knew trouble was upon them. Bailey tightened his hands on the hackamore and waited. Whatever was out there in the dark—the thing that had scared his horse—was like no other animal Bailey understood; he could smell the pungent musk of men in the air. A sudden light flare from a lantern confirmed the horses' warning and Bailey's nose.

A line of men blocked the road to Culver Tusk. H.G. rose from the carriage seat, snatched the curtain back, and thrust forward. The carriage lantern illuminated the shock on his face; H.G.   called out. "What in the hell is going on?" His question went unanswered, not from the men or Thomas. H.G. clumsily fell back into the carriage seized with alarm. What could this mean? Maybe they were Southern men of clergy traveling to lecture the morality of slavery to captured Union soldiers.   H.G. stiffened, waiting for Thomas to explain the prominent figure seated in the carriage to the men. Instead, he heard Thomas speak in familiarity.

"Gittin' worried ya'll was lost." The word *ya'll* ran a cold chill in the air. H.G. grabbed his pistol and pushed out of the carriage, enraged. The lantern was passed from one man to another, finally to the Son of a Bitch, the devil himself, his lawyer smiled.

Nothing could satisfy the murderous flame that ignited inside H.G. less than death.

The smell of his body musk mingled with the rush of cold sweat ascended to his nostrils, and he welcomed it. This was not the smell of a coward.  His brother Grove was not the only man of courage in the family. "God damn it all to hell!" H.G.'s words were staggered and laced with anguish.

He blinked rapidly, tears burning his eyes; he pushed further out the carriage window, nearly tumbling out. H.G. attempted to unlatch the door, but it didn't move. Contemplating if he could shoot Thomas from this angle or aim and kill the Son of a Bitch.  H.G. heard a gunshot. The exact shot that sent the occupants at Culver Tusk into panic.  The force of the bullet to his chest forced him to drop his gun and knock H.G. back inside the carriage. The bullet did not hit his heart but was close enough to visit his impending.  H. G. was between the veil of living and dead. He whimpered, "Eloise, I...been shot." His mind searched desperately, racing against the fiery sensation from his chest to his innards. There was a sensation of tiny nerves in his bottom being soothed by the warmth of his bladder releasing. H.G. whimpered helplessly, "P…lea…se." He died thinking of the pleasure Miss Eloise offered with that one single word of surrender: "Please." To which he added, "God, please."

# FIVE

The trial of H.G., the accused killer, Thomas, took place less than a month later in a room filled with spectators. Thomas C. Latimer, overseer known for his emerald eyes, was indicted.

While preparing for the trial, Thomas confessed to his attorney, Lee Edgar, without remorse; indeed, he had "set H.G. up. H.G. was planning on stealing back what he promised me, but…" He added, his voice filled with conviction, "So yeah, I'se agreed to lead him to his enemies to face his fate. I'se had no thought his lawyer was setting me up." His eyes blazed with anger as he continued. "It does no good for me to kill H.G., much as it would've given me pleasure to gouge his eyes out with my thumbs."

Mr. Lee flinched; he did not like this man, Thomas, or the unnatural color of his emerald eyes. However, given that he knew the outcome of this legal drama and his considerable monetary reward, he played along with the conspiracy to convict Thomas. He knew his client was not guilty, but that was not his concern. Lee Edgar had both the gossip of H.G.'s death and inside political information; H.G. had been set up. Besides, Attorney Lee Edgar was paid to "Just show up for the official legalities of it all."  Edgar amused himself by drawing stick figures on a notepad.

Thomas's attorney stopped drawing and reminded Thomas without mincing words, "Fact is, Thomas, no jury is going to believe these honorable men offered you money and property. Now…you can fix your mind to believe that!"

"Dey gotta believe me. I'se found out dat H.G. faa-alsifi-ed the papers and had me working for nothing! He had no intentions of *ever* giving me property and dem slaves, ever!"

"Let's be clear with each other, Thomas, before you shame yourself and make a fool of yourself in court."

"Whatcha mean…shame?" Thomas was genuinely baffled.

"You can't make claims that H.G. falsified the documents just because you like the word *falsified*." Lee Edgars knew his client had been intensely listening to the accusations of falsification of the documents concerning the other parties. Hell, everybody, including the Governor of New York and the Governor of Arkansas, was making claims to the property. Thomas had asked him more than once what the word start with fa…meant and how to say it. Lee Edgars, for his entertainment, listening to Thomas stumble with each letter was like watching a drunk trying to stand up.

"What shame?" Thomas's skin crawled. He felt light-headed and was about to call the guard to take him to his cell. But Mr. Lee spoke before Thomas could open his mouth.

"The question is, Thomas, how would you know if the papers were falsified?" Thomas's lawyer glanced slyly up from his writing pad. "You ever hear the word *illiterate*? Edgars wrote quickly across the page and placed it in front of Thomas. "Point at which one is your name… go ahead, pick out your name." The daylight coming into the steel bars of the jail window rested on the letters. Edgars waited. His client's head was tilted down towards the paper. Thomas had a full head of hair; shame Lee Edgar thought all that thick hair was wasted on a man about to be executed. At the same time, his hair seemed to be disappearing every waking day. Mr. Lee had become afraid of combs of late. Thomas's head raised; their eyes met.

"You can't read or write. You're illiterate! As illiterate as those Negroes, you oversaw!"

Thomas hadn't cried since he was about three years of age, but the unbridled truth of Lee Edgars' words cut him open like the prized whip he used on Negroes. His wrists shackled, he slammed with great force his two fists tangled with steel into his face, splitting open the skin on his forehead, the pain causing his involuntary urge to cry to evaporate.

"What in God's name !?" Edgar Lee gasped.

Thomas howled with satisfaction at the rush of terror in Edgar Lee's eyes as the blood of the gash ran into Thomas's open mouth; he opened it wider. Thomas's howl became a growl. He was vindicated. His lawyer, who, with all his fancy learning, was wearing a hoop skirt under his pants

A week later, Edgar Lee returned to the jailhouse, determined to act as if nothing repugnant had occurred. He picked up where he left off. Whiskey helped. He averted his eyes from the gash on Thomas's forehead. Edgar looked down at the stick figures and read the few notes he had bothered taking. He would not let this ignorant animal deprive him of the money promised to ensure this beast was found guilty.

"It's your word against the good men of this county, Thomas. Even the Negroes running the horses that night couldn't back your claim!" Thomas went pale. *Good*, Mr. Lee thought. He knew beyond any doubt bringing up the Negro testimony after Thomas's arrest would be his revenge for this animal gashing his head open in his presence.

No Negroes were allowed in a courtroom, so the meeting was held in front of the jail in the sheriff's office. The sheriff, swollen with arrogance and reeking of whiskey, asked questions like he was reading a list of supplies that hardly kept his interest.

"Thomas, you'se say der was two men dat shot and killed H.G., one being his lawyer. Da fact is dey got word white folks were being held against their will, and it might've been Union soldiers, hiding out at Culver Tusk." The sheriff rested his buttocks on his gnarled oak desk and folded his arms over his protruding belly. "Hell, we in da middle of a goddamn war, and da went to investigate! Now, let's see what da Negroes running da horses that fateful night got to say."

The Negroes were brought in unshackled. Each weathered wall of the room and dreary dull furnishings were of no consequence until the two men appeared and stood in the flicking light of the oil lamps. Dressed in tattered clothes, their powerful muscles and taunt chests beneath the frayed garments highlighted how outdated and frail the jailhouse structure was.

The sheriff's office, including any official building, under no circumstances, had ever had a Negro come through the doors. Now, for the first time, there were two. The Negroe's quickly and with discretion glanced at Thomas, then to the sheriff, and dropped their heads. Thomas thought, *Good! Niggas know their place.* But before he could linger in that satisfaction, one of the Negroes bobbed his head up, looked over at him, and then at the sheriff as if he wanted to say something.

"Bailey, dat your name, boy?" the sheriff asked.

"Yes, sir." Bailey nodded.

"Y'all know who shot H.G.? What happened dat night, boy?"

"Sir…it be so dark we'se couldn't tell. We'se hear Master H.G. call out to Mr. Thomas, sir, but he don't answer him. "Several deputies were spaced around the room while gas lights revealed the photos of wanted criminals. Thomas leaned forward to see if he might spot his brother Robert among the faces. The deputy behind him gripped Roberts' shoulder firmly. "Sit back."

"Go on, boy," the sheriff directed the Negro.

"We'se worried cause Mr. Thomas shooting off his gun."

"What about da men on da road?"

"Sir?"

"Was he shooting at da men on the road?"

"No, sir, shooting in da air let us know he'd kill us."

"Make a whole hella sense." The comment came from one of the deputies, who, too, found it disgusting for Negroes to be discussing white folks' business, especially murder. He sucked his teeth, hoping one of the Negroes panicked, just for a moment. He had his hand on his gun just in case his wish was granted.

"We'se hear one man holler, 'Don't do it.' Den..." Bailey heard something in the corner of the room, like a rat scurrying about. He had sat up all night because of the rats running in the cell.

"Den?"

Distracted by the rat sound, Bailey noticed a man behind the desk. The little man had pushed forward from behind a stack of papers, looking out. He was writing. The one thing Bailey wanted in his life was to learn to read and write. He did not forget where he was, but he was curious about the man's oddness and what he was doing. It seemed each time somebody said something, the man wrote it down. Bailey bowed his head to not upset the sheriff but turned enough to watch the little man. "Sir?"

"Den, what happened?" The little man went back to the pad.

"Gun goes off."

"H.G. was shot dead?"

Bailey wanted to talk, excited that his words might come alive outside his head. He spoke. "Dat might be right, sir." And sure enough, the little man's hands moved. Bailey's voice nervously penetrated the air. "I'se suppose, sir, I reckon." He was scared, but he knew this was a white man's problem. *"Dem white folks dey after one another, not me and Sam,"* he told himself.

Bailey continued. "Just fo' da gunshot one 'em says, 'Fo' the life of you,' while the small translucent hands moved on the pad. Bailey thought the hands looked like they had rocks under the transparent skin. The veins were the color of the sky. "Dat's what one of da men's say, it be so dark, can't tell which."

The sheriff walked over to the window and looked out. "Um-hmmm. 'For da life of you.'" He leaned over to talk with one of the deputies.

"Something's wrong with dat man, real wrong." Bailey hoped he had not said it out loud as he returned to the conversation.

The sheriff coughed. "Said 'For da life of you'? Whatcha think he meant by dat?"

Thomas, less than five feet from the Negroes, shifted his weight on the hard chair. He didn't hear what the Negro Bailey's answer was. He didn't care. Thomas had stopped listening. He was glaring at the other Negro, the quiet one, and was shocked at what he was witnessing. The temperature of his blood was rising, heating the tips of his ears. One of the deputies was handing the other Negro a tin cup of water. The bowed head of the Negro rose slowly, and he almost made eye contact with the deputy. "Thank you'se, sir." Thomas could see him clearly from where he sat, he could see every one of the deputies leaning up against the wall or standing half attentive, and in the middle, two Negro's not showing the kind of fear he was used to evoking in Negro's. The flickering of the gas lanterns on the two Negro's skin highlighted their features and disturbed Thomas. He didn't need details of Negro's planted in his mind. Thomas stared down at his shackled wrist while this unshackled Negro drank water. The temperature of his blood rose to his eyes. His raised head when he heard someone cough.

Thomas caught sight of the Negro's head tilted back, his dark Adam's apple moving up and down in the light from the lamp. His throat was smooth, not even hair bumps. The Negro finished drinking and sighed his satisfaction. The last gulp of water going down his throat made Thomas furious more than the thought of prison or death. At that moment, he was overcome with rage. A white man handed a darkie water to satisfy his thirst while he was chained up like an animal. But then, the Negroe's tongue came out of his mouth. Thomas was taken aback by the contrast of his pink tongue on his dark lips, moving slowly and deliberately in satisfaction and taking the glistening drops of water off his lips. Thomas leaned forward, his lips trembling, searching for the best vulgar words to shout at the Negroes. Nothing the vilest of curse words he favored were shackled tighter than his shackled wrist.

The blood that rose started boiling and had nowhere to go. Thomas sprang off the chair. With hands cuffed tucked to his belly, he bent his head and charged at the Negro. The sound of his chair crashing, hitting the cement floor, ricocheted off the walls. There was the noise of boots scuffling and more chairs falling amid the anguished growls from the prisoner. The sudden outbreak was matched by other inmates in the back calling out from their dark cells, "Escape, escape," clanging anything to make noise, including their heads against the bars.

A shrill, high-pitched cry of alarm rose from the corner among the burst of violence. Bailey caught sight of the little man running from behind the stack of papers, eyes bulging with terror.

Thomas headbutted Sam's midsection with brutal force, knocking him into Bailey. The deputies wrestled to get Thomas under control; the room was small enough that the deputies were falling into one another to avoid the brunt of Thomas's boots. "Get hold of da prisoner, now!" the sheriff demanded.

Thomas twisted his head through the deputy's hold. "Niggas, shittin' niggas." If Bailey could have, he would have struck a blow to his former overseer, but that act would be the death of him and Sam.

Bailey looked straight into Thomas's eyes—something he had never done before. It was brief, and it proved enough. Beyond the rage, he saw the fear Thomas had of what the white folks were going to do to him. Bailey hoped his glance told Thomas what was on his mind: *Dey gon' git you! Yes, sir, dey gon' git you good.* He kept himself from smiling.

He watched as they dragged Thomas out of the room, the overseer's boots hitting the cement like metal door knockers. The thick door to the room closed behind the guards and Thomas. Both Negroes dropped their heads in silence. "Y'all boys did good," the sheriff ordered one of the deputies. "Get 'em on outta here, ya'll try to escape you'se dead!"

"Yes, sir."

"Take 'em and shackle 'em to the outhouse."

They passed the little man on the way out. He was hunched over, crying in the corner. The smell let Bailey know the man had more than peed himself. Out of sight of the sheriff and deputies chained to the outhouse, Bailey spoke his thoughts out loud to Sam. "Some 'em wrong with dat little man. Wrong."

Sam didn't answer, as he was busy with his thoughts. He had seen Thomas watching him with devilish eyes, and Sam had taken a moment to lick his lips, hoping it was enough. It was enough, and it was worth the headbutt.

Thomas was executed by hanging on January 8, 1864. His brother Robert came to his cell that morning to say goodbye. Thomas asked Robert to promise him two things: get the Culver Tusk land owned by H. G., find H.G.'s daughter Sarah, and put a child in her. I want a nephew!

The Civil War ended. At last, the Negroes were freed! Southern whites, the haves and have-nots, finally reached the bottom of the barrel, and the bottom fell out. Scarlet fever took up residence in Grove Lane. H.G.'s widow willingly accepted her fate. Succumbing to the disease seemed easier than enduring the humiliation of her life. Her sister-in-law followed. In their dying days, they instructed the remaining servants to burn what was left of all written documents. It was the one business allotted to women to clean up the men's mess. Grove and H.G.'s widows agreed to burn all evidence and shame found in letters or documents. It was assumed Miss Sarah perished in a matter that was not relevant to ponder. The wealthiest brothers in Springfield, Arkansas, were dead. Who was getting all that rich land was on the minds of the ordinary people. The pages of history became so thin and fragile that words like *ownership*, *property*, and *freedom* were hard to adjust. During the first years, it was more than enough to try to keep up with burying the dead, keep the ghosts at bay, and find a pot to piss in. The South and white Southerners were devastated, their minds desperately seeking new laws. And for the freed Negroes, the end of slavery came without direction. Rumors began to swirl that five negroes' women were residing in the second-largest plantation house, Culver Tusk, the first being Grove.

Springfield, Arkansas, residents cried this fortune reversal could only be attributed to a curse.

# S I X

Miss Eloise's sisters arrived on the ship *Mary Ann*, which sailed from Ireland to New Orleans, with titles of ownership of Culver Tusk; they barely survived the worst days of their lives among the other Irish immigrant passengers. Two-thirds of the passengers died during the voyage. In New Orleans, they spoke nightly about finding their way to Culver Tusk and seeing what sounded like a palace to their humble lives back in Ireland. They knew it would be a while before reaching Springfield, Arkansas; they were too ill to travel further. The documentation of their property inheritance was neatly folded in the letters from Eloise. Their sister was dead; their nephew was dead. Was it the war that killed their sister and nephew? Disease? The grieving sisters sadly could relate to disease, as they were nursing themselves for months after the voyage: persistent coughs, loose-running bowels, and constant low-grade fevers that seemed to pass from one sister to the other.

In the boarding house, the overly made-up landlady who left a trail of feathers fleeing from her gowns in every room scrutinized the sister's every move. At the end of each day, she was perched on her chaise sipping port. Her brother floated behind her, wearing long, colorful house coats and reeking of sweet magnolia. They nursed the sisters with home remedies for their illness, listening greedily to the details of the sisters. The landlady offered to find good, strong American men for a small dowery for each sister.

Four men came into their lives one by one, with minimal courtship. "It will take strong and willing men to travel to Springfield, Arkansas, to care and protect us while learning to help us undertake the American ways," the eldest of the sisters said after weeks of counsel from the landlady.

"What about love?" one sister asked.

"What about it?"

More than a year after they arrived in America and years after their sister and nephew's deaths, they made the trip to Little Rock, Arkansas, in the summer of 1870. But it was not summer weather that greeted them. Cold winds forced them to wrap themselves in layers of shawls and head to the courthouse.

Upon their arrival, the city clerk informed them, without as much as a sympathetic glance, that their concerns were not a matter to be taken before a judge, as they were inquiring into business without legal cause. "You can't come in demanding to get the title to Culver Tusk and several Negroes! Haven't you heard about the worst war in American History?"

The clerk took out his glasses and put them on as a matter of arrogance, although the group before him misunderstood this as interest in their dilemma. The eldest sister's husband laid the signed papers before him; he did not bother to glance at them for more than a few seconds. Before chuckling, "The papers were invalid." The sisters, stunned, stood in the courthouse next to their husbands with eyes wide and teary. "It is simple; you have no rights to the property," he assured them. "Unfortunately, the owner, H. G., never filed the legal documents. Nor would it have mattered. Your sister Eloise was not a legal heir in marriage or relation." The clerk looked closer at the papers out of curiosity, then said, "More so, the names of the Negroes on the paper mean nothing. This name here"—he tapped the paper— "Negro Mary, her son's dead." He added, "Mary was held and questioned, let go, and probably run off. He pushed his glasses back over the bridge of his nose. He knew the case well. The clerk walked to a file, ruffled around, and returned with a newspaper. It was the least he could do, seeing it was their sister. He directed them to where they were buried, Eloise and the son, Peter, in a pauper's grave. Although unmarked, he assured them it could be found. "Someone," he stated, "put a makeshift marker and planted a rosebush that has not bloomed over the years."

"How might you know of this?" the youngest of the sisters asked. Impressed by the clarity she spoke, the clerk glanced for the first time at her. He blushed, stunned as if a clap of thunder had sounded in his belly. Her face was specked with freckles near her button nose; he found her quite pretty, stirring a feeling he'd thought lost. Her overcoat was unbuttoned, exposing her long, pale neck. He knew he'd be making intimate gestures that night. His wife would be pleased. He cleared his throat and turned his attention back to the men.

"We get more than enough gossip concerning the dead." He patted the newspaper's face and folded it to the article. He read it out loud and without sympathy.

"November 8, 1863, H.G.'s Mistress Kills Her Son and Takes Her Own Life.

Upon arrival, the soldiers found the body of Eloise McAllister lying next to her child." The sisters let out gasps and cries, which the clerk ignored as he continued. "While it appeared at first to be a mother and son sleeping, it was soon discovered that both mother and child were deceased. It was ruled officially death by poisoning. Near the boy's body on the floor was a Negro child, also deceased. A hysterical Negro slave named Mary was arrested but released.

"A note was found in Eloise's possession confirming she had taken her own life and the life of her son, Peter, and her son's playmate said Negro child. In the note, she wrote she was sorry for the Negro child's mother, Mary, but felt her son, Peter, would not want to face death without his servant and playmate with him.

"All Negroes and servants had disappeared from Culver Tusk Plantation."

The city clerk secretly found pleasure in reading the story of the deaths. A religious man himself, it proved God's command over sin. He thought, what sort of woman would seduce a man astray from the holiness of marriage? And to further give birth to a bastard? He glared with contempt at the paperwork before him. It indeed was an abomination!

But now he was getting bored with their tears and could see the ill-tempered nature of the husbands was losing footing. The men, he suspected, had thought these marriages would open the door to a prosperous life. *Huh!* Foreigners, and Irish at that! He had looked at the marriage certificates before him and laughed, thinking, *If the rumors were true, the couples standing before him had been married indeed by that Negro pastor, passing for white that was chased out of town!*

But what would be the point of further shattering their lives? He shook his head. He was getting hungry, as it was near his lunchtime. He pushed his glasses back over the bridge of his nose; they slid immediately back down. The clerk angrily drew a small circle on the other side of the road on the map.

"Here." He pointed. "What's inside that circle is what you can live on and make a living if you can. It's the only property for immediate sale." The clerk watched their faces for any recognition of knowledge of the circled land. Nothing! Ah, they had not heard of the rumors of ghosts and curses that had plagued these parts since the war. Just as well, he thought. Just as well. The clerk had a usually high level for gossip, but the outrageous rumors of ungodly stories were all he could take.

Despite his explanation, the pretty one asked, "What about Culver Tusk, our sisters' home?" He took her words as a direct attack on his religion. "How dare you suggest a harlot and her bastard son have any legal property rights!" He leaned forward, his voice shaking. "We don't take well to strangers or the ill manners of foreigners. We are God-fearing people. He went to his desk and brought out the documents for the land. The cursed bastard land was divided. The husband, McGregor, Donaldson, Harrison, and Evans handed over the last of the sister's money, signed their names on the paperwork, and left. The clerk locked the office door, walked into the back office, and down three steps, where the air was cold and musty. He waited a moment to adjust to the dim light, then, seeing the hunched-over figure, turned away and threw the papers in his direction.

"Jed…?" The hunched-over figure did not respond. "Damn it," the clerk mumbled, then commanded, "File these!"

He could have handed the file to Jed but avoided him by averting his eyes from his disfigurement, instead looking at a spiderweb hanging from the ceiling. Nor did he risk waiting for the bulging eyes of the little man to glance up to respond. The clerk quickly returned up the stairs and closed the door between them. He washed his hands vigorously, scrubbing at the thought of the Irish immigrants near him. At last, he felt cleansed of the unfortunate task of his morning. The clerk meticulously rearranged his desk. Neatly stacked the paperwork in the far corner before laying a cloth. Satisfied, he opened the wooden lunch box. The smell of onions and garlic greeted him. Smiling, the clerk lifted the biscuit and unwrapped the small container of pigtails and potatoes, ready to enjoy his food in peace.

When the door shut, the small man in the basement office edged his chair away from the wall. Jed was excited to get to the paperwork. He had heard the women in the office crying and the shouts of their husbands. The names the clerk spoke through the thin door were familiar to Jed. They brought back an exciting part of the past that involved him. A history he knew in more detail than most anyone in the office. Jed had taken the notes of the Negroes' comments and then the trial of Thomas C. Latimer. Finally, although even now still regretfully, only Jed and the deceased's brother Robert attended the execution. It bothered Jed, as he'd had no idea that dying men lost their bowels. Throughout his life, Jed didn't always have control of his bladder or bowels; he'd always thought when he died, his body would be at peace and not further shame his mother. That hope was gone.

# SEVEN

The small community of yeoman farmers remained secessionists even after the war ended, a war that left them feeling as if they had been treated like livestock by the government. There were court documents that recorded the testimonies of these yeoman farmers, statements that spoke exclusively about "the curse." It was their opinion that during Reconstruction, the government had intentionally placed them on cursed property and offered the best land to more suitable white Northerners. The families disdained politics and politicians and believed in the Constitution, which protected a man's property. And now that honor was broken. When the Arkansas General Assembly approved the 13th Amendment to the U.S. Constitution, their lives were over and now cursed.

All they had to cling to was the goal of forming a town reflective of the prewar South. So, they wrote letters, convinced that the area surrounding the river, the eastern side, to be exact, was cursed. Cursed! Furthermore, they declared the land adjacent to them on the other side of the river was undisturbed by this ungodliness of happenings. It was believed, on all accounts, that the unaffected people on that land were the sole cause of their own broken life. Culver Tusk was occupied by Negroes with curses and Indians, and the government ignored this violation.

The letters continued to come in from the farmers, as well as wives and families of the dead soldiers, and even from the folks committed to the freedom of Negroes. The testimonies ranted and raved, starting with similar stories. One of the first letters was dated one year after the war legally ended.

The letters started sad and, over time, became increasingly angry and violent. Some people's lack of literacy made it difficult for the reader. The letters penned by more educated authors were even more vile and violent. There were packages stuffed with military remnants and boxes filled with pellets of farm-animal feces. The words replaced primal screams from mothers, wives, and grandmothers rising from the pages. "Our dead soldiers are not ready to be defined by medals of honor, ribbons, or flowers on graves. We lost the goddam war! But we shall ne'ver give up! Our sons' cries cling to the darkness of dry wells and empty rain buckets." The words stuttered and staggered off the pages at times with the eloquence of a drunken poet. "Anything that offers a portal for their once-lived lives has become home to their desperate souls, something as small as the poke of a needle to cloth if enough for their ghost to enter."

Most office workers found the accusations of cursed land laughable and entertaining. They were southerners first and government officials only because they were lucky enough to be working. To them, a ghost was a part of Southern life as the humidity.

June 1869

To Whom It May Concern,

We were walking away from a long day of labor past a bush the three of us saw together and are willing to testify. A shrubbery changed itself for a moment into the face of the assassinated President Lincoln, and just as quickly, the bush turned back into a bush as a lantern light being blown out. But still, the leaves were left holding drops of blood. There is something ungodly about these parts.

Samuel Parker, Abolitionist

December 1870

Dear Sir,

Please read the last letter of the soldier meant to be the father of my children, whose lives will forever be unborn. My deceased husband appears to me on what I cherish to be my best sleepless nights. He carries from the grave, in the palm of his hands, the last light of the moon he gazed upon before dying.  I beg him to stay with me even though he is dead, made of blood and moonlight. He cannot; he moans; the wind's howling interprets his words. He tells me death is a journey he must endure alone.

Please, I beg you, our elected officials, to help us regain our past. Five Negroe women are rumored to live in the plantation house, Culver Tusk. You must immediately send the sheriff to investigate. So, I might share this good news when his spirit returns that his death was not in vain. Please read with compassion his last correspondence.

Sincerely,

Mrs. Sheila Clark, Wife of Sergeant Clark


Dear Sheila, my beloved wife,

I pray you are well and that your delicate fingers receive this letter. I write each word, knowing they are more permanent than myself. We have lost so many in combat I can no longer pretend that my own life is history than life itself.

Forgive me if thoughts of my mortality rise more readily than my faith in this war ending.

I begin my days with prayers of returning each night. If I do not return, may the moon watch over you.

Eternally yours in love forever, your husband, Sergeant Clark, May 11, 1864.


The boxes of letters took up space in the basement of the city clerk's office and nothing more. Before the arrival of the Irish sisters in the area, some families decided to talk to the new mayor in person. They carried the land's dirt on their faces and wore the shabby clothes of sharecroppers. They agreed that the elected officials needed to see their lives after the war.

They set out in early winter, the challenge of the weather causing the long journey even longer for the families in the four wagons. The men smelled of homemade liquor and belched up foul remnants of their near-empty stomachs when they talked. Their eye sockets sagged and were covered in dark circles and broken veins. They looked exactly like the letters that were written—terrified and angry. At least, that's what the men looked like to the mayor. The children and women looked worse. When Mayor Simmons met the families in the street, they appeared as foreign to him as hunger. He descended quickly down the courthouse steps and held his palms up to stop them. "Don't bother getting out of the wagon, you good folks…come all this way, let me come to you." He opened his arms politician wide like he intended to gather each of them, including the kids, in one swoop. When their faces remained unimpressed, he clasped his hands together and gave them his most trusting smile. It made his cheeks hurt, but that smile got him elected twice.

"The least I'se can do comes down to greet you." He could not imagine—the thought sickened him—having the distasteful-looking visitors inside the walls of his court building stinking up the rooms. He stopped smiling; his face grew serious. "Now, what seems to be the issue?" The mayor and the sheriff listened not so much to the complaints but to any possible threats. He found the stories of ghosts and the cursed land boring but continued to act interested.

"Dem fields, mayor? It be's winter or summer, da fields don't give us nuttin but grief.' Da weather come and go like it don't belong to God's reasoning. And our wells, da water ain't proper. Old folks say it's filled with the bitter tears of da devil. It's poison. We send letters, but ya'll don't respond."

A little girl held out a jar with a tin lid; the contents had started the journey as snow. It was her proof, a child's proof, that snow and ghosts exist. The snow was what they had begun to drink because the well water wasn't proper. The mayor stared into her oversized blue-green eyes and smiled. "You brought snow all this way? What's your name?" When she opened her mouth, she revealed a crooked smile with jagged, rotting teeth. He regretted asking her.

"Jamie Lou, sir."

"Well, Jamie Lou, let's look at this snow, little dawling." He chuckled and pinched her dirty cheek, making a mental note not to wipe his hands in front of the onlookers. *I pray I don't catch something*, he thought.

The mayor unscrewed the lid with enough force that the water splashed over, wetting his fingers. He grimaced. "Well, looks like you got water now! Too bad. I thank you anyway, Jamie Lou." His voice was agitated as the girl dropped her head to investigate the jar with disappointment. It flashed through the mayor's mind that, out of spite, the men might have spit or done something worse in the cloudy liquid. It made him angry.

He dismissed the broken families with sacks of flour, salted meat, and dry beans. He gave the kids small treats and the men tobacco and whiskey. To the pregnant women, he smiled and handed them bundles of cloth to sew. The wagons moved away, back home with a promise from the mayor to send someone from their office to personally investigate the land.

Later, in his office, the mayor's staff entertained him by imitating the voices of the families. The sheriff was pitifully dramatic. "Seeing dead soldiers without their flesh, not quite skeletons, they said, but without their flesh."

One of the deputies piped in. "What da hell does dat mean *without flesh*? But not skeletons? Stupid poor trash!" Everybody nodded while the sheriff continued to bring them to near hysteria.

"More wound den flesh." He threw his hands in the air, fanning his fingers and letting them shake like the metal jingles on a tambourine. "Ain't dat what the woman with the red hair cried? More blood than bones."

His hands dropped from the air, and, pulling his gun out, he pretended to shoot. "Pow-pow, there you go, more blood debones and ghosts!"

The mayor threw his head back and howled, "Go on!" He slapped his thigh.

"Dey marching over our crops, killing our land…Dey, dey said we cursed! Son of a bitch, you cursed, all right." The mayor closed the office early that day and took his staff and the sheriff to dine at Little Rock's finest restaurant. It might be snowing somewhere in the county, they laughed, but here in the capital, it was crawfish season. The families were foolish, and the letters were ignored.

But alas, one employee read the letters with sincerity and committed to their safekeeping: Jed, assistant to the town clerk's office.

Stacks of files surrounded Jed, and a lamp light barely covered his minuscule work area. The solitude of the basement didn't relieve the haunting voices in his head since childhood. *"Are you busy?"* the voices asked as he opened one envelope after another. His oversized head, too big for his small frame, would rise as if expecting company, only to realize it was the voices.

Insane, lonely Jed was what he called himself, insane, *lonely Jed.*

He occupied himself between reading and studying the deformity of his hands, which resembled doorknobs. His spine, when most distressed, would curve into the shape of a C as if he were bending to pick things up, even when nothing was dropped. He was not the color of white people. Jed was transparent. He felt a kinship to the letters.

Jed was spellbound by the events described in the letters, as he was born strange. The bloody bones and unexplainable acts narrated in the letters gave meaning to his life. Jed read them with the seriousness in which they were written. Jed believed every word written. His hands trembled in the right places, and he knew when to gasp softly in disbelief. He was as devoted to the letters as a preacher is to the Bible, and he could quote letters from years past since the letters had been arriving steadily since the war.

Jed took the letters to heart, weeping over them. He understood what it was like to live in a state of hopelessness. Jed believed every word written just as he felt the voices of the people that lived in his head, voices that no one, not one person but himself, could hear. The voices asked him questions no one dared ask him. *How you doing today?* The voices were not male or female; they were sometimes nice but mostly not so nice. *Jed?* the voices asked, with no hint of their true intentions. *How you doing today, Jed?* The voices had been with him since childhood, keeping him company in the shadow of his parents' shame. Jed had been thrust into the arms of a Negro nursemaid after his mother survived a difficult birth. His parents had felt betrayed by their doctor, who had guaranteed their son would not live to see his first birthday. He did, and along with his survival came the voices.

"Fine," he would answer with trepidation.

*Who gives a shit?* The voices would laugh. *Who gives a shit?* He could not tell how many people lived in his head, as they all spoke together as a family.

In the end, the other officials laughed at the letters. Most letters concerned the land of Culver Tusk, the blessed land, as it was referred to, and the former plantation house, where it was claimed five Negro women lived. This claim alone, they argued, validated there was indeed a curse on the white Southerners.

Jed felt—in fact, he knew—that the letters would be helpful one day. He did not know how or when. Jed put them away with the documents, treaties, and titles that went back nearly one hundred years, from a time people dismissed as unimportant. This made the documents and letters even more precious to Jed. He knew claims that events and people deemed unimportant had nothing to do with truth.

He sometimes imagined, when his body had enough strength and the weather was accommodating, making the trip to the cursed land to see with his bulging eyes the walking dead figures and to hear the voices that called out to their mothers from the drinking wells and pails. He examined the maps accompanying the letters, memorizing the course he might take. More than anywhere, he wanted to see this place called Culver Tusk and the blessed house. Secretly, he dreamed if he offered the Negroes the papers no one deemed necessary, they might cast a spell to undo his twisted body. He planned his visit, month after month, sitting in the dim, damp basement.

*You're too weak,* the voices whispered. *Too soft, Jed.*

And then, in the late summer of 1870, a telegram arrived for Jed to send off. A telegram that convinced him it was time. The voices in his head jokingly egged him on. *No one will miss you. No one! Maybe you should take the devil for company.* The voices laughed out loud: a hysterical chorus. Jed became angrily defiant and laughed back. No longer feeling afraid of the voices, he engaged with them. He cursed at them, "Kiss the morning roosters' ass!" He waited in dead silence for a response but got nothing. He felt encouraged by their silence and was guided by that alone. "Maybe I will take the devil with me! Maybe I will."

He picked up the telegram and reread it. A Roman Catholic nun, Sister Elizabeth, was coming by train to meet with Evening. Jed had heard stories of the Indian woman named Evening, mentioned in the telegram. But why, he wondered, was the telegram addressed to the man named Hargrove? Jed sent it off but added a warning to Hargrove and Evening. The officials knew the nun was coming, and he knew more. It took many long, tedious days searching files for hours, which left his frail body weak, but he meticulously went through the dusty boxes until he had enough of the pieces to tell him a story. Ten boxes labeled "Tusk: Government Treaty of Indian Property, 1798." Jed inhaled the dust of history, nearly eighty years past, rising from the box. It held the notes of men with significant legal and political standings, men in his own family with blood on their hands. He wept openly. Jed's eyes devoured pages of notes, gasping at times, other times covering his mouth in shock and shame.

Hargrove! Hargrove was Grove's only son and H.G.'s nephew. It was widely rumored behind political doors that Hargrove murdered his father. Jed found the document of one female slave named Lena, who was the property of Master Grove. Why, he wondered, with all the negroes Grove owned, why this one document with just one name? Reading on, he discovered more. It described in legal words and personal notes written in the margins Grove and the former governor had both been involved in the murder of a legal, free Negro man for his land. Jed realized more blood was on their hands than he'd originally thought.

He took out a pine box of papers that one of the horsemen had found on the road where H.G. was murdered. The box contained letters from Ireland addressed to Mistress Eloise, but amid the letters was H.G.'s diary. Jed realized he was holding nothing less than a room of gold bricks. Had anyone bothered reading his last entry, they would have seen that the overseer, Thomas, had not lied; he did not kill H.G. despite the damning evidence that took him to his execution. H.G.'s diary held many answers, going back to before the Civil War. Jed covered his mouth; afraid he might involuntarily yelp with joy. His eyes watered. He wondered if someone had intended for all of this to be saved, and if so, why? Blackmail? Trembling, he asked if his own life could be in danger, but this quickly passed as he realized he had no life to be endangered.

He seemed to have been waiting for this moment during his dreary life. Voices or not, Jed and the devil, were going to Culver Tusk. Jed did not bother to close the door leading outside. He hoped the cool air brought snow, imagined or real, to bury the city clerk while eating his daily lunch of pigtails and boiled potatoes.

It was an uneventful Friday when the clerk felt the cold. He lifted his head. "Who's there?" He greeted the silence with the stomping of his feet as he looked once outside the office. Nothing. He closed the door, walked past the stairs leading to the disfigured man, averting his eyes, and returned to his desk. The broth the pigtails were cooked in had soaked through the cloth and onto his desk, causing a frown.

Jed rushed to his waiting buggy as much as his slight frame would allow.

The sack and case he threw in first. No one who saw his twisted body pulling itself up onto the seat could have differentiated him from a small child. Only the expert snap of the whip told them he was much more. He reviewed the plan, knowing the road east would eventually take him to Culver Tusk. He first would have to get past the yeomen farmers, the ones who had come to town last winter, and then the sisters of the dead woman, Eloise. His eyes rolled in his head. Should he be scared? Jed wiped the sweat from his forehead. The cursed land each family farmed joined directly at the junction he needed to travel. It worried him what they might feel about him if they knew he was the mayor's relative. Would they take their anger out on him? Twist his frail body even more? The voices in his head agreed. *They go' git yo ass and burn you over an open fire.* The laughter rose into the cold air. He thought of turning the buggy around. *Go find Mr. Shelton Wyman,* the voices told him. Jed pulled the wagon over to the side of the road and wept, for it seemed finally the voices were showing him compassion.

He opened the case and pulled out an official letter. In the documents, he prayed for some sign from the heavens that in the very end, he, Jed, would survive and for once feel like a man, and his prayer was answered. He read: Mr. Shelton Wyman leading a group of one hundred armed men assigned to the border of the county east of the Ozark Mountains. The cold sweat poured down the back of Jed's neck as his eyes rushed over the names of the Negroes assigned and living on the land. His mouth popped open, and the cold air rushed in and dried his throat. He thanked the voices for guiding him, finally whispering something in his favor. *Go find Shelton.* There on the list of Negroes was the name of the Negro Bailey. Bailey, he remembered, had been on the road when H.G. was killed and was the one who spoke in the jail. Jed had never forgotten the sympathetic look the Negro offered when he saw Jed had peed his pants. He felt that Bailey was a good and kind man. Jed snapped the straps of the buggy. He did not know why but thinking he might meet Bailey made the journey less frightful. The voices laughed, then agreed.

# E I G H T

Bailey went to the river, rolled his frayed pants, and walked in. Nothing of his feet was soft; the bottoms were as hardened as the water rocks they encountered. Bailey had never known shoes for over a month during his enslaved life. This day in freedom was no different. It was late afternoon, and the only hint of shade rested in the wide patch of trees on the other side of the Harden Grove River. Bailey was feverishly hot but not much interested in the promise of shade offered in the distance. The cool movement of the water was enough.

He took a tin cup from a loop made of hemp from his pants. The loop held all he owned: the tin cup, a small knife, and a pouch with a few seeds from squash. Bailey bent down to the river and dipped the cup into it. He then turned, facing directly into the sun. The sun felt new to him in freedom, and he closed his eyes to let it in. He was still getting used to the sun and being friendly with him. It was too hot sometimes, yes, and gone too soon sometimes. Yes, he agreed with himself, but it was, after all, the sun. It laid itself on everything it came upon, and each thing it touched had its understanding. As an enslaved man in the fields, Bailey often cursed the sun's fiery spirit. A prayerful man always, he begged forgiveness for his ignorance. But then, he told himself, he was bent under the command of another, and when the sun laid itself upon his broken flesh, he cried inside of its betrayal. "I cursed your sun, God, forgive me." He knew God would forgive him for that misunderstanding. Too many times after being chastised by the slave master and his flesh torn open by the whipping, his pain was made worse by the sun's heat. God saw that as well.

Now freed, he got to know the sun differently, and in this new understanding, he did not need to curse it. He knew the sun, as God intended it to be, was a service to the earth and all its family. Bailey respected that. As he headed away from the river, the sun went with him.

Not far, less than a quarter mile away, was his woman, Mary. She was standing in a field of lotus berries. She had been occupying herself with the print of her dress, thinking she could cut the bottom and put it in the quilt she was making. She looked up at the sky around her and saw the field was just as empty as it had been at first glance. In the last few minutes, Mary had taken to worrying about Bailey, asking herself, "Where did he run off to?" She cupped her hand over her eyes to shield them from the sunlight and looked towards home. "Nah," she said, "he ain't gone home without me." She looked around to see if he was hiding in the tall, willowy grass stalks, playfully watching her.

Mary waited while tiny trails of sweat ran slowly from her scalp, tickling her head under her twisted braids. The day seemed hotter than most. She reached to pick one flower from the lotus stem to place in her hair. The stem scratched gently; it felt good. Mary heard something rustling and turned. She saw him coming, walking with ease toward her and parting the tall stalks with his arm and smile. His broad smile was as much of her body as her breath. She exhaled but could not return the smile. Mary was determined not to let her man think walking and leaving her alone was okay.

Bailey had not asked anyone, not the man who oversaw the land, not Mary. He had just walked off and hadn't brought his pole for fishing. That couldn't be it. Now, here he comes, smiling as if the act of his leaving was like any other day he had ever known. He got close enough for Mary to look into his eyes.

"Here you'se go." Bailey reached out the cup towards Mary. Mary gazed up at him with as much intensity as the sun on his face. She did not take the cup at first. She was waiting for him to tell her something about his leaving. He said nothing. Instead, he touched her braided hair close to the flower with his free hand and smiled. "Pretty."

Still pulled tight with worry, her face was satisfied that Bailey was back. She asked, "How's you'se know I'se thirsty? I didn't even know it myself." She blinked twice rapidly, pondering her question. "But I am."

He was squinting, blind from sunlight, and smiling simultaneously. "You'se never ask for nuttin." Bailey saw Mary was still pondering her question. She was confused, and Bailey understood her confusion. Mary's body wanted a drink of water. But like others enslaved, Mary learned to save her life, which meant forgetting her basic needs. Thirst be one. What she or others wanted didn't matter. Bailey thought, it matters *to me, Mary.* He bent and kissed her forehead, hoping what he didn't say out loud she felt in his affection. She smiled, and Bailey took that as a yes.

He would not know what to say if a kind stranger asked him what Mary looked like. Bailey could say Mary is pretty, but the prettiest things can become ugly. A man's heart is smarter than his eyes, for the heart is always looking for the truth, and the truth is beauty. This he knew for sure. He did not know how he realized it, but he did.

"My Mary's face," he would tell them, "Is da same as dat sun coming up dat let me know it's morning and da sun going down to tell me it's night. Dat be God's truth." He would add, "And be'tween the two, her face let me know I be awright." If Bailey could have shared his thoughts with Mary, he would have, but he did not know how to speak of everything his heart knew with only a handful of words to choose from.

Still perplexed, she asked, "How's you'se know Bailey?"

"Cause I'se wonder sometimes what I'se can give you'se."

He wiped the sweat from his forehead with his free hand before it got to his eyes. He lowered his voice and put a bit of a song to it. "Dat attt… mouth full of rrriver called on me, and say, Bailey! Give yo woman dis water." Mary squinted her eyes and smiled up at her man.

"Dat what da river sounds like?"

"Yep, dat's how it sounds to me."

She laughed, forgetting she was upset at his absence. Mary took the cup and drank.

"Err'body gits thirsty, I figure." He paused. "I thought…it be time," nodding his head up and down, "dat it be the time you'se know your thirst." Bailey was a good foot taller, providing enough shade for her turned-up face.

"Me?" Tears rose in her eyes.

"You'se, Mary, and whatever else your body calls for."

Mary pondered the question for a moment, saying to herself, "Err'body gits thirsty?"

She was interrupted by another question, which rushed in and quickly vanished. But not before giving Mary that funny feeling under her skin, a piece of unattended grief. Mary looked at the ground. Mary wondered if her son felt any pain when he drank the poison. Seizures followed her grief. The seizures felt like tiny bugs crawling under her skin, racing. When this happened, she knew her nerves were ready to act up. It was a sign she hated, and Bailey did, too.

Mary felt the nerves go into her hands, tingling her fingers. In the past, her mind would fill up with tiny lights, and everything around her would run into a black hole until she disappeared. She'd wake up sometimes with pee on her.

Bailey steadied her shaking hand, holding the cup. "Drink, baby, I'm sorry." He tried never to call her *baby, as* it might bring up her child. He had slipped. Bailey would do anything to stop one of the attacks on Mary. He started humming what he thought might soothe Mary.

Sometimes, the word *baby* spoken in her presence made the spells appear. He hoped it would not be so today. Bailey hummed until he saw Mary's body relax; she held the cup steadily. He stopped.

"Err'body gits thirsty." She repeated it as firmly as the ground beneath them. There was no wind moving in this part of the day. The only sound beyond them was a lone bird singing in the sky. Nothing answered the bird's song.

"Err'body," he repeated.

"Humm."

A thought crossed his mind, and he followed it. Looking out over the field to reassure himself they were alone; Bailey unbuttoned his pants but did not take his eyes off her. Mary was looking at him over the rim of the cup. Before she could summon up the question to ask what he was doing, he was naked from the waist down. The small space between them closed as he kneeled on the earth.

"You'se going to ask me to marry you naked, Bailey?" she teased. Mary knew soon as they found a Negro preacher, they would be joined in God's eyes. But it didn't matter any. Mary knew they would be together forever.

Bailey reached under her dress and pulled down whatever piece of torn-up rag she had covering her privacy. It was a hot, wet rag, and he took pleasure in that fact. He pulled her to the ground. He was careful and gentle with Mary, as always. His voice was hoarse. "You'se my wife when I first see you. God told me dat."

Mary straddled over him and took herself down to rest her knees on opposite sides of his warm body, arched above him. She adjusted his manhood with ease, still holding on to the tin cup. Bailey peeped at the dark hair between her legs, smelled her body's warm, familiar scent, and closed his eyes momentarily. He inhaled her smell deep into his nostrils. Both the heat of the day and her scent filled him.

"I'se feel better, Bailey." Her voice was huskier than before. Mary's eyes were half-closed. It seemed to Bailey that Mary's private part had enough moisture to fill her cup. "Bailey?"

"Mary?" She took her body all the way down on his waiting hips and let him go deeper inside her. She tilted the cup and took the last swallow. He reached his hand to take the empty cup from her.

"I'se missed you'se, Bailey." The words were barely audible, but he heard them and the meaning inside Mary's words.

"You think youse know when youse git thirsty agin?" The soft skin of her lips pulled gently into a smile. She nodded yes. "Den, it was worth me going, so you'se git to know your thirst." He let the cup fall to the ground. Bailey wanted nothing between him and Mary, not even the hot air. The cup's job was done.

He placed the palms of his broad hands on each side of her fleshy thighs, feeling a different heat from her skin than he had felt from the sun. "Don't git jealous, sun, but my woman is hotter," he joked. His mind traveled with that thought and wondered if this was what the sun felt when it lay on the face of the water, hot and wet. He trembled. Maybe that's all we are as people: the sun, water, air, the earth. It's funny how my mind works sometimes. He thought, *We's not meant to be slaves or masters, just be part of everything else on God's earth. Doing what it is supposed to do. Just minding its own business.*

Bailey's eyes watered under the weight of his thoughts. He wondered if a man could be smart if he couldn't write his name or recognize it. Bailey came out of these thoughts and went back to his woman. Mary's body demanded his full attention in a field held together by the scent of lotus flowers. He blinked, and the tears ran freely down his temples.

Mary's full hips moved in minuscule circles. Bailey's hands reached around, taking hold of her butt cheeks, squeezing gently, guiding his hands to slide up and down her thighs, back and forth. She moaned and tilted her to the side. Bailey's eyes moved over her face, satisfied with the pleasure he was giving her. Mary's lips parted.

"Water, water, wa,' err'body, thirsty, water," half-singing the words matching the movement of her body. "Err'body, thirsty, water, err'body, thirsty, watererbodythristywatererbodythristyerrrrrrrr."

At that moment, Bailey's desire to shorten the distance between them took over. The air between them was an imposition. He wanted to taste her mouth. "Come to me, Mary." Mary pulled her dress over her head and let it fall. Bailey knew her nipples well, all swollen and ready for his hands and mouth. *They'd have to wait a bit*, he thought. He was thirsty for her lips and let her breasts rest a moment on his chest.

He tasted the sweet berries and river water her mouth offered. He did not know how long he could hold back his pleasure. She pushed her tongue with tenderness and urgency, and he knew she was asking for more. Mary rolled her tongue like she rolled her buttocks passionately. Her kiss asked for more than he had ever imagined he could give, but he was determined to try. Bailey asked his body to provide Mary with what she was calling for.

*Give*, he pleaded with his body. He was torn between begging to please her and begging not to let go of his pleasure too soon. Because of her movements, all the strength he had to hold back his pleasure was leaving. *God*, he called out in his mind, *give Mary all of me dat I'se got to give*. The more he begged, the more Mary's body asked for more. She pulled her mouth away long enough to gently cry, "Err'body, thirsty, water, err'body, thirsty, waatererbodythristywaterrrbodythristyerrrrrrr." She was stringing the words together as one. When she was done, her body covered itself with goosebumps of satisfaction; Mary kissed Bailey.

His pleading to God and his woman ran the words together, swimming in the warmth of their kisses in between. Bailey did not know how to read or write, but he knew the taste of God's River and his woman that he knew! He cried inside. They were not wet tears to be released but moans of a good cry, giving your prayers to God and making love to his woman. To him, his moans were like thunder falling away from the rain.

Mary raised her face from his. Her top and bottom lip pulled inward, pressing tight, with her teeth biting down into the flesh of her mouth. Her nipples, poking out fat and dark, looked out at him. Bailey trembled at the vision; the sweat glistened on Mary's skin, the sun soaking into her brown skin with gold undertones, and her sweet smell shook every part of his body alive.

Bailey couldn't hold on any longer, just as the rain could not hold on to the sky. He squeezed her thighs and let go in one, two, three breaths. Bailey shook so hard that his back and hips rose and arched off the ground. Their pleasure met. Mary opened her eyes and spotted a red-breasted bird flying into the air with blue-black wings. Mary imagined herself like the bird: lifted in the air. Her back arched limber as bamboo stalks, her hips and buttocks still straddling across Bailey. Without warning, it began to happen. The second wave of the spell was coming on. Mary felt the dizziness and a tingling feeling in her head, like a swarm of bees looking for a flower to land upon, a dance that stung her brain.

Then, the black door appeared above her. Her hands began to flutter like the bird's wings. "Sing, Mary," a voice called from behind the door. She opened her mouth and sang… "Watererbodythirstywatererthirsty, watererbodythirstywatererthirsty." But nothing could keep the spell back. The door was waiting. The door Mary learned was all the voices of mothers and children singing in the choir of the dead. Mary figured not many folks could hear the choir's songs if they didn't know the truth. Mary knew the truth, the ugly truth. A mother's womb holds the soul of their child. The door opened, and Mary saw another world.

A sky filled with fat clouds and timeless rain fell constantly from the sky. The clouds spoke to Mary for a split second, because of her love for Bailey and her need to be okay for his sake. Mary denied the voices were talking, yet she knew in the same breath that the clouds were talking, and they had a list of promises and one wish.

"Sing, Mary."

She was sure that Bailey could not see what the clouds offered her—Mary's son. *Yep, dat be my baby, no matter how long he be gone and how he was taken from me*, she thought. Now, he was laughing in the clouds. Her son was calling to her, waving at her, face wet and rain hanging on his dark lashes. She looked to see if the calluses were gone from his hands. He had loved it so much when she kissed each callous, rubbing them with animal fat stolen from the kitchen.

She realized the images in the clouds would erase her child without notice, like he did not exist. The rain would go away, the choir would be muted, and fat clouds would disappear, like always.

Mary felt Bailey beneath her, moving the earth. He was not in the sky with her; Bailey was resting. The red-breasted bird above them froze in flight and watched Mary. At that moment, Bailey's sperm was vigorously inside her, seeking life.

Mary fainted when the door shut. Warm pee ran from her body and confused Bailey with its warmth. It was a minute before he knew she'd peed herself. Mary's body was limp. Bailey rubbed her back, listening to her breathing. "Mary?" Her chest rose and came down heavy, sinking against him. "Mary?"

His body shifted to adjust to her weight. Mary stirred. "Err'body gits thirsty, err'body gits." Mary was coming back. She felt she would throw up, so Mary turned her head away from Bailey. She spotted the bird still sitting on the branch watching. "Pretty birdie." Mary smiled. The field was full of everything that made itself a field: grass, wild lotus flowers, and trees. She had no idea that Bailey had been rubbing her back for some time or that she had peed herself. Bailey was still beneath her, waiting. She opened her eyes to the tenderness his face offered. Bailey's skin was smooth except on his forehead. "Whatcha thinking, Bailey?

"If I had da words, I'd tell you'se, Mary." Mary felt almost like her old self but still had a tingling in her head.

"You'se good, Mary?" She said nothing. Searching her face, Bailey wondered if she had come back yet. It had been a while since the spells had come on her. He regretted leaving her alone in the field, thinking that might be why. But then he slipped and said the word *baby*. "Dat might be what started it," he whispered to himself. Mary got up and started to walk away. The warm summer air was suddenly cooler, with her no longer on top of him. Bailey felt a sense of panic rise in him. He had been foolish to risk loving his woman in an open field. Anybody might come along, and now Mary was walking naked as her birthing day. He got up and reached for their clothes.

"Mary!"

She turned over her shoulder with tears in her eyes. "I'se didn't mean to break da sky," she said sorrowfully, then repeated it as if she needed him to answer. "I'se didn't mean to break da sky. I'se didn't mean to break da sky. I…"

"Oh, God." Bailey came alive, jumped, and began wrestling with his pants.

"Sky broke, help me, Bailey." Bailey watched Mary, hopping on one leg, struggling to get his pants on. Mary held her palms.

"I don't see nuttin'; I swear, Mary." He knew the spell was lying and making her see things ain't there. "Mary ain't nothing on your pretty hands, please, Mary."

Mary looked down at the tiny bright blue sparkles of the broken sky in her hands. She walked back to him. "Looka, what have I done, Bailey?" In her mind were small fragments of the sky, so tiny Mary couldn't imagine she'd be able to put the sky back together again. "Oh, God, where my son gonna live if da sky is broken, Bailey?"

Bailey looked at her tormented face. "In here, Mary." He laid the palm of his hand on her chest; her heart was racing. "Right here, Mary." *Come back to me, Mary. Please come back*, he begged, hoping Mary could see his love for her.

Bailey had witnessed the madness that took over in folks too many times. The madness sprang up to break their faces in half. One minute, they looked like he'd always known them to be. The next minute, another face took over; the new face was always twisted, something gawd awful. He had seen the foaming and frothing of their mouths, barking sounds coming from their throats. Louder than the dogs that chased them down. Bailey had felt madness once. His face had trembled with such force that he thought his face would shake loose from its bones. But he, with God alone, had fixed the madness before it got to barking or foaming.

*Not my Mary, God. Not my Mary.* He listened to the gibberish from her mouth about a broken sky. Bailey figured Mary saw the blue sky as a big window; her son looked down at her through it. Bailey saw how that might be comforting to Mary. But lord, what possessed her mind to make her believe she broke the sky? Bailey couldn't figure it out and didn't have the time. He took her underpants and quickly wiped the pee from between her thighs. He looked up at the blue sky. "Something as beautiful as dis can't be broken," he mumbled more to himself than Mary.

"All day, daylight, nighttime, ain't go' be either one now dat the sky's broken," she wept between the gibberish. Bailey stood up from wiping her thighs and, taking Mary by the shoulders, shook her as easily as he could so as not to hurt her but shake her senses back. He waited. Her head rolled back; her chin pointed up at him. Then her head flopped forward and dropped down. She wept harder, this time turning her wet face to him accusingly.

"Looka what you'se done, Bailey!"

"Looka, what I'se done, Mary?" Bailey didn't know what she meant or what he had done, but he would take the blame from his Mary. He paced his words with deliberation as if he was hitting a nail into wood, "Look… wha…I na done, Mary." His words seemed to settle her. Bailey pulled her face to his chest. She rested momentarily, looked up, and whispered, "Looka wha you'se done."

"I'se know, baby." He bit his lip for slipping again. Mary's body stiffened.

"I'se sorry, Mary, I'se sorry. Look what I na done." She never mentioned her son being poisoned by Mistress Eloise. Never. He would've been willing to listen to how Mary felt since his death, but Mary rarely mentioned her son. Bailey had met the boy a few times, standing silently by Miss Eloise's son, Peter. They could have been the same child except for the slight color difference. Bailey immediately knew how the child came about. He just hoped H.G. hadn't hurt Mary too severely in the act. The thought made him grind his teeth and blink back tears. Bailey could and would listen if Mary could talk to him. No matter how the child came about, he knew how deeply Mary loved her little boy. Bailey took some comfort knowing the child's tender flesh only knew the affection of his mother's hands and never the affliction of a whip. Bailey knew that if the boy had lived, he would have shown the child love. Sometimes, he wondered if he should tell Mary through her silent grieving for her son; he, too, grieved and not only missed the boy but had learned to love him. But again, he wondered how to speak the thoughts of his mind to help Mary understand.

Bailey scooped Mary up and cradled her against his body to take her home. On the walk back, the sky began to fade to gray. Bailey looked up. "We gon' git rain, Mary."

He sounded happier than he felt inside, for Mary's sake. She was pulled tight in his arms like a child. Bailey heard her laugh softly. He could see their cabin just ahead. When her laughter ceased, he listened to see if Mary had settled down into sleep. She was quiet, and then, as if somebody was listening for her voice, Mary poked her head from under his arms and opened her mouth wide. He saw the hole where he had recently pulled out her aching tooth. It was healing properly.

"Errrrrrrrrrrrrrrrrrrrrr'body." At first, Bailey worried that somebody would hear and take it the wrong way. But her mouth wasn't foaming, and she didn't bark. Mary was singing, "Errrrrrrrrrrr'body." It was the sweetest sound he'd ever heard. His heart was beating fast, yet he knew it was not from the walk but from the sound coming from Mary. Bailey didn't even know his Mary could sing. Maybe they'd find a church someday and let Mary sing behind the preacher. "Errrrrrrrrrrr'body," she went on for a while on one note. He hastened his pace.

Bailey wanted to ask her, "How you'se hold on so long to dat sound and not take da time to breathe?" But he didn't. He just pleased himself with his thoughts. *It was a small thing in a big way, giving my woman water if water led to her singing 'stead of barking or foaming at the mouth,* Bailey thought. *I'se can handle dat!*

Mary stopped singing, whispering what seemed like a name, and Bailey stopped. He pulled her higher. His arms had begun to tremble with excitement, and he leaned himself in. "Wha' dat you'se say, Mary?"

Mary bit down softly into his shoulder and peered up at him. "My son's name was not Peter, Bailey."

"I'se know, Mary. I'se know." Bailey held her closer and waited to hear Mary speak her child's true name, but for the rest of their journey home, Mary slept.

# N I N E

Matters of the summer seasons worsened, where once there was foliage, long heavy icicles hung from the sycamore trees. With that offense, the bees disappeared, leaving vacant hives for the spiders. The crisp air hinted something else just as strange as the deceitful weather was on its way. Folks complained that the air touched their skin and bit at them akin to insects. The habit of scratching and spanking their exposed bitten flesh became normal. The families living on the cursed land saw the change of color on the edges of the low-hanging clouds, sitting on the treetops of icicles as a warning from Mother Nature.

Their children didn't have the childhoods their parents and grandparents grew up with. They were breastfed with the milk laced with the open wound of losing the war. The land's beauty was gone from the memories of their parents and grandparents. The children were growing up with snow drifting on southern land.  As the first generation to inherit the Civil War legacy, their imaginations struggled to act out a childhood that did not exist. Already wounded to the bone by war stories, the children romped through frozen fields, enacting nightmarish tales. They bypassed games of hide-and-seek, kicking up the dirt, or skipping rocks. Their tiny bodies imagined the movement of rigid soldiers falling backward, sabotaging child's play. It was a game of war, in which the cold wind carried the children's angry screams across the fields of unproduced harvest, sometimes snow, "You'se a damn Yankee." Or another familiar charge, "Yo family is white trash. You'se don't even own a nigga."

When the birds arrived, breaking up the low clouds, they came as an uproar of more than a thousand displaced, unrecognizable fowl across the Mason-Dixie line. They came flapping against the cold, brutal sky. The collective sound of the birds made folks' faces pull back as if caught in a windstorm. The old people thought this was the end, if not for them separately in their declining years, then for the small community. They prayed for the end to be swifter and kinder than the war.

The children found sticks, rocks, or, unbeknownst to them, human bones of soldiers to throw at the foreign nests. The screeching and flapping birds ascending into flight made the children scream with ecstasy. They won the game if a nest fell, and the eggs broke, exposing her vulnerable insides. The old folks rubbed their aching joints, sucked their remaining teeth at the unruly children, and advised their parents, "Hitting at a helpless bird's nest's bound to bring more bad luck." The parents laughed the old folks off, but then they, too, secretly worried.

A half mile from the first farmhouse, a golden-breasted rooster sat facing his hens in silence on a hill separating the east from the west. Like the last soldiers of war, the rooster had led them away from the new birds, defeated. The hens followed him to the arch of the hill. The hens laid nothing but their heads, their beaks resting on piles of foreign bird shit. One old man joked the hens were trying to kill themselves in foreign shit. It got a good chuckle, but nobody laughed after days of seeing their hens becks thrust in the piles.

The families took to their porches with axes, lynching rope, and shotguns cocked. Their fears were multiplying, and the feeling of madness was without direction; everything and everybody was suspect. Southern accents deepened, segregating those souths of the Mason-Dixie line from the transplants and transients.

"Wh' air dem birds come from?"

"Don't know, but do know migra'ng for anybody, too early. Dem birds' songs ain't right."

"And dem da wrong birds. Dis, not dar sky, dem Yankee birds!"

The birds hung around, not more than a half mile east of the hub of the road, leaving fields full of feces as their calling card. Each daybreak, the rooster would keep its cock-a-doodle-doo locked in silence. Near the man-made water hole, the goose would cackle, and the mockingbird would lose itself; it imitated the goose so well that the geese left the formation. A mockingbird cock-a-doodle-dooing, bouncing from branch to branch while the geese swam separately in silence.

The farmers and sharecroppers, whole and broken families, gathered at the hub of the road leading toward town, becoming a pack, waiting for the world's end to appear.

"Dem birds a warning."

"A sign, colder coming."

"Remember when it snowed last year for months?"

"If we git another freeze, we'se might as well throw our palms up to da sky." They all nodded in agreement, even the children.

"Yep, da devil is living among us."

Southerners, devoted to suspicion, were left to ponder, "What is da sky doing, giving us snow and hail in August? Dat ain't natural." They were left preparing to drop dead, if need be, from hellfire and pride. They had no one to turn to but one another. The government ignored their cries, letters, and telegrams. Writing a letter about foreign birds and icicles would be useless if war ghosts had not gotten the mayor's attention.

So, they waited again and watched the slow sunset, questioning the layers of colors before the sky turned black. Sometimes, the land was soft enough to allow their sticks to twist and turn into shapes that told a story. Amid the bird droppings, the changing of the season, and the dead not ready to be dead but ghosts, there was nothing else to do but wait. A lucky day passed quickly. Then, another anticipated unexpected happened. A song came down from the Ozark Mountains, crossed the river, and drifted out of the woods. It came late at night, stretching into predawn. The sky offered no promise of a breeze, just its stillness of heavy cold air, but the song became the sky's breeze. It lifted the curtains and entered the house, reminding them of spring. The song shimmered like the moonlight on the Mississippi River covering the long faces of the occupants; their eyes glistened with hope. Leaving smiles on every face, even the newly born babies. *No, it wasn't gas*, they agreed. Notes of the song shook the leaves of trees vigorously, big and small, as if icicles were a minor detail. And when the song was present, no ghosts were seen or heard from. The old stood upright again without complaints of sore joints and aching bodies. Their minds skipped like rocks before the war to the other South they loved. They wanted their South back. Teeth or no teeth, they smiled big at the memories the song offered. At the hub, they argued in a friendly way about the song's words. *Err'body*, some could agree on. None of the farmers or sharecroppers liked *err'body* without reason as to why not. Err'body, what? But that ain't making sense, they concluded and left it at *err*.

And this next thing was vital for them to agree on, and they did. In the beginning, it seemed the song brought melancholy. Some memory you needed to forget to move forward. But they agreed that after a while, the sadness turned sweet. Soon, only good things seemed to happen after the song was heard. Things so small they might have gone unnoticed, but the song came first, forcing them to look outward and wait. They figured, in good humor, that maybe the devil was taking a break or just liked music. It felt good to laugh together, to make light of it. And good things did seem to happen.

"Well, like dat rooster finally taking to his chickens. A few of da farmers got eggs."

"Yep, sho' 'nuff is true."

"Chickens took dar beaks out da shit and laid eggs." They laughed heartily.

"And…and…what bout dat damn goat? Come moseying up da road like it don't know it's a goat, coming to be eaten! Huh, what about dat?" Oh, they laughed hard on that one and ate well for days.

"And don't forget dat piece of worthless land. Out of nowhere, greens harvested so big you could wrap the leaves around yourself."

For days and nights without worry, they enjoyed the relief. Having run out of things to gossip about, many families still went to the hub, as there was nowhere else to venture. There was no point tending to fields that refused their services. One day, they saw from a distance two people approaching.

Something about the woman looked familiar. She was pretty despite the worn-out life her body carried, and she was drunk. Her blue eyes were sunken deep into their sockets, but her long lashes demanded attention. Parts of her hair were matted, parts stringy; somehow, she'd managed to keep a patch on top in gold ringlets. She was pretty.

When the man spoke to the men in the group, his voice had a bitter, unfriendly edge. "My name Robert. I'm looking for a man I'se used to work for before da war." He didn't bother introducing the woman. He continued. "We na lost everything. Like everybody, like y'all, I'm sure." He nodded at the woman with him. "We's be willing to do anything to feed ourselves. Been all down the delta. Any work around here?" His left hand moved when he talked, and his right arm hung loose next to him like it was useless. And he had a slight accent, one of the men noticed. "Sound like it been a long time since you na seen dis man? War has been over for years." Sam watched Robert closely, thinking *Something about him was a bit from the truth. Whatcha hiding?* Sam wondered.

"Yep, sho' has. A lot of life na been lived since den, but da debt is still unpaid. Thangs have changed now. I'se got to look him up. Meantime got to find work.... Ya'll got anything?"

"Nope. I'm hoping to get a crop in, though." A redheaded boy came around from behind the man's leg. Then he opened his mouth to speak. Robert noticed the boy had missing teeth.

"We'se cursed. Darkies cursed us." The words whistled through the gap of the missing spaces in the boy's mouth.

Robert took his hat off and looked at the child. He wore a slight smile of amusement on his face. The boy was cute. Robert wanted a child of his own, and a nephew for Thomas, one that would say any old shit out of nowhere. The man in front pushed the redhead child back behind him. "What brings youse here? Don't take much to see. We'se just waiting to die from starvation. You say a friend?" Somebody in the small group chuckled.

Robert sensed the sarcasm and continued: "Dey was having trouble on dat last farm we's at, but we's"—he nodded at his wife— "got things moving a bit."

"What kinda help you'se say ya'll good for? Look like you been hurt?" The man was looking at the limp arm hanging at Robert's side. The woman made a sound like she was about to say something,

"Aaaaaakkkkk,erraaaaakkkerrr."

The odd sound moved around them like the beginning of a song. Robert felt the shift of feet among the group, the alertness of the men's shoulders, the leaning in of the women. Nobody spoke, just waiting for what the sound would do next. The redheaded boy's head came back from behind the man.  The sound stopped.

Robert was used to her odd sounds. He took a pack of tobacco out of his pocket and a flask, which might as well have been gold. "What dat boy means, da darkies cursed ya?" He held his tobacco out for them. They nodded respectfully to accept. He moved with the men away from the women to talk.

A strong tobacco smell rode the cool air to circle the women left standing together, plus the woman who came with Robert. "She seems dim-witted," one of the women whispered to the others. The woman without a name staggered away and found a tree to lean against. She pulled her hair away from her face and closed her eyes.

"Wait…hell, no, you'se know who she looks like?"

One or two tried to place her face. Could it? Never! No matter how or what the circumstances. One of the women, not ready to let doubt betray her, mumbled, "H.G.'s daughter's dead. Scarlet fever killed em all."

"No way in hell or heaven could dat be her! Dat gurl was named after a flower, right? Dis thang looks like a cactus." They laughed together.

"Nah, ain't nothing delicate about dat woman."

"Pretty, though, sorta."

Robert's companion's name was Sarah. She listened as they passed their speculations, like serving tea on the veranda, on fine porcelain Sarah had once known. Sarah gazed at the women without envy or need for friendship. There was no room left inside her for friendliness. Their gossip was as bitter as the underside of overripe rhubarb. All Sarah wanted was a drink.

Sarah pushed back her stringy, dirty hair. She had no itch but scratched her neck to look at how much dirt came off her flesh. Her bitten-down nails were packed with grime. More amused than bothered, she moved the back of her tongue back and forth to scratch her throat. It sounded like a piglet. The women shot her a look of disgust. It cast away all doubt; she could not be related to H.G.

"I am little Sarah Grove." A wide smile broke over her face, to which some of the women raised their eyebrows in shock at the pride in this dimwit's tone.

One of the women adorned with her dead husband's tattered war coat addressed the rest of the group, her eyes roving over Sarah, "She ignorant. Dat ain't no Grove. What da hell was dat sound she was making?" They had each worked, in some way or fashion, as tenants moving toward ownership of Grove property. To whom his widow had given them useless titles to small plots on the Culver Tusk property.

"Maybe, dat's what da man Robert is talking about. Dey got a property title." They named off the number of folks with titles, including the sisters and their husbands, now these two. The land promised to folks wasn't even a fourth of what the family owned when the brothers were alive. They whispered these two might be spying for the government, seeing what little we know about why our titles are ignored. Yep, they concluded these strangers might be spies; *we broke and broken, not a pot to piss in, but we ain't stupid.*

The women finalized the conversation with a laugh and turned their backs to the woman. Quietly, Sarah mentally shouted at their backs, *Swagger baggers!* She spat on the ground and spotted an ant walking with a crumb on its back. *That ant got more food than I got*, she thought. It reminded Sarah of her daddy, H.G., sitting at the head of the dining table behind a juicy, plump roast. How many days had she nibbled tiny portions to maintain her tiny waist? "Sarah, dawling, you'se eat less than a purple finch. You ain't a bird." Her father's complaint was halfhearted, as she knew he preferred women light as a feather.

The image of a plump roast was so vivid in her memory that Sarah laughed with such force the sound shot out of her mouth like a cannonball. Caught off guard, the women turned clumsily as if they had been attacked. The sight of Sarah reeling back and forth with laughter made their faces grimace and twist in total disgust. She approached them with an uneven walk, still laughing.

Robert looked over at Sarah and cursed her in silence. He moved quickly toward her, and the men followed. Everybody, including her husband, faced the lone woman with a crooked smile plastered to her pale face; she was the center of their disgust. Sarah leisurely took out a rolled tobacco from her pocket and held it to her lips. None of the men offered her a light, not even Robert, which allowed the group to feel more comfort in their disdain for her. Sarah watched the faces of the women and knew there would be no tea and crumpet conversations among them. Sarah didn't care about making friends, anyway. She took a stick, poked at the fire, and lit her cig.

The man with the little boy spoke to Robert, ignoring Sarah. "You'se keep on dat road, ya'll be on. Ya'll gonna pass by four farms—dem the ungrateful fellows we'se work with sometimes. Mostly McGregor. Ignore him if you can. He a mean drunk, and dangerous. Together, dey might as well be animals in a pack. Da wives are sisters from Ireland.  We'se don't trust 'em even if we'se are forced to work with 'em. He continued. "Ya'll follow da river da further east you'se get bound to run into Shelton or one of his men. He's da head of dem good-doer northers.  We'se heard he and his men determined to interfere with lynchings and even threaten to shoot. Dem damn northerners ain't got no business down here. Anyhoo, dat Shelton fellow got a big cabin off Creek Rd. He'll help you'se find who you'se looking for."

"Henry's old fishing place?" a redheaded woman who could have been the boy's mother asked with concern. "Is ya'll friend Hargrove, H.G.'s nephew?" She looked at Robert with disbelief.

Robert watched the woman's face closely for a reaction. He took out a flask and handed it to Sarah. He waited for her to take a few steps away. "Yeh, sort of. I'se used to work for his father. He still owes me from before da war."

"Grove! He been dead! His son, not sure, might…own dat land now, but ain't sho, cuz can he legally if he…we think…might as well be owned by a—" Robert glanced at Sarah, but she was lost in drinking and had missed this last piece of information.

"Yep," the woman continued. "Might as well be owned—"

One of the men cut her off. "Leave it be, woman!"

The woman took offense. "Ain't said nothing." She finished the conversation in her head. *It might as well be owned by dat Negro Lena. Folks know he killed his daddy for dat Negro! What kinda of world lets you kill yo' daddy and take his property?*

"What?" Robert looked the group over, then let his eyes settle on the woman. She looked once at the man with the dark hair and then away. "Whatcha know about how Grove died?" Robert felt his skin crawl and wondered how much he might have been implicated in the murder after he ran off. He saw nothing in their eyes but curiosity; he was sure they knew something.

"I'se been here a long time." The woman who spoke had no teeth or eyebrows, and a collapsed face walked forward. "Anyways, I'm saying it; it gon' seem like a lie, but I'se telling ya'll dis."

Robert waited, studying the woman, and then noticed Sarah had returned. He sensed the others in the group were amused by something they shared that he and Sarah were not. Even the little boy seemed to know something. "What?" Robert asked the woman.

"We'se know a lot, and at da same time, we'se don't know NUTTIN!"

The shrill laugh jumped out of Sarah's mouth again. If there was a secret among them, she laughed like she was in on it. Sarah stopped laughing and looked towards her husband for a moment, her head tilting as she pushed the hair back off her face.

She offered some advice to Robert and the group. "Why don't we'se leave, huh? Go somewhere, anywhere but here," Sarah's voice was lovely despite her worn-out look. "I'se hear dem Indians in Oklahoma is hiring white people to—"

"Shittin' Indians?" Robert broke the group's line to snatch the tobacco stick from her mouth. Her cracked lips remained open while a smoke trail escaped. If he'd slapped her, like his good arm wanted, no one would have bothered to say anything—the looks on their faces suggested he should. Sarah's face was turned up toward him, her cracked lips still open as if she were waiting for a slap. Her eyes were smiling; she batted her eyes up at Robert. Robert held the tobacco stick with his good hand. His limp arm remained by his side.

"My name is Alberta," the woman without eyebrows said. She was observing the woman. Alberta didn't take to the woman, but she took to defiance. She'd lost a mouth full of teeth to it.

Everybody waited for the woman to speak, even Robert. Sarah shifted her unsteady body and pulled her shoulders back gracefully. "My name is Sarah, dis my mean husband, Robert. My mother…yes, was named after the flower, Iris." The delicacy of her words and her pride in speaking dispelled any doubt of her identity. Many in the group had seen the woman in her youth being paraded over the land in her daddy's carriage. They remembered the exemplary high steps of the horses, under the commands of the Negroes, and how she would, pull back the carriage curtains, lean out to give the same salutation to the people working her daddy's land. As if the group before her requested, Sarah leaned forward and, with the wind rustling her oversized pants, gave them what they desired: a curtsy of curtsies, her lashes faster than hummingbird wings. "How be yawl doing on this fine day? It's a bit on da chilly side dis afternoon. Bless ya'll hearts." The pages of history turned backward. It was little Sarah all grown up…They paused, not knowing how to finish that thought.

The women's gasp buckled the air around them, and the wind stopped blowing. The boy knew this kind of abrupt silence between grown-ups. They were stunned. He moved from behind the man and went to his mother. When the group caught hold of their breath to speak, no one bothered to take turns. They looked at Sarah but directed their wing-flapping questions to Robert.

"I'se thought you'se said…?"

"A friend…?"

"Don't dat mean…?"

"If you'se married…?"

"Is dat…?"

"Who…?"

"Why is she…?"

"Who are…?"

"What da hell?"

The redheaded woman spoke the final sentence. "H.G.'s daughter? Den you'se should know what happened!"

Something about "what happened" didn't settle right with Robert. No one noticed Robert's reaction except Alberta. She saw the sudden glaze of his eyes that turned to pure hatred! His brownish-green eyes were more wicked than a barn cat, born of the devil. Looking hard at him, Alberta decided that he must know what happened. He said his name was Robert, but he reminded her of somebody else.

The others were busy looking at Sarah, starting to make a spectacle of herself, spitting out a singsong riddle, her voice breaking like dry chicken bones. She took to moving, circling the group. This song did not come down the hills into the valley. This song came in choppy notes as heavy as the swing of an ax, and it scared the children in the group and gave the men chills. Her eyes crossing and then rolling around her head made them wonder if she might be possessed.

> *"I am Sarah of southern sweets.*
> *rising from da land*
> *bloodred suns rise just for me*
> *Me, me, me eeeeeeeee*
> *moonbeams keep me company*
> *while darkies fan the summer heat*
> *banana leaves*
> *Shoo fly, shoo!"*
> *meeeeeeeeeeeee*

Sarah was weeping, snot coming out of her nose. She used her tongue to catch it. The men's heads dropped in disgust. "H.G.'s daughter!" Sam spoke to no one in particular. "By Gawd! Thank God he's dead and probably rolling in his grave." He glanced over to see how Sarah's husband was reacting, thinking any decent man would stop her madness.

Robert was behind the bolted door of his mind's eyes with a memory from before the war. Robert's wife could have taken her pants off and danced naked, and he wouldn't have noticed. He was back there in memory. And the more his wife circled the group with her loud chanting, the more his memory was served to him on a platter and slammed in his face.

Robert was back in a blazing-hot summer, years before the war. Grove owned the land and was God to him. Robert wanted to tell this bunch of nitwits that Grove was God. Robert served him as his first-in-command overseer. The day Grove died, the South died, and Robert had seen it end.

The chestnut-colored horse named Glider was the first to ride up to his memory. Having trained the horse himself, he remembered how the horse's front legs lifted so that his horseshoes blazed with the sun's force and rose into the hot air on command. The day was hotter than the devil's breath, and Grove's whip was a black snake rising in the air. Sweat rained off the horses.

Robert was on the horse beside Grove, his arms working the reins. He was trying to keep his horse under control; he had a good arm then. The horse Glider jumped and bounced under the weight of the whip. And then the gunshot, and there was nothing, nothing anybody could do about it. The day was sliced in half. In the first half, they were riding in the hunt for an older female pregnant slave named Lena, and then abruptly, in the second half, Robert's God was murdered.

Grove, the man he had come to love as a father, took a shotgun blast to his stomach. Time came to a halt. Robert saw the look in Grove's eyes as he was knocked off the horse into the air: his eyeballs bulged out of their sockets in utter disbelief. When Grove's body hit the ground, time began; Grove was dead. It was then Robert became Godless.

The memory burned to his bones a red-hot prong of relentless agony. He wanted to get away from these people and take his crazy wife with him. He cried out in agony. "NOOOUO." The group barely heard it over the sound that was coming from Sarah. It was a collision of pain and madness between the husband and wife.

Robert was the only witness to Hargrove killing his daddy over a Negro wench. In the parlor days later, the grieving widow shed no tears, handing Robert five thousand dollars for his silence. "And what about my brother arriving from England, ma'am?"

"What of it?"

"Your dead husband gave me his word he'd give him a job," saying the word *dead* very carefully to bring the total weight of his threat. Her mouth tightened. "My brother-in-law, H.G., will be arriving soon with his wife, Iris, and daughter, Sarah. I will mention his need for employment when they arrive next week."

"Mention, ma'am?" He bore his eyes into her face.

"I will insist on his employment now that you're leaving." Her eyebrow rose to seal the deal on his departure. "What is his name?"

"Thomas C. Latimer, ma'am. Thomas C. Latimer."

Grove's widow had kept her promise; it was years before he saw his brother again. It was at Thomas's execution. Thomas's emerald eyes had gone to a milky green, almost gray, but Robert still saw the ferocious spirit in them. He listened and promised to follow Thomas's dying wishes.

Robert's memory left. He glanced over at Sarah, who was still stomping on the ground. "Your damn daddy H. G. is da reason my brother was killed," he said to himself. The rage in him rose. *I need to beat her. Dat's what she needs.*

Sarah had stumped up enough dirt to cover half her body. "Sarah!" Her body went limp to the ground. Robert walked over, bent, and with one arm scooped her up, more to weigh him down from the memory than to help her. Sarah held on.

Alberta walked to Sarah's weak body and gently pushed her hair from her face. "Follow da road he told ya about." She let her hand rest on Sarah's cheek. "You'se won't get lost." Sarah's eyes watered. "If ya'll stumble upon four men with Irish wives, don't tell 'em who you'se is, Sarah. Dem women hollering bout property rights and issues with ya'll family!"

She did not know if Sarah knew about her father's mistress, Eloise. *Best leave it alone,* she thought and kept talking. "If you'se stay on dis road, ya'll might run into a Negro named Bailey and his woman, Mary. She bout ready to be birthing —if it ain't born already. Dey work under da man's we'se told ya'll come down here to save Negroe's, Shelton.

They were a small group, but they parted like the hundreds of curtsied ballroom processions of the past that Sarah had been accustomed to. The wind began to blow again, gently bringing the scent of honeysuckle flowers. The smell of honeysuckle was fitting; it was a cool towel to the fevered thoughts in their heads. They'd poorly behaved to the daughter of H.G. The men tilted their hats and bowed slightly as if under the scrutiny of her father's eyes. Wishing they had lit her tobacco stick, they thought that if she got that land back, they might be messed up for sure after mistreating her.

Robert half carried his wife down the road and then set her on her feet. When they disappeared, Alberta looked at the group. "Maybe I'se shouldn't a said we'se don't know nothin'."

"Yeah, maybe, but you'se didn't know she was H.G.'s child," Sam replied.

"Hell, Robert never said who she was. We'll see what happens."

What happened next shocked them. The sun popped from behind the clouds, and the redheaded boy pointed to where Sarah had stomped up dirt. There lay a nice-sized black and gold sack. Nobody knew how to negotiate who should pick up the satchel, but Alberta did.

"It can't harm us no more than what we none has done, to look inside." The entire group nodded in agreement without hesitation. Alberta walked over and brought it over.

With more delicacy than her fingers were used to, Alberta began untying the knot. The impatience of the folks around her was heard in the shuffling of their feet and a cough from one of the men. "Damn, tie y'all be patient."

When the pouch opened, she gave out a small gasp. The heaviness of the pouch was from the gold nuggets, her eyes watering at the sight. Among the gold pieces lay a diamond necklace surrounded by sapphire stones. There, too, was a strand of pearls. Alberta had never worn pearls in her life. If alone, she would have put the pearls around her neck. It was a sight she thought more beautiful than any sunrise. Without teeth or eyebrows, she took it all in and, for a moment, imagined herself a queen.

At the sight of her tears, everyone gathered closer to see. This woman, who never showed weakness, was bent over a satchel in tears. Shocked, they only passed the pouch through the men's hands and let the women peep in.

"I'se heard dat song last night," the man spoke up to the group, but his eyes were on the sack. "Every time some 'em good come right after that song."

"Yep."

"Now we'se got a sack of gold and diamonds. Dat song magic." Several amens echoed the joy in his voice.

"We'se can't keep it, though," Alberta glanced around. Shocked and offended by her suggestion, one or two rolled their eyes in disbelief. "Dey know it was dropped here or might have been." She watched their faces think it over a second, then firmly pressed on. "Either way, we'se can't keep it."

They waited silently, each thinking of Sarah's family's power and not knowing who else besides her and the uncle was alive. Finally, they agreed. "But," Alberta was pleased to add, "We'll take a nugget a few coins to divide among us—a few, but not so dey miss it." The heads of the group bobbed up and down.

"Dey cants' be far off, just around the bend." Not a hand moved to volunteer to chase after them.

"You'se a big boy, ain't you, son?" Those words spoken by one man in the group set a course of action that would later become a bitter feud over which man spoke the words that would eventually haunt them all.

The boy nodded eagerly, smiling at the group. "Go and give it to da woman, not dat man, and say thank you. You'se hears?"

"Yes, sir." He was looking up at the man with the dark hair, his new father, but he was thinking about his daddy. He'd gone down that same road and never came back. Maybe he'd find him, too. His new daddy placed his hand on the child's shoulder.

"Tell 'em you'se found it, and we'se sent you'se after dem."

"Yes, sir."

"Now, whatcha gonna say?"

The space in his mouth whistled the answer. "I'se saw it…and say look, and my new daddy said you'se take dat to 'em now."

The little boy noticed his new daddy's smile when he said *daddy*.

"And what if dey says something missing?"

The boy shuffled his feet and glanced over at his mother. "I don't know."

She leaned down and kissed his forehead. "Say you'se tripped running after dem bag fell, and something mightta fell out."

Alberta chimed in. "Yeah, dat's good. Say you'se fell."

"What you say if dey asked if we's opened it? What you'se say?" His new daddy leaned down, looking the child in the eyes.

"No, sir. Dey says go, boy, take dis to dem nice folks."

"Good boy. Dat's my boy." Everybody in the group smiled down at him. With Alberta's approval, Sam took out a couple of small pieces of gold and coins and tied the sack. Sam rubbed the boy's head. "Go." And go he did, running fast like he was in a race, looking back to see them waving him on. He stopped once, putting his hands on his hips to catch his breath, and then, thinking he saw something ahead, he took off again.

The group took turns deciding what to spend the coins and nuggets on. "What about a cow? Do ya'll think we got enough for a cow?" They sat on the ground in a circle.

"Oh yeah, two cows and feed."

"Some staples, of course," one woman pitched in. Nobody argued that a celebration was called for, and the Sunday coming was about as good as any. It felt good to laugh and plan together and not spend the time fretting over the curse that now seemed to be lifting. We'se go get supplies."

"We's can't go back to Little Rock. We's got to go farther and get supplies." Every agreed head nodding yes.

"Oh yeah, we'se go back with gold, and we be digging our graves. Dey thinks we'se got gold on dis cursed land dey snatch it away; we left with nuthing!"

It took a while before they got uneasy with time passing and the boy not back. His mother had dozed off, her head leaning on the man's shoulder. They woke her up and asked. "Is he a clumsy boy? What if he dropped it, though?" one woman asked, which started a series of questions that took time to sift through.

"What if dat man Robert wondered why we's send da boy and not a man? Dat Robert ain't got trusting eyes!"

"What if da boy got scared and told dem what happened?"

Alberta placed her tongue in the space of her mouth, making a clucking sound. "He git scared easy?" The question, directed at his mother, seemed to open a can of worms.

"What kind of mother am I'se to let him go alone? I'se shoulda gone with him. What kind of God-fearing mother would tell her boy to lie?" She looked up at the boy's new father with tears. She wondered what kind of woman he thought she was now. Her fears of her new husband leaving her, like the boy's father, swelled up. She prayed her son did well and showed his new father what a good son he'd be.

Sam patted her hand. "We did da best thing sending him alone. Anyway, he's got to learn how to be a man. Dat's why I'se here to teach him." She relaxed and smiled at him.

They sat on the ground, waiting for the boy to come down the road. Anxious, they tried to distract themselves with the same question: How much could they get for the gold? The conversation continued until a woman spoke and said, "It's gittin' dark, my kids waiting on der supper."

"Where my boy Sam. Dey got my child." She looked up helplessly, her face pulled in tight, eyes open wide, tears welled up, waiting to release.  Sam pulled away from her eyes and directed his eyes to the road.  "Go home and wait, woman."

Something in his voice, firm and solid, like he was going off to war, and the descending dark sky scared her even more. She heard in Sam's voice that he was worried, and she screamed.  "Oh…God, my boy, Sam, my boy!"

"Take her home!" he instructed the women. "Now!"

# T E N

It was late when Robert and Sarah spotted a cabin in the distance. The cabin belonged to Bailey and Mary. Robert noticed the contrast between their fields and those they had just traveled past. The corn stalks were high, and there were signs that other vegetative life was pushing out of the ground, including a young peach tree.

Lousy weather hadn't taken such a toll here, Robert thought, his anger rising. The voice of the little boy came to him. "The Negroes na cursed us." That's precisely what the little boy said, but to look at this land, it was anything but cursed. Then again, it was Negroes and not whites on the land.

He stared at the Negro who stood up to greet him. The pregnant Negro woman got up as well. She inched her way forward slowly despite her husband's extended arm to caution her back. "Evening, sir," Bailey greeted them. Robert grunted. His face contorted with anger. *Here I am standing at the foot of a porch of a Negro man and Negro woman, and I ain't got a chair to sit on.* He rolled the tobacco juice and spat on the bottom step.

Bailey spoke again. "Can I'se help you'se, sir?" Bailey did not have to wonder how the man felt; the man's hatred hung heavy in the air. Robert surveyed the house and surrounding area. Bailey kept his smile on his face, the muscles beneath the smile aching. He kept his head lowered. He couldn't afford trouble with Mary about to give birth at any moment. "You'se lost, sir?" Again, he made sure he kept respect in his words. Although she seemed familiar, he didn't dare look directly at the white woman wiggling around in the dirt beside the man. He repeated his question. "Sir, you'se lost, sir?"

It was the word *lost* that made Robert's teeth grind. *What kind of world?* He thought. *Is this what da damn war did?*

"How in da hell a nig—" But before Robert could finish, a white man came around the corner leading his horse. He was a large man in height and weight, and his skin had a history of harsh weather. Across his chest was a holster and, on his horse, a rifle. By his size and eyes, Robert knew guns were a last-minute thought and only if needed. This man could well take care of himself. He seemed as wide and tall as the door of the cabin.

He spoke to Bailey first, not taking his eyes off Robert, sizing him up. "Evening, Bailey. I come around to see if Mary had ya'll baby. See, she ain't." Shelton Wyman didn't have a problem with Negroes, and never took to the thought of owning a person, not even a wife. He had come to like Bailey and Mary more than most folks.

"No, sir, Mr. Shelton Wyman." Bailey was glad Mr. Wyman had arrived; this stranger seemed bent on trouble. "We's waiting on nature to call dis baby out—got my chores done early to wait with my Mary."

"Well…ya go on in the house while I talk to this gentleman."

Bailey put his arm around Mary. *Dat man don't know nuthing about being a gentleman.* He took a glance at the stranger. *I be a fool not to see him look like that devil Thomas.* Bailey's heart began to race at the possibility. As he and Mary reached the threshold, even before the door closed, Mary looked up at Bailey with her face squeezed tight. "It be time, Bailey," Mary said with such ease Bailey didn't know if she was teasing him. It was only in that next moment, when he felt warm water rushing over his naked feet, that he repeated and confirmed to himself what Mary had already told him.

"It be time." Bailey had already prepared the side of the fireplace with blankets and clean clothes. His hands were sturdy, and he prayed they stayed that way. He was scared but would not show it. Bailey had been prepared for a long day or night of helping Mary to give birth. Ultimately, it was not needed, nor was much required of him. Not long after he closed the door to the white folks, his daughter was born. Bailey cut the cord with his knife and put the afterbirth in a bowl as instructed. Finally done, he sat on the pallet by his Mary while their daughter drank hungrily on the swollen. *I am a daddy just like that*, he thought, smiling—*a daddy.*

"You'se okay, Mary?" She nodded.

"She thirsty." With that, they both laughed.

"Bailey?"

"Yes, Mama Mary." Mary laughed. He wiped the sweat from her forehead with his clean cloth. "What, baby?" Bailey felt he could finally say the word *baby* without breaking her heart. He began to tear up when he realized this little girl would never know her big brother. "What, Mary?"

"Err'body gits thirsty." The light of the fire glowed on her face, her arm around their child.

Their little girl would always know that truth. He whispered, "Err'body gits thirsty." He kissed the wet top of the child's head.

"I'm need you'se git me cleaned up," Mary whispered. "Git the bucket. I'm going to bury her birth sack tomorrow." He smiled and followed Mary's directions. When done, Bailey got up, took down one of the cups, and poured water from the pitcher. It was dark outside. He held the cup to Mary's mouth, listening to the sounds of both his woman and daughter satisfying their thirst.

When mother and child dozed off, Bailey figured he'd satisfy his thirst. It wouldn't hurt to fill his tin cup with whiskey, go out on the porch, and smoke his tobacco while they rested. He had forgotten about the white man and woman. He put an extra log on the fire. Looking out into the night sky, he wondered if becoming a mother would stop the fits for his Mary. For all her pregnancy, things had been quiet. He looked down at his woman and his daughter. Mary had the baby lying on her stomach. Bailey knelt closer to the pallet, the light of the fire illuminated dancing on their skin. Bailey shook his head to ensure his eyes were right, and his baby girl smiled.

"Mama." It had been a long time since Bailey had called out to his mama. He leaned as close as he could without disturbing Mary from sleeping. "God, youse giving me part of my mama?" He looked again; sure enough, his mama's eyes looked out at him through his daughter. He crossed himself in prayer, whispering, "I'se promise you'se, daughter, I'se going to give you'se da best life I'se can. You gon' have a better life den yo mama and I ever had. I promise you dat." The tiny head of his baby girl jerked a bit as if she understood. Her face turned slightly; her mouth latched onto her mother's nipple. "Seem like life should be dat easy, daughter." Bailey got up, smiling, and headed to the door. He was crying.

Within a week, as many feared, the worst winter was in Springfield, Arkansas. Those who prayed for rain had never imagined balls of hail causing bodily harm to those running for shelter. There would be no crops; nearly everything but the trees got up and moved away. Two families in the group took their share of the money from the gold and headed north to get a handle on industrialization. The mysterious song that had visited the trees and hills was gone. Nobody had heard it since the last gathering at the hub when the boy had chased after the couple and never returned home.

The gold had given them a bit of hope, but the price they paid was higher than they imagined. They wanted the gold to help them forget the misplaced birds and the ghosts.

Sam had not returned with the redheaded boy. The boy was lost, and Sarah and Robert had also disappeared. Sam told them the couple had made it to Bailey's, but that was as much as Bailey could say. Sam questioned him thoroughly, but because the man would not look up, he had to guess if Bailey was lying.

"No, sir. Dey came stood right dar." Bailey had pointed at the spot on the ground; Sam followed his eyes to the place, thinking Bailey might be showing him foot tracks. Sam only saw dirt. "Den Mr. Shelton Wyman come 'round da corner, he took em on away from here. My Mary gave birth. Dat kept me tied most of da night, sir." The man with the dark hair asked one last question and got the answer he wanted least. "No, sir. No boy with red hair was with 'em. No boy at t'all. Yes, sir. Dat be da truth."

Bailey watched the white man slowly walk away. He called after him, "Sir, you'se got enough wa'ter or food for da journey back? Sam got on his horse without another word and headed home.

# ELEVEN

The redheaded boy had gotten lost. After running down the road for some time, he saw a small canoe sitting on the shore.  He got what he thought was a big boy idea and decided to get in the canoe and paddle close to the land as his real daddy showed him. Once in the canoe, he forgot to keep an eye on the shore, the thrill of the adventure distracting him. As he held the pouch of jewels in his hand, the rest of the world spread before him. He had at first been excited to catch up to the man and strange woman. But now they were nowhere, and he did not know what to do. The canoe had floated away from land. The boy was unsure when, but he was soon lulled to sleep. Awakened by a strong thump, he opened his eyes and realized he had made it to land. He did not recognize the area. There was a different family of trees with white bark, startlingly contrasting the dark skin of the trees he remembered. When he got out of the canoe, his legs wobbled. "I'm lost," he whispered, trying hard not to get scared. Maybe he thought the man and woman were lost, too.

The thrill of the adventure went away, and the bag of jewels held no interest. It was getting dark, and he was hungry. He had not thought about how young he was until he saw how big the world seemed. He saw nothing but trees that looked scary. "I will follow the river, and it will take me back home," he told himself, and this comforted the nervousness in his stomach.

"What if da Indians come and git me?" All the stories that once fed his imagination when he played with his friends became a nightmare. The boy felt as helpless as the bird's nest when they knocked them out of the trees. He began to cry. He knew enough about dying to know it hurt. He fell to the ground and wept into the cloth of the sack. "Mama."

He gave himself a good cry. Then, standing up, determined to get home, the boy saw ahead of him a horse approaching. The horse was trotting slowly. He waited to see if the horse was alone. It was not. As the horse got closer, he thought it was a child riding. The rider and the horse got close enough for him to see it was not a boy.

Jed fell from the horse; his eyes were closed.

"If he is dead, I will ride his horse home."

Jed opened his eyes. "Where am I?" The voice sounded strange to the boy.

"Sir?"

"I'm…lost. Where am I?" His voice was weak.

The boy smiled a toothless smile. "I'm lost, too."

Jed looked up at the sky and away from the boy with his wet, red hair. Jed wondered if he had met his first ghost, but none of the letters mentioned children. "What's your name?"

"Junior. What's your name, mister?"

"Jed." Jed looked at the boy. "Where's your folks?"

Junior thought about the sack he had placed near him on the ground. He lied. "My new pa went to catch us some fish."

"How you get lost, then?"

"I'se was looking for some kindle for fire to make my new Pa proud. How's about you, mister…? Grow-ups get lost?"

The voices in Jed's head piped in because *he's stupid!* Junior saw the sudden look of rage cross the small man's see-through face. The man's eyeballs popped forward like they were running out of the sockets; simultaneously, his jaw jaunted forward, saliva forming in the corners of his mouth.

Junior nearly peed himself but held his pee, remembering he was a big boy, so he lied again. "My Pa will find us; he's a good fisherman," his lie invigorated him. Once, my pa caught a catfish more giant than a shark."

"Good. I'll wait. I think I'm hurt." Jed's body ached from top to bottom. In his adult life, he had not ridden a horse for longer than a few minutes at a time. The wheel on the buggy had broken, so he'd had no choice. He regretted his decision almost immediately after starting the journey. But he could not turn back and let the voices win. Besides, he wanted to meet the families, and even more, he wanted to meet the woman they claimed to have put a curse on them. The woman called Lena. It took him a while to realize he was going for selfish reasons. Yeah, he wanted to see the folks that talked of cursed land, and he wanted to see ghosts. But his hope was if this Negro woman named Lena put a curse on land and people, maybe she could undo the curse that penetrated his body. He would rise six feet tall, and his skin would darken to cover the blue and green veins on his hands and face. Besides, he could offer her the letters and documents that stood between her and the white people. He had the documents found on that road leading to Culver Tusk among the letters.

It was not long before it got dark. All that was left was the song-like sound' Errrr' coming from the hills through the woods. The sound rose and fell everywhere around, giving no hint of the direction from where it originated.

"What...is...that?" Jed asked the child. The boy was quiet for a long time. Jed could barely make him out in the dark.

"We'se heard dat sound for a while, mister, kinda like somebody singing. Good luck follows it."

"What kind of luck?"

Junior thought of the jewels and decided to find a way to hide them from the man. "Like food." He was barely audible.

"Well, you're in luck. I got some scraps in my saddle." He knew the boy was hiding something. Nobody left a child in the middle of nowhere. *He* thought these folks were different, and *the letters proved it.* "You believe in ghosts?" Jed fussed at himself, realizing the question might scare the child.

*Stupid Jed,* the voices agreed. "Hey, Junior, I got food and matchsticks. We gonna be okay. Your dad be here soon." Jed didn't believe much of what the kid told him or that his dad would be back. What he knew was that he and the kid kept each other company and the lies between them. Together, they'd figure something out. "We'll get a fire going and eat."

Junior nodded and went to the horse. Indeed, with the song, he was thinking something good would happen. He found the wrapped meat and bread when he heard rustling behind him. Junior dropped the food and ran to the other side of the horse. The shadow of the man approaching was more significant than the small man waiting for food. "Pa?" excited Junior ran back around the horse; glad his new paw had come to find him. Junior stopped in his tracks and looked at the man. The last light of daylight let him recognize the face. His heart dropped. It was not his new paw. He glanced past the man on the road behind him. "Sir, where's da rich lady Sarah?

# TWELVE

The cold breeze didn't offend the five Negro women as it chased the fallen leaves on the road outside Culver Tusk. They agreed, "Dis pump water sweeter, thank you, Jesus!" That same breeze crawled into the house's yellow pine floors, making walking barefoot a treat. The women of the house knew weather and how to read the woods, and the woods told them an early, harsh winter was coming. They did not believe in asking God about his earth or its doings. "Hummp, dat's not our business."

What was their business were the twelve deputies that rode up pulling a wagon of dogs to arrest the women—or, with little or no provocation, kill them. The white men came down off their horses, hands on guns, and stood among a gang of hound dogs that lunged forward with madness. Thick chains snatched the dogs back, chains the women personally knew the weight of. Between the shouting of the sheriff and the dogs' barking, the women could hardly make out what was being shouted at them.

The women waited, seemingly unafraid or even undisturbed. They waited until two deputies could settle the dogs by taking them down the road near the woods.

"Sir, can we'se help you'se?" said the thick woman, dark as molasses, sitting on a wide chair draped in a beautiful silver and green shawl. Her voice was without concern, but the truth was that letting these men see her concern could probably make things worse.

"Who runs dis house, gal?" The sheriff looked back toward the dogs in the distance, jumping and lunging in their direction. He was making a point to the women. The sheriff turned back. I asked you a question!"

"Nobody, sir. It runs itself."

The sheriff looked around at his deputies. "You gittin' smart with me, gal?" They placed their hands on their guns. "No, sir. I just answered you'se question."

"Is der a white person in da house I'se can talk to?"

"No, sir."

"Dat right! Hear y'all practicing witchcraft on dis land, worshipping the devil."

"No, sir. Ain't never heard of such a thing." She couldn't help but smile inside at his words.

"What da hell ya'll be doing on dis plantation? He demanded! Dis used to be da home of H.G." He called one of the deputies, and they leaned into one another and talked. "Which one of you'se name is Mary?"

"Nobody, sir."

"Lena?"

"Dat's my name, sir."

"Your former slave of H.G., right?"

Lena leaned forward against the rail of the porch. She could feel the ache of her back starting up, and if she didn't get the other women to get her to bed, she'd pay dearly for days. But with these men bent on causing them harm, for now, all Lena could do was take a moment to rearrange her body. "No, sir, Grove was my master."

The sheriff leaned against the wagon. "And who you'se other Negroes belong to?"

The smallest of the women, Sylvie, stepped up to the edge of the porch, her shoulders pulled back. The rag on her head covered her forehead and nearly her eyes. But the sheriff, seeing the strong bone structure and jawline, knew there was nothing small about the Negro woman. The shape of her mouth let him know it was filled with tobacco. Sylvie turned to the side and, sure enough, spit a straight line off to the side, not a drop hitting the porch. "Sir, we'se don't belong to nobody but ourselves…and each other. We's free."

The sheriff whipped his gun from its holster and took aim. "Come here, nigga gal!" The eye of the barrel was pointed at her forehead. It was the first moment since their arrival that any sign of fear rose, and it was not in the woman herself but in the sheriff. His hand trembled. Sylvie stepped with ease off the porch and walked to the sheriff, her mouth moving the tobacco around like he'd asked if she'd caught any fish that day.

"Sheriff Samuelson, " a voice boomed. The sheriff had seen the man's shadow before he heard him. He turned to look at Hargrove, who spoke the sheriff's name without a dog hair of respect. There were more poisonous rumors circling Hargrove than a barrel full of rattlesnakes.

Sheriff Samuelson spoke, showing none of the contempt he felt. "How you'se doing, Mr. Hargrove." Over Hargrove's shoulder was a line of men on horses, far outnumbering the sheriff's deputies.

"You'se can put your gun away, Sheriff. What brings ya'll this way?" Hargrove looked over at the women on the porch. Seeing no apparent harm done, he nodded his greeting to each. He looked at the gun and waited until it returned to its holster. "Sheriff, you'se got a reason to be on my property?"

"Folks around these parts been complaining. Just come to see what the fuss is about."

"You'se on my property—you know that, right?" Hargrove glanced at each man, mentally noting who they were.

Sheriff Samuelson wanted to say, "Hell, your family owns most of Springfield. Where can anybody stand and not be on your property?" But he kept that to himself. "No reason at t'all, Mr. Hargrove, no reason at t'all."

Hargrove got off his horse and walked to the sheriff. "It won't be a good idea if you'se come on my property again, Sheriff; for you, you deputies, but especially you."

"Now, Mr. Hargrove"

"You heard me get your men and dog's way from here!" The deputies didn't wait for the sheriff to give directions; they were already mounting their horses. Both men were close to eye level and of similar weight and age. Hargrove tilted his head back, eyeing Sheriff Samuelson, ready to tear up the earth beneath them in combat. The sheriff turned and mounted his horse.

The sheriff took another quick look at the small Negro woman, who had not moved. He rode off, thinking about the line of tobacco that Negro wench spit. It was longer than any man he knew. He hated not being able to see her eyes with her head rag because between the eyes was precisely where he was aiming to shoot her dead. He stayed up half the night hearing those words in his head, which filled him with a violent rage, "Sir, we'se don't belong to nobody but ourselves… and each other. We'se free." Nigga woman speaking to him like dat! He was sure, under that rag, she was staring him straight in the eyes. She could see him, but he couldn't see her, and that was wrong. He didn't eat his supper that night, nor sleep, nor did his wife. His wife got the brutal force of his rage, from her buttocks to her private part. When he finished, she lay naked in a fetal position on the floor.

# T H I R T E E N

The women of Culver Tusk couldn't count on the weather to tell them what season they were in or how the brutal winter had made its way from the North to the South; they depended on events to mark time in their memories. The women remembered the sheriff had come before the foreign birds, which may have been late spring or summer. They remembered clear as spring water Sylvie's words, "Sir, we don't belong to nobody but ourselves and each other; we'se free." That very evening, they'd made a pot of collard greens, drank sweet tea and fried fish caught by Sylvie, and savored her words for dessert. Their days were free, without time to fight or think about dying. Sylvie bravely faced the barrel of the sheriff's gun, and her words spoke to a truth no one had claimed out loud before. Folks wanted freedom dead if it was meant for everybody. The women knew the worst of this life and the best that existed in the silence between two musical notes. The women chose to exist between the notes where joy existed.

They woke when their bodies told them to rise. Time was marked by seasons, and the seasons were mixed up, so what? The earth listened to our cries toiling in the fields. Then come war and death. Mother Earth is speaking her mind; let her talk and listen. So, when the misplaced birds came, the women stood on the porch and prayed for the bird's safety. They were grateful the birds might find homes in the trees. They did not take it as a warning, as other folks in Springfield did, but more of a promise. In the very end, they claimed, the trees would become homes for wherever birds migrated there because their eggs needed a home! Hargrove enjoyed the ease with which they lived. But he firmly reminded them once the folks of Springfield found out the sheriff came and left without the bodies of the women, they'd take it upon themselves to do what the law couldn't.

Two women of Culver Tusk, Sylvie and Claire, had taken the daily task of keeping a watch on the road through the front window. Claire always cleaned the windows. Although it was a tedious ritual, she enjoyed doing it. Nature mixed up or not, they just had to pay closer attention. While the wind whistled, there was little stirring most days, and the woods were peaceful. The women sat quietly, listening to the wind, rain, or whatever voice nature chose each day. Occasionally, they remarked on the family of trees around them.

On this day, Sylvie had been curt with Claire earlier, so Claire was especially quiet. They sat in silence. The woods in the near distance appeared serene. Sylvie pushed the rag up off her forehead, her eyes nearly squinting closed.

"I'se escaped in dem woods with my husband years ago. We'se run to Canada to live out da rest of our lives free, we'se did." Claire was closest to the window and thought of napping before Sylvie spoke. She was tired of sewing and babysitting the woods for the day.

Claire looked up to see Sylvie's lower jaw moving as if she would continue her foolish story. Perhaps explain what in the world she was talking about. Claire had never heard Sylvie mention a husband, let alone escape. But instead, Sylvie's jaw unhinged, and all sound stopped as Sylvie's bottom lip began to distort. Claire groaned, realizing what was about to happen. *Why, why, why?* Claire's mind shouted, *does Sylvie act out?* Claire believed it was directed at her.

Sylvie's snuff can was halfway across the room. Disgusted, Claire watched a trail of tobacco stream into the air, unbroken, before it hit its target. *Splat!*

The delicate shawl around Claire's shoulders dropped away. She swallowed her saliva, fighting the urge to throw up, knowing it would be unladylike. And indeed, she refused to allow Sylvie the satisfaction of seeing her displeasure. "You promised not to do that in the house. You promised!"

Claire was precise and passionate about the cleanliness of rooms, history, and truth. She looked cautiously at Sylvie, her birdlike features. Sylvie's keen eyes rested on a subject or scanning the area, ready to take flight. It was Sylvie's contradictions that both confused and drew Claire to her. Sylvie, who often showed despicable manners and a habit of saying questionable random thoughts, was not always pleasing to hear. With all her contradictions, Sylvie was as delicate as a hummingbird in her emotions. With little or no provocation, she would burst out crying, speaking gibberish with the quickness of the hummingbird wings, leaving her hysteria to be sorted out by the other women in the house. Yet in moments like this completely unprovoked, Claire wondered what had angered Sylvie to talk of this mysterious husband or the woods from which she claimed she had escaped to Canada. It didn't matter. There was no excuse to spit tobacco across the room. What would it hurt for Sylvie to make the trip to the tin can, turn her back, and rid her mouth of the foul, dark substance?

It was hard to determine whether silence or fighting back was better to negotiate Sylvie's anger. The accusations that sometimes came out of her mouth made no sense; Claire suspected there were valid reasons. With her index finger shaking vehemently upwards, Sylvie would insist that God was going to send them to hell for one thing or another. Slamming the back door, Claire thought, was more than a show of her anger; it was bad manners. And worse were her long absences with no explanations offered. There was no concern over the worry it caused the women. How they quietly fretted at her absence. Or, Claire confessed, "I silently weep with worry." They all loved Sylvie. Yet, as much as they loved her, they did not seem to understand her. All the women in the house knew Sylvie said things that did not always seem true. Yet they put up with it. Now, here she was announcing to Claire that she was married and had escaped to Canada.

Claire's frustration overrode any concern over Sylvie's fragile nature. "Then?" She sat forward in her chair and defiantly pulled the shawl back over her shoulders. She decided not to address the disgusting act of tobacco spitting. Not one word. Claire placed the embroidering needle into her cloth—the bird she was making was nearly complete—and smiled at Sylvie. "What are you doing back here in the sad toils of the South if you escaped?" Her words were intentionally accusatory. "The South is a picture of horrors beyond the imagination." Claire picked her needle up and went back to work.

Sylvie looked down at the delicate needlepoint coming alive under Claire's fingers. The images Claire created were just as lovely as their creator. She gazed at Claire, trying to hide her affection toward her, an affection not diminished by the anger she felt now. The dark braid sprinkled with silver strands that curled around Claire's head was like a crown. Her skin, unblemished by time, glowed most days. She was the exact color of an acorn, Sylvie thought, and her face was also shaped as such, with its dimpled chin. Sylvie had heard that a dimple in the chin was a kiss from an angel at birth. She tilted her head up as if she were embarking on a thought.

"Hummp..." Sylvie's anger was fanned by the thought that Claire was suggesting she was lying. "Cause dat road said to come back to you'se, wench!"

The needle in Claire's hand paused a moment in the air. She wondered if she had heard Sylvie correctly. "What do you mean the road said to return to me?"

Sylvie shot up from her chair, knocking over a stool, and headed to the other room. Upset, Sylvie reached over the top of the cabinet stand. It took her a few careful movements to get the ledge of the bowl. Her fingers touched the delicate fabric that covered it. Claire had given her the cloth. It was enough time for Sylvie to calm herself, but just barely. She took down her prayer bowl and removed it from the fabric covering. Sylvie kissed the crystal bowl, marched out the back door, and let the door slam behind her.

Claire stood, flustered from their interaction. She went to the back window and watched Sylvie stroll toward the river. Claire had no clue what Sylvie meant when she said, "Because the road said to come back to you." She went back to her chair and took up her embroidering. Thinking of her own life or what little she could remember before the war, she tried to summon a memory that might have included Sylvie. Nothing came to her, yet her hands were trembling. Why?

Claire did not believe in going back through her past since it could not be changed, and even more so because she honestly could not remember much. But Sylvie's comments made her curious. How could she have returned to me when I didn't know her until she arrived at Culver Tusk? Come back here? Here, where? Distracted, she pushed the needle in the clothe piercing her finger. "Ouch! Darn it, Sylvie!!" She'd been so consumed with what Sylvie meant that she'd ruined her work. Watching her blood soak into the fabric, she mumbled, "Sylvie, look what you made me do!"

Claire had long suspected that everything Sylvie said was not as crazy as they thought. Something told her Sylvie knew more than she told them but offered tiny bits like crumbs for birds. *And now,* Claire thought, *this odd statement that she came back to get me. Get me? Even my memory is vague of how I…got free.*

Memory was useless to Claire, and what she tried to write of those days only caused her heart to break. One or two words pushing into her mind, or a name did nothing to sort out her history. She stuttered, "I…I…I don't think Sylvie knows how to read." Claire thought *My journals would be useless if Sylvie tried to spy.* Claire wished she had answers to her past life, but she didn't. Claire vaguely remembered that someone had come for months and given her food through a tiny crack. She was imprisoned in a shed. Claire had no idea how long or why and the war came. Claire thought maybe a Union Soldier had carried her out of the dark cell. "But then what?" she whispered. "How long was I there, and what was my life before being imprisoned?" The tip of her finger was starting to swell, the pain excruciating. The needle had gone deep, maybe to the bone.

The river was far enough for Sylvie to walk out her anger and stop fussing at Claire. *Besides*, she thought, *ain't good to fuss over my blessing bowl.* She got to the stream, knelt, and began filling it, sometimes using handfuls of water and letting the waterfall droplets from her fingertips into the bowl. She had not meant to say what she did to Claire, thinking it best not to bring up what Claire seemed not to remember. "Me?" she mumbled. "She does not 'members me!" Sylvie's reflection appeared in the water, reminding her of how different she looked now. Her face was thinner, her eyes deeper, and she was older now. *Sometimes,* she thought, *even I cans't 'member myself from all those years ago. So…how I 'spect Claire to kno's me?* This comforted Sylvie. She did not mind now, at this moment, being forgotten by the woman she's always loved. The water calmed her.

Sylvie regretted spitting tobacco before Claire, who had become even more of a lady than she was when they met enslaved. Being educated, Claire had tried to teach the others to read. When she was caught, their master ran up to her with the ax handle, hitting her with great force. The scar on her scalp, beneath her dark hair, was where the weapon had opened Claire's skull up and maybe, Sylvie thought, closed her memory. Did Claire not remember the blood splattering onto the children at her feet? Or the howling of her voice when the master ripped her baby, soaked in blood, from her arms?

Sylvie thought *I'se helped save you when dey buried you in dat room. I'se knew where da hid you and how he came to you to harm you'se body. You'se calling for death, but he keeps you from death, only 'cause he tink he loves you. I'se da one dat comes to feed you. I'se teach you to walk agin. And when I'se run off, I come back in war 'cause I'se know you locked away. Now you'se free and a lady, even more so.*

Sylvie smiled to herself. Did Claire not remember each time she opened the slit on the door and handed her food? How I'se dug a hole to crawl inside to teach the teacher to walk again. She wanted to say to her, "Claire, you in dat dark, musty room reeking of your shit. Rats running around you, yet you always say thank you. Don't cha 'member looking at me each time I'se come and you'se whispering those words still trying to teach me's?"

*It is us*

*Chained together*

*With only the smell of the Atlantic to remind us of our journey*

*Thousands of dark souls*

*Lives tortured on foreign soil.*

*Our collected adrenaline*

*Who but us could know the meaning of freedom*

*When it comes*

*Not on paper nor law of man. But us.*

Sylvie continued. "Dem was your words, Claire. You'se, cry to me over and over while I was fighting fo' yo life. Dem very words become my strength when I'se decide to return to git you. Dat is what I'se say over my blessing bowl now. Words you'se no longer 'member."

Sylvie saw folks coming down the road. From a distance, everybody looked colored, just dark lines distinguishing themselves from the light. It was the singing back and forth to one another, pacing their journey, that told Sylvie they were Negroes. She sighed with relief.

Sylvie rose, leaving the blessing bowl on the ground, and headed to the smokehouse. She took what was needed from the shelves: a large piece of smoked meat. She hurried to the storage, hoping they hadn't gotten to the house. *Okay,* she thought, *what might hold 'em? A jar of honey, a loaf of bread, sweet potatoes, and apples.* She rushed back to the road. The wagon came to a stop. "How's y'all be?" she greeted the folks.

"Fine, ma'am." The man lifted his hat. "We'se doin' fine. Seen better days, seen rougher—mostly rougher, though." The grown-ups summoned up a bit of laughter.

Sylvie offered the sack to one of the women. The woman's mouth tightened, trying to hold back the tears in her eyes. She gave herself a second before she spoke. "We'se thank you'se, ma'am. We'se sho' thankful, ain't we?" The children bobbed their heads up and down.

"God bless you'se."

If the family didn't all belong to each other by blood, they might as well have. The dirt, hunger, and dust of sharecropping had a way of reorganizing features into one picture of starvation. Sylvie looked warmly at the first generation of free slaves snuggled together under a blanket.

"Thank you'se, ma'am," they chimed in together.

"Ya'll, be careful."

Sylvie watched them for a while and thought of how many folks had left with their backs to the land they had once tried to make a home.

After gathering several fallen apple blossoms to drop into the water, Sylvie picked up the blessing bowl. As she walked toward the back of the house, she passed the garden where Claire had planted African tulips. Although Claire claimed the seeds were not tulips when she first got them and put them in the soil, they had come up tulips. The women had laughed at her confusion when the flowers emerged. "Where'd you get da seeds?" they asked.

Claire told them, "A woman on the road had a pouch of seeds and said they were a gift for me. I was shocked by her kindness and thanked her for her generosity. She said they were another sort of flower—a name I can't recall now, but it was certainly not *tulips and blue at that*!"

"Well, dat explains it!" They laughed lovingly. And now and then, a tulip broke the ground, still as shocking to Claire as the first one.

Sylvie set the bowl down on the earth, knelt, and took out her tobacco pouch. She kissed the earth and sprinkled the tobacco. "Tank you, Spirit

God, tank you." She spoke with conviction, closing her eyes. "Tulips, daisies, roses, lilacs—don't matter, God; we receive 'em."

She asked for blessings for all living things and those dying or dead. She asked to be forgiven by Claire. She had not intended, she told God, to upset Claire and let her see her frustration with their friendship. *But how, God, can Claire not 'member even my voice?*

She paused momentarily, then continued the most challenging part of her prayers. As always, she spoke this one out loud. "God, forgive me for da souls I killed. I'se used to seeing us killed. I had to learn to kill. You'se know dat, right God? It was not for me but for freedom." She was suddenly overcome with grief, covering her face with both hands; "I'se ain't a killer, God, but I 'se did kill. God, let me know da difference between da two befo' I'se die so I'se might understand."

So heavy were her sobs that her body heaved up and down as if the earth were lifting her. It was a while before she could stand up, gather her bowl, and walk to the porch. She felt exhausted, but a sudden anger rushed over her, delivered like a slap. There she was, back mad at Claire, whom she loved deeply. *Forgive me, Spirit God.*

Sylvie bent her head over the blessing bowl. The cherry blossoms had opened their petals. When she turned to the back door, she saw the lace curtains of the window move. Claire. They looked right into each other's eyes. Sylvie saw that Claire had also been crying.

Before Claire and Sylvie's arrival, the three other women had been living in the home. Isabel and Izabal came with Hargrove six months after the war ended. It took them months to get used to the enormous spaces and rooms. The ballroom shocked them, especially the chandelier. "White folks na stole stars from the sky?" they whispered upon seeing it. They had worked in the fields and had never been inside a plantation house. Isabel and Izabal were identical twins, and finding a thread of difference to tell them apart was impossible. They intended to keep it as such. "Just as one cans't separate da darkness from da night and da light from da day, our lives are da same."

One twin had seen snow for a brief time. She had been sold off from her sister by their master. The other twin had heard of snow only when her sister returned. The enslaver took the one away and soon after returned her. Each woman was useless to the seller and the buyer without the other. While miles away from each other, one in the Carolinas where snow fell upon her and the other back in Arkansas, they had stopped eating. Their mouths had shut to food, their bodies unmoved by beatings or verbal commands. Dying was their preference, rather than suffering life without the other.

The time spent away from each other was made up in their private conversations. They filled in the details of what the other had missed in the weeks apart. They shared every thought, every act, dream, wish, and tear. It was as if each had fallen into a dark hole when they were separated and reunited with one question directed to the other—what happened? They initially answered each other's questions, taking turns, but then the stories blended, and they couldn't tell who had left and who stayed. Soon, they began speaking of themselves as *I* or *we* for those listening to them. Between them, it was impossible to tell which of them had experienced whatever thing or incident in their separate lives and now shared the same memories. Claire remarked not long after meeting the sisters.

"I think there are times I envy their memories and how intertwined they are." Claire's voice cracked, then fell silent.

"We's all got memories, Claire. Yo's might be too painful to come. Da twins...well...no matter der memory, dey lived dem together! Dat might be da difference, just having somebody to witness yo life. Dat might be all it takes."

To the twins, memory was freedom. "Y'all ask too many questions!" Sylvie often told them, and they responded in the same way.

"If you'se got a memory, then you'se alive, and if you'se telling somebody about a memory, dey a part of dat living. Ain't dat right, sister?"

"Dat right." That was what Isabel and Izabal believed as truth. For this reason, they had a difficult time with Claire, who did not seem to have many memories to share. The twins loved Claire like the other women, but she had a mystery to her that didn't sit right with them. She didn't remember much and was vague about what she remembered. She avoided questions like the questions themselves were the problem.

"Somewhere, she's taught to read and write and talk like she does," the twins told each other. Claire, the twins decided, had never worked in the fields. Her delicate brown hands, on both sides, were smooth as river stones. "She says…she was enslaved but never said where," they whispered to each other. They had asked Claire that question on the first day of her arrival at Culver Tusk.

Hargrove had told them very little, except they should expect a woman named Claire. When she arrived, the sisters asked, "What plantation are you'se from?"

"Not more than a week's journey from here." Claire's dark lashes blinked rapidly. They waited. "I never want to speak the name of the plantation or who was my master. I would rather forget." *Or that I could fully remember*, she thought. Claire's eyes watered. Or even that she could remember at all. Her head had begun to throb.

Claire was quietly observing them, her face set, her hand ready to turn the knob to leave if they felt a need to press her further. Her pensive look did not stop the searching glances on their faces. The twins seemed determined that knowing her past would make her welcome easier.

Claire was ready to turn around and walk out the door she entered when a commanding voice just off the entrance broke the silence. "You'se mind taking a room with a lot of sunlight coming in?" Claire looked at the two identical women and leaned forward in the direction of the voice.

"Not at all, ma'am. I like sunlight in the morning." Claire knew, without meeting her, that was the woman Hargrove had told her about. "You Miss Lena?"

"All day and all night." Lena's laughter filled the hall. Dat room has a lot of light. I'se heard it was the woman's room, Miss Eloise's, but she kept the drapes drawn shut. Sad a person feels so bad she closes out the sun."

"What a shame. Maybe she was sad, but I love the sun, thank you." Claire lowered her eyes and said nothing more.

"Izabal? Isabel?" Lena called out.

"Yes, Lena." Lena did not miss the tone in which they responded. *Noisy women,* she thought. "Y'all gon' show her da room? You'se know I can't." She sighed; she'd have to find another way to avoid telling yet another person the full story of her broken body. "My body paid the price for freedom. Some days, the cost is higher than others." The day Claire arrived; Lena's body was suffering something awful. "Show Miss Claire da room."

"Yes, ma'am."

During her first week, Claire walked around the vast home and discovered the beauty of the detailed woodwork. Most of the rooms of the house were closed off. The expensive furniture of the room's history was covered and left unattended between cleanings. Claire loved her bedroom's expansive windows and immediately decided the curtains would remain open day and night. Initially, she divulged no more than her name, but she wrote feverishly, hunched over at the desk in the drawing room. Trusting only her private thoughts to paper, even the thoughts she couldn't speak to herself. The twins discovered at least one thing more than her name: there had been a baby. Isabel and Izabal saw her naked, and the stretch marks on her belly told them there had been at least one child.

Morning light had just broken up the last hue of night, and most of the house was asleep. A rooster's neck stretched his neck to call the day in. The twins walked in as quietly as ice melted, carrying fresh water for Claire. Thinking she'd still be sleeping like other mornings; they found she was not. Light poured through the open window, spreading across the room and on Claire. Claire was standing naked in front of the mirror. The sisters stood watching her as if she were a portrait to be admired. The sisters' eyes poured over her body, searching for any signs of physical scars of former beatings; the distance and the light gave them nothing. Claire's skin was smooth. There was very little not to admire. Claire's body was not as firm as they noted from hard labor yet sturdy. Her breasts were more prominent than her dresses revealed. It took Claire a minute to realize their presence. She did not try to cover herself; she smiled.

"Water. So, it's you two who've been bringing fresh water for me to wash myself with. Thank you." She pointed out for them to put it on the side of her bed. "But from now on, you don't have to serve me."

"We'se all serve each other as God intended."

We know she is a mother. Isabal and Izabel agreed later as they walked into the garden. They nodded and, looking down at the fat leaves of the greens sprouting out of the ground, said together, "She got to have memories of her baby or babies." A shadow crossed over their faces. Whatever thoughts or the talk of babies stopped abruptly, and they began picking the vegetables in silence.

Lena was the first to arrive at the house and was told the plantation was her property after the war. The near-fatal injury from another time in her memory left her barely able to walk more than a few steps. Yet the authority of her thoughts was felt throughout every room that her bare feet imagined walking.

It was unclear to the other women how the plantation had become Lena's or how she became hurt. But she was there, and the one man who made sure it remained as such was Hargrove. Fate found the woman over the first months after the war in different circumstances on his path. Hargrove invited them to come to live at the plantation as free Negro's with Lena under his protection. When he told each, "Lena is a Negro, she owns and runs the plantation, but her body is permanently broken," He might as well told them he'd had supper with Jesus. As far as the woman was concerned, it would have been more believable. A Negro woman owned a plantation. Humph! Hargrove saw in the twin's eyes God had brought the right women to live with Lena. They didn't bother hiding the fact; they didn't believe a word from his mouth. They took the invitation because he told them about Lena's broken body. Hargrove found Claire at the end of a Quaker meeting. She was sitting alone, holding a book and a small bundle. She looked lost. Hargrove told her the story. Claire nodded yes; she'd come to Culver Tusk as she had nowhere else to venture.

The women learned quickly; Hargrove and Lena spoke and enjoyed each other's company as if no color sat between them. They smiled tenderly, and Lena would avert her eyes to some other room detail. Hargrove watched her, waiting until her smile returned. When Lena was fussing about something, Hargrove was just as quick to jump at Lena's words as a leaping frog from a pot of boiling water. Lena, as dark as a cast-iron skillet and as beautiful as any sunrise, could melt you into a soft place of love or toss you to the wind. Claire immediately took to the darkness of Lena's skin, making her the prettiest shawls to wear around her shoulders. "You are my canvas, my inspiration, Lena."

"If da keeps the shawls coming, let me be your canvas. I love 'em!" Claire smiled. "Claire?"

"Yes, dear?"

"What in da world is a canvas?"

Claire was delighted with the question, pondering for a moment how to explain it. "Lena, you know how God's night sky is a story of stars and moonlight?" Claire's face lit up with excitement. "And…and in the day, the sun, clouds, all sorts of beauty, just showing up in glory!"

"Lord, yes, what glory," Lena added.

"Well, that is God's canvas! God puts everything beautiful in the sky. Your skin is my canvas."

"Sho' 'nuff." Lena enjoyed the images Claire was putting into words, and hearing that she was a part of the images, she repeated the only thing she could think of to say. "Well, I say."

Smiling and pleased with herself, she did not notice Claire's perplexed look or hear her whisper, "How is it that I even know what a canvas is myself?"

Lena didn't talk much about ownership of the plantation. The house did not matter to her, but she was aware of the folks in the countryside. It was a matter of life and death to them, including the sheriff who had come to the house. Not being able to walk far did not stop her from knowing what went on outside Culver Tusk. Folks blamed her for what they called a curse, and now that the other women were here, they inherited the blame. Lena looked down at her dark hands and talked openly with God. "It ain't me dat put a curse on 'em. It's dere thinking about me and my people." Lena had not wanted to stay in the former plantation house, let alone own it, and said as much when Hargrove announced it.

"I know you'se don't care, Lena," Hargrove had told her, "But I do. This is your home." She said nothing. "Lena, trust me this one last time." Still nothing. Lena sat watching Hargrove as he continued struggling for the right words. "My protection, Lena, is all I'se have left to offer you and my life. Please, for your own sake and mine." Under his breath, he whispered, "And my love, from which you seem to have turned away." Hargrove talked, and until finally, he asked one question that settled it all: "Where can you'se go and be safe in this world, Lena? Tell me, I'll go with you'se if you have me?" Hargrove apprehensively placed his hand over Lena's. He waited; Lena didn't bother pondering where she could go. She scrutinized the details of Hargrove's hand on hers. Lena gazed into Hargrove's eyes; she wouldn't allow herself to succumb to the love she saw in them. Lena needed Hargrove to know that his understanding, not his love, was most needed. "Hargrove, my first memories of life, I'se barely walking age; I hear grown folks around me talking and praying *God give us freedom*. Lena squeezed his hand. "I'se didn't know what free meant; I was barely walking. I'se learned soon as I could walk out into the field what not being free meant. I'se started praying like err'body else *God give us freedom*." Lena paused. "Hargrove, da law says we'se freed, and I can't get up on my own from dis chair and walk into my freedom." Hargrove's heart burst open with a fiery emotion rushing to his stomach—gut-wrenching sadness. The truth shook him to the core. He lifted Lena's hand and held it to his lips. Hargrove got out of his chair and scooped Lena into his arms, "Then I'll carry you'se into freedom, Lena, and I'll find other women to keep you company in your home."

He kept his promise, traveling throughout Springfield and beyond. He asked God to guide him; he was led to each woman, but the last. Sylvie had arrived without Hargrove's approval or knowledge. She was carrying two squirrels she caught, and the smell of the woods on her clothes. She came with a heavy knock. And now, as Claire had watched Sylvie praying over her bowl and weeping, she too began to cry. She felt sorrow making its way into their lives, disturbing what peace they had gathered.

Claire had glanced around the room as if it might reveal an answer. She could hear Lena snoring softly in the parlor, and she had no idea where the twins might be off. Her finger began throbbing. How, she wondered, could such a small thing cause such discomfort? There was no use continuing her needlepoint. The blood had ruined the cloth.

The nervous feeling in her stomach indicated something more would happen—more than Sylvie and her question of how Claire could not remember her. The question only opened a portal for the uncomfortable feeling to reveal itself. There was something Claire felt in the air coming toward them. Claire sat momentarily to list what could harm the women. It was more than the threat of the sheriff. Was it hidden in the unseasonable winter they were enjoying? Things that even the woods could not know. If the thought of displaced birds worried folks, something told her that would be minor compared to what was ahead. But what? She threw the needlepoint in the rag pile. It was useless to her. The delicate golden bird she had worked so hard on, now discarded to the rags, was looking up at her. "Do you know?" she asked the golden bird jokingly, noticing the blood from her finger had stained the cloth just under the bird's feet.

A bird is standing in blood. That can't be good! Claire snatched the cloth up and tossed it into the dying fire. *What is going to happen?* she wondered. The flames rose suddenly with new life, dancing wildly, devouring the bird. *Is one of us going to die?* she thought, which made her begin to cry softly. But then, what did they expect but to pass on? Claire felt her heartache. None of them had ever spoken of leaving one another in any way, let alone dying. Who? Lena, who struggled to get in and out of bed? One of the twins? Sylvie? Myself? The thought of her death frightened her.

"I want to live, God. I want to live long enough to finish my writing and to remember my life before it is gone." Speaking aloud was the first time Claire admitted to herself she wanted to recover the past—the past that eluded her; Sylvie seemed suspiciously aware of it. Claire cried out to the flames ravishing her needlepoint. "I want my memory back, no matter how painful."

# FOURTEEN

The twins found the squash embedded with the face of a baby. Maybe if they'd blinked, the upcoming events would have remained in the world of the unspoken. But they stared. The squash was partially buried in the densest part of the garden, under a considerable patch of strawberries; the squash's skin was dripping with strawberries' blood. "Go figure, who would leave a bab—" Alarmed, they frantically began to seek out the mother, then abruptly stopped. "Oh, my, it's a squash!" They tried to laugh at the trick their eyes had played, but what came out was more like a series of hiccups. The sound brought Sylvie to them. Just as amazed at the finding and not ready to call her eyes a lie, Sylvie took off running to the house and carrying the baby…squash close to her breast. Whatever it was, it was a sign. The twins ran close by, arms flaring, screaming at Sylvie to wait.

Lena could hear Sylvie shouting her name from the road and something about the twins and a baby. Out of breath, Sylvie ran into Lena's room, clutching the thing to her chest. "Looka, Lena!" Lena sat up in her bed and looked out the window. "Don't see anything."

"Here." The sisters rushed into the room as Sylvie handed Lena a beautiful golden squash about the size of a two-month-old baby. *Trees got faces like people and mountains, so why not squash? At least I can hold it! Sylvie was thinking. Found among rocks and sweet dark soil, squash had features. Eyes…nose… see my mouth? Skin is just as soft. The baby likely was left years ago and decided not to die but become part of what was growing from the ground.*

"What…da heck? Where dis…baby…I'se mean, where does squash

come from? Cause it's too big to be a regular squash.'"

"I'se know it's real big—weighs as much as a big baby." Sylvie sat on the bed to touch it. "Look like a person, too."

The squash lay soft and undemanding on Lena's thigh. Lena's fingers gently turned the squash over, poking on the skin. It surrendered just enough to make Lena wonder, "Dis squash?"

Sure enough, the squash seemed to be looking outward, with eyes, nose, and mouth. The skin of the squash was golden brown. The red juices of the strawberry dripped down the sides like it had been crying blood. There was so much pent-up laughter at the sight of the women gushing over a squash that Lena burst out laughing.

Lena investigated what appeared to be eyes on the squash. "My, my." "Lena?"

Sylvie questioned, "How squash grow in a patch of strawberries?" *And why are strawberries growing in August when everyone knows they come up in May?*

"'Cause dey want to. I guess t'aint no explaining some things."

"Huh!" Sylvie folded her arms.

Claire reached over and poked it gently with her index finger. "You know, sometimes the wind brings seeds from far away and sets home on whatever dirt they find, like the rest of us in the house. You know, like how I used to travel." Claire continued. "Home is where you find yourself." Again, Claire had said something from her mouth that she had no memory of. Travel.

All the women were as close to the bed as they could, sitting or lying on it. Each leaned forward to look at a young child's face on the squash.

"And I think I loved traveling, I might add." Claire still wanted to add more to her thoughts. Something about the sight of a baby imprinted on a squash felt like a message beyond the veil or memory.

"True…" Sylvie smiled to herself. She fully understood what traveling meant to Claire. She repeated herself while she gazed fully at Claire. "True…"

Lena turned her face away from the squash, not sure if it was her thoughts about her dead baby or if she was exhausted from the conversation. "Git it off the bed. Put it somewhere till we decide what we want to make of it. Something's going on." She pointed her index finger to the ceiling, her eyebrows raised in exclamation. "Somebody talking."

The other women nodded in agreement. Claire started to speak. "We—"

Lena threw her a glance that begged her silence. Shaking her head, she said, "Claire, we'se have plans to make! We's got to let da spirits what we know, or better yet, what we'se don't know. Pour some liquor on the front porch for those beyond." She slid her more able leg over the bed. "I think I'll cook tonight if ya git me out of dis bed."

Isabel and Izabal made it happen, lifting Lena so she could drape her arms over their shoulders. No one remembered who took the squash off the bed. The twins just remembered pulling the blankets back off Lena and the smell of her warm skin rising to greet them. Lavender!

Lena was out of bed and dressed in her house gown, sitting at the table preparing the meal. They ate together, cleaned the house, and sat resting at the table, entertaining each other with small talk until they heard the distant sounds of horses. Lena put her finger to her lips to warn the women; *shhh.*

# FIFTEEN

Hargrove was more than aware of the feud brewing in the countryside. It did not involve many, but it took only one person to kill another and more. And with the arrival of the four men and their wives, things had gotten stirred up again. Rumor was that the women were related to his murdered uncle's mistress.

When Hargrove rode into the city to speak to the mayor after the sheriff had come to Culver Tusk, the mayor laughed, saying they'd been getting letters of complaint regarding unnatural things happening since the war. Hargrove asked to see the letters. "No, no, we throw that kind of madness out. Probably burnt 'em," he said, laughing. Yup, we don't keep foolishness." The mayor offered Hargrove a seat and a cigar.

Declining, Hargrove asked, "Why did the sheriff and deputies come out to Culver Tusk asking about black magic and threatening the women?" The mayor took a deep breath. Hargrove knew he was about to lie.

"Well, hum, Looka here, Mr. Hargrove, you'se got to understand the situation as we'se see it."

"We?" Hargrove tilted his hat back.

"We'se, the people. Mr. Hargrove, I am the people. The folks voted me in. I'se got to say we!" The mayor became uncomfortable with the whole conversation. "Folks around here been broken by the war in ways only time will tell. Like it or not, it's true… And Hargrove, I hear you'se got Negroes living in Culver Tusk. Tell me it dat taint true?" The mayor waved his hand hurriedly at the smoke he was blowing away from Hargrove. "The sheriff was just trying to keep the peace."

Hargrove smiled inwardly at the foolishness of that statement. He looked right into the eyes of the man he had known most of his life. Hargrove never liked him. There was no pretense of who between them held absolute power. Hargrove's family was old money with deep connections. If the mayor liked his job, he knew how to keep it. They stood watching each other in uncomfortable truth. The mayor was a political puppet.

"I don't take these folks seriously…You know dat, right, Mr. Hargrove? But I got to ask questions. The years since the war don't mean anything to people. You'se know that, right?" For a man whose speeches could inflame a crowd, Hargrove noted how unsure the mayor sounded. Hargrove tilted his hat back to let the mayor know the conversation was ending.

"Mean it or not, I 'se got enough men on my land protecting da women."

The mayor dropped his head and dusted off his jacket. He thought, *you'se mean dat nigga Lena.* He looked up with a smile. "Mr. Hargrove, let me know if you'se need anything from me. Anything at'tall. You'se should come by and have dinner with me and my family. Mother asks about you'se all the time."

"You give your mother my regards." Hargrove left and headed to Culver Tusk.

He decided not to mention his visit with the mayor to Lena. Hargrove had another urgent matter to discuss with the women.

The door opened before Hargrove had a chance to knock. Lena had shushed the women with her finger to her lips when she heard the horses, and she relaxed when the cowbell signaled it was Hargrove. After greeting the women, Hargrove hung his coat on the hook with the ease of familiarity. As always, he quickly assessed the room's mood, and everything seemed good. Good! He sat at the table, took his hat off, and sat it on his lap, holding on to the news as long as possible. He finished the last of the four tea cakes with red jam set before him. He ate four because he knew Lena had made them. "Best tea cakes I ever had."

Claire rolled her eyes good-naturedly. "You say that every time, Hargrove, but Izabal"—she paused— "or Isabel make the best tea cakes to me." Claire mustered a playful look. "I mean no harm, Lena, but you said it yourself."

Lena shrugged. "No harm taken. I'se agree. Tis up to da taste of the one eating da cakes. Besides, Sylvie made the jam. Might be what Hargrove is fussing over."

"No, Lena, the jam was good, but it's the tea cake. See—I ate four, two without the jam!"

When they set the jar of white rum in front of him, Hargrove took a long drink, burning his mouth. When the fire went down to his belly, he was ready. He laid the telegrams and a letter on the table. The route number on the telegram, in bold print, was down the road from Culver Tusk. He secretly hoped the news would not change the cheerfulness of the room. He missed coming over more often, but now, with the rumblings of the Confederate families and the four men with wives related to his uncle's mistress, he was kept busy just staying ahead of any potential threat.

"It says…she should be here next week. Coming from Ohio."

"Who's she, Hargrove?" Lena took the telegram off the table to look at it. Hargrove tried to remember how much reading Lena had. Hargrove had taken it upon himself to read documents to her. He questioned why he hadn't asked her if she could read. Hargrove watched the movements of her dark fingers gently turning the telegram over. Lena let it rest on the table, pressing it down with her palms. She spoke to the women. "It says she got news about Evening's daddy. It makes no sense; Evening Daddy has been dead sixty years now. Who is she, Hargrove?"

"She's a nun, Lena, Sister Elizabeth. Dat's what the head of the convent put in the telegraph. A Negro nun. Anyway, she is of the Catholic religion, which is different from Baptist or Pentecostal." Hargrove watched how each woman took in the information and then added it. "I'll pick her up from the train station and bring her here for ya'll to welcome her and get her settled in before she meets Evening. I thought that would be best." Hargrove glanced over at Lena since the women seemed uninterested.

"And?" Izabal asked, or perhaps it was Isabel. Hargrove couldn't tell which twin was asking the question. Irritated, Hargrove threw her question back, "And what?"

Sylvie matched his agitation. "And what dat got to do with us? She ain't coming to see us. Dis Sister Elizabeth! She ain't no kin to us; she comes to see Evening. You'se know where Evening stays." Sylvie poured another taste; drinking made her even bolder sometimes. Beads of sweat glistened on her forehead.

"What do…nuns do?" one of the twins asked. Both were twirling their rum in their glass in the same direction.

"Isabel?" Both women took a sip at the same time. Damn it, he thought, dey drive a person crazy and probably don't know their selves apart.

What do nuns do? Good question, he thought. Hargrove didn't know the exact details but was just as satisfied with not knowing as knowing. Let the women ask him what he didn't know. The liquor made him want to talk, even if to hear his voice. He looked from one twin to the other. "You ask what nuns do…" he was waiting for one to acknowledge. Both responded, "Yep." At least he tried, Hargrove continued, "Well, dey live to serve and suffer. Dey takes a vow of poverty."

"What's dat?" Sylvie insisted.

"What's what?" Hargrove turned his attention toward Sylvie. She was a spitfire at times, and he saw the fire now in her eyes, ready to fight.

"A vow of poverty." Sylvie leaned forward, eyebrows raised, "What da hell you'se talking about, Hargrove?" Lena could hardly contain herself. She covered her mouth to stop laughing.

"Where you promise God not to want anything, and if you got everything, you'se give it to others. Strangers don't matter; even da clothes you'se are wearing, the food in your mouth. Your life is to work for others' happiness, serving 'em dawn to dusk."

"Whatcha say?" Claire saw the movement of Sylvie's mouth after she spoke and noticed how her body stiffened up. Claire wondered what Sylvie was thinking, as Sylvie's thoughts concerning any situation could never be anticipated. Sylvie, taken aback, asked, "Dem nuns wanna be slaves, and a slave coming to see Evening?" Sylvie tapped her fingers nervously on the edge of the table.

"Leave it, Hargrove." Lena knew if the direction of the conversation took them down that road of being enslaved, nothing good would come out of it. "Please, Hargrove." Sylvie stopped tapping and perched on the edge of her chair, waiting.

"Well," Hargrove took Lena's advice and added another exciting fact he had heard about nuns. "Dey ain't like preacher wives who go to church, sit in da front pew, and come home to look after the kids and der preacher husband." The five women sat still, waiting for Hargrove to say what they knew to be true. Hargrove was afraid to knock on Evening's door with any foolishness from the past. "Nope," he continued. The drink had made its way to his head. He smiled. "Nuns grow up and get married to Jesus. Dat's what the nuns do: marry Jesus." Hargrove missed the look on Claire's face, followed by the roll of her eyes.

"Dis Sister Elizabeth got married to Jesus." He pondered in thought for a moment before he continued. "Probably never been with a man, not even courted like Jesus's mother, Mary. Mary was a Virgin."

"What dat word virgin mean? Dat her last name Sister Elizabeth Virgin?" Sylvie asked.

Lena gave a hearty laugh. "Nah, it means she never had sex." Hargrove agreed with a low, long sigh. He couldn't imagine a woman or man living their whole life without having the proper affection.

Claire shifted at the sound of what she deemed Hargrove's arrogance, her shoulders defiant. Hargrove, she knew, was a decent man, and it was clear he had his affection for Lena, but still, in the end, Claire Hargrove was a white man. She resented the slow movement of his hands on the glass and thought, *like rubbing a new untouched piece of flesh, a nameless soul you don't even know, but you want it cause nobody else na sniffed it.* Claire felt dizzy as a flash of something familiar ran across her mind.

The twins erupted laughing. The ripple of laughter from the other two women surprised Hargrove. The zigzag motion of their bodies rocked the table. Hargrove lifted his drink just in time to save it from being knocked over. He was slightly drunk, and the movement of their bodies rocking back and forth didn't make it any better. Both laughter and their words circled in and around his mind like birds trapped in a barn searching for an opening. The women's words blended when they poured words onto their laughter. He had difficulty sorting out who was talking and who was laughing.

"She ain't…"

"Lord, I na heard everything. First a squash or a baby, now this mess."

"She might be a virgin!"

"But I guarantee she na felt her thang howler at some point."

"You don't need any man in da room to feel something." Lena fell back on the chair, laughing and gasping for air.

One of the other twins said, "It helps—can't lie about that!"

"Hell, some men can make you feel like you are flying."

Sylvie, intoxicated by the drink and the conversation of sex.

"Yaa sho got that right!" she shouted.

"But I na been so good to myself. I pulled my hair." Izabal or Isabel stood and started moving her hips in one direction and then the other: all that movement and no music, just the rhythm of their bubbling laughter.

"Woman…shut up." The bottle was being passed around, and the voices blended.

Hargrove could no longer distinguish which of the women were singing praise to sex now that Sylvie joined in. "Nice be a man in the room, but lord knows he ain't needed. My husband was a wild ride!"

"Ain't lying to you, woman. One day!" One or both twins hit the word *day* with conviction and jumped in the air. Her cotton dress rose over her thighs. Hargrove sat in shock, watching her body jump almost as high as she was tall and come down wide-legged, feet planted on the floor like she had mounted a horse. The brown color of her dress was lit from behind by the fire. The outline of her inner thighs parted. Hargrove's eyes widened, sure that undergarments did not cover the image between her legs. She was naked under her dress; the light of the fire highlighted her private part. His breath caught as her hips moved side to side and then back and forth. Hargrove was appalled when the flickering thought crossed his mind if both women had identical private parts. He shook his head to clear his mind as one or the other twin kept talking.

"I went swimming, got out dar water. Lay on the grass, naked as a new day."

"Oh, Lord."

"Sun so hot it drank that water off my skin and…befo' I closed my eyes to rest; I'se pulled a small branch with fat leaves to fan my naked self."

Sylvie looked at her reflection in the window and smiled. The twin continued, " You'se know how we's like our feet tended to."

"Yes, we's do!"

"I'se got to fanning my feet, got to fanning my legs, my thighs. It was an apple blossom bud right near da top. I'se gently fanned my thighs; bristles touched, tingled, if you will. And I…"

She stopped moving her body from side to side and arched her head back to laugh. The sound of one twin's robust laughter and the other calling out, "Sho nuff, sho nuff we did," was even more intimate than the story's details. Claire blushed, but she did not want the story to stop. All her imagination was employed, and she loved it. Isabel or Izabal, one or the other, had done things to herself that Claire did not know even possible. She found herself looking with admiration at both women. How confident and satisfied they were with their happiness. At that moment, she wished she had someone to reflect on in her life. But just as quickly, she released that thought. No one, she told herself, that she loved should endure what her mind refused to remember. Claire put her attention back on Isabel or Izabal.

"Da leaves tickled my thighs, and my nerves jumped like flames. I'se waited to see if I had nerves in my belly; I sucked my belly in." Hargrove glanced over at Lena to see if she had lost her mind for not stopping this untamed behavior. Lena was smiling and fanning herself with a dishcloth. He wondered if Lena had ever known such pleasure had he ever given... his thoughts were interrupted.

"Dat branch had me feeling as good as it gits!"

"Do declare, did it?"

"I's reached up and my hands tangled up into da thick naps of my hair." Hargrove's eyes widened in shock, but it was not over yet.

"I'se hollered cuz, I'se wet, the river wet, my skin from the sun wet. I started pulling my hair hard till the roots hollered."

The disbelief of her words snatched Hargrove up from his chair, tumbling it backward. "I'm going to pray for each one of you. Y'all should be 'shamed, 'shamed for talking like that in front of a man. And your age! I say shame!! What's the total of all ya ages together? The Bible ain't even that old. Ya'll wrongs!" He heard his hurtful words and hated them as they spat out his mouth. But he was shocked, and still, he kept talking even though they did not seem to pay him any attention; their faces were cast downward, giggling like children. He wondered, for a moment, what they were staring at.

"And I'se got a grove of apple blossom trees." Addressing Izabal or Isabel, whichever of the two was standing. "You'se took a tree branch and did *what?*" His words rushed out of his mouth, and spit flew. "Now, what I got to do? Cut down my trees lest I am reminded of your wild sexual behavior with yourself!?"

"Suit yourself, pig face. Git your ax, and git started chopping." Sylvie said it with so much drunken carelessness that the women howled.

"I'm starting to see why folks that ain't hateful but care about ya'll don't bother to come out here; even the Negro's hesitate. Where's my hat?" Hargrove snapped his head around.

The laughter got louder. Through their tears, wide-open legs, and laughter, Lena pointed her finger at him and said, "It's hanging on your lap."

Hargrove looked down. By God!  A full erection held his hat. He gasped. The rocking of the women's bodies and the raw laughter rising from their bellies was like a song he did not like, yet his body had responded to it. It had been a while since his manhood had felt alive. Humiliated that he was being laughed at, the heat of his shame rose in his face. What hurt most was that Lena seemed to be leading the laughter. Her head was thrown back, arms loose by her side, her whole body shaking under her green dress.

Near the wood-burning stove, one of the twins was still standing with her fingers in the grips of her dark hair. He saw her body beneath it in the light. He took his hat off his lap and threw it on the table. He was ashamed of the hat and himself. "Keep it as a reminder of da shame you'se brought me tonight. Shame on you." If Hargrove meant to bring any sense of stability or gain an apology. It didn't happen. Lena put the hat on, tilting it to the side. That sent the women into a frenzy. The women were as happy as he'd seen them in a long time. He did not turn to say goodbye or even acknowledge the playful good nights they threw at him. The door swung open, and Hargrove snatched his jacket and took off, enveloped by the dark and his shame.

Hargrove got in his wagon and removed the cowbell, as he did not want the women to know his direction; despite his shame or the strong drinks, he knew he'd sleep nearby to watch over the house. He took off toward the road and checked on two of his men guarding the back road before circling back to the woods. Hargrove tied the wagon to the tree and walked back through their property. He made it to the shed to rest. Drunk or not, he knew he had to keep an eye on the women. After tomorrow, he decided, he would put another two men to watch in the shed. He had gotten a report of another attempted lynching Shelton, and his men had stopped. They'd gotten the family safely out of the county.

The laughter dissipated into silence after Hargrove left the house. The women had no idea he had circled and was in the old, abandoned shed. They were exhausted from the night. The telegram and the letter to be discussed lay between them on the table. Sylvie rested her arms on the table and then her head but assured them she was still listening to whatever they had to say about the news. There was no sound from the others, so Lena aired her thoughts.

"I'se can't walk to Evening, so one of you'se got to go down to Evening's house."

Claire insisted she was not the best person to deliver things of this delicate nature, although she did not know why she felt this way. She cleared her throat and looked over at the twins. "I think you two should go."

"Why?" The women were seated together on one chair, sharing one glass.

"She might react badly to the news. Two people is better than one." Sylvie lifted her head off the table. "We'se don't know one thing or da other about her daddy might stir up something, make her act out."

"Evening's a gentle spirit. Claire, it would help if you didn't suggest such a thing, but of course, we can go," both women answered.

"Claire, stop being such a fool. If two people need to go, den I'se volunteer, me and you!" Sylvie said.

"How did that work out the last time we went together?" Claire found herself ready to battle with Sylvie.

Lena took the telegram and folded it into fours. "What da hell happened last time you two went to Evening's? I'se don't remember anybody saying nuthing." She tucked the paper in her pocket.

"Dat's 'cause we'se never discussed da matter." Sylvie glared at Claire.

"We'se don't mind going," one said, and the other chimed in, "We don't mind at'tall ."

Lena still tried to remember why Claire and Sylvie had been down to Evening's house. They came back too quickly to call it a visit.

"One of y'all fools tell me da last time you did anything together 'cept fuss." Lena laughed. "I got to git some sleep. Hurry up and tell me what happened." They ignored her request.

Lena wished she could carry the news to Evening, but her broken body wouldn't allow it. Claire and Sylvie were too far into their fussing, so Lena asked the twins to help her settle in. "Dat nun ain't coming dis week. We'se git Evening da message in da next day or so." Lena put the telegram on her nightstand. "Blow da light out for me." Lena lay in the dark, gazing at the night stars. She spotted the North Star. There were no clouds in the sky, just a sliver of the moon. "God's canvas." Lena's eyes watered. She thanked God, her broken body, and all God gave her the grace to be still alive. Lena felt the goodness and pleasure of listening to the night rituals and chatter of the other women preparing to settle in for the night. Lena closed her eyes and turned her thoughts to Hargrove.

# SIXTEEN

Sylvie burst into the back door out of breath, feathers in her hair, fussing as the chickens had gotten out of the coop again. "Somebody messing with da latch. I'se made dat coop myself! Who mess it when I'se not around." They wanted to ignore Sylvie, but they knew she was in a fighting mood. The twins said we did it, Claire said I did it, and Lena said no; I got my legs back and went out and unlatched it. It worked. They laughed and picked the feathers out of Sylvie's hair.

By afternoon, the women were moving about, each in their world, when Lena heard a knock and leaned forward toward the sound. She whispered, warning the other women, "Somebody's at da door." They had not heard horses, Hargrove's cowbell, or anyone approaching by foot up the road leading to the house. Each woman tensed up.

They did not wait to see if Lena was right. Sylvie reached for the shotguns and handed one to each of the twins. Lena took her pistol from her housecoat pocket. Claire's gun was nestled in her knitting bag. She reached down and pulled it out. Sylvie picked up a third shotgun leaning against the wall by the door and turned to the women, one hand on the doorknob. Lena nodded the command with her loaded shotgun pointed, cocked, and ready. The sound of the hinges creaking would be enough for her finger to pull back the trigger.

"It's me, y'all." The tension in the room eased up like spring rain. The weapons were put away as quickly as they had appeared. Sylvie opened the door open.

Evening stood on the porch against the fading light of the sky. Her hair hung in four long braids past her shoulders, and she was dressed in dark trousers and a man's shirt under a beautiful jacket. She was smiling and carrying a woven basket covered with a cotton-dyed line with intricate patterns. Sylvie thought *Dis cloth is something Claire would like, all dat tiny stitching around da edges.*

"You'se look nice. We's musta talked you'se up, Evening. Come on in." Evening stepped over the threshold.

"Is dat true?" Evening's voice was deep and velvety.

"Always to's me," Sylvie replied. Evening chuckled, which seemed to challenge Sylvie's true feelings.

Sylvie squinted her eyes till they were barely slivers searching Evening's face; what if Evening didn't think the women missed her? She felt *dat ain't right.* Sylvie let her eyes slowly glide over Evening's face while seconds came and went. The only odd thing for the women watching was that neither bothered to close the door, and the cool air poured freely past them into the room. Claire quickly went and put another log in the hearth.

It was nice to hear Sylvie having an emotion beyond anger. Claire, too, missed Evening. Evening, as Claire saw it, was one side of the bookend of their lives, like the day; Lena was on the other end, like night, holding their stories together. Claire blushed to admit she felt jealous, seeing how intimately Sylvie was taking Evening in. Evening's presence felt natural whether they saw her once a month or every six months. Evening was as much a part of them as they were to each other. "Sylvie dear," Claire didn't want to give any hint of jealousy, "I've put another log in the hearth. I'll have to add another if you close the door much longer?"

Sylvie stepped aside. "You'se believe I'se missed you, Evening!" My goodness, Claire whispered; even affection became a battle with Sylvie.

"Come sit with us. Ain't seen you since the quarter moon." Sylvie closed the door behind her, leaned back on it, and sighed. "It's good to look around at ya'll makes a good feeling rise in me." She added, "We'se being together like dis." One of the twins made room on the table. "Sit your basket down if you'se want." Turning to Sylvie, she replied. "Me and sister feel da same it's a good feeling. It's a feeling of being complete, ain't dat right, sister?" They both nodded yes.

Lena cleared her throat, sighed deeply, and nodded toward the table. She was ready to be moved. Claire and Sylvie went over to help Lena take the painful steps to sit at the head of the table. Lena, leaning heavily on each woman's shoulder, moaned with every step. "Jesus, thank you'se for err' step even if I'se can't take on my own."

"We'se just about to have peach brandy. Evening, join us. What's in da basket?" one of the twins asked. Evening knew it was Izabal. She could tell them apart but would never let on to the other women. Regarding the sisters, she always spoke to them as they wished, as one.

"A dozen Goose eggs."

"What you'se say?"

"Yes, ma'am, got goose eggs. I'se know y'all be hearing dat water song circling."

"Yeah, we'se hear it. It's been a while. Whatcha, think it means?"

Evening searched out each woman's face before speaking. Her life under her mother's spiritual guidance taught her that not everyone was open to the truths of the universe. Each was eagerly waiting. "It comes from the story of water. Errrrrrrrrrrrrrr means one soul, errrrrrrrrrrr."

"Maybe dat why we'se drink more when we'se hear it."   Isabal and Izabel exclaimed. "Tis not a familiar thirst; much deeper thirst, like our bones thirsty."

"And the water is sweeter," Claire added.

"Yep, dis song is the story of da unexpected in life. It comes from da memory of the mother earth; it shows up to provoke either a personal lost memory or a collective memory trying to come home."   Evening waited before continuing.   Good, the women weren't looking at her like she was talking foolishly, so Evening continued. "Even if you'se, or we'se not ready for da memory. It'll be waiting, not on time, but in time. Like a ghost in the room, you'se don't have to acknowledge it for it to be there. Ghost ain't leaving till its time to go." The women nodded understandingly, except Claire.

Claire started frantically digging in her sewing basket. "I don't know where my gold thread is. Has anyone seen my gold thread?" Evening took a deep breath, placed the palm of her right hand on her chest, and patted. She directed the following words to Claire's heart.

"Song comes, and no memory comes to you'se. It leaves you'se a gift to remind you or encourage you to know the soul of our memory comes not on time but in time." Claire looked up from the basket. "Here's my gold thread. It was tucked in the fabric."

"We'se got a gift! The song gave us a real baby, but it's a squash, too." Sylvie's voice was trembling, waiting for Evening to give meaning to the squash. Evening snickered at the notion until she saw the serious look on Sylvia's face. The clicking sound came from Claire; she'd sat her basket down and got up to fill the glasses with peach brandy.

"Evening, don't pay Sylvie no mind," Claire leaned down and whispered, pouring some peach brandy into her glass. "Please."

Evening looked around the room, plucked a goose feather off her jacket, and took Claire's advice. She recalled the last time the two had come to visit her, warning her that the white people were planning on attacking. She had listened and reassured them she was safe in the house and would not leave. Evening shared with her that a family of wolves had decided to befriend her and that they came around when they sniffed danger. It was not her first battle with white people. But Claire and Sylvie had spent more time fighting about how to keep everyone safe. Evening took Claire's advice and did not ask more about the baby or squash.

"Sho' is cold out. This brandy is perfect."

"Yep." They drank in silence.

"Well…I was bringing eggs over, and ya was talking me up. I can feel some 'em in the air."

"Yep."

Sylvie let out a deep breath but had no intention of answering. Claire asked, "You know what a Catholic nun is?"

"No, what's a Catholic nun?" She took a drink, and her eyes widened. "Whoa."

Evening was a beautiful woman whose head full of gray hair was braided and twisted into four long braids. Most days she came to visit, it looked like she just tossed her clothes in the air and let them fall on her, but tonight Evening looked like she had put thought into it. Lena shook her head and pulled the telegram from her dress pocket.

Evening, having paid Lena's words no attention, slowly looked around at each of them. Smiling and waiting, she figured the paper had something to do with her. Lena, nervous about this news, hoped she might better explain it than Hargrove. "It's a woman living not as a woman but for da Church, praying all day and helping people when she can." She pointed at the telegram. "Da head of da Church sent you dis message. The nun is coming from Cleveland, Ohio. Her name is Sister Elizabeth, and she is traveling by train."

With a whimsical smile, Evening sipped her drink and gazed, showing no interest in the paper in front of Lena, who continued. Lena tapped the paper, ready for whatever was about to occur. "She comes to see you, Evening—dat much we know. Tis bout your daddy!" The muscles around the smile on Evening's face twitched. "She'll be here sooner din later. It must be important to come all dis way. You'se want da telegram?"

Evening locked eyes with Lena. "Can't read—you'se know dat, Lena."

Lena leaned onto the table with both arms folded. Her hips ached. She turned away from Evening. "I'm tired. Claire can read it, but it says exactly what I'se told you. dat woman, or whatever she is, is coming from Cleveland." Lena sucked her teeth and began rubbing her aching hands. She was tired, and her body hurt, and nobody seemed in the mood to talk anymore. *Good,* Lena thought. *Sometimes, it's good to be quiet.*

They waited while Evening took in the news. Outside, there were loud yowls and screams from Coyotes traveling from the woods. Evening started the conversation back up.

"News about her husband?" Evening asked, looking around at the women as if they should understand what she meant by "her husband." How would they know since she had never told anybody?

She heard Lena say, "Your daddy," but Evening could not remember him. She only knew her mother's husband. Nobody at the table said anything out of respect, figuring the news was a lot to get used to.

Him. Evening rolled the thought around in her mind. She never talked about him, her mother's husband. She never told the women that her daddy's presence was never absent from their home. Or at least not until her mother died. Then, both their absences were felt in every corner. Her mother's husband was more than a ghost, just never flesh and blood for her to see. But her mother saw her husband in their home, which left Evening childhood with the burden of bearing witness to the unexplainable. Yes, she wanted to tell the women my mother cooked his favorite meal every Sunday, set his plate at the table, and ate with him, her husband. *As if their daughter—me—was not there.*

Evening looked at the women sitting around her, seemingly occupied with their thoughts. But she knew they were just being kind to her, given the news. How could she explain to them what had mystified her for sixty years?

Her mother ceremoniously pulled his chair back, his plate..., and his favorite things every Sunday. She refused to drink from a separate cup. She shared his...sip...after...sip. Her mother would ask the empty chair to "Pass me the..."

Nothing ever really passed from the empty seat, but her mother reacted as if it had. Once, a bowl was toppled, and warm soup spilled, causing her mother to jump. But there was no bowl that Evening could see, no spill, just her mother cleaning up the invisible spill and assuring her husband it was okay. Over the years, she, too—their daughter began to see a pot or dish moving in midair.

"Thank you. Just what these potatoes needed: more salt." Her mother did not have an imaginary friend. She had her husband, who occupied an empty chair. Only her daughter knew that. And nobody—not even their daughter—could see him, pots and dishes moving in mid-air, but not her daddy's face. As hard as their daughter tried, she could not put her daddy in the house, at the table, let alone in the chair.

Or in her heart, where the singular note of loneliness sat waiting.

Even at age four, imaginary friends are a dime a dozen to a child. As hard as she tried, no bones or flesh of what her daddy looked like announced itself. So, she politely asked one Sunday, "What does my daddy look like, Mama?" Her mother was taken aback.

"What do you mean, daughter? What does he look like? Do you mean if you look more like your daddy or me? "Well, sometimes more like your daddy, when you get frustrated, and your face pulls in," her mother laughed. "And when you sleep, you look more like me. That's what your daddy thinks, huh, Daddy?" Evening cried, feeling more alone, and got mad at herself for asking the question. Her mother wiped the tears off her cheeks and said, "When you get sad like this, I can't tell who you look like. Don't cry."

When Evening turned five, an imaginary friend showed up, granting her childish wish to see her mother's husband. The season could not have laid a more welcoming path for his arrival. The whole earth burst forward with every strain of gold that it possessed. The hills were full of flowers, and the smells, coupled with the scent of the river, came into her bedroom window. She got up and walked quickly to the river with her mother's permission. A friend was standing in the water, wet and smiling. He stood wrapped in a ray of sunlight, a little boy with eyes as dark as the center of the woods.

"I'm almost six years old," he announced proudly, brown skin new, no bumps or childhood scars, shiny and wet. For sure, it was her daddy when he was a boy, she thought.

"Where you been?" Excited, she did not wait for an answer. "Want to come to my"—she stopped herself— "our house?" He nodded. The drops of water on his lashes sparkled in the sunlight. *My daddy's beautiful*, she thought and reached for his hand. "Come on." The happiness in her voice rippled with emotion like the waters from which he had emerged.

The plants they passed in the fields were plentiful, with names like Hygeia herbs and Hops. She called out to each one as her mama had taught her. The sweet smell of honeysuckle was everywhere. "Mother gets mad at the honeysuckles 'cause they smother her plants." As the boy, her daddy, walked alongside her. Evening found comfort in the swish of his wet pants, telling her that he was indeed real.

She led him up the back porch and through the unlocked door. Her mother always left the door slightly ajar for her, letting her know she was nearby. A rattle sat on a small stump to protect the home. Evening rattled it.

"Remember da kitchen? Mama made new curtains. This is da table. Mama…" Her voice was filled with pride. "She made it with you." The boy smiled at the table, gently moving his wet fingertips across the wood.

"Y'all chopped da tree down, but first, she prayed to da tree." Her head filled with everything she wanted her daddy to know. "Mama, say we's pray and ask permission before we chop, cut, or pull things from da earth to give thanks." He nodded in agreement.

"You'se talk?" His dark eyes looked at her through the water hanging on his lashes. He said nothing. "You helped her. It took a long, long time, right?" She moved her head up and down, hoping he'd agree. She was willing to settle for a nod. He watched her but offered nothing more than his eyes had already told her in silence.

"I'se eat with my mama and…" She did not know how or what to say to all the Sundays with the empty chair. "Daddy?"

She had eyeballed him closely, his skin and clothes wet from the river.

Evening fought the invasive truth. Her daddy did not come home.  Her heart sank. The chair her daddy sat in on Sundays was too big for this little boy. Nothing in his kind eyes hinted that he knew her or this house.

Maybe…She touched his face. He smiled. She knew he belonged to somebody else.

"We'll eat something." Her throat was hoarse. She took down what she knew would be in the pantry: a saucer of food to share. After they had eaten, they went hand in hand back to where she had found him. The river sat quietly waiting.

But Evening was not ready. She got them sticks to play with. He drew a picture of a boy sleeping in a bed next to a woman. For a long time, they sat together until it grew late, and the air became cool. The daughter knew somewhere her mother was watching, as she always did—watching from between the trees on a hill, moving like the wind, watching her.

"You'se not my daddy, are you?" Her throat burned with the amount of sorrow swelled with each word.  She cleared her throat to move the burning away so she could say something to make the pain softer.  He stood up, eyelashes still wet. The river had not yielded to the sun nor the wind. He hugged her hard until her bones felt the hug. The little boy kissed her mouth until her teeth felt the kiss, and her tongue tasted the river. He turned away. First, the sun took his image, forcing her to shield her eyes, and last, the water took him under.

With the sunlight dancing slowly, the water rippled where he went in. She pretended the ripples were his voice finally speaking to her until all went silent. Then, the daughter waited in the quiet and tried not to listen to the thoughts in her mind. Her mind knew nothing of what her heart begged to understand. She thought, *He might have stayed if she'd given him all the food. He would have understood if she had drawn a picture of her and her mama, the empty chair, and…sip…sip.*

It was dusk when her mama came to where her daughter stood and held out her hand. They looked at each other for a long time. The daughter began to cry as her mother gathered stones and placed them in a circle around the picture the boy had drawn in the dirt.

"Is he coming back?"

Her mother broke the stick in half and threw one half towards the mountain and the other towards the woods. "Things come back differently, and you got to know them differently to let them in."

"I miss him, Mama."

"I'm glad, daughter; things that are good for us we miss when gone; things not good we turn our back. They are not worthy of missing." She bent to kiss her daughter's forehead. "Those are tears of missing, so cry." A boy, not her father, came from the water and went back into the water. Sip…sip…

The years ran ahead of her after that. Six years old, like the boy… seven…eight…nine…

Her mother walked with her through the woods, showing her the ways of the woods and plant life as if she were undressing herself, revealing her own body. "See here, daughter." There was not much more to learn.

As her mother promised it would, her bleeding time began when her feet had been on the earth for thirteen turns of the sun. Her mother got up and washed Evening on the exact day her blood came down. "Why, Mama?"

"Why what?"

"Why you'se washing me? I'm not a baby?"

She strung beads upon her daughter's neck with a sack of herbs attached. "Sit on da bowl." The steam ascended from the bowl. The smells of marigold, thyme, and burdock root. While she sat, blood poured from between her legs. Her mother nodded. "Dat's the river of blood of our ancestors, daughter. The bleeding story of women marks time and life."

After that, mother and daughter sipped the bitter tea and star gazed during the monthly. The tea gave her visions. Evening learned not to fear the dreams that came to her during her bleeding time or the people who brought the dreams. Some came on horseback, the woven blankets burned with gold threads, bursting with the intricate patterns of the past. Others danced in Evenings dreams, stomping the earth until smoke rose to join the clouds. Her favorite dream came to visit when the moon was full and only on the third day of her bleeding.

In the dream, a giant wave from the ocean far away would lift her from her bed, carrying her down the path and through the woods, under the watchful eyes of the Ozark Mountains, singing to her in a language where the tongue rolled the words like drums. She would be set down at the lip of the earth and told to look across the waters that led the ocean to her. Evening knew the line in the far distance was one her father had crossed. These dreams did not frighten her. What scared her was what came after when her body changed: her breasts pushing through the threads of her dress. She grew restless. Tired of tasting the salt of her tears, she wanted the salty kiss of a boy who lived in the water.

Some days, she caught herself begging for the wind to come calling. Her favorite season was autumn. With the fierce winds and naked arms of the trees, she would bury herself in a pile of leaves. That wind would raise her dress, the leaves rustling the edges of her underpants as delicately as her desire. On the best of an autumn day, she'd roll on her back, and the wind would come with a mouth full of sunshine, hot and heavy down her throat.

Not knowing her feelings made her do stupid stuff for no reason. Her mama, paying her no mind, seemed rather amused until her daughter decided to sit in her daddy's chair and eat off her mother's husband's plate.

The daughter felt a need to pass the food to her mother, to touch her mother's fingertips with each dish…from his chair! She sipped from the cup her mother had shared with the space, a space her lonely self knew all too well.

*Sip*…staring at her mother defiantly. *Sip*…staring at the butter melting on his fried bread. Fried bread with peppered corn that his wife had cooked for him. Yet her mother merely smacked her lips, enjoying the juice of the collard greens, and plucked up a dab of meat with her fingers, seemingly undisturbed by her daughter's audacity to sip from her husband's cup.

*Sip…sip…*

The daughter waited until her own body began to tremble with unanticipated nervousness, hurt that a sound from her mother could break her feelings and leave her heartbroken and trembling.

*Sip.*

After a moment of silence, her mother whispered, "Pass the butter, husband."

Evening plunged into defiance and handed her mother the butter, intentionally touching her fingers. 'Do I'se have your husband's fingers? ' She wondered, not daring to look at her mother but allowing the touch to linger.

"Daughter?"

"Yes, Mama?"

"Your daddy…" Her mother paused and chewed her last bite, then sucked the remaining food out of her teeth. "Your daddy and I'se were just talking dis morning. We'se realized da days of sitting on your daddy's lap are nearly over. Her mother gently wiped her mouth while gazing directly at her daughter, one eyebrow raised to the mountaintop she was looking down from. There were flames in the mother's eyes that her daughter thought must be coming from the sunlight through the window. Evening caught herself praying for her mother's forgiveness for the foolish act she committed as the flames rose.

"Do you'se know dat…one day, you'se will leave your daddy's lap, leave our arms, leave our home, and marry?" To whom or how? Evening wondered, living so alone with only rare visits from her mother's people's tribe.

"Your daddy and me…"

When her daughter defiantly pushed her plate away, her mother said nothing. Instead, she asked her husband if he wanted something sweet. Evening shot up from her chair and ran out the back door. Her mother watched quietly from the window, not rising from the table. She watched her daughter stomp down the porch, across the yard, and to the well before returning her eyes to her husband.

Evening climbed the well and let herself go in headfirst. No one heard the impact of a thirteen-year-old girl's body, with dreams running through the veins, hitting the water, nor the splash that followed. Her mama might have seen the giant splash if she had looked away from the chair. Instead, she passed sweet bread to her husband as her daughter's head hit the water.

The water entered her nose, rushing up Evenings' nostrils, disorganizing her brain. *Holler,* her brain shouted. *Call your mama!* Evening gasped for air and got water, and she choked. *Holler child, you dying, call your mama!*

But she was distracted by the sweet call of the water, the bubbling sounds filling her with music. Water on her face, neck, and back—water warm and cool simultaneously, heavy and light. The possibility of being touched was wrapping around her imagination. One day, the water sang to her, "Someone's hands will touch you: you'll be long into your journey. Your hair will have turned silver. A touch strong enough to chop this pain down and gentle enough to call you home."

A sudden force of sound shot down into the well, bringing her back to her drowning. Evening's mother's robust and full-of-life laughter swirled around her, making the water in the well bubble up. Curious about the depth of laughter, she forgot how good the water was and began to wonder what her daddy might be saying to her mother, which was so funny.

The meaning of her mother's laughter made its way through the water: *There are many possibilities in life before you at such a tender age. Dying should not be one of them.* Like a baby's last turn in the womb before heading down that final path, the daughter turned and followed her mother's laughter out of the well. She left her wet clothes on the back porch. The rattle on the door was quiet as she entered.

She walked naked to the table and sat down, not ready to set aside the boldness of living now that dying was not an option. Starving, she ate off her plate in her chair as the sounds of her mother warmed her wet skin.

*Sip…sip…*

Now, with her mama dead and gone, she sat with the women she loved but to whom she had never told the story of her mother's husband. Nor had her mother shared any stories of her daddy's life. All Evening knew was that her mother's husband had Sunday dinner with her mother until her death. Evening realized she had never mentioned or heard the women say if they believed in ghosts.

"Listen." Her voice was smooth as peach liqueur. Lena stopped humming to listen. "My mother's husband has been gone over sixty years. What can anybody tell me bout my daddy? Evening waited. "Ya'll sure you'se don't know what dis woman coming to tell me…?"

"No, ma'am." Claire stood up and took her sewing basket to the shelf.

"So, he might still be…" Evening's voice sounded flat.

"Evening!" both twins spoke firmly.

"You'se said you didn't know, so why not that?"

Evening's eyes filled with tears. As soon as they began to fall, she swiped them away. Her words came out harsher than the women had known. Lena shook her head at the women to let her be. It made sense for Evening to get out whatever feelings she had about this news.

Evening shouted, "You'se tell this Sister Elizabeth not to come! She got to pass dis house first. Tell her…not to come if she's NOT bringing what I'se don't remember. Tell dis nun to bring me da bones, blood, and flesh of my daddy, or bring me his ghost!"

Lena sighed with some satisfaction. Evening had finally called him her daddy, although that didn't make it any less painful to see how hurt Evening was. Despite Lena's signal to let Evening get her feelings out, Claire moved towards her. It was only natural, she thought, to give her some comfort.

Evening shot up from the chair. "I'se thank y'all." She walked to the door and turned to look again at the five of them over her shoulder.

Always that smile, Sylvie thought.

"He'd be near eighty-five by now. And look at me—I ain't been a child in a long time. A daddy at my age? Guess it ain't never too late to have a daddy or a ghost?" Isabel and Izabal took the other's hand in comfort. With that, Evening was out the door and gone. A slightly drunk woman jumped down the porch, running down the road to the house covered in shadows, still with no idea what news Sister Elizabeth was bringing. She shouted: "Either my daddy or his ghost."

The women sat for a while looking at the door after Evening left. "Let's call it a night. Say our prayers." Lena was exhausted. The covers of her bed were pulled back where the squash rested. Still pushing its presence to be more than squash, it stained the sheets pink with strawberry juice. "If I didn't know better, I'd think my monthly had come on." She said it lightly to the women, but inside, the wound of her child was not even a scab, no matter how many years had gone by.

She looked at the red-stained sheets, then, after a moment, waved her hand. "Just put a towel over it. Change da sheets tomorrow. I'm tired."

Lena woke up the following day after a night of pleasant dreams she was aching not to forget. She felt her whole face smiling. She rose onto both elbows, noticing the abundance of sunlight pouring through the window, but the air in the room was cold. Lena glanced at the hearth, wondering why nobody had started the morning fire. Somebody had been moving around. Lena spotted off to the side of the fireplace a baby basket with a beautiful yellow and blue knitted blanket draped over it. Lena gasped and covered her mouth. Who in the hell, she wondered, brought a baby basket into the house, and from where? The blanket had to be from Claire, but she did not think Claire's mindset leaned toward being foolish. So, who? But that didn't explain where they got the basket from. *Lena's mind shouted, but it ain't a baby, and to think it's a baby isn't right!* She forgot about the dream that woke her up with a smile. This squash thing was getting out of hand.

Lying back on her pillows, she imagined the others moving around the baby basket, tiptoeing in hushed tones as if there were nothing wrong with a squash in a baby basket sitting near the fire to keep warm. *Serve 'em right*, she thought, *if dey looks in the basket and da squash is a…*She stopped the notion before it was complete. Somehow, it didn't feel right to make light of the situation.

Lena slowly removed the covers with care and noticed no discomfort in her body. "Humph." Her feet weren't swollen, and she had not felt this comfortable in a long time. "God?" She wiggled her toes. "I'se thank you'se, God, but I'se got a feeling dere's more to dis story."

Lena pushed herself a bit more and arched her back off the mattress. "Lord, dat feels good." She smiled. This would be a good day, baby basket, crazy or not. Lena could feel it.

One of the women called out; Lena couldn't make out whose voice it was shaky: "I'se got a feeling about dis baby squash. I'se think it brought spirits. Dey na brought us something from behind da veil?"

"Good or bad."

"My bones say good."

"Good, who dat I'm talking with?

Silence followed.

# SEVENTEEN

Where was this nun? Claire had given Lena yarn and needles, but Lena found knitting distracting. She focused on the bedroom window where she had tried to rest most of the day. Rain mixed with snow was a lie-down day for Lena's body. But lying down did nothing for Lena's worries.

When she heard the horses, she determined they were less than a mile. She rose to see the burst of light bouncing in the dark, knowing it was Hargrove's buggy even in the dark. She waited until she heard the cowbells.

Her authority came in full bloom, her commands running like anxious children. "Here dey comes, and in dis weather. Git da tub ready. Boil some water for a bath. Need more fire? On second thought, git da fire blazing hot! I had a feeling dey git here tonight, of all nights." She pushed the blankets off her body. "Light da fire on the kitchen stove, too." Her commands were as fierce as the winds outside. "Git blankets and open dat side door for Hargrove to change privately. He got some pants in the pantry and a shirt."

Lena pressed her face on the window. Hargrove was close enough now that she could make his face out. His beard was fuller. "Put something down by da door to catch da weather coming off em and whatever else da bringing in this house. Light at another lantern. Get my shawl!"

Sylvie chimed in, "Mine too!"

"Boil some water for coffee." Lena was unsure if Claire was asking a question or making a statement.

"Who wants coffee dis time of night Claire?"

The ladies' movements were quick with nervous excitement upon the nun's arrival. All other visits were from folks up to no good outside of Evening and Hargrove. This was like a celebration of sorts. All their questions since the telegram's arrival would be answered. What did she look like? What was a nun? Was she pretty? How old was she? And what did she know about Evening's daddy?

"Get some rum!" The horses had made it to the porch.

"And for God's sake, somebody *open* da door!"

Sylvie opened the door; the women's bodies formed a semicircle around a blanket on the floor. Behind the nun, they saw Hargrove's buggy turning away toward the mountains away from the house. They didn't know what to make of the person in front of them, except she was soaked to the bones, and her wet, pale face was peering out of a strange head wrap.

"I'm Sister Elizabeth. Mr. Hargrove said to tell you he'll stop by tomorrow." Sylvie grabbed and pulled her into the arch of women, onto the blanket, and closed the door.

Lena spoke first. "Come on, let us help you. Dat's all you got?"

"Everything I need, I got."

"I'm Lena, dat's Claire, and dis here is Izabal and Isabel—as you can see, dey twins—and den you got Sylvie! And, of course, we'se know you are Sister Elizabeth."

"Yes, ma'am." They were removing her soaked garments during introductions. Sister Elizabeth had little to do but lift and yield to the hands, pulling her wet clothes off.

"Ain't no men in da house. Don't worry. We'll get you'se into a hot bath and put extra firewood in da stove to keep you warm. You'se wanna drink? We got peach brandy or rum. Or can you drink?" Lena had not even considered the last option until the words came out of her mouth.

"You'se going to hell for asking her," Sylvie spoke under her breath, but everybody heard.

One of the twins had hidden the bottle when she saw the horses and refused the command to refill the glasses, but now she thought maybe she'd better and went off to retrieve it.

"Is dere a hell?" Sylvie wanted to know if this nun had an answer.

"Why you'se want to know, Sylvie?" Lena spoke before Sister Elizabeth could. "What I na did dat requires a trip to hell?" Lena sounded agitated. Claire was glad that Sylvie was not in disagreement with her but still embarrassed that these two would fight in the company's presence. Claire was relieved that Sylvie was not dipping snuff tonight. Not yet at least.

The women continued peeling away the wet layers of Sister Elizabeth's clothes, down to her slip, underpants, and bra, which came off in a snap. A naked nun. Claire put her arm around her. "Come on, let's get you into the bath."

Sister Elizabeth suddenly felt ashamed. Not of her nakedness, but that she had allowed the women to serve her and not the other way around. She could have taken her clothes off but hadn't. It felt so natural, letting the women undress her and take over what her hands could do.

Her vow of servitude to the weak, the poor, the sick, and the helpless was broken. She felt the scorn of Mother Superior's face. How many prayers on her knees would be administered because of the sin that she had committed just by having several women serving her needs? And Sister Elizabeth reminded herself that not one, but several women had served her while she had done nothing as they removed her habit and stood her naked on her feet. Sister Elizabeth's life was devoted to service. She had failed within the first few minutes of her duty in their home. She was fussing at herself when the women effortlessly lifted her in the air and lowered her body into the makeshift tub. Once lowered, Claire guided her head to rest on the neck of the galvanized tub, where she'd placed a thick cotton towel for her neck.

"Oh, God." Sister Elizabeth closed her eyes, the hot water soaking up her body and her resistance. "Goodness gracious, this feels so heavenly, and the smell." Her words made the women smile. They clasped their hands together in happiness.

"That's the lavender I put in the water." Claire looked around into the other women's eyes. Seeing their acknowledgment, she smiled. *It's the small acts of thoughtfulness that bring us joy.* They waited as the steam rose and the firelight covered the dark room, the woman's limp body telling the story of her travels. She surrendered and fell immediately to sleep.

"She's 'sleep!" Sylvie looked at the twins.

"Let's git a drink and let her sleep." Lena looked around for the bottle. Isabel or Izabal went and pulled it from the shelf behind the wall.

The liquor was nearly empty. Another bottle would have to come, this time homemade white rum. Meanwhile, a pot with beef bone, carrots, onions, celery, and herbs was simmering. They took water from the tub, threw it out the back door, and put more hot water. The room was lit with fire, lanterns, and curiosity while they waited for her to wake up.

"She blind, you'se know." A log fell in the hearth.

"Who?" the twins asked.

"Her...she blind, da nun."

"You'se drunk."

"Yep, but dat don't make her less blind 'cause I'm drunk." Sylvie snapped back.

"Why in da world would you'se say she blind?"

The water splashed as the nun sat up. "Because I am blind. Whoever said it is right." The short, cropped hair on the head of the white-looking woman spoke from the wood-covered, galvanized tub. "And yes, could I have just a little of that liquor you offered earlier?" She laughed softly. "And no, I don't think anyone is going to hell for asking me if I want a drink. Thank you for the bath. Mind if I stay here a bit?"

"Nope!" Lena reassured her. "But somebody got to crack dat back door a bit let the steam out.

The cool air came in through the door while the raindrops fell. "Listen," Lena instructed them. "D'air's a lot da rain can tell us about days past and those ahead."

Sister Elizabeth took her drink of the homemade white rum. The first sip made her choke. Claire leaned over and patted her back. It didn't take long before the choking turned into a deep sigh of relief. Nobody said anything for a while and seemed to be enjoying the peacefulness of it all. They listened to the sound of rain drumming on the house and the porch and one another's breathing.

When Sister Elizabeth started to cry, nobody was urged to do anything except pour more hot water into the bath. Sister Elizabeth closed her eyes and took in the room's offerings: lilacs, rum, soup, and rain. Sister Elizabeth thought briefly of saying a prayer and just as quickly realized she was indeed inside a prayer no words could replace: the blessing bestowed upon her. Her crying, to the women, didn't seem to matter. Their comforting sounds encouraged her.

Sylvie stood up and walked toward the door to close it but hesitated and turned to the women. Her voice was thick. "If you'se can cry, you'se gon' be okay. It's when you'se can't cry, dats a problem." Instead of closing the door as planned, Sylvie pulled a coat from the hook and put it on.

"Where you'se going in dis rain?" Lena asked.

"Git some smoked meat for da morning, bacon. Be right back." In Sylvie's absence, the woman spent a good hour carefully drying, massaging, and oiling Sister Elizabeth's body before getting her dressed for bed.

They were all asleep when Sylvie returned two hours later. Three on Lena's bed—well, Lena, Claire, and the squash. The twins got tangled up in a blanket on the floor. The sofa was where Sister Elizabeth was curled up, clutching one of Claire's handmade pillows. Sylvie went to Sister Elizabeth to gently snuggle herself opposite and let their feet touch, feeling more relaxed than she had in years. She exhaled one long breath and was asleep.

None of the women awakened or even heard when Evening entered the room. Her shadow loomed against the wall. Evening placed her palm on the shadow and prayed. She put the extra logs on the fire and straightened up the remaining disarray of the area. Evening pulled a pouch from her pocket. The contents burned the tips of her fingers. Not a muscle in her body moved as she inhaled the room's air. She spoke in her mother's voice, holding the pouch close to her heart.

"It will come upon you to call out." Sip…sip… "And when it does, listen for the answer." Sip…sip…

She lifted blue, black, and brown seeds from the pouch and threw them into the fire. Over her back, she tossed the seeds into the air. The light of the fire flickered with images. Evening read the images as her mother had taught her. What ascended was the blooming of dark tulips, the symbol of hope. Evening's heart quickened in joy. Reaching into the space where the seeds lit up in full bloom. She had no fear that the women would awaken; their world belonged to the seeds. Evening had no fear of the fire's flame.

In the light of the fire, she knelt on both knees ceremoniously and dropped her head back. It fell back as if detached from her frame, the light of the flame dancing on her throat. "I give my voice to you'se, Mother. I give my voice to you'se, Father." The sound that left her throat, indeed, was not her own. It was the sun calling out on one hip of the road and the calling moon at the other hip. This was the truth, where day and night meet once a year in full regal—not bleeding one onto the other but facing each power source. Evening's voice left the room and traveled until it had exhausted the miles it traveled.

# EIGHTEEN

"I thought you were going to git meat last night?" Lena looked around at the spotless kitchen, wondering who'd gotten up and cleaned without making a sound. Sylvie, she suspected. However, it looked like she had just opened her eyes.

"I changed my mind. We'se need to stop eating so much meat. Chasing after my food cravings like a dust storm chasing dirt."

Annoyed, Lena sighed before telling Sylvie, "Well, change it again, 'cause you'se got me wanting some of dat smoked meat and strong black coffee. My head aching." Sylvie rubbed her stomach. "You feel, okay?" asked Lena.

"I'm awright. Who making da coffee dis morning?" Sylvie started toward the door. She pointed at the stove. "Somebody got water on."

"It's for my hot-water cornbread." Sister Elizabeth stood in the doorframe. "If that's okay?"

Sylvie put her hands on her hips. "Whatcha know about hot-water cornbread?"

"Who you think raised me? I wasn't born a nun. I listened to what my mama and grandmother talked about cooking. Put a pinch, two eggs, half of this or that. When you can't see, your memory holds onto stuff to show you the way. You can imagine doing it yourself. I look white, but I'm not. Who's the darkest in this room?"

"Lena is dark as da night, and she has big eyes. Make me wonder what she saw dat surprised her so."

"Why?" Claire came into the room. "Good day, women."

"My mama was on the darker side of brown."

"How you know?" Sylvie sounded confused.

"'Cause I remember her face. I could see then. My memory has kept some things in here and here." She pointed at her head and heart. "That's what I was telling the gentleman, Mr. Hargrove. He's a lovely man. Made the ride here pleasant." The room fell silent, no rustling of clothing or humps from Lena. "Did anything happen with Mr. Hargrove? It seemed like the last thing he wanted was to come in the house with me."

Lena looked down, straightened out the wrinkles in her dress, and smiled. "We'se leave dat alone. Go on, finish telling us 'Bout ya folks."

"Well, I can't remember my papa's face, but I know the inside of his hands. Like he had small stones under the skin—rough too." She sighed. "But I loved his hands. Sometimes, I feel his presence when I pray on my beads and roll them around on my fingers. He sang when he talked." She laughed. "He didn't end his words; they blended." Sister Elizabeth stopped talking for a moment. Her head bent forward; then she lifted it toward the women smiling.

"Something like, 'We'sbe alls right with diskindameal, Mother.' That's what he called my mama, Mother. He takes three or four words and makes one word." She sighed deeply, feeling the loss of her family and her childhood—a feeling she had avoided in the convent. She gently pushed her feelings to the side. "I was born in New Orleans, and the first years of my life were filled with food."

Claire sat down in her chair. She did not miss the sorrow on Sister Elizabeth's face. She heard the twins' steps as they entered. Claire greeted them then to their guest, "Sister Elizabeth, we don't mind if you cook. Just let us know how to help you."

They listened, and the pots seemed to move easily under the direction of Sister Elizabeth's knowing hands. Her fingers moved across the countertops, feeling along the walls with little guidance needed from the women. She stood in the sunlight coming through the window. "Tell me where everything is according to sunlight." They spoke at once and were happy to accommodate.

"The pantry is to the left of the brightest sun coming in the window, the stove to the right. If you walk into the sunlight and reach your left arm, that be the door to the back porch. When you turn around from the porch door, take six long steps to get to the table.

"Yes. And please leave the kitchen door open. The breeze will tell me I'm in the center, and the sunlight is near the pantry."

"Well, the basket of eggs and butter is on the table. Skillets all sitting on the stove—' course you would know dat 'cause you got water on."

"That's right." Sister Elizabeth moved smoothly to the pantry. She got a large platter and turned to the table to place it. "All right, Sylvie, you get the meat." Her fingers glided across the table, the walls guiding her.

"I did a lot of the cooking and cleaning at the convent and learned how to get around. A lot of bruises and burns was my teacher." There was not much for the ladies to do beyond hand her things and enjoy the unraveling of her story. Everybody was happy with the meal put before them, the scents of bacon and coffee permeating the room. The convent didn't always fare well enough to round out a meal of hot-water cornbread with bacon, greens, smothered potatoes, and coffee.

They were so busy eating that nobody paid much attention when Sister Elizabeth stood up. But everybody did notice when she found her way to the baby basket.

"The baby still sleeping?"

"What baby?" Lena's coffee went down the wrong pipe, so she choked out the question. Sylvie patted her back.

"Boy or girl?"

"Squash," Lena coughed. She patted her chest quickly and cleared her throat.

"That's the baby's name, Squash?" Sister Elizabeth turned in the direction of Lena's voice. "Squash, that's an odd name for a baby."

"It's too early to drink, Lena." Sylvie piped in.

"Who said anything 'bout a drink?"

"'Cause I know ya'll, Lena." Sylvie headed to the cupboard. *She thought, I need a drink!* She went around, putting each woman a good splash of liquor. She didn't need their permission.

"No, it's real squash from the earth. It just looks and feels like a baby!"

Words from the book of the Prophet Ezekiel walked like a ghost across Sister Elizabeth's mind. She spoke to them out loud, urged by a calling to do so. "As for the likeness of the living creatures, their appearance was like burning coals of fire and like the appearance of lamps."

"What?"

"I am not sure. Maybe we all still…"

Claire called her on it. "Still, what?" She glanced at the twins for input since they'd found the squash. Their heads were down. Claire wondered why. Neither was prone to praying in front of the other women, so why now, if that was what they were doing?

Sister Elizabeth reached into the basket and gently picked up…*Baby!* The smell of her baby sister, Casey, rushed up from the delicate bundle. *She is soft like flesh. Squash got eyes, nose, and mouth?* She gasped. "Who's baby is this?"

"We don't know!"

"Spirits." The twins spoke firmly, convinced of this notion. Claire's eyes went back to the twins, wondering when they had come to that conclusion and, for all their sake, why they were just now telling them!

Lena waved her arms in the air. "Dey come in here, put dat squash on my lap, and…Sylvie hollas, 'It's as big as a baby!'"

Sylvie jumped in. "Still is!"

"Dat's enough, Sylvie! Later, in the middle of the night, *somebody* comes with a basket weaved with green satin ribbons and covered with a yellow blanket. Claire claimed she'd been up most of the night and couldn't say who'd done it if you believe that! But she liked the fabric! Lena glanced over at Claire, seeing if she wanted to add something. *Hu-humph,* she was busy staring Sylvie down.

Lena went on, desperately trying to dispel the twins' notion of spirits. "Somebody did it, and it wasn't me!"

Isabel's and Izabal's heads popped up, ready to take on the accusation, believing.

Lena was placing the blame on the sisters. "Somebody or somebodies?" Claire had been so busy watching Sylvie that she couldn't tell if Isabel or Izabal had asked the question. Their faces were equally distressed.

Lena finished what was in her glass and said with conviction to Isabal and Izabel, "Somebody or -bodies, don't matter! Madness is happening in dis house! Madness!"

Lena hoped they didn't hear the fear in her voice. She remembered her dream now, or a sliver of it. She had dreamed of the veil between life and death. Somebody, or somebodies, from the other side, was coming to visit. Lena feared it was her and Hargrove's dead baby, and her useless body might not be able to pick up her child if the baby wanted to be held. As if the thought of her inability to pick up her child wasn't enough, what if her child was hungry? Lena's hands went to her breast, and her eyes watered. The women had laid the squash or baby on her lap. Was her lap enough for a child gone too soon?

"You wr-r-rong, wrong f-f-f-for dat, L-l-l-Lena." Sylvie hadn't stuttered in a long time.

"Whatcha you'se are blaming me for now, Sylvie?" Lena was in no mood to consider what Sylvie's stuttering meant. Lena feared what memories this baby-like squash stirred up, and it unsettled her. Lena was plenty aware she was about to be nasty to Sylvie but could not stop herself. *If I go to hell for anything, it's not for being unable to stop my words.* Her anger was jumping inside her limited body, doing what she couldn't do with her legs: Jump the hell up and run out of the house if a ghost entered. Just above her was the room where a white woman had killed herself, her child, and a small Negro child. Now, decades later, a squash had her grieving her and Hargroves dead baby, and only God knew what story the other women's wombs carried.

"Sylvie, tell me, wrong for what? All I ask you, fools, is who did it. Dat's all I'se want to know. Who wrapped a squash in a baby blanket?" Lena knew she had full attention in the room. Lena let her eyes roam slowly over each woman. "Who did it? Somebody answer me!" She shook her head. "And I'se got to be wrong? I will not be wrong today!"

"You's wr-rong f-f-for de-ee-escribing da basket to somebode-ee dat can't see?" Lena realized it would take more than a notion to figure out what Sylvie was mad about. Her mind flashed back to the dream. It made her dizzy. "F-f-f-f-first, you—you—you'se ask her if she wanna a drink!" Sylvie shouted the last word toward the ground as if spitting tobacco. "Now you…"

"Now she what?" Sister Elizabeth asked Sylvie gently. "Asking me to picture a basket somebody lovingly put together for a baby or asking me to imagine why somebody would think a squash is a baby?"

"HumphHumpHumh, thank you!" Lena slammed her glass on the table. "You'se said it, Sister Elizabeth. Who could mistake a baby for a squash?" She caught her words. "What da hell did I say? A squash for a baby." She half-heartily laughed. The other women did not. *Hmmm.* She pushed back on the chair, adjusting her back.

"Help yourself, Sister Elizabeth. Turn dat squash into supper! We's fighting about a baby." She caught herself again. It made her angry. "We'se should save our strength and wait when dem fools come charging at our door!" There, she said it! "Dem white men intend to kill us." She said out loud what each knew. She continued. "Sister Elizabeth, you ever make squash soup?"

Lena was ready to end the madness that this squash had brought into the house. She thought that's what started this, a squash and then Hargrove bringing a letter 'bout Evening's father! "Cook the squash, Sister Elizabeth," Lena insisted.

"You—you go-going to hell, Lena!" Sylvie was trying to catch her breath, thinking of cutting into the squash, baby, whatever was troubling her. Claire wanted to rush and comfort Sylvie, seeing how her hands were shaking.

"Ain-n-n-t-t-t-ta right to hur-hur ta somethin' dat look like a baby!" Tiny drops of spit flung from Sylvie's lips, the bottom trembling with agitation. She was just as angry at herself as Lena. Claire forced herself to stay still, watching it all. Sylvie started walking in small circles, looking down at the floor as if searching for something. A button, perhaps, or a thought. In her following words, Claire realized the stuttering was gone, and her pacing had stopped. Her words came out determined. "Just like it ain't right for snow to show up in August and spring to come in fall and the earth bleeding human blood, and…"

Sylvie stopped talking. Something called her attention to the wall nearby. A quick movement, like a shadow, had moved across her face. She lifted her head to see images on the wall, slowly traveling upward. The shadows were different in size; they were children. Sylvie looked out the window to see if the shapes of the trees were making the images. She turned back.

Lena, looking in Sylvie's direction, paid no mind to Sylvie gawking up at the wall. She figured Sylvie was ignoring her by turning her back. "What tis with you lately, Sylvie? You'se thinking all day about hell. I can't go to hell but once! Why don't you'se say what's bugging you, Sylvie?

Isabel and Izabal were not listening to the argument nor witnessing the shadows moving on the wall. They watched the beautiful, wrapped bundle pressed against Sister Elizabeth's chest. The green lace with yellow ribbons was almost hidden in her arms. She swayed. Good, they thought she'd rock the baby, but instead, she started walking to the door.

"Wh-ere you'se going?"

Claire saw the twins had straightened up in alarm. She followed their eyes to Sister Elizabeth. *Oh, God,* she thought. "Sister Elizabeth." Claire had not meant to whisper but figured she must have since Sister Elizabeth did not respond. Sister Elizabeth did not hear her. Therefore, she could not hear the warning laced in Claire's tone. With deliberate, careful steps, Sister Elizabeth continued moving with the bundle cradled in her left arm. Her right arm extended and moved in the air until she found the door handle to turn. It turned and began opening. The hinges made a sound Claire would later write about in her journal.

*September (Even now, my bones shake uncontrollably)*

*The door hinges called out with distress, a warning of the unknown waiting on the other side. It was as if the very touch of Sister Elizabeth's hand to open the cedar wood was a portal for our memories that were no longer willing to be tucked away by denial or silence. There were children with cries only a mother could interpret. I did not have to question if it was real or if ghosts were walking over the threshold. The ghost was hand in hand with memories, ready to be recognized as such.*

*The door being pulled open sounded like the cry of a woman with grief centuries old. A wailing at first that quickly turned to the moans of hard birthing labor. I watched and listened through senses I had never been privy to, which many call the veil between life and death. I wrote frantically despite my shaking fingers. Dipping the pen into the ink, letting it stain my fingers. I feared the men and women of Springfield were outside the door armed with the task of our death. Those who wanted the house, the land, had arrived. I was terrified at that moment that the wailings were a sound we would join, in one manner or another, in death. Yet somewhere within, I knew it was the door itself; the door was crying.*

*I wrote to say goodbye to this world, but all I had were circles on the paper, which I now labor to make sense of. The door was coming home to the memory of when it was a tree. I was unable to prepare myself for what was about to happen, nor could the other women I could testify to. First, I saw Lena fold her arms across her chest, her eyes steeled toward the door. Sylvie squeezed her hands into fists, ready, it seemed, to fight. Yet, no one ran toward the guns. Perhaps we knew this was not war.*

*I could not move. I kept my knitting in my lap, my needles lying on top of the cloth, my journal. As light as it all was, it weighed me to my seat.*

*We were waiting, stopped in time, laboring. The air in the room became our teacher. It blew in the winds of the mountains, the ocean we had crossed, the trees we hid and rested on, everything in the room, the tables, chairs, and the children on the wall watching us.*

*"Don't…. please don't." These were the first words I heard.*

*Claire.*

I think Isabel reached out to grab her sister but caught air. Her palms, momentarily and as if slapped, fell back to her sides. Izabal cried out. Or was it Izabal reaching for Isabel? "Sister!" Both stumbled toward the open door. "Don't hurt her, Noooo, no more. Don't let her die."

Sister Elizabeth turned over her shoulder in the direction of the distressed voices of Isabel and Izabal, "Die…who?" Sister Elizabeth asked frantically.

The shadows of children on the wall sat down and crossed their arms and legs obediently as if they were at the feet of their parents. The wind came in the door with such a force it knocked over a chair. It brought the leaves from the outdoors and, even more, the stories the leaves had been carrying forever. Whatever memory the wind was serving, it caused Lena to choke. The taste of salt water rushed over Lena's tongue, holding her to a time when she was running for freedom.

The air was shaping and reshaping itself. The air formed balls of fire and fell upon Sister Elizabeth's flesh as she held tighter to the bundle in her arms.

Claire's forehead began to pour sweat until she remembered she had once been stripped naked in a rainstorm. She rose from her chair, the contents on her lap falling to the floor. "Sing something, Lena." The insistence in Claire's voice did not make Lena sing one note. Lena's face softened. Her fingertips were stretched, webbed in the air, reaching for what only she could understand. The air before her was shaping itself. Lena snatched a handful and pushed it greedily in her mouth. She choked again.

Claire staggered across the floor toward Sylvie. "Lena!" Why, she wondered, was she calling out to Lena when it was Sylvie she was moving toward?

A high-pitched wail circled the room. "I was going to get a little air. Nothing else, I promise," Sister Elizabeth cried out to whatever force was present and realized her wish for air was granted. The air was everywhere. She leaned her body against the wall and dropped down to her bottom. Everything she knew at that moment was cradled in her arms. Squash baby. It was God's seed. She felt every prayer she'd ever counted on her rosary; each Hail Mary, full of grace, came into the room, revealing what was written between the lines of the prayers. God had opened the door for them, as any suitable truth seeker would.

"I must be blind drunk," Sister Elizabeth said to no one in particular. She chuckled, hoping laughter would sit her upside down. She'd settle for anything, but it didn't. She held on. "Though I walk through the valley of death, I shall fear no evil. The Lord is my shepherd." "Thy Lord given me my sight to be thy witness." Each word marched out of her mouth with deliberation. "Lord, let me be thy witness."

The children on the wall unfolded their hands and clapped in unison momentarily. They were being seen. The children who lived long enough to speak and those who were learning were being seen. They had been away in death too long with someone's memory to rely on their existence. The wind rushed to every corner of the house, knocking loose things over until it reached Miss Eloise's bedroom and the adjourning room of her son Peter, where the memory begged the wind let it be for now. *Wait for Mary.*

The corners of Culver Tusk had long been waiting to tell their story despite the dusk and neglect collected. Every wooden thing in the house began the journey of coming home. The children clapped faster, egging the story on. First, the pine floors parted and rose till the branches tilted the house's roof—the tilt of a gentleman caller hat, southern style. The kitchen table laughed into its memory. Once, the pine floor was known as the proudest oldest oak tree, and with the first strike of the axes, it released its pride in the sky.

Sylvie looked up at the jubilee children, laughing and clapping. She joined in and jumped barefoot, springing as close to the children as possible. Lena's chair pulled itself from beneath her warm body, and the air set her gently to where once there was a floor. On the earth near her sat a polished teapot. She lifted the pot to her face, Lena's face softened, and the years drifted away; *this was my face when I was a child; my child looked as I did.* In her gaze, she saw bits of Hargrove. Before she could thank the wind, she was leaned against the trunk of an elm tree and was overtaken with comfort in her bones. Lena sighed, "I don't know when I felt dis peaceful." Her voice was soft. She looked around to see who had taken the pot and had handed her a fresh drink. The rum mixed well with salt water, she thought.

The cherry rosewood bed Lena slept in each night, and the cedar rocking chair she sat on went back in time. It was not long, maybe a blink of an eye or two, before Culver Tusk disappeared behind the veil of life and death and turned into a family of trees.

A cool breeze circled the room, carrying the familiar smell of red clay dirt, pinecones, and the flesh of tree bark. "I'se know dem woods," Sylvie whispered sweetly. A split second later, she saw her husband, and joy washed over her. He was as handsome as she'd remembered. He was wearing his favorite brown hat cocked back over his head. He was smiling at her with all the pride he could muster. "You'se ain't mad at me for running off, husband? "

He shook his head no. "Can't be mad at a woman who taught me to run to my freedom." His chuckle rose and washed over the room. "I'se just wishing you'd told me you'se leaving. I missed you'se. I reckon I'se knew da way you loved up on me dat night, so tenderly."

Sylvie turned, searching for Claire, feeling somewhat righteous and worried he'd be gone just as quickly as he came. "Der, Claire, see in da shade? See, Claire, dat be him, my husband. I'se didn't lie to youse." It dawned on Sylvie that if she could see her husband, he was dead.

It did not matter if Claire's eyes couldn't distinguish what Sylvie was pointing at because soon, she heard a man's voice. "Pleased to meet you, Miss Claire. We's escaped into the dem woods, but I'se reckon my Sylvie comes back to git you. You'se all she's ever talked about." Claire gasped. There he was, Sylvie's husband, the prettiest man Claire had ever seen.

"Oh, please to…" She turned to ask Sylvie his name.

"Claire, look!" Claire followed the direction she was pointing. A narrow trail parted the trees, and the voices coming from behind the trees were speaking as one.

"Hard for us to run with a newborn."

Isabel and Izabal moved out from behind the trees on wobbly legs. Fresh blood, the color of cherry juice, covered them like they wore aprons. Their voices echoed, "You'se caint tell a newborn to stop crying." They were angry, and their words and eyes were two sets of twin barrels loaded and fixed on the bundle in Sister Elizabeth's arms.

Standing in the place that was once Culver Tusk, a thick forest of displaced trees had erupted, and the dreams and veils erased all lines between ghosts and memory—effortlessly, time collapsed to where time goes for people, gone. And time was running out. Claire's tears streamed down her face, and her body shook with great agitation as she clasped and then unclasped her hands frantically. She cried, "Who's baby Isabel and Izabal!?"

# NINETEEN

Sarah was a seasonal drinker, and now that the seasons were blurred with displaced birds and snow in August, Sarah stayed drinking. She had a constant three-word conversation with God. "God help me."

She often thought of the woman without eyebrows and the toothless redheaded boy. Sarah thought, out of the group, they seemed the friendliest. The dark-haired man who talked for the group was handsome, yet he looked at her as if only flies would be attracted to her. *He's probably right*, she thought. *My daddy and mama would not even know me!*

It was rare that Sarah caught a glimpse of her reflection. And when she did, it knocked her into grief. Her teeth had grown crooked and were stained tobacco brown. One of the front teeth was chipped. Her skin was as tough as a horse saddle; at least, that's what Robert said on the occasions his good hand touched her body. The porcelain skin her mother kept from the sun was embedded with dirt. Her pores were the size of pin tips. Her hair had fallen out in patches, so she had to part it with her fingers to cover where the scalp could be seen. Sarah had gotten used to her ugliness over time but could not get used to what happened to her eyes. Hollow and lifeless, the pupils milky, and the whites of her eyes were now yellow. Her eyes were once the last reminder of her mother. She remembered how much like her mother she had looked, and now, even this previous remaining feature had been drowned in sorrow, Robert's beatings, and drinking.

She smiled, thinking the dark-haired man's opinion had changed once he'd found out who she was. Miss Sarah of Grove Plantation, her daddy's dawling. She could not remember how many years had passed since she'd left Grove. How long had the war lasted? The years were a tragic blur of war, illness, grief, assaults, and drunkenness. The soldiers had passed Sarah around for their pleasure like a wet rag. And on her daddy's land! *How old am I ?* she wondered. Her face answered back, and at every chance, she saw it reflected. *Old.* Sarah couldn't tell you when she got married to Robert, but she knew why. On the road away from the hub, Robert found a big rock and told her to sit. He took out his flask and offered it to her in a friendly way. They passed the flask between them in silence. Robert had a smile on his face, Sarah thought. *The curtsy, for me, must have done something for Robert that only brutality could satisfy him.* Robert spoke; the smile never left his face. "Because of H.G., my brother is dead. You'se own us land and a baby." Robert stood over her and raised his good arm. Sarah lifted the flask and realized the flask was the last thing on Roberts's mind. She held on tight to the flask, lifted her face, and received his slap. Robert left her to sleep it off, returned, and headed back on the road when they came to Baileys.

Shelton Wyman, the white man, had come around the corner when Robert and the Negro Bailey were talking. He had no idea who Sarah was, but he gave Robert the small shack and a bit of work, if for no other reason than to keep an eye on him. Shelton stopped a week later. He knew little about Grove and Culver Tusk's history and told Robert that nobody except Hargrove was left in the family. Robert had moved Shelton away from Sarah's earshot. Shelton's last piece of information was most satisfying. "Hargrove's niece's body was never found, but folks pretty sure she died. Piles of scarlet fever bodies had been taken off in wagons; most likely, hers was one of them. It was brutal." Robert half nodded, thinking *Well, now she got a husband, and legally, what's her is mine.*

"You sure interested in them, folks. Why's that?" Wyman wasn't stupid; Robert was up to no good.

"I'se worked on his property on the other side of Arkansas for years, with a promise of land. War came. I fought. We lost. I went up North."

"That so what about your wife? Is she sick or something?" He glanced over at the limp body of Sarah on the ground. He felt pity as she rolled over on her back. Her legs flopped wide, and the long sound of gas followed. "I be damned." Not even an "excuse me" was offered by her. Pity!

Since they arrived, Shelton Wyman had not heard much come out of Sarah's mouth. He wondered, looking at her crumpled in the dirt, if the poor thing could talk at all. Maybe she was mute. He'd met a man like that once. He was also pitiful, drinking and grunting at the world. But, Wyman thought, that mute was a hella good shot with a gun.

Robert's laugh caught Wyman off guard. It sounded strained. "Traded a man my saddle for her up north." Wyman looked at Robert, wondering if he'd heard him right and, if so, whether he was joking. He couldn't tell by the smirk on Robert's face. He watched him spit on the ground, turn to nod at Sarah, and then back.

"Sure, miss my saddle, though!" They both laughed. It was funny to Wyman, but he didn't like laughing at such a helpless creature. "You?" Robert asked.

"I'm here." Wyman knew his following words would make or break the two. But judging how Robert had postured himself with Bailey and Mary, he already knew the outcome. "I'm from up North. The government hired us. Most folks are gone. Many people stayed on this property until the legalities get sorted out. Rumor has it Culver Tusk is in the question of its rightful owner. Some of the men part of the time hired by the man who..."

Wyman watched Robert carefully, certain this fellow would have fought against the Union if this man had fought. He decided not to say Hargrove hired some of his men. "I know you say H.G. owes you, but he's dead." Wyman meant to sound less accusatory, but it didn't come out that way.

"Dat's right."

"Seem like a few folks were promised land. Sisters from Ireland.

A man named Thomas, executed for the murder of H.G., went to his grave saying Culver Tusk belonged to him." Shelton chuckled. "That's what I heard; there are a lot of rumors going around. Hard to sort out what's true." Thomas's name brought the limp body of Sarah to a sitting position. Wyman looked over at her. She was looking at him from behind her stringing, filthy hair. Sarah felt sick and heaved so hard her ribs felt like they would break. Sarah dry heaved, and liquor ran over her bottom lip.

"Bro, orb, oter." She pointed desperately in Robert's direction. She's disgusting, Shelton thought. Maybe a saddle was more than she was worth. "Brrrder." She was still pointing at Robert.

"What she say?"

"Who the hell knows? I stopped listening to her years ago." He picked up a rock and threw it at Sarah. He missed. Sarah fell back as if she had been struck.

"Ahgggggg."

Shelton put his hat on to leave. "Farmers say the land is cursed. Maybe ya'll have better luck getting some crops going."

"Dat's what da boy said." Robert had not meant to speak out loud.

"What, boy?"

"On da way here's, a redheaded boy said da darkies cursed us." Robert looked down at the ground.

"That right?" Shelton's body tensed. He had given Robert a shack, but his instincts told him he might be housing something evil.

Robert took his eyes off the ground and back to Shelton.

"Yep. Dat's right."

"Well, sounds like that was the same dead boy they found floating in the river?" He observed Robert's face for the slightest movement.

Robert's face tightened.

"Bout the same time they found the dead boy, a government official went missing. His broken buggy was nearby where they found the boy." The image of the shriveled man with hands like doorknobs and transparent skin rose in Robert's memory. He remembered a brown sack the man had under his arm.

Wyman continued. "That was Jed. He is the son of the mayor's sister. Wyman got up to leave. He took a step down onto the road. He turned back, thinking he might have said too much. All gestures of kindness were gone from his face. "Long as you keep to yourself and work, you can stay. Any trouble, though, you might as well start back down the road you came."

"No, sir, won't be any trouble. I'm just marking time to see how to get what's due me." Shelton Wyman left. Robert left Sarah where she lay.

Each day followed the other, with the destruction of his anger and the image of that boy floating away from him downstream. I didn't kill that boy! Might be my fault, he admitted, but I didn't kill him. The river did.

Sarah, in the meantime, continued as she had since the end of the war to turn her rage inward and poured anything that appeared like liquor down her throat. She hated Robert, but she hated her life more. Her rage burned like an unattended fire in a dry field. Her sorrow crawled up her spine as if it were a staircase. At times, memories of the Grove Plantation suffocated her. She drank, yet it only left her drunk. She wanted to forget her life. She enjoyed the rare times she vomited, and her vision blurred, the world spinning while her belly's contents jumped from her frail body. When the spinning stopped, she'd hope, and she wake up from the violent heaves, maybe she'd be back at Grove with her daddy teasing her for being bold with him. Instead, she awakened to her life and Robert. His mouth was as nasty as the worst outhouse.

She would have settled for his silence, but she was never that blessed. She knew he was up to something, which was likely violent. Robert would settle for nothing less: his coming and going for periods, riding the horse into the ground, smelling kerosene when he crawled on top of her. She hated the days as much as the nights unless he was absent.

He'd got a dog and named it Lincoln. "Maybe dis damn Lincoln can learn to do right by us!" Sarah said she didn't like dogs, and they scared her. She said her daddy had them for hunting Negroes. They were mean dogs, and her daddy kept her away from them. "I don't like 'em, Robert."

Robert shouted, "Ain't nobody asks you if you like dogs!"

Lincoln had tan ears that lay flat. They never moved, even if he got excited. The edges of his ears were black, matching his nose. The rest of his body was a deep, rich brown. He was a wide-eyed hound, chasing the wind between hunting days. Robert waited till the dog got devoted enough not to run off. Lincoln would come to lie on the porch at Robert's feet. The dog slept on the porch; sure enough, he heard Robert Lincoln sit on his hind legs, panting, waiting for Robert to command him. One Saturday, their hunting trip brought home a rabbit, yet both the dog and the master wanted more. Robert wanted more for his life, and the dog wanted more for his master as he trotted along, looking up at the rabbit dangling upside down.

Lincoln's tongue hung out of his mouth, and he panted, his eyelids drooping. His head popped up when he thought his master was going to speak. "Good boy, Lincoln. Good boy." Waiting on a command, waiting for anything that sounded like "Go git 'em, boy." Robert looked down at the dog's eagerness to please him and got angry that day. "Be nice if that no-good wife of mine was mo like you, huh, boy, maybe if that damn President Lincoln's wife had been a good wife to the president, we'd won the war?"

The acid of hunger that lined his stomach rose to his throat. He vomited. Suddenly, the thought of rabbit meat put a flame on his anger. "You shoulda caught me more, you worthless dog!" During the remaining steps to the house, he cursed at Lincoln. He tossed the rabbit on a tree trunk. "What a mess dis world is in now. What a mess, ain't it?" Panting, the dog tilted his head to understand the command. "What a mess, President Lincoln."

He shot the dog in the head. "That's what traitors get Lincoln wagging your tail for Negroes."

The sound of the shot rocked the shack's weak frame. Sarah had been watching through the cracked, dirt-stained window but did not see that act coming. She only saw a dog and the mean man she had to lie beside in bed at night, walking home. Sarah had been hoping he had caught a rabbit, as she had a taste for it. Sarah waited for the door to open, preparing herself for whatever misery he was bringing home.

Then the shot. Sarah turned abruptly from the sight and gasped. She crumpled to the floor and covered her face in horror. She could still hear his voice and the echoing of the gunshot. But the dog had not made a sound. Sarah wondered if the dog knew he was about to die. Robert's voice came through the door while talking to the dead dog.

"Good boy, Lincoln." Robert pulled the dog back off the porch. The dog was heavy. "Good boy, Lincoln."

Some of the life in his arm was coming back with time, but it was still mostly useless. He knocked the rabbit to the ground and sat on the tree stump to rest momentarily. The trail of blood from the dog had followed him. He laughed and took out his canteen of whiskey. "Funny thing, Lincoln, funny thing."

The dog's eyes were open, and the top of his head was gone. Robert searched around for the brains, spotting some small gray matter. "Funny thing is, Lincoln, yo blood, my blood, or da rabbit all 'bout look da same." He took a long drink. Robert did not want to bury the dog or go into the house. Robert decided he had a lot to think about. What to do now? He had met the men who were married to the sisters from Ireland. Robert thought this might be a good time to ask them to join his plan. He doubted they'd have any problem killing.

Robert got up, pulled out his pistol, and shot it in the air. "This one is for you, God."

The tin cups on the table settled from the sound of the second gunshot ringing out as Sarah waited. Her husband's outhouse mouth faded away into silence. Sarah broke the silence by putting the liquor bottle in her mouth. The bottle hit against her chipped tooth. It hurt, but it didn't matter, as she was busy running toward drunk.

Now, living in a house that threatened to cave in with every movement and working in dried-up fields that were cursed, she had not a pot to piss in.  She wanted out like the dog. Sarah knew she had lost the bag of jewels that belonged to her mother.  Her mother's jewels had been her only possible way out.

So, when Robert finally came into the house hours later and reloaded his gun, she was utterly baffled when her mother's pearl necklace fell out of his jacket. Robert was busy cussing at his weapon to notice. Sarah crawled to the necklace and stuffed the pearls down her pants into her underpants.

"Whatcha looking for?" She wanted to distract him while she straightened her clothes.

"Life."

"There's a biscuit in the jar and a slice of ham in the cool box on the back porch." Robert looked at her curiously, wondering why she was trying to speak like a lady. "The Negro, Mary, brought half of a ham by and food from Wyman." This eased the tension in his face.

"Here." She opened her hand with a silver dollar in it. "It's your pay." Robert frowned and snatched the coin. A Negro bringing him money and food made his blood rise. He took the money and said nothing of his feelings.

"She come alone, without dat man?"

"Wyman brought her. She came to give me material for clothes and some herbs to relieve my sickness. Wyman must have told her I was sick."

He took off the jacket and replaced it with a heavier one. "Well?"

"Well, what?" Sarah asked.

"Git me some in' to take with me to eat." It was a relief he was going. She hurried with the task; the pearls of the necklace rubbed against her private part when she moved. "What da hell you'se smiling bout?" Robert put his pistol in his jacket.

"That you got something to eat and got paid." They both knew she was lying.

"Clean up dat blood and brains on da porch. Dog died! I'se got to bury him in da woods." He laid a canteen of liquor on the table for her. "You sick?" He had a smirk on his face as he looked down at the canteen and back at her face.

"No." Sarah tried, but she could not take her eyes off the canteen. What if Robert was in the mood to snatch it back and leave? She didn't have much left in her bottle.

"I'se didn't think you was. And…if so…ain't no medicine gonna help you'se, woman!"

With that, he walked out the door. "You'se right, Robert," she whispered.

Robert had no idea about her mother's jewelry. She had never told him that she had dropped the sack. She felt sick with worry. How and when had he gotten ahold of the necklace? She had been confident that she dropped it at the hub of the road. She tried to trace back over the weeks that had passed. Robert might have gone back to the people. Maybe they found the sack and gave it to him. They would have known it belonged to her.

Sarah went to fetch the wash bucket and filled it at the pump. If she let the dog's blood sit overnight, it would become permanent. It would be a double curse to have a bloodstained porch. Sarah scrubbed rigorously. She felt hopeful for the first time in a long time. If Robert had the rest of her mother's jewels, she would ask him for them. Sarah felt she had the strength to kill if he refused her request. Yes, she thought, I can kill, not for myself, but for my mother's jewels.

Sarah got off her knees and walked to the water pump to wash the blood off her hands. She desperately needed a drink.

# TWENTY

There were twenty-five people armed with the conviction that the government betrayed them. They were ready to stop meeting, writing letters, and starving. They were going to remove the curse by killing the women. Something the law could not or did not care about. The group had been convinced by the husbands of the Irish sisters and, even more by Robert, to go to Culver Tusk and take the plantation and land. Not another day should go by; night had been tucked behind the Ozark mountains, and nothing in the blue sky warned of bad weather.

Robert glanced over the group, "Whatcha gonna do?" He was burning with anger. "I ain't sitting around talking with cha bout ghost, on cursed land! Robert smiled inwardly, watching, savoring the words he was ready to unleash. "Negroes living free at Culver Tusk." And he added for spite, "Dey probably killed da boy, too!" All faces turned to the boy's mother in disbelief. Sam put his arms around her, pulling her tight protectively against his chest. Sam wanted to go and knock Robert to the ground. He whispered to his wife.

"I'll be back, and things gon be better, best you'se believe."

Her eyes were vacant, her cheeks hollow. Her son's death had stolen her appetite. She spoke slowly and deliberately, "Sam, bring me a part of der flesh; let me know dey dead. Some fingers be good." The boy's mother looked away from Sam, missing the horror her words provoked. He gently pushed her away towards the other women. "You'se women go home."

Alberta stepped away from the women. "I'm going with ya'll."

Robert chuckled. "You'se ain't going, don't need no darn women even if she looks like a man."

The rifle came down off her shoulder. Alberta had a bone to pick with Robert, which was picking time. "I'se married a no-good man. He knocked my teeth out. You'se remind me of my late husband. May he rest in hell! You'se can call me what he used to call me: *Trouble!*

Robert stared at Alberta's collapsed face and hairless eyebrows for as long as he could. He was trying his hardest to see what, if anything, her face knew of pretty. Her cold stare told him she'd earned the name trouble. He turned to the group, "Come on! Git in da wagons. Git on your horses. Now!" They rode in silence with their jaws set, Alberta alongside them. The weather was good traveling the first few miles; they were thankful it wasn't snow or hail. They got off on the first road leading to the plantation. "We'll walk from here!"

"How far?"

"Just over dat hill yonder. We'se don't want 'em to know we's coming!"

That's when the weather took a turn; they chose to ignore it. Stiff winds rolled down the mountain, pushing them back toward the hub. When they reached the hill, the wind came at them harder. Two steps forward, one back, but they moved on. It took a while, but they were close to the final road leading to Culver Tusk. It was faint, but they spotted smoke rising, which had to be from a chimney. They moved forward, knowing that, according to the map, Culver Tusk was around the bend.

"What da hell?" Sam asked no one in particular. He was sure they should have been standing on the road facing the house. He looked around, shaking his head in disbelief. Sam spotted a family of loblolly pine trees in front of them. The trees stretched on either side of them for miles. *So, where is da road to Culver Tusk?* Sam wondered.

Donaldson, Evans, Harrison, and McGregor kneeled on the ground and spread a map between them. Evans put his finger on the circle the clerk had made of their cursed land and walked their fingers to where they stood.

"What's dis—God or da devil?" They stared at each other before putting their eyes back on the trees. They stood staring from one to the other, then back at the trees. One farmer with an ax raised it violently and smashed it to the ground.

"Damn it!" The urge to kill was too much to settle on looking at trees.

"Look," Sam pointed.

"What?"

"Ova der." In the distance, standing looking at them, was an older Indian woman wearing colorful clothing.

Robert mumbled, "Kill her." He raised his rifle as did the others. The woman vanished. Then, the loblolly pine trees vanished, and there was Culver Tusk. The sprawling porches of the plantation home, with its enormous Grecian-style pillars and columns, elaborate balcony, and evenly placed windows. Alberta gasped and put her hand over her mouth. "What in da heavens." Alberta started running towards Culver Tusk, the elaborate balcony called to her. She ran with her toothless mouth open, her eyes fixed on the balcony. Suddenly, Culver Tusk disappeared, and the loblolly trees were in their place. The scream that fell from her mouth sounded more like a slow growl. Alberta raised her rifle and shot. Sam grabbed hold of her shoulder. "Don't waste ammunition. Trees ain't harmed you." It was the second time he'd seen Alberta with tears in her eyes, the first being the sack of jewels. Alberta was making a new sound, this time a soft whimpering. *"Dat house is made for a queen."*

Sam didn't have time to figure out what she meant. "Let's get the hell outta here!" The group needed no command or direction. Each turned, stumbling over one another, holding on to their useless riffles, seeing what had just occurred. What was the use of bullets when witchcraft was involved? They stumbled towards the path leading to the hub.

"Where da hell y'awl going?" Robert shouted in disbelief.

"Home 'fore we end up dead." They ran away unsteadily, looking back over their shoulders. They were glad the wind was pushing against them and not in front. "Git to da wagons!" The man with the ax was outrunning them. A heavy dose of disbelief and fear had replaced the urge to kill.

Robert decided to wait. He watched them moving away. Then he, too, looked over his shoulder at where the woman, the trees, and the house had appeared and disappeared. Suspicion rose in him about the group's intentions.  His distrust of what had occurred rose slowly like the first shade of night falling around him. Moving swiftly, he chopped a tall branch off a nearby tree and returned to the road's end. He removed a cloth from his sack and tied it to the branch's top. Robert then stabbed the sharp end of the branch deep into the ground as a marker. Satisfied, he took one last look over his shoulder, and the 300-year-old trees looked back. Nothing in his life taught him how to win a stare-down with trees. Robert ran to catch up to the group.

When he caught up with them at the hub, he chose his words carefully. "Whatcha gon' do?" Not sure who to look at, Robert looked toward the mountains. The last of the sunlight was leaving, making the tops of the hills in the distance appear gold. He saw the distinguished shapes of the Ozark Mountains losing to nightfall. Soon, he thought, the sky would be one flat wall of blackness, impenetrable to the human eye. "Ya'll say you'se been living with ghosts and hail, snowballs breaking yo' windows. Why you'se run from trees disappearing? Huh! If you'se say de negroes got a curse on us, it makes sense what we saw and didn't see." Robert looked at each one of them, measuring their fear. "It was a spell. Whatcha think a curse is but spells?

We'se got to kill 'em, or dem trees gon come with der branches and beat our behinds like we kids!' Shocked at his words, they mumbled a bit until the possibility formed images in their minds.

"You'se right!"

Evan responded, "We'se git some rest and head back in another direction. I'se want to git this over with. I'se say we take dynamite."

The others nodded in agreement. They decided they would start again in two days, this time headed in the opposite direction. If they had Indians with them, they would need more ammunition. Robert offered to take care of the guns. "But my horse ain't been well lately. Lucky to have made it this far." He took out the coin from his pay.

"You'se plan to ride all night?"

"Don't have to. Got ammunition at the house." Robert rushed his words out.

"Take my horse." They watched Robert as he left and headed to their home.

Sam began the walk to his home to the grief-stricken mother. His steps were heavy; the boy should never have been sent off with a bag of jewels. They were cowards, so they sent a young boy with a lie. All he had was a lie and a bag of jewels to face his death. Sam did not know how much more pain he might have felt if the boy had been his flesh and blood. But if his wife's grieving was any indication, he did not want any part of her suffering. He had no children of his own.

When he got to his house, it was dark outside and inside, making the sobs from within more sinister than human. He inhaled the night air, hoping the smell of pine from the trees would calm him. He paused at the door before turning the handle to open it, realizing he felt physically weak.

Sam had been heartbroken to be the one to tell his wife he could not find the boy, but at least then there was hope. The news of the boy's death flung devastation into her world. Now he had to tell her they had found the house, but it disappeared.

The knob was wet and cold as he turned it. It was just a matter of time; he realized as the damp cold permeated his finger, reminding him of her request for the fingers of the women; Sam knew he was leaving. A father figure was no longer needed; he failed, and the boy died. The door opened, and the warmth from the hearth barely met him. Adjusting his eyes to the dark with just a bit of help from the dying fire, he gasped. His wife was on her knees, inhaling desperately, clutching for dear life a pair of the boy's undergarments. The heaving of her body, rising and falling, made him realize he could never lie with her again without feeling her pain swallow him alive. He'd drown, not in the Mississippi, as the boy, but in her grief. Sam knew it was best to take off heading north at dawn.

# TWENTY-ONE

A merciful sky allowed the evening light to arrive much earlier than expected. It topped the trees with a gold hue. A tad more sunlight, just a bit, would have forced the women to squint or not look directly at what they were seeing. Indeed, they saw it all! It was happening. They did not call it black magic or think it was a curse that a family of trees had just announced they wanted to come *home*! After all, Culver Tusk was made of the flesh of trees. Claire cries, "What are ya'll about to tell us? We might not wanna know!" Well, the telling unfolded in the collapsing of time; hidden memories were freed from the dusk assigned to collect centuries-old stories.

"Whose memory is this?" Claire's cry went unnoticed. Isabal's and Izabel's hands, on opposite sides of the tree, stretched to find one another. They said nothing. After all, the trees were three hundred years old and swollen with history. "My God!" Lena cried out. "What am I witnessing?" The sisters' arms stretched with great effort to reach around the 300-hundred-year-old trees! In the rising dust, they were no longer held by flesh, blood, and bones; they were daughters of memory. Isabel's and Izabal's fingers touched, then clasped together. The tree softened enough for truth to return, friendlier this time—the children on the wall buried their faces in their palms, peeping out between their fingers.

Isabal and Izabel unclasped their fingers to dance, their repetitive movements.

Their feet stomped, forcing the earth's soil to rise. Their voices chanting and bodies circling were intoxicating. The tree itself stretched to lengthen and arched accordingly, like a dancer waiting for her moment to defy space beyond the limitation of minds into imagination.

Lena lay against the tree that was once her favorite chair. She was grateful that she had never thought of her baby as belonging to anyone but her. Lena had been on her way to freedom. Hargrove knew that! She leaned into the tree trunk, feeling each detail of the bark imprinted on her back, enjoying a memory of showing Hargrove her growing belly, "Feel my baby kick." Hargrove hesitated; a collision of thoughts ran through his mind. He placed his hand on her stomach. "Our baby." With that, Lena dared to tell him despite being owned by his father, Grove. "Me and our baby gonna run to freedom, Hargrove. I'se can't bring a child into life, and that life is of a slave." Hargrove said nothing, and Lena didn't bother to read his silence. It didn't matter. Lena had freedom in her mind. Now, Lena sat with her broken body against a tree, and her baby was dead. She turned her attention to the twins.

Sylvie took hold of Claire's hand. Sister Elizabeth allowed a disobedient thought to enter her mind without wondering about the wrath of God or what the Mother Superior or bishop would think. She said, "The stories of mothers enslaved are being told through the trees; more truth than I've known on my knees. I want to hear God."

"We'se was caught dat day anyways." Isabel and Izabal spoke regretfully, holding desperately onto one another. Memories etched in the lines of their faces were as deep as the tree's bark between them. Lena knew the story of snow and fire was about to be told. Isabel and Izabal were pressed together like pages in a book. Gazing deep into each other's eyes, their tears were as thick as the tree sap they clung to. "It don't take a newborn…long to die…even if she is suckling her mama's milk." The words came out harmonized.

"Free." Lena bowed to give grace to a grave where her child rested.

Both women continued. "The other runners whispering 'hurry.' They whisper… '*Hurry!*'" *Hurry* means to those headed to freedom, "Kill dat crying baby, fo' we'se all git caught."

None of the runaways knew one sister was with a child until she raised her skirt and squatted. The other moved so quickly that they didn't have time to sort out what was happening until the newborn was suckling on her mama's tittie. Terrified hands dug a hole for the afterbirth. The hounds would smell the blood if left unattended. They poured a fair amount of pepper over the dirt to repel the dogs. Traveling silently was the only way to freedom, and they demanded that the sisters do what was right. It was the baby's life over theirs. What else was there to do but the unthinkable? *Hurry.*

"We held her."

"Tight."

*Hurry!*

"Baby between us."

*HURRY!*

Claire whispered, "Right there among the trees near the window."

"What?" Sylvie asked.

"Sylvie… they killed the child. Dey both hold da baby's death as one. Look how fast  red sap is running from all the trees."

Lena picked up the pot, looked again at her past, and sang.

"Claire later wrote as much of the truth as her mind offered: *As if sparked by your song, Lena, we chanted you, yooouuuu. We chanted until the ouuuuuu surrounded us, and we became one like Isabel and Izabal. We knew it was all our story one way or the other as mothers of stolen children. The words of your song completed us as a family. Then…*

*Sylvie walked away, weighed down by her tears. She left the song, the trees. I cried out, "Sylvie," but she was gone. I found my writing pad to unscramble the circles. The circles could not be broken; it chose to be released. Write what happened or what appeared to happen when babies die with the taste of their mother's milk on their lips. I looked up to ask the children on the wall, but they were gone. What language will they speak when they return?*

# TWENTY-TWO

Sister Elizabeth rose off her knees, her body trembling in the aftermath, still cradling the squash against her aching chest. The wind had come with an unrelenting clarity, tossing time into nothingness. Now, its gentle breeze was less than a child's whisper. Whatever had just happened was becoming no longer. Sister Elizabeth's heart was breaking as all that had appeared was now contained in a child's whisper. Time was calling her back to the story of now. The trees slowly returned to what they had evolved: tables and chairs just as they were when the story started. Lena sat back in her chair and smiled; the world of the unknown had given her curiosity back. The door was the last to turn back into a door, just in time for the insistent knocking of the determined fist to get in. The knock was relentless. The hinges were silent. The twins had collapsed into one another, and movement was out of the question.

Claire wept quietly while writing, a journey Lena knew was Claire's understanding of God. She realized she would have to drag her broken body to the door, as the caller was not going away. Lena saw Evening peep in the side window. She took a deep breath and looked around. "Lord, you put trees and memories in this house; now git me to da door." Lena took hold of the back of the chair that was an oak tree moments ago. Lena pushed and then pulled her body. She said, "Hold on, Evening, I'm coming." She barely turned the handle before the door carefully opened. The outside sky filled the room with sunlight and a cool breeze. *Lena wondered if a whole day and night had come and gone.*

Evening walked in. She had waited long enough and now had come up the road to meet up with her past. She had witnessed the house turning into trees and waited until the house came back. Evening did not ask any questions, knowing what had happened. She was glad they seemed okay with how the spirit moved in the world.

Evening took Lena's arm and helped her back to the table. Lena glanced over at Claire. "Put the squash back in the basket." And then to the twins, "Get da glasses and a bottle. Call out back to Sylvie?"

Evening interrupted, her eyes settling on the new face in the room. "Where's my daddy?" she asked firmly. Sister Elizabeth handed the bundle to the women. "My name is Evening. You be the one, right?"

"Yes. ma'am."

"Call me Evening. Well, I haven't slept since they told me you were coming. I might have nodded off but not slept."

"I'm sorry you had trouble sleeping." Sister Elizabeth's voice was shaking, and she could not stop it. "I have something for you."

"From my daddy?"

"I never met your daddy directly, but it's about your daddy. I come to tell you a story."

Lena eased back into her chair. This was the second time she'd seen Evening upset, and even now, her face had a hint of her smile as she asked Sister Elizabeth, "You'se got a daddy?"

"Yes. What I remember about him is his singsong voice."

Evening watched the delight in the woman's face; the nervousness left as she talked about her daddy. Evening's heart ached for such a memory. Evening's eyes watered. Each woman noticed and respected whatever was crossing her mind. They sat in silence. Now and then, the sound of the wind rose close to a human whistling. Claire got up to peep out the window, hoping she'd see Sylvie.

Sylvie had not returned. No one seemed ready to talk about what had happened in the house. This very floor on which she now carefully walked was dirt earlier. And the house had made room for the woods where they had all, at one point, run away. This thought startled Claire as she realized she had just included herself in running away in the woods. She placed her hand on the cool glass of the window, thinking of Sylvie's words. "I'se come back for you!" *Me?* She thought, *oh, God, why can't I remember my life?* Claire wanted to run up the stairs to her room, sit at her desk, smell the fresh lilacs, and write about what had happened. But what words could explain the unexplainable, and to whom was she writing? Words skipped quickly in her mind:

*Who but hundreds of Africans chained together under a sky filled with spirits' bright stars? An uncharted voyage. A people's skin covered in ocean salt and the smell of those bodies that hadn't survived the voyage. Who but them must speak of freedom?*

"Pardon us?" One of the twins touched Claire's shoulder, startling her.

"Who's you'se talking with?"

"With?"

"Yes, Claire, you'se were saying something, but to who?"

"No one." Claire opened her mouth to answer, but she'd already forgotten the words she had spoken out loud. She thought: *It was not who I was talking to but who was speaking to me from within.* She could barely stand the quizzical stares from the sisters. Claire turned away.

"Evening, we seem to have lost track of time or day." Claire glanced at the window for guidance. "Do you… know?" The question from Claire was a lie; she didn't care. She was anxious and cared what would happen now that Evening had come to find out about her father.

"Don't let the bright sun fool you. It's on its way to dusk. Don't matter the day you know it ain't yesterday or tomorrow."

Evening responded to Claire, but her eyes stayed fixed on Sister Elizabeth.

"So," Claire said, "I… don't know what you mean *it ain't yesterday or tomorrow.* But certainly, we might as well have an early dinner."

Isabel and Izabal went in the direction of the kitchen. Lena noticed that one was off in her walk—not much, but enough for her to notice. The other put her hand around the waist for her to lean on. "We, okay?"

She spoke to her sister with concern. Lena thought *I was right—one moving differently in her body. I wonder what's the matter.* Lena rubbed her thigh and turned her aching body back to Evening. "You want to stay for an early dinner, Evening?" Evening was still watching Sister Elizabeth.

"Thank you, Lena, but I cooked for me and her."

Sister Elizabeth felt strong emotions from Evening. "What did you cook Evening?"

Evening put both hands in her pants pockets and proudly lifted her head: "Smother rabbit, soft potatoes, fried bread, snap peas, okra, tomato cobbler, white potato pie. Spring water with just a bit of cherry juice to sweeten it. I put some ham in the peas." She threw out the menu quicker than water to put out a fire. The list made her smile even more significant; she added, "I got pickled peppers if you like heat to your food."

The women laughed. Sister Elizabeth rocked her body in her excitement. "I love spicy ." Claire smiled at the childish way Sister Elizabeth spoke. Evening decided right then that she liked the woman. She could tell she meant no harm. Evening permitted her frustration to ease away; there was no way this woman meant anybody any harm. Evening was glad she went out of the way to cook everything she could get her hands on.

"I know it's cold, but I made ice cream. I went up in the mountains and got some snow. Ice cream is my favorite."

"Up in the mountains, for me?"

"For us. You like ice cream?"

"I love ice cream, but I hardly had any at the convent." She laughed. "I can't even remember how it tastes."

"Sho' 'nuff."

"' Nuff." The two laughed. Evening, slowly and with deliberate steps, walked over to Sister Elizabeth. She waited for any reaction in her body to be this close to the woman who had news of her father. Evening wanted to be angry. But she felt something unexpected, a sense of longing pulling at her. Hardly what she had imagined or prepared herself for; with no time to think about what was happening, she sat close to Sister Elizabeth. Claire, confused at Evening comfort with Sister Elizabeth, shrugged her shoulders at Lena.

Evening and Sister Elizabeth spoke quietly to each other as if nobody else was in the room, and the women let it happen. There was no denying there was an immediate ease between them. The smells began to come from the kitchen, along with the sounds of pots and pans. Lena sniffed the air. Yep, she thought, rosemary, garlic, and onions. She thought *I'm famished!* She continued straining to hear the two. Lena was delightfully surprised as Evening talked more than Lena was used. She must be nervous, Lena figured.

"Almost made just as much desserts as I did food." Evening laughed. "Got me a sweet tooth. My mother told me Daddy had one, too." Lena smiled, hearing Evening call her father, daddy, not just her mother's husband. Lena caught Claire's attention. Claire nodded at Lena, letting her know she'd heard it, too.

"I shaved a bit of lemon rind into the ice cream."

"Sounds like it's a meal for Jesus himself."

"Sad to see you blind."

Lena quickly glanced around, thinking she would hear Sylvie say, "You'se going to hell for dat!" Where had Sylvie run off to this time, Lena wondered.

"Yes, it is sad, which I thought I'd reconciled myself to, but today, I feel the weight of my loss. How did you know?"

"I can tell. My mama treated a child and a woman in her tribe for blindness with her medicine."

"It work?"

"Everything my mama did worked." It was the first time Evening stopped smiling. Evening knew Sister Elizabeth's blindness was much worse than the woman her mother treated. That woman's blindness came from a virus. This woman before her was not the same.

Nobody spoke out of respect for the tears coming down Evening's cheeks; her crying was barely audible. Sister Elizabeth asked, "What brings you to tears, my dear Evening?" Her words were like music; each word meant to touch the very core of Evening. Evening rose and walked away from Sister Elizabeth, struggling to gather her thoughts.

Evening, who lived in a house so lonely that it was covered in shadows year-round, was startled. Since her mother's death, Evening had welcomed the days; her shadow appeared on the house's walls, offering her a chance to talk. Her shadow loomed over her, and when she sat, her shadow sat, and Evening spoke to her own shadow. How could she explain to the women of Culver Tusk that she'd sat and watched two insects caught in a spiderweb struggle to be free because loneliness kept her awake?

But now, this woman came and asked her why she was crying, she said dear Evening. Evening had not heard words spoken so intentionally with such truth in a long time, not since the last days of her mother's dying. Now, to listen to these words," Why are you crying?" spoken to her soft as churned butter, made Evening aware of herself in a way she was not used to. She felt alive. Most days, she put on whatever was nearby to cover herself—a pair of pants, a shirt, and a jacket.

"Tell me, Evening." Sister Elizabeth said.

Evening found herself fidgeting with her clothes. She thought back to the well when the water became hands on her body. Just as the laughter entered the well, this woman's voice gave her the urge to live. She stared at this woman they called Sister Elizabeth with wonder. She had traveled all this way with only shadows to guide her. What story about my daddy would make her risk her life?

The light from the window pouring on Sister Elizabeth's face was dancing. Her lips were like the red of the Trumpet Honeysuckle flowers outside Evening's window. Evening did not understand the feelings that moved inside her. It was like her body was a jar of still liquid, suddenly shaken, and she was waiting to see what would rise before settling to the bottom. This made her wildly uncomfortable, and she wondered if Sister Elizabeth might be able to tell as much. Evening wiped the tears away with the backs of her hands. "Evening, come back closer to me. I don't mean you no harm; if I do, I will take care of you."

*Was dem words or a kiss?* The question ran across Lena's mind. Lena looked around to see what the other women were doing if they heard the intimacy in words. Izabal or Isabel came to the table with a large bowl, the steam rising. Claire was writing in that journal of hers. Writing and embroidery were all Claire seemed to need. She watched Claire for a moment, her hand moving across the paper. Lena thought, *I'se got to remember to ask Claire; if she doesn't remember her life, what is she writing about?* It occurred to Lena she might want to be careful what she tells Claire.

Lena felt a rush of loneliness come over her. She had wished the determined knock on the door had been Hargrove. If nothing else, she and Hargrove had learned to love each other as a family despite the laws and without their child. Lena watched Sister Elizabeth and Evening; they were in their world.

Lena learned to read the space between people as a child. Her mother taught her. The space between people is the unspoken word, the ghost of the past, and…even more, what is and isn't going to happen. That is the truth: more than a mouthful of words folks speak to you or their so-called kind eyes; it's the space you must learn to read; it can save your life. Lena squinted her eyes.

"Here, sit down here." *Here* was on the floor in front of Sister Elizabeth. Lena gasped at what was in the space Sister Elizabeth was calling *here*. Lena looked over at Claire, hoping she was writing this down! Better yet, draw a picture! It was a space full of flowers blooming and bees buzzing with a determined obligation of their own!

*Here* was between the nun's legs. Evening sat with her back to the woman, draping both arms over Sister Elizabeth's thighs.

"Here you go." Claire sat in the chair next to Lena and handed her a short glass of dark liquor.

"Oh, I didn't see you'se move. I'se need this. My legs are on fire."

"I know, dear. I saw you rubbing them. It's been a long day—or night, tomorrow, or yesterday." Lena took a deep breath. Finally, one of them acknowledged in their way something had happened in Culver Tusk. They turned their attention to Evening and Sister.

"You ever seen fingers move that slowly and deliberately? Make you question if they are moving at all?" Claire whispered.

"Working out da memories." Lena smiled at her own words.

"Yes, ma'am."

Maybe it was the warmth of the medicine in the glass or just the gazing at Sister Elizabeth moving her hands through Evening's hair, but Lena's body began to feel at ease, her bones settling. Lena was just about to say as much when the back door opened. The cold wind from outside shook them from their tranquil state.

"We'se gon' have trouble. Da people of da cursed land are coming." The voice was solid, familiar, but different. At first glance, the figure appeared to be a man of short stature and petite frame. Lena thought she saw someone else, an even more petite figure shaped more like a tree stump off the porch. Maybe, she thought, it's a shirt on a stump?

"Sylvie?" Claire could barely contain her body, which was usually poised and controlled. She rose from the table and walked forward, her knees weak. "Sylvie?" Framed in the light of the open door, Sylvie, dressed in tattered Union officer clothing, closed the door behind her. She leaned the rifle against the wall.

Lena saw madness behind Sylvie's eyes and waited. She was glad the rifle was out of Sylvie's hands. She tried to read the space in the room, but the air was filled with images of blue tulips. Lena went back over the past weeks and days, rising in her mind's eye distinctly as omens. She whispered the events to herself, "First, a squash that looks more like a baby, Hargrove, and the telegram about a nun coming. Then here comes the nun who is blind, and today, every wooden thing, including the floors, has turned back to trees. And now!" Lena folded her hands on her lap and looked each woman over carefully. "Is any of us real?" Lena pinched her thigh. Maybe freedom fell into a dream like we'se imagine freedom should be freedom." Her name is freedom, and she's a dreamer; she is nature's mother." Evening said. She watched the slow rise of anger in Lena's eyes.

Why is it interrupted by this nightmarish hell? Not waiting for an answer, she continued. "Sylvie comes in dressed as a soldier, saying we'se under attack!"

Nobody moved in the moments that followed. They listened as Lena continued. "We'se knew dis time was coming. Negroe women living in dis house." Lena looked at each of their faces, offering each a chance to speak. Nobody responded. The fire crackled in the hearth as a log fell. "We'se trying to do what?" There was much sorrow in Lena's voice. "Live out whatever days God gives us left on dis earth. What we'se thinking? Dat time go by and we ain't hated! What we hated for, tell me? It's da same as if dey hating da wind, da sky, sun, and da very earth herself."

Lena hit the table with the palm of her hand. She was not mad at the table or the women but at Hargrove. *Where he at now?* she wondered. Where was he when I'se was trying to run to freedom? She turned to Evening and Sister Elizabeth; the beauty of their image had not left. The space between them was safe. Not even the thought of attack could tamper with them. It was in God's hands now.

Lena spoke on behalf of herself and the women. "Spirits, it's up to you'se. We'se do what we'se can, but in da very end, it will be up to you'se." It was said. Lena exhaled. She turned her question to Sylvie. "Is it going to happen tonight?"

"No, but we'se must get prepared."

"Done!" Lena voiced with sheer determination, turning to give directions.

"Evening, y'all go ahead. Sounds like a wonderful meal." She chuckled to herself. "You'se two gon' be all right, right?" Lena knew it was up to her to ease the tension in the room, and she was prepared to do it. She knew things would work out just fine if a room could be a forest. Yes, Lord, just fine!

"Let's take a moment to pray together." And they did. Isabel and Izabal led the prayer in harmony and blessed each moment that offered them life. "Spiritual universe, in your wisdom, gives us the knowledge our spirit can hold, and may we move with that understanding in your world. Let us not focus on war but on da gift of life. Thank you'se for this gift."

"Y'all go ahead, Evening. Go." Lena pushed back against her chair to slide away from the table. She was not sure if Sylvie's words were the truth or just her madness acting up. We'll take care of Sylvie."

"I'm famished," Sister Elizabeth chuckled. Her eyes were closed. "It would be nice to eat, sit, and talk to you."

"I am prepared for battle." Sylvie ignored any resolution Lena was trying to put in front of them. She turned to Claire. "I'se returned once, and I'se here agin to protect you."

Claire's voice rattled when she finally answered. She felt Sylvie's words pushing her off a cliff: "Sylvie, you're scaring me. What did you see while you were gone?"

Ignoring her question, Sylvie commanded, "Claire, it's cold outside! Get da shawl you'se finished working on and give it to Sister Elizabeth to wear."

"It's not finished. I want to put more tulips—"

"Give it to her, Claire. It's an order!" Sylvie took off her hat as any good Southern gentleman would. "Please, ma'am, it's cold outside." Sylvie's face looked physically exhausted and long with worry. While Lena hoped that whatever Sylvie saw had occurred in her mind, Claire seemed dumbstruck.

One of the twins went to where the shawl was lying and handed it to

Evening. Evening took the wrap and admired the delicate flowers before gently wrapping it around Sister Elizabeth's narrow shoulders. Evening spoke to the women. "Darker tulips mean love that does not die." Sister Elizabeth thought to herself, *I pray you are right.* Behind them, Claire's eyes suddenly widened, and her mouth opened to speak, but instead, something told her to stop. She picked up her journal, flipping the pages frantically, turning until she got to one she needed, which was of her and Sylvie's previous fight.

> *Dear Journal,*
>
> *I fret over the fight that I had with Sylvie this morning. She is delicate and means no harm. But when I asked her, "If you run off, how did you get back here?" she snapped, "I'se come back to get you, wench!" It left me confused at first, and then I was torn with a feeling of despair for the rest of the day. It's as if I have blocked something horrid from my mind that Sylvie is aware of. But what?*

Claire's journal fell to the floor, and she collapsed on top of it. She cried with all the agony her body could find. "It's you, oh, Sylvie, it's you." Her upturned face was streaming with tears. She glared up at Sylvie, then buried her face in her hands. Her sobs rocked her frame.

"Yes, ma'am, it is I at your service." Sylvie saluted Claire's collapsed body.

"Go," Lena called out to Evening firmly. "Please, now…go!"

After putting the shawl around Sister Elizabeth's shoulders, Evening whispered, "I realize I have been waiting for you all my life; the water spoke of your arrival." They left quickly; Sylvie bolted the door just as Claire began to rise, ashamed of her outburst. She wanted to run and apologize even if she did not fully understand the memory that came to her.

# TWENTY-THREE

Culver Tusk was off in the distance, less than a mile. Hargrove saw the sun's glow resting on the edges of the roof. It gave him some peace. He wanted to check on the women but decided to stay away. Hargrove seemed tired, more than usual. His stomach was uneasy, and his nerves were unsettled since taking Sister Elizabeth to the women. The smell of his dirty clothes and body rose to his nostrils. He had not taken a bath in over a week.

Hargrove lay on the ground, which was hard and cold. Good, he thought; he needed something solid to hold him up. For the moment, the earth would do. Hargrove did not want to go home. His home was one mile or less at the south end of the creek, and it waited for him. He had four white servants that attended the house, twenty-five Negro families, primarily farmers, and twenty whites that lived on and worked earning a good living. Hargrove was lonely.

Tonight, the ghost of his family was on him. He did not miss them. Everybody was dead and gone, except there was word of late that his niece, Sarah, might be alive, in trouble but alive. He rubbed his tired eyes and listened to the sound of his rough skin. He was full of loneliness and missing, but it was not for his birth family. Not his mama, his daddy Grove, or his uncle H.G. He wondered if he'd ever loved them or if they loved him.

Hargrove tilted his head back to the sky and shouted, "No." He missed not having his own family with Lena. He tried hard not to think of the one child who had almost made it but had died. Lena and his child. Tonight was filled with the memory of the baby. Hargrove had, over the years, given the unborn child a name to make it more real as time threatened to take it all away. Tonight, the baby's name was Sam. Lena, he thought, would have called him Little Sammy, maybe.

Over the years, he had given the unborn child a gender and changed it once or twice. It depended on his mood. When she lost the baby, Lena said that it was a girl. Her heart said such. Lena never saw the baby, but he had. He saw the shape wet with blood; the body of the baby was curved over like it was in prayer. The doctor shook his head and handed the lifeless baby to the nurse attending, but not before Hargrove saw soft, wet, thick dark curls on the baby's head.

Hargrove had been hell-bent on saving Lena and turned his attention to the doctor working on Lena. It took a long time for Lena to forgive him for saving her life. 'I'se can't take away da life God gave me on my," she said when well enough. "But I'se won't fight if you'se or somebody else take my life. God won't hold that against me."

*Dead* was the first word out of her mouth, barely audible when Lena lifted her head after near-death labor. "Dead?" Her agonized face poured sweat, but her body shook with the chills of her fever. The doctor announced, "Nothing else I can do!"

In and out of consciousness, Lena whispered, "Dead." Sometimes as a question or statement. Hargrove thought Lena was asking the fate of the child. "Yes," he whispered as gently as he could, "*Our baby's dead.*" What rose in her dark pupils was as hard and cold as a tombstone. Her voice was just as low as his. "Me, Hargrove, kill me now." He pretended not to understand, "You're going to make it, Lena, I promise."

*Dead.* Knowing he had failed when she said she was running for freedom was the hard truth. A truth: Lena's body paid the price, and now their child was gone— *Kill me.*

"No." His voice quivered. Hargrove could have easily put the bottle of morphine to her willing lips to sleep forever. His willingness to consider giving Lena the lethal dose of morphine tragically sat within him momentarily, but that thought was not alone. There would not be enough left for him to follow her in death. The fading looks in her eyes told him the pain medicine was pulling her under. Barely audible, she asked, "Please, Hargrove."

"I can't live without you. I love you, Lena."

It had been settled without any more words. Hargrove knew he would have to live without Lena's open affection from then on, but he was determined he would protect her. Tonight, he chose to believe the child was a boy and was named Sam Hargrove.

Hargrove listened to the noises of the night around him. He was utterly alone except for his horse tied to the tree nearby. This kind of aloneness of the land crept inside him. "I'm getting old." Sadly, he could only half chuckle. The thought was like a stone skipping water. His thoughts took him farther with each skip into melancholy.

His heart was racing. Hargrove felt discomfort in his bones as he moved his body about on the ground. He sat up. Looking up at the sky. It would soon be dark. It was his least favorite time of day, as it made him nostalgic. He inhaled the cool air. He did not like to fall into those moments of what his life might have been and what if he could have stopped Lena from running or left with her. He was a coward. She'd had no choice but to be brave.

He had lived to see the world of enslavement end legally, but it was not enough. It was not over, not by a long shot, as each day, the laws and, worse, the people's minds were figuring out ways to go back to enslaving the Negroes. For that reason, he could let the memory of his child ease up. Sam would have been half Negro. He wept inside for the life Sam might have lived, even with the money and education he would have provided. Their child, Sam, would have been a Negro. Sister Elizabeth's words rushed over Hargrove. *No matter the stories of the South, I will understand it, not what anyone perceives me to be, but from what I am, Mr. Hargrove, I am a Negro!* Whatever part of Hargrove's heart remained whole; he'd filled it with his love for Lena. It was broken pieces that

Sister Elizabeth's words fell upon. He wanted to believe if Sam had lived, he'd have spoken those words or similar with as much unbridled self-love. Words a father could be proud of.

Hargrove reached into the side pocket of his jacket and took out the small bottle of dark liquid. He drank it and coughed. The heat of the liquid burned, and the effects quickly traveled to his brain. He felt dizzier than usual, then felt the light sensation of the dreamlike state the medicine offered. His eyes closed. In the dreamy state, Hargrove could hear Lena's voice rising as clear as the wind whistling in the distant trees. Her voice was trembling. "Master Grove and Overseer Robert killed my child. Dat's your father who killed my child." The pain belonged to the truth of the words. Hargrove would have preferred a more pleasant hallucination, but this was what was offered, so he took it. His views on slavery had caused him to sever ties in his heart with his father and mother, and he now wondered why. *Why God? I grew up to despise the world of slavery. To resent, with boiling blood, the very structure of my own life and see the beauty of the Negro. Beyond beauty, God, to love. But why, God, had I failed in my belief and Lena? Lena chose freedom, and I hesitated. Why? I was planning to take her and our baby to freedom. While I was preparing for their freedom, Lena took her freedom.* Hargrove stared at the night sky, searching among the few stars; it was the North Star he desired most to appear. The flat side of darkness stared back.

# TWENTY-FOUR

The loblolly pine and live old oak trees lined the road from Culver Tusk to Evening's home. Claire, still weeping, had jumped up from her heap, wishing to kiss Sister Elizabeth and Evening goodbye. She stood at the window and watched Evening and Sister Elizabeth until they turned at the bend. Claire watched the gentle swaying of the tall, graceful loblolly pines, which proved a pleasant distraction. Wiping the last of her tears, she decided to go to her room before anyone called out for her.

Evening and Sister Elizabeth walked briskly away from Culver Tusk Evening, guiding her steps. Evening was pleasantly surprised Sister Elizabeth didn't question their quick pace. It was still light outside, but moments after being guided down a steep path, Evening said in a foreboding manner, "We're almost there." Sister Elizabeth started to ask if anything might be wrong when whatever shadows she saw disappeared, and darkness enveloped her. *Had it turned night that quickly?* Sister Elizabeth asked if they might have come upon an entryway into nature, like a cave. In just one step—all it took—it had gone from light to darkness as if they had walked into another time and space. She instinctively glanced over her shoulder. With her faint sight, she saw the path behind her still carried daylight. Evening watched silently, barely guiding Sister Elizabeth's elbow, trusting the nun's senses.

Sister Elizabeth stopped and took a few steps backward into the light, then forward again. The contrast was startling. She took one more step backward into the light, testing her reality. Having just left a house that had turned itself into trees, she was still shaken but unafraid. She stepped forward again; whatever this was, it was not an enclosure.

Evening watched her and understood what she and the women knew and what Sister Elizabeth was experiencing firsthand. Since her mother's death, the sun could not compete with the loneliness of its occupant. Sister Elizabeth felt the desperation of the sadness as they approached the path leading to the house. It had an existence of its own. With her sight limited to shadows and the movements of darkness, she had, over time, developed an intimacy with darkness. Darkness held as many shapes and stories as light and even more. The shadows surrounding the house were like useless open mouths, willing but unable to cry out. Several times, Sister Elizabeth stopped on the path to hear whether this dark had anything to tell her. It was as silent as the stones on the path.

Evening cautiously watched Sister Elizabeth as she stopped, standing poised and waiting, her head slightly tilted and her eyes closed. Never removing her hand from her elbow, Evening wondered if she should have warned her before they left Culver Tusk. But how can you warn someone of the loneliness you carry of your mother's broken heart and your own? The dry grieving, she called it, for she could not cry. Evening was used to the sadness. It was hardly the vibrant, mystical house of Culver Tusk. She wondered if this nun could bear what she barely noticed anymore: muted screams. Evening listened to birds chirping in the trees and thought Sister Elizabeth must know if the birds were singing. Shadows or not, it was okay.

At that moment, she decided to guide Sister Elizabeth to the water and let her hear the beauty of the brook talking. Indeed, once she heard the delightful chatter of the brook, she would know she was safe! Evening realized she did not want this woman to turn back toward Culver Tusk and away from her. Finally, Sister Elizabeth inhaled deeply and turned away from the talking water. "Let's go to the house, Evening. Thank you for taking the time to let me adjust. It's okay." She squeezed her hand gently to show she meant it. They walked the remaining distance in silence.

Upon entering Evening's house, Sister Elizabeth smelled a bouquet of spices and aromas. She felt sure the hands that prepared this feast were anything but sad. Somewhere, the spirit of this woman she had traveled to meet was waiting to reveal itself. Sister Elizabeth wanted more than anything to be there when it happened. She began to hum, then sing one of her favorite hymns to herself. The words delighted Evening.

"Lord, Lo-orrd, Lord

my home

is where thou sends me

Lord, Lo-orrd"

Evening positioned Sister near the fireplace and fed the fire woodchips, then off to prepare plates. By the time the song looped around for the third time, Evening joined her. The words were complete in their simplicity and made whole by the women's ability to naturally harmonize together. Within the first hours, the house began to awaken. The candles' light, the kerosene lamp, and the flames from the fireplace flung light onto the porch through the windows. The scent of pinewood filled the air, along with the delicacies. It was no more than the simple acts of two women whose hearts wanted to listen and be heard in a song. Neither spoke this aloud to the other, but both were aware of the desire in their hearts. It seemed they had been waiting for each other's company their entire lives. Each new day or night offered validation their waiting was over.

It had been nearly a week since Evening and Sister Elizabeth walked through the door, sang together, and sat down to eat. Both women, in their own way, pondered the events at Culver Tusk. Was it magic or some act of God? How can a chair return to its life before the ax man came? Is that the purpose of existence, memory? Does the wood have memories even when it is no longer a tree? They asked each other these questions like shooting stars, unprompted, out of the blue, and sometimes interrupting a mouth full of food, being so eager to know about the unimaginable, imagined. God or magic, it was the same. Yes! It was the same; it was decided. They would not worry if answers did not shape the world into something they could understand.

"The world I have known is not one I could ever understand." Sister Elizabeth spoke during one of their nights of inquiry. "And what is understandable about slavery?"

*"Harrumph!"*

The questions became a way in which they tied themselves into a knot and became one—no mention of Evening's father. Sister Elizabeth and Evening were both enchanted by the other's company. It was like a friend had come to visit, a friend you loved and missed who knocked on the door just in time! Just in time for what? Evening was unsure, but nothing urged her to ask for news about her daddy. She wanted more of this blossoming friendship.

They had gotten so full of the meal the first night they went straight to bed. Evening offered to sleep on a pallet on the floor near the bed, but Sister Elizabeth would not hear of it. Evening rarely opened the door to her mother's room except to dust and open the window on Sunday mornings, returning to close it at night. Ten years had gone by since her mother died while the pain sat patiently, waiting to be heard. Evening had never cried over her mother. She laid next to Sister Elizabeth in her mother's bed. Her body told her it was safe now to time to cry. *Not now*, she begged silently. *Not now.* Evening inhaled and then released her breath. She had washed the sheets in lavender petals in the cold river the imaginary boy had once walked out of and back in. She'd dressed the bed earlier, and before Sister Elizabeth entered it, she had put hot stones wrapped in cloth under the quilt. When Sister Elizabeth got into the warm bed, she started crying.

"I have not in all my life, since my mama, daddy, and grandma, been this cared for, and those memories have faded every year," she shared.

"First, Lena and the others undressed me from my soaked-to-the-bone clothes and…lifted me to lower me down in the scented water. It felt like—God forgive me for saying this, but—it felt like a true baptismal. I passed out with relief, listening to their playful banter like they were speaking as the Bible said in tongue. I have been serving God since I was six, and most of those years have been spent on my knees in prayer.

Evening stroked Sister Elizabeth's hair like her mother once did hers in this bed, just as Sister Elizabeth had played in her hair at Culver Tusk. "What broke your heart, Sister?"

The kerosene light danced on the wall. Evening watched the light, waiting while Sister Elizabeth's soft cries filled the room. Finally, she heard her weakened voice. "It was not that I was on my knees for glory, but for the Mother Superior and the others handing me unwarranted penance. A few nuns knew I was a Negro and would not let it go unpunished" She squeezed the bedcover in her hand, wrapping it tightly as if wringing the suffering from her body. *No*, she thought. *I must keep silent! I am here to bring Evening comfort, not the other way around.* But she heard, despite her inner begging, the words of her anguished voice continuing and the soft, encouraging "hmmmm" from Evening. Evening's fingers lightly squeezed her tight curls for a moment and then released, soothing and intoxicating. Sister Elizabeth's scalp rejoiced.

The light of the kerosene had gone out twice, and the room had chilled. Each time, Evening rose, added more logs, and re-lit the lantern: Sister Elizabeth's story or this the beginning came to an end. Sister Elizabeth had been molested by several priests, starting soon after her arrival. Later, she gave birth to two babies. The other nuns carried newborns off—secrets hidden in their vows of silence. Evening allowed her tears to run silently down her face. She pulled the cover higher on them both. The wind outside was picking up, and she wondered if another blanket would be needed.

"Evening, would it be too much to ask you to hold me till I fall asleep?"

"No, I need it just as much."

"Yes."

"I used to sleep between them, on this bed, when I was a baby."

"You remember that?"

"No, but Mama told me the story over and over. It seemed for her, but now I know it was for me. She told me stories of him, of them, so I'd have their memories for company." She squeezed her eyes tight, willing herself not to cry out but to let this woman beside her feel whatever was passing through her heart. *I do not know what religion is,* Evening thought, *but I do know evil. And evil happened to Sister Elizabeth and her babies…and my daddy.* She wrapped her arms tightly around Sister Elizabeth.

"Closer, please." Sister Elizabeth was barely audible. It was a long night and way into the morning before each awakened.  Evening took out the chamber pots after each relieved themselves. She guided Sister Elizabeth to her mother's wash basin, which she'd filled with warm water and a cloth.  They did not exchange words as each cleansed their bodies and dried their skin. The pleasure of being comfortable with such personal details with one another spoke for itself. Evening couldn't resist the glances she stole at Sister Elizabeth. What she saw made her tremble. She heard her breath quicken. *I want to kiss her breast.* Her thought startled her, and as if she'd heard her thoughts, Sister Elizabeth's nipples hardened.

"Here, put this on."  Embarrassed, Evening handed Sister Elizabeth a dress that had fallen off the shelf the day before while she was dusting the room. She had picked it up and replaced it on the shelf, and it had fallen back to her feet. *"Svshki."* She had not understood why her mother's spirit was dropping the clothes at her feet, but now it made sense.

*Chi, hullo li.*

Evening helped pull the turquoise dress over Sister Elizabeth's head, watching Sister Elizabeth's fingers delicately touching the beadwork on the neckline and sleeves once it was on her body. It felt right for Evening to see her mother's dress being worn.

"How…do…I appear to you, Evening?" She felt embarrassed asking such a vain question. Even if she wasn't blind, a mirror in the convent was prohibited. She imagined the other nuns might have caught a glimpse of themselves when they polished the silver or washed the plates.

"Like a woman that been in hiding! You beautiful like the sudden bloom of a flower." Evening thought her words would please Sister Elizabeth, but she turned slightly away.

*Hiding*…That word struck a note with Sister Elizabeth, something she had begun to ask herself of late. *Am I hiding my life inside religion?* In the beginning, it was obvious that she had gone to the convent because she was useless to the plantation. What other choice did her family have? They were her parents but did not own her.  But what did she want now that she was grown, she wondered. What if I just left the order and never returned? Yes, she loved to serve people, but she knew she could not live alone, seeing only outlines and shadows. She realized that despite the suffering from the priest and her Mother Superior, she still believed in the man Jesus. He was made to carry his cross. What did the wood remember of Jesus's journey? Sister Elizabeth blurted out before she could stop herself, "My birth name was…is Diana." Her body was shaking. Diana's naked feet were planted firmly, yet her fingers nervously patted the dress. Her upper body was trembling. Diana's face glowed in the sunlight. Her lips were parted to speak, but no words came forth. Evening had played in Diana's hair throughout the night, twisting and untwisting, leaving a lovely, untamed, short, wild bush of thick curls.

"From now on, with your permission, I will call you Diana!" Evening knew whatever turned Sister Elizabeth away from her compliment gave her back her true self. She was pleased, "Diana, do I have your permission?"

"I am trembling with happiness." She whispered her name, trying to give it the matter-of-fact tone that Evening had. "Diana." The whole world seemed to be turning upside down, and she was unsure when she had decided to stop resisting and turn with it. 'Yes, yes, you have my permission. Anything you ask of me, Evening." There was nothing to deny in those words the hunger for intimacy was upon them. Evening felt the tenderness each wanted to share would have to wait for the right time. To understand that time, Evening felt she must first learn to bow down and ask her soul to guide her to Diana's body, which had been harmed. She realized she hadn't asked Sister Elizabeth when her train was headed back North, or maybe Diana had no desire to return. "Are you hungry?"

They still had leftovers and ate like they were tasting the food for the first time, barely stopping to talk to each other. The water was thrown out the back door when the morning dishes were washed and put away. They finished feeding the chickens and geese food scraps. Diana and Evening spent most of the day in the woods picking herbs before returning to the house. When she next spoke, Evening heard the insistence in her voice, light but there. "Evening, take me around your house and show me the details. Over the days, I have gone from each room, and now I want to know the stories of the rooms."

Evening questioned whether anything had changed in the house over the years except the curtains. She looked at her father's empty chair. She wondered if Diana knew she had misplaced her word by saying "show me," she being blind and all. *How can I show you the love that was once in this house?* Love that I resented as a girl. How can I show you the safety of love, knowing my mother was always watching? In the middle of a war, I always knew I was safe. My mother kept me safe. Now she is gone, and feeling secure is something I work for each day.

Nothing in the room had changed but her mother's presence. Her dying had left behind shadows of longing. The weight of her thoughts filled her with sadness. Evening knew she was about to introduce Diana to the world she had lived in, both with and without her parents. That world was still trying to find balance in her heart, and Diana had part of that balance.

For the first time, Evening felt a sense of fear of the unknown. What did this woman know about her father? She sat down, unsure how to show

Diana the only world she'd ever known. "Diana?"

"I like the way you say my name, Evening. It reminds me of home."

"Home?"

"Yes, it does. Show me…your home, Evening."

"The bedroom we shared was my mother's, where your stories and our story now live."

"Yes."

She heard Evening's chair against the floor. "Stand up, Diana."

Diana took her direction and rose. Evening went behind Diana, she was taller. Diana inhaled the smell and closed her eyes. She trusted this woman, whatever she was doing.

Evening wrapped her arms around from behind and lifted Diana, then placed her feet atop her own, with Diana's backside pressed against Evening felt a sensation tingled between her legs. "Give me a moment, Diana; I feel lightheaded." Diana's silence told Evening she might feel similar to her body. Evening always knew she was strong, and finally, it made sense why she had such a strong body, besides needing to chop wood or carry water from the river. Her big feet and strong body had found a reason to exist. To carry Diana. They were pressed together, front to back, with no room for a feather to get between them.

"You lighter than I thought." She whispered. Diana wanted to press her buttocks into Evening's hips.

"Am I?"

Since she was taller, she could place her chin on Diana's shoulder, so they were cheek to cheek. They walked, and Diana's hands went out to touch everything near them: the panel of the walls, the doorframe. She jabbed her fingers in corners, wanting to feel every detail, every nail in the wood.

When Evening's feet needed resting, they stopped and sat down. "Put your feet on my lap, Evening. Come on. I rode 'em. I wanna rub 'em." Evening laughed and complied. "Here you go." Her feet were cold. Diana rubbed her own hands quickly until her palms were warm. Satisfied, she let her fingers acquaint themselves. She noted the hard bottoms of Evening's feet and thought, *I would love to rub them soft again every night before bed. Every night. I will be leaving here soon. I am going to be leaving.*

The thought burned in her stomach, and she felt her heart aching. *Stop,* she said to herself. *Love her feet while you can.* She thought of her tiny room at the convent. *I will cry when I get to my room. For now, I'll make the most of it.* She rubbed the bottom, kneading the arches. Evening had fallen asleep but soon awakened, embarrassed. "Was I snoring?"

"Yes."

"Come on, let's finish. I got to show you the sitting room." *Home,* she thought. *This is my home.* She looked around and realized she was searching the corners for her mother. As much as she was enjoying the touch of Diana's hand kneading deeply yet tenderly into her feet, she wanted to show her things in the house she had been taking for granted. *Besides,* she thought *this might be the last time I'll be happy in this house. Whatever Sister Elizabeth—Diana,* she corrected herself—*has come to tell me about my daddy, it might change my life and what I know about my mother's husband and my father.* Would anything change if Diana gained her sight? Each night after the painful stories, Diana lay asleep; Evening had learned the pattern of Diana's breathing.

She asked her mother's spirit to guide her hands each night as she gently raised Diana's eyelids. The dark brown pupils looked out at her, showing no sign of acknowledgment. Evening squeezed the top of a tiny tube she had carved hollow. It was filled with a gold, cloudy liquid she had mixed and prayed over. She watched the drops touch each of Diana's irises. The pupils were motionless as they absorbed the medicine. Not once did Diana awaken, not even a stir. Her breathing remained even.

# TWENTY-FIVE

Hargrove arrived looking as exhausted as anytime they'd seen him. He had aged, it seemed, in less than the two weeks that had gone by. "Whatcha knows, Hargrove? It's been a while," Sylvie said as he entered the door.

Lena smiled up at Hargrove. "More den a while. Sorry if we's." She paused, her eyes resting on his face. "I'se hurt your feelings." Hargrove didn't miss the affection in her words. He rested his eyes on Lena long enough to assure her he was okay. Lena winked.

Hargrove came into the house and removed his hat, ensuring he hung it on the rack this time. "What yawls know that's good? I rode past Evening err 'day."

"Nothing yet," Izabal or Isabel answered. He didn't care anymore about sorting the two out.

"Whatcha mean nothing *yet?*" he said. Lena nodded to the chair near her so he could sit down.  She added. "Sister Elizabeth and Evening took off to her house nearly a week ago. Most we'se hear is laughter in da morning. Sylvie says Da, run and jump in the water."

"Yeah, I heard it when coming out of the woods." Hargrove chuckled. "laughing and squealing in that cold water scattering the birds from the nearby trees.

"Guess we just got to wait." Lena hunched her shoulders.

He watched Lena's face, searching to see the young woman she used to be. What was it in her dark skin that erupted and dismantled his thoughts? And her eyes, even darker than her skin? He finally found the words and strung them together in his mind. *I look at her and feel like I am falling and being born simultaneously, a phenomenon I cannot explain or ignore.*

"What's wrong?" Lena asked. Her silver and white hair parted down the middle and twisted into two braids, contrasted against her dark skin. Her cheeks seemed to have gotten higher over the years. She smiled, and the width of her mouth stretched her lips, showing her nice teeth. She spoke as if she read Hargrove's thoughts. "Walnut bark." Hargrove nodded and continued taking Lena in.

She was pretty in her younger days and lovely as she got older at Grove Plantation. Hargrove had left the plantation on and off for years, and Lena was always there on his return, working in the field. Her not bearing offspring for the plantation was an issue, but his father never sold her. Hargrove saw that. Lena was barren until they secretly laid together.

But now…She broke his imagination with her beauty. He rubbed his cloth over his face and wanted to tell Lena how beautiful she was. Maybe, he thought, freedom did that to a woman. Hargrove put the cloth back in his pocket. He wished he'd shaven.

He took a good bottle of cognac out of his sack. Claire got the glasses. Not much of a drinker, she decided tonight would be a good night to be one.

"I got something to tell ya, and I don't want you to be upset." He waited till each of the women came to sit around the table. He noticed that Isabel or Izabal was helping the other, as one had a limp. The thought of that dang berry tree branch story crossed his mind. He coughed. They sat and drank a moment while the crickets seemed noisier than usual, or likely his silence was loud; he couldn't hold onto it any longer.

"I've been away, but not really. I have been coming around and sleeping in the shack near the barn or sending one of my men down at night."

"I'se already know!" Sylvie jumped in. "Either you'se or dem moved my wooden box and put it in da corner."

"Sorry, Sylvie. There's a strong chance folks are set on coming to Culver Tusk to harm ya'll, but…

"But what?" Lena did not require a lot of explaining. She just wanted to know. Sylvie had already told them of the trouble he was speaking about.

"Just let me get through this, Lena." Hargrove saw on Lena's face he had spoken too harshly. But there were delicate details he wanted to be careful with.

"Is there going to be another war?" Claire heard the fear in her voice. A sudden wave of desire to jump and bolt out the door came upon her, which was foolish, she knew. The danger awaited outside the house, away from the land.

"Not really, Claire…but anything is possible. War can only accomplish what can't be resolved: death."

"Not really? Are you'se listening to yourself, Hargrove? What does *not* mean to you, 'cause I'se know what it means to me."

"I'm sorry." Hargrove saw that Lena was watching him intently. He was dancing around the truth. She knew it. He chastised himself with the thought of the last time he'd danced around the truth. It had cost two lives and broken Lena's body.

"Yes, I'm listening, Lena. And it won't be another war, but that doesn't mean the violence won't continue! This group of folks has gotten in their head; this property belongs to them. The fact that Negroes are living in the house makes the matter." He paused and forced the truth out of his mouth. "Deadly! They figure on getting y'all out of the house and squatting on the property while they fight the government.

"Hargrove, dis is your land, right?" Lena slammed her palm down on the table. "I'se got the papers you'se gave me." Claire pushed the matter, not trusting the look of uneasiness on Hargrove's face. "Your land right, Hargrove?" she demanded.

"It's complicated. The wives of the men were the sisters of my uncle's mistress. They are making claims to those who will listen. The man who supposedly killed my uncle, H.G., was his overseer, Thomas. He also claimed a piece of property belonged to him, but Thomas was executed. Now, his brother believes it is his property. H.G.'s lawyer has legal documents that were suspiciously signed by my uncle, which turned Culver Tusk and the surrounding land to him and his partners. My lawyers are handling that case. And to their credit, to our advantage." Hargrove didn't think it was time to tell the women that documents dating close to a hundred years might hold the answer to the partial rightful owner of Culver Tusk property. That would be their friend. Evening. Hargrove intended to make sure all wrongs were right by Evening.

"So, if the man killed your uncle, his brother can't claim the land, right? And…you *are* or, as you claim, *I*, the rightful, legal owner?" Lena asked Hargrove, but she looked at Claire. Unfortunately, Claire looked deeply distressed. Lena glanced down at her hands, then back at Hargrove. Hargrove realized he had been right. Lena had not shared the earlier part of their life with the women. She had not told them he killed his father over her. He studied her face carefully, nor had she told them it was because of his father their child died. Lena and Hargrove's eyes were locked several minutes before he answered.

"Not quite. Claire, pour me a small drink."  Hargrove did not want to dull his senses. When Claire poured the drink, he took a small sip. He noticed that the twins hardly touched the one glass before them and had not said a word. They were not even looking at him but toward the window. *Maybe I have frightened them*, he thought. He quickly added.

"Ya'll will be okay. I have a small army of men stationed around the land, and they are ready to do whatever it takes. You're safe. And I plan, if it's okay, to stay here in the house. I expect a confrontation will happen sometime next week."

"How do you know it's next week?"

"We have an ally living among them."

"A spy?" Sylvie spat her tobacco into the can. Hargrove nodded yes.

"This is the part that makes it a bit complicated. One of the men who got involved was Thomas's brother."

"Da man executed?" Lena leaned forward. Something in Hargrove's face told her he'd requested another drink for courage. He was holding something back.

"Yes, and he's supposed to be married to H.G.'s daughter, my niece, Sarah. If that's true, it becomes another legal battle." Every mouth, including the twins, dropped open and stayed open. "I just got this news tonight from one of the men. Sarah's husband left the group to get more weapons." Claire spoke of her confusion out loud. "If your niece married the man that murdered your uncle." She gasped. "Then legally, he, being her husband, could own whatever she inherits. Her voice is useless in the matter."

"Hargrove, what's his name?" Lena asked.

Hargrove took the rest of the liquor down his throat and lied. "I don't recall, but it doesn't matter." Lena searched his face, wondering what he might be thinking of or whom.

Hargrove inwardly scolded himself for lying. It did matter; Robert was the overseer who had beaten Lena, while the other man on the horse was his father, Grove. He felt he could not share this with the other women. Hargrove had no idea how this might affect Lena. He did not even know if Robert knew it was Lena in the house. Robert had been the only witness to what had happened to Grove. Robert had taken off before the sheriff arrived, which remained a mystery to Hargrove. Later that night, in the solemn parlor after Dr. Wilkens had left and while waiting for the sheriff, Hargrove had spoken the truth to his mother. "I shot your husband, my father, and would have shot Robert, but he rode off."

"For...that Negress, Lena?" His mother put her finger to her son's lips and stroked his cheek with her other hand before he could answer. She smiled a wicked smile. An asset she'd learned over the years. "It was a hunting accident. Do you understand, son? That's what we gon' tell the sheriff. It was like the accidental drowning of a beautiful man I used to know." She placed her hand over her heart. "You have his eyes." Her words stung Hargrove but did not shock him. A strange relief rushed over him, explaining the undertone of resentment he'd always felt from his father. "Yes, son, your father was with him the day of the drowning *accident!* I was engaged to your father when the accident occurred. Her head turned sharply away as if some notion of truth awaited her attention. "It was the annual garden party".  Slowly, she turned her attention back. "Please do not ask me his name. It is eternally in my heart and on a tombstone in Philadelphia. The only man I truly loved! He drowned, and the only witness was your father. Your dear father was pleased and full of triumph to carry his dead body in the back of the wagon on the road near my parents' home for everyone's viewing, especially mine." Her head turned sharply again but landed with intention to her husband portrait on the wall. "On the day of Mother's annual garden party!  Are we clear on what happened today?" Those words were said to the sheriff when he arrived, emphasizing, "It was a hunting accident." The sheriff was suspicious seeing Grove was killed in the middle of an open field. What possibly were hunters hunting in the open? He questioned. Who was the other hunter?  But the sheriff nodded yes; he understood. His mouth remained clamped shut. The wealthy have their sayings, he thought. *Money makes the common man nod the way money calls heads or tails, yes or no.* The sheriff nodded yes and nodded again so there'd be no misunderstanding. He privately took pleasure in introducing her to her new world with a jab. "Yes, ma'am, Widow Grove." The sheriff left, thinking another woman would have collapsed under the word *widow;* hell, it hadn't been a full day since her husband's death. But Grove's widow stood on the balcony overlooking her beautiful land like any other day.  He learned something that day: money makes some woman's grieving period shorter than it takes to flutter her lashes.  By the time he rode back to Grove's body, deputies had loaded the body on the wagon.

Hargrove's mother turned to Hargrove after the servants let the sheriff out. "It would be best for you to leave…son. A few months, maybe…" Her hand rested over his. "Whatcha expect me to do with that half-dead nig—"

He interrupted her sharply. "I'm taking Lena with me!" Hargrove left, taking Lena and a prayer that she would survive her injuries until they got to Boston, despite Dr. Wilkens thinking otherwise. Hargrove found a Negro healer to travel with them who disagreed with Dr. Wilken's diagnosis, assuring him Lena would survive. It was the last time he saw his mother. They met only in letters till her death.

*July*

*Dearest Son,*

*I hope this letter finds you well. I will get directly to the matter at hand.*

*A distant cousin tells me that the Negro Lena survived and lives in your home, not as your servant but as hers. Tell me this is a vulgar lie or that you have gone mad. As situations are undoubtedly different there in the North, matters of living among Negroes, I still can't understand nor choose to imagine what has taken over your mind. My brother-in-law, H.G., has taken over affairs and resides over both plantations. He has hired a man named Thomas.*

*Thomas's temper reminds me of my late husbands, but I must admit it is necessary in these times of unrest. Due to the cruelty with which he oversees the plantation, he has gained the reputation of an iron man. H.G. has promised this behavior will not go on forever.*

*He is a handsome man with emerald eyes, which has caused a stir among many, including some of the wives of our dearest friends. It amazes me the attraction so many women have to the troubled souls of men. Even my niece, Sarah, has taken a fancy to him. You would hardly recognize Sarah, as she was just a tiny child when we last visited, but she is growing into quite a beautiful young woman. Unfortunately, her rebellious nature far exceeds her Southern charm. For which, of course, she can hardly be blamed, given her father's doting on her every need. He says that boarding school is not an option currently. This time! What better time for a girl to be educated about her responsibilities and duties? Indeed! He calls her activities harmless when she oversteps Southern charm and etiquette boundaries.*

*And her poor mother, Iris, bless her soul, seems indifferent to anything beyond drinking and the extravagant gatherings she throws for entertainment or charity. And in the middle of this bloody war! She refuses even to consider anything regarding war. Leave that to the men of education and politics, she cries. I can hardly disagree. I worry this war will not end soon. Thank God it's contained in the distance.*

*Not that matters of war and politics are a woman's concern. Still, it infuriates me that she has no worries in that direction. On the other hand, I would be interested in hearing about their discussions in the North regarding this bloodbath. I don't imagine you will enlist, and I warn you not to, for I know what side you would join and shame this family further into humiliation.*

*The construction is done at Culver Tusk. They will be glorious additions, no doubt. I am going to take up residency when it is completed. Away from all the festivities in which I am no longer interested. The events here at Grove Lane now seem to blend into one another. Many a sunrise has met the glow of the gaslights when our guests leave. Unfortunately, for reasons only you and I understand, it is too soon for your return. I have suffered wearing black. It washes out my delicate skin.*

*As ever devoted,*

*Your mother*

Hargrove stood up slowly from the table. He could not believe the turn of events since his departure to Boston and return to the South after the war. He was not sure if he was exhausted from the layers of memories or the anticipation of the ensuing attack. He doubted he would get a chance to talk alone with Lena tonight. "Where should I sleep?" he asked no one in particular. Indeed, he felt he did not want to direct the question to Lena. "Two men are arriving soon. I have instructed them to sleep in the barn."

"You'se can sleep in the room off da parlor with Jed." Lena saw the shock of her words register. Hargrove's eyes swept across the room and went back to Lena. He pulled his gun from under his coat.

"Who the hell is Jed?" *Here,* he thought, *I am sitting with my back to the door with the threat of an attack. How could they…? How could Lena not tell me a stranger was in the other room?*

"You'se trust me, Hargrove?"

He did not answer her but shouted at the door, "Get out here now with your hands in the air!" His words flung with such force the chandelier shook.

Lena realized she had not seen a gun drawn by Hargrove in years, and then it had led to murder. "Hargrove!" Pushing both hands on the table, she tried to raise her body but collapsed back onto the chair.

Sylvie rushed to the parlor door, standing as straight as she had in her uniform.

"What?" Hargrove's instincts told him that any man of dangerous intent would have emerged by now from behind the door. He let his arm lower, the pistol still in his hand.

Lena spoke firmly to him. "You'se think we'se let somebody in here dat would harm us?"

"Lena, you should have told me!"

"Told you'se what, Hargrove?"

"A *man* in this house!"

Lena turned away from him but not before he saw pain in her eyes. "What is it, Lena?" Lena did not respond. The door began to open, but not entirely. Sylvie, hand on the door, was looking into the dark. "Open the door fully, Sylvie," Hargrove commanded.

"Put dat gun away, Hargrove." The twins' voices were urgent. Sylvie stepped to the side. Hargrove waited, and still, no one exited. At first, he thought this was a trick, and the women were up to some foolishness to have a good laugh at his expense. But then Claire called out as if she were comforting a child, "Please, dear, come out."

This confused Hargrove. A child? He thought back over Lena's words. Jed? Lena had only said the name, not man or child. He felt nearly as foolish as on his last visit when he'd been laughed out of the house with his hat hanging off his lap. This was another trick! He turned to Lena to confront her. Hargrove didn't care whether the other women in the house understood, but Lena needed to realize he was here to protect her at any cost.

Before he could speak, he heard a faint, fearful voice in the dark. "Is he going to kill me?"

"No, Jed, he's a friend. He didn't know you'se were here." Lena looked at Hargrove. "Put dat gun away." She called out to the person in the room, "Come on out here, sweetheart. It's okay."

Jed had arrived muddy, and his clothes nearly shredded, half-dead with exhaustion. Sylvie had discovered him lying on the ground near the house. She got him cleaned up and put a man's shirt on him. The shirt went down to his ankles, fitting him like a dress. She cut the sleeves over his wrist; otherwise, they would have fallen to his thighs, leaving him with his arms and hands drowning in fabric. She had never seen a grown man inside a body fit for a child yet twisted up. He came out of the dark room.

Hargrove stared at him in disbelief, at a loss for words. He looked at the abnormally short man with sparse facial hair and bulging eyes. Even though he stood half in the dark, the man's skin was translucent.

Filled with trepidation, Jed looked around the room. His bulging eyes rolled loosely in one direction and then the other. Sylvie was the only one who had come to know him well. He trusted her. Sylvie had found him, and only in the past few days had she introduced him to the other women. Jed looked over at Hargrove, his eyeballs rattling back and forth.

Hargrove tried not to, but his face showed disgust. The man was…? Hargrove calmed his voice. "Where you from?" He put his gun back in his holster.

"Little Rock." Like a woman, the little man's voice was low and soft.

"Why are—"

Sylvie interrupted the conversation. She pushed her shoulders back, reminding herself, *"Dis man is under my protection.* "He brought legal papers and letters of importance with him. He worked for the mayor. And he knows who's you'se are, Hargrove!"

"This official business you here on?" A mild sense of worry was in Hargrove's voice, as he did not know what business he might have or what it could mean.

Jed looked at Sylvie for direction. She nodded to him to respond. "I got copies dating back decades ago. They were being hidden under the courthouse. I think most folks thought they were lost. And I got some more recent papers filed just before the war. I was there years ago when they got the man accused of your uncle H.G.'s murder, or at least who took the blame."

"Accused, blame?"

"Yes, sir."

"Thomas, the man they executed didn't kill my uncle?"

"Dat's da Thomas you were talking about, Hargrove." Hargrove could not tell if it was a question or a fact from Lena, making him wonder what else this man knew. Did this man, Jed, know that Thomas was the brother of the former overseer Robert? Hargrove decided to halt the conversation immediately before too much was revealed. He wanted to talk with the man privately in the room. *Wait… the ominous note with the telegraph regarding Sister Elizabeth signed Jed. The documents this man mentioned included the legalities of the Evenings family owning the land within the papers.*

"Would you like a drink, Jed?"

"I can't drink."

"Why?"

"You'se going to hell for dat." Sylvie pulled her shoulders back defiantly. She felt protective of the small man before her. She saw the beads of sweat and the trembling of his small frame.

Lena laughed. "Well, looks like we'll be in hell together, Hargrove." She hit the table lightly.

Jed explained. "My innards are weak, and I get sick. My skin gets flushed, and I sweat more than normal." Jed had a long list of things that went wrong with his body and would have continued, but the voices inside his head interrupted him. *Just tell him you are a prissy little girl, and good girls don't drink.* Jed's body jumped, as he had not heard the voices since he arrived at Culver Tusk. He shouted before he could catch himself, "What! Where yawl been?" He spun around, searching the room as if the faces of the voices would finally appear, but nothing.

The voices answered his question. *We were right here watching you. And we know you helped kill the boy with the red hair. You murdered that boy!* Shocked at the accusation, Jed felt his bladder soften, and the sound of his pee poured onto the floor. He glanced down, pulled his shirt dress up to his knees, and began weeping. *Murderer,* the chorus of voices in his head, shouted. *You ran away! You might as well have killed him. You…you, murderer.*

The women watched Jed but refused to allow his actions to sink in. Madness, they had learned, was best ignored and might be contagious. Saliva ran down his cheeks like a baby teething without a sign from him to consider wiping the spit away.

Hargrove took pity on what was in front of him: a pint-sized man with bulging eyes peeing on himself and shouting to someone or things no one in the room could make out. God help his tortured soul, Hargrove thought. "Give me some rags to clean this up and get water for the tub." His instructions were fatherly, although he had no personal knowledge of fatherhood except in his imagination.

Lena instructed the women. "Put another log on da fire. Let's git him cleaned up. Come on now, hurry."

With such a small body, it was not long before the tub was filled to accommodate Jed. Claire smiled, watching the small man, naked and seemingly unembarrassed, go down into the warm water. This was the second time strangers were bathed in the fire-lit room within two weeks.

The twins left the room discreetly after the water buckets were poured into the tub. Hargrove was there in their place. Claire wrote in her journal.

*First, it was Sister Elizabeth, nearly as white as Hargrove, without the sight of her eyes, with news about Evening's daddy. This man Jed, not even white but transparent, whose eyes bulge as if falling from the sockets and burning with madness, has come with papers that might reveal the ownership of this house and land. I wonder if Evening and Sister Elizabeth know the likely imminent danger we are all in. Indeed, by the robust laughter that runs up the road, it isn't very likely.*

# TWENTY-SIX

Neither Sister Elizabeth nor Evening knew the details of Hargrove's arrival to guard the house nor about Jed with his legal documents. They had not spoken to the women at Culver Tusk since departing that day.

They were caught in a dream. In the tiny moments that had come and gone within the past days of unexpected journeys, a world of happiness was upon them, unlike the world outside Evening›s door. Separately experiencing what was happening between them, they turned to each other for confirmation, as they had developed trust and intimacy. It was three in the morning; neither was sleepy; they knew it was time to bring Evening's father's story home. Evening poured two cups of wine, the identical cups her mother and father drank from *Sip, Sip*. Evening started the conversation by returning to a place she struggled with and missed.

"Mother fed her husband every Sunday. Mother talked to her husband like he was there: blood, flesh, and bones. Sip…sip… She drank from the same cups; she alternated each."

Evening took out her pipe and lit it. The smoke's heat filled her throat, and the smell of the tobacco was sweet. Looking up at the soft dance of the smoke, she remembered the day she fell headfirst into the well and her mother's laughter coming after her, requesting that her daughter come back and join the living.

"I didn't know you smoked."

"Sometimes, rarely. My mother smoked. She told me she and father smoked in the evening together." Evening, let the smoke drift in the air for a few minutes. The silence felt good, but she knew it was time. Tobacco was in her parent's honor. "Tell me what you know about my daddy, what my mother refused to say. Tell me with the truth of honor in which I deserve"! Diana closed her eyes. Her lips pursed inward. She took a deep breath, beads of sweat gathered on her top lip.

"Evening, your father was taken from your mother, from you, by five men. They desperately wanted this land. It was your mother's tribal land. When they married, she legally gave the land to your daddy. He was never enslaved. I'm going to tell you the story as I was told.

The men wanted the land. Your father said no."  Diana paused to listen to the sound of Evening's body and see if she moved or if her breath quickened. Nothing, not even the inhaling of the pipe.  "They came one or two more times. In between, they warned him by setting fire and burning part of his crops. They demanded that he sign the land over, but your daddy refused. That's when they decided to kill him."

"Do you know if some of these folks at the hub are kinfolks of the men that killed my daddy?"

"I don't, but…Hargrove is."

"Hargrove?" Evening sat back in the chair, shocked. She set the pipe down on the table nearby. Evening looked down at her hands; her mother often said she had her father's hands.

She remembered the times she and Hargrove had discussed the land. Recently, he asked permission to have his lawyer investigate some legal matters regarding the property. He assured Evening it would be beneficial. Evening assured Hargrove it would benefit others to stay away from her land.  "Sister Elizabeth, was one of the men Grove?"

"Yes, is that Hargrove's father?"

"*Was* his father!" So, Hargrove had killed the man that killed her father. The thought brought no relief. She watched the smoke rings rise in the air. Hargrove had no idea she knew the story of what happened in the field with Lena. Evening picked her pipe back up.

"Keep going. I mean to get through this story tonight."

"The third time they came, he never bothered to answer. He was working the land."

Evening quickly sat the pipe down and clapped her palms together, "Scratching the back of the mother."

"What?"

"When you work Mother Earth, you are scratching the back of the Great Mother. This pleases her." This was how she learned to love caring for the earth, feeling how much pleasure Mother Earth must feel.

"I see." Diana laughed. "Language is beautiful, stories are beautiful, sometimes painfully beautiful. I said I see, but I…"

"What, Diana?" The movement of Diana's eyes and the tiny lift of the corners of her mouth told Evening that Diana was unsure of what was happening. "Tell me, Diana."

"I'm not sure, I see; I mean…it brings me comfort knowing he was scratching the earth. Your mother's husband looked each of them in the eyes and went back to his work, ignoring them. They told him he'd never see harvest time. He said, ' I don't need to, but I plan to. But if not, the earth is gone do precisely what it's gone do, with or without me.'" Evening interrupted her. "What was the man's name, the dying man?" Evening was on the edge of the chair, her body was pulsing, she felt the veins of her forehead swelling. Hargroves's daddy killed my father. She willed her body not to betray her; Evening did not want Diana to hear any sound of the swelling storm in her body.

Diana's emotions struggled momentarily; she did not want to hurt Evening more than needed. She could not tell in her voice how or what was happening in Evening, as her tone was even. Diana was relieved to be able to share the anguish that had been alive in her for so long: a dying man's story of violence, murder, and pain. "Evening, I know this might sound strange, but I don't want to say his name. I feel like saying his name would burn the flesh of my mouth."

"What?"

I had to say his name day and night. I slept on a cot in his room. The stench of a dying body, no matter how I washed him. I wanted to leave with no memory of the sound of his voice and ever to call his name." Evening watched Diana's body closely to sense what might be happening inside her. Diana seemed lifeless, as if defeated. Her hands were loose on her lap, and her shoulders slumped forward. But her face was most troubling. Diana looked like she'd been washed up on the riverbank. Her eyes' rims were red, her face's skin moist with tears, and even her short curly hair seemed to have lost its luster.

"I don't know, Evening…It seems I still struggle with the part of me that feels anger or, worse…maybe hate. I don't know if that anger or hate is his or mine. Praying has not released me." A thought came to Diana that she realized might help both understand. "It's the part of me taking back my name, Diana. Sister Elizabeth, bound to the church's duty, would say his name, but I, as Diana, can't. Saying our names, Diana, and Evening in this house to one another is my blessing, my freedom."

"And his name means what?"

"The opposite. I don't want his name in this house! I can tell you the story of what happened to your father cause it happened. But…"

It was more than the cracking of her voice or the tears. The tobacco taste could not distract Evening anymore from the knowledge Diana suffered. She set the pipe down on the plate.

"I don't want to know his name for now; keep going."

"Thank you. The man gladly confessed his stories one after another. Each began with a desire to want your father—a piece of him just as much as the land. There were times during his confessions I heard what sounded like ecstasy in his trembling voice. It sickened me. "Screw the land; he'd say as loud as his weakened state would allow; we wanted him. They wanted what was inside your father."

"Inside?"

"His courage, his love for your mother. They wanted to know what was contained in his silence."

"His silence?"

"Yes." Diana laughed gently, a sound that came to Evening as a shared caress. Diana was discovering what Evening Father's silence might have meant. "Please forgive my laughter, Evening. I learned much about your father's beauty, mother, and you. I laughed because I was nervous about my affection for you, which grew through the stories. Now, I realize it is even deeper being here with you." Evening went to the window not to look out but to gently touch the curtains her mother had sewn in silence before she died. "His silence."

"It's what he didn't say to them they were faced with. They could never possess his soul. They couldn't buy it; with all the money, they couldn't buy a soul from him or buy one for themselves." Diana felt the heaviness of the air in the room. Evening held on to every word until she alone could embody the wholeness of this truth.

"The man telling me this story was wrestling with that at the end of his life! Done dead, goodbye! He didn't understand the beauty of living, and his life was ending. He said there was something about your daddy. He said the men argued and cussed! Burned his crops. Threatened him with unthinkable acts, and your father never responded except to stand firm in his silence. I asked why they kept coming back to burn or threaten him for so long before killing him. I don't know what possessed me to ask such a foolish question, but I did."

She signed. "He couldn't answer that directly, but the pieces I gathered about your father, he was bigger than life, and they wanted to keep him alive as long as they could to bear witness to a force they did not understand."

"My mother, my dear mother," Evening now understood her father. She openly wept. "Give me a moment. I'm glad we spent the time getting to know one another, Diana. We made room for his story to be told." Diana understood. She recalled the nights she and Evening slept nestled with each other. The next morning, they ran outside to the low bridge. Diana had trusted Evening to take her hand and jump into the water.

Evening looked at the chair her mother had sat in for years, thinking, *"Mother, you were sitting at the memory of my father and feeding me my father's memory.* "Just because you kill something, or someone does not mean you are bigger than life. It means you have no understanding of life." She closed her eyes and thanked her mother for that lesson. "Diana, tell me something."

"What?"

"You say…part of you hated him?"

"Yes, or maybe his hate crawled into me. I don't know." Diana thought deeply momentarily, searching for words to make sense of her inner struggle. How long did she, as Sister Elizabeth, listen to the teachings of the Bible before she began to believe she should suffer? She must suffer for those she served. *I must ease the suffering of others.* How long? How long in listening to that man tell her how much he hated Negroes and then cry out for the gifts he saw in Evening's father before dying? He never once regretted the horrid acts he committed. Diana tried desperately to share her confusion with Evening. How did she know what she felt when she pulled the covers over his cold shoulders? Or her hands learning every detail of his room to move without him knowing she was blind and pouring water and holding it to his lips with certainty up to the day of his death. He was a vile and horrid man begging God to forgive him but never saying for what? Asking her to guide his forgiveness. I offered him Matthew 16:26: What does it profit a man to gain the world, but lose his soul? He spat in my direction. Forgiveness or hatred? Did it crawl on her skin? Did she hate him and more? Was there a difference in their hatred? Evening's words broke into her thoughts.

"How could you care"—her pain was not missed in her words— "for someone you hated?"

The question was fair, Diana thought. "It was difficult."

Diana thought but did not share with Evening that *I was Sister Elizabeth, not the woman I am with you. With you, I am free. I can feel what I desire. I can rise off my knees and drink if my throat is parched. As Sister Elizabeth, I vowed to silence. I had no thought of asking what I could or could not do. But me traveling here now, I know it was worth the pain I suffered caring for his dying body to know you and carry as Jesus the cross, carry this story to you.*

Diana was confident her life had led her to this room. She folded her hands together. Diana had not counted her beads since the train ride, and her fingers did not miss them. But she often thought of the young boy Samuel and his mother.

"Evening, I prayed for salvation from hatred for both of us." This was accurate. There were moments when Sister Elizabeth felt no hatred while caring for him. Such as the nights when his body was more bones than flesh, and his skin stretched so thin that it tore open. When he didn't even have the strength to close his mouth to bugs, the dry rattle in his throat as he choked on them. The other nuns had to help her clamp his jaws shut. On nights when his eyes dried from staring back at his life calling out, his eyes were on fire. Diana remembered her hands being her true sight, moving over his body to heal or manage his remaining life. On those nights, in silence by his bedside, moonlight came in the narrow window, giving her sightless eyes some direction. She knew the light covered her and the murderer without discretion. It shined, teaching her that everything in the room was covered in the beauty of moonlight despite the horrific acts of humans. She did not hate or love. On those nights, she wondered how or if she would ever meet the child he described. That child, now a woman in her sixties, was waiting for answers.

"I listened to a dying man tell his story relentlessly. Clear at times, sometimes through delirious from the medicine. He came to the convent for the last three months of his life to die. Evening"—her whole body began rocking back and forth. Diana's anger rose in temperature with the flames in the hearth— "I washed that man's face while he was telling me how he murdered not just your father but many negroes. I combed his hair while he told me about your father. I gave him medicine for his pain while he was telling me a heart-wrenching, aching, painful story that I had no medicine to take for my breaking spirit."

Diana was near hysteria, and yet Evening refused to go and comfort her. Even though the urge called her, she could not. She sat watching and listening, almost from a distance from her own body. Diana's once lifeless arms were flung in the air, her body rocking with force.

"He was dying, and he had no other story to tell, not of his mother or father, not of love of wife or children, only the story of when they came and took your father away." She willed her body to stop rocking. "He thought he was confessing to a white nun. He thought I would understand, regardless of my religious orientation. But what he did not know was because I was a Negro, they assigned me, and my white-passing skin wouldn't tell him otherwise. They knew of his hatred of Negroes. It was another way for them to remind me.

Diana had the intruding question: what would happen when the story ended? Would this new world of her as Diana end? Would she return to Sister Elizabeth? Would Diana disappear under her habit? And even more, would the tenderness of feelings between her and Evening leave them both? It had not occurred to her that Evening might hate her for caring for him. *I must not let this happen;* her mind called out. *I must find a way for Evening to understand my duties. Please, God, let her not hate me if you listen to any prayer, grant me this.* She called out desperately in her mind. She heard herself pleading between sobs, her head spinning around, not sure where Evening might be in the room. Her eyes were flooded with tears. "What use are my eyes if I can't find the woman I love and beg her not to hate me." she clawed at her eyes.

"P...lease... Evening help, I... was assigned to him. Evening, I beg you. That was my duty." Evening still could not move or speak. Instead, she quietly watched Diana's arms fling, sorrowfully tearing at her eyes. She could not bring herself to go and comfort her.

Diana's voice rose with frustration. "I asked the question in my prayers, *what am I to do, Jesus? What am I to do?* This was my assignment—that's what my rational mind told me. It was part of my orders Evening! Mother Superior's orders, and I did what I was told. I prayed to the Holy Mother, Virgin Mary, for strength to do what Jesus would have me do. Prayed for the strength to be as obedient as thy Lord Savior." Diana's hands came from her lap and began to rise, palms up, reaching into the air before her.

Evening watched the rise and fall of Diana's hands, begging for comfort. She still could not rise to comfort Diana. The very thought of this woman before her, whom she had come to love, had touched this vile man with those same tender hands rising in the air. The man who helped to murder her mother's husband…and "my father." She had not meant for those last two words to be spoken aloud.

"Yes, your father. Whatever part of me might have been whole was gone. I knew that much. I was empty. Indeed if Michael, Angel of Death, would have come and reached out his hand for me, I would have gone without protest." Diana's cries circled the walls, and the only thing that answered was the crackling of the wood in the fireplace. Inside, she begged Evening to break into her words with some sign of tenderness, to let her know hatred was not in her heart. Nothing but the fire dancing offered any level of warmth. Her heart was saddened even more, but she continued.

"I begged! Angel of Death, come to me. It would have been welcome to die—that's how alone I felt. On a few occasions when I was relieved of my duties of his care, I found my lips would be swollen from biting them. I could not eat for days. I broke my fingers, squeezing them to endure his words. Then, a miracle happened. Evening?"

"A miracle?" Evening rose from her chair. She was exhausted, as she knew Diana was. She had never spoken as much or heard as many words in all her decades on the earth. There were a few words a day she exchanged with her mother. Evening's mother did not believe in talking for the sake of talking. Each conversation was deliberate in its delivery. This room had been filled with hundreds of words in the last week, tenderness at first. Now, the words came as heavy as the boots of soldiers and as rapid as the tears of the children and women left to cling to life after the war. She lifted a log and inhaled. It was the solidness of Mother Earth. She exhaled.

"Can we sit near the fire next to each other, Evening? I need you close to me."

"Yes. Let me put more wood on it." It was true she felt anger, but she had also felt love for Diana since the first time she saw her. Evening knew she needed a few minutes to gather herself, and the smell of the earth always helped her with this duty. Evening spoke with as much kindness as the wood had offered her. "I know you suffered, Diana."

Diana continued. "My vow to the church all came down to those few months of caring for him. I realized I was keeping him alive to hear the story to the end. God had me there to hear and deliver your father's story to you. And I did not even know if you were alive, but I knew I would find you if you were. In the very end, I felt this was a love story."

Evening watched Diana's face in the firelight. The pores of her skin were moist with tiny beads of sweat. Her head was tilted slightly upward, waiting. Her lips partially opened with her last words, *a love story. This is the face*, Evening thought, *that listened to the man that murdered my mother's husband*. Did Diana's face appear to that man as it did in this moment? Beautiful. A sudden rush of anger crawled up her throat. She took a moment to calm herself.

*A love story*. The oddness of Diana's statement halted the anger in Evening. Nothing in her mind or her experience living alone in this house over time offered her understanding to accept what Diana said. Her bottom lip trembled, but she was not close to tears. She wanted to break something unbreakable. *Love story?* She wanted to break something that was meant to be whole, to break it in half. This thought was foreign and did not please her. It was not her nature to harm. There was nothing to prepare her for the story of her father's murder and, in the same breath, "How dare you call anything about this a love story." The words made it out of her mouth.

"Yes, Evening, a love story. For me, it became a love story." The palms of Diana's hands burned against the edge of the table where she had, without knowing, begun tapping it rapidly. Something she had not done since childhood when she first started to lose her sight. A signal to her parents of the difference her world was becoming. "Yes, a love story."

"They murdered my daddy!"

"Yes. they murdered your daddy 'cause they couldn't kill him! They couldn't kill him, Evening."

In the space between them sat a bowing down of humble understanding. Evening looked around the room. She looked at the carved bird on the windowsill, the deer rack where her father's clothes hung, and her mother's curtains on the windows. She saw the paintings, the table and chairs, and the beadwork, all illuminated by the fire and the lantern light.

Minutes ago, the smoke had danced, and the air had lifted and been clear. Diana saw the look of tenderness rise on Evening's face. She smiled up at her in recognition. Evening was taken aback for just a second. Realizing how precious this moment was, she smiled back. Oh, Great Spirit, she prayed, she sees me! She wondered if Diana knew what was happening in her hysteria. She chose not to say anything now. It was true, and her father was never gone.

"They could not kill him." Evening sighed deeply.

Diana said, "No, they made Jesus carry his cross, then murdered him, but they could not kill Jesus."

"I don't know Jesus, and I don't know my daddy." Evening dipped her fingers into a bowl of blueberries. She squeezed and let the berries' blood release and stain her fingers. All the while, she looked at Diana's face. And then, as if it were the most natural of acts, she took two fingers and wiped the warm, dark juice across her cheeks. Diana's quizzical look and slight shock spoke of the answer Evening was seeking; the medicine worked.

*Now,* she thought, *I know this truth to be.* She went to Diana and reached her hand out in the space between them. "Come, let's go to the fireplace, as you requested." Diana didn't search the space as in previous times. Her fingers gently found and curved over Evening's.

Evening offered her father's chair to Diana with a hand gesture. Again, she saw a smile of recognition on Diana's face, but still, Diana said nothing. Evening refused to doubt what her eyes saw three times to be true. Diana's sight was returning, but her mind had not caught up to the miracle. They sat across from each other. Both admitted to being exhausted, but both agreed they must go on.

"You cared for him?"

"I *took* care of him." Diana's voice was clear and direct—she had not cared for him. "They dragged your daddy away from his home, beat him, cut him, and left just enough of him to hang! I could not care for someone so vile and callous. I took care of his dying." The agitation deepened. She took a moment to adjust her lower back, which had started to ache. Often, this happened when she felt stressed.

"But I thought about the part of him that returned to the tree. The tree that witnessed the murder. I took care of the man who cut your daddy down and buried him. I cared for the man who listened to the better part of himself. He returned and carried out your father's wish. Your father's dying wish was to protect your mother's eyes from the horrid sight of what those men did to her husband and your father."

"You washed him?"

"Yes!" her voice begged. She wanted Evening to forgive her, but she did not know for what.

"You fed him?"

"Yes."

"Prayed with him?"

"I listened to his prayers, yes." *My duties of attending to a dying man,* she wondered, *is this enough to make you hate me? What now, Evening, what now?*

Diana was suddenly afraid that she had soiled the love they had discovered between them. She panicked, scrambling for words to offer.

"Evening, I listened and thought about you. I was worried about you. l worried about the little girl your daddy left behind." There was no indication that her words were getting through to Evening. *It is the truth,* Diana thought, *and I must make you understand.* "Your daddy left worrying about you, and I seem to have picked up that worry. That's why I had to come and see you. Not knowing even if you were alive."

"How do you know he worried about me?"

"The last thing your father said to the men before he died was, 'Bury my body. I don't want my wife to find out how you have left me. She is a hunter, and she will find me.'"

Diana paused, then added, "He told them, 'Everything walking on two legs ain't human. One of you has got to have enough humanity to bury my body. Now, let's git this dying over with boys.' The man I helped crossover said he came back later and cut your daddy down from the tree and buried him. It's the only human thing he felt he'd done."

"That was my daddy's worry, Diana. What is your worry?"

The question came out of nowhere and startled Diana even though she remembered confessing that she, Sister Elizabeth, had taken over the worry. But the concern she had before coming to the house near Culver Lane and her worry now was different. Now she wanted to admit to Evening that *My worry is who I am in your company. I have taken back my birth name, swam naked in the near-freezing water, and now something is happening to me physically. I feel a fire in my body calling for you. Its flames are most ignited between my thighs. The world has turned upside down, and I am with it. I love you, and my sight is back.* Instead, she answered as a coward. She responded, "Maybe later I will have the words for my worries, but I'm now confused."

"There is a lot to be confused about. I'm sorry if I seem angry at you, Diana. Tell me more."

"His whole life was wrapped up in that night of your daddy dying. It took that man his whole life to try and crawl out of that memory."

"Did he make it out with your counsel?"

"No. I heard him take his last breath. He was still trying to tell me more. I did not want to get any of it wrong. I knew one day, if you were alive and I found you, you and I would be here. And that was the one good thing about being unable to see then." Evening sat watching the light of the fire on Diana's face.

"I never imagined what it would be like to find you and talk. I had to feel inside the story through the images he was giving me. And being here is more than I prayed for; it's what my heart has wanted. I knew this home was filled with love." Pausing, Diana listened to Evening's labored breathing. "Evening? I promise I will stop if it gets too much. I promise."

"I have been waiting sixty years. Talk to me."

"The men had come to the house, they agreed, for the last time. They didn't see your daddy's horse or wagon. Thinking maybe nobody was home, that made 'em even angrier. 'Come all that way with killing on their mind and nobody home,' he had said. The house looked empty, but they saw a brown child lying on the bed asleep through the window."

"Me." Evening smiled.

"Yes. He said you were the color of a late autumn leave. That's what his memory served him. Your hair was wild upon the bed. You were lying on your back, your arms and legs spread wide. A gold-colored cloth tied around your bottom." Diana stopped momentarily reflecting and said, "You just trusting the world to look out for you."

Evening heard tenderness in the last words and asked, "That what he said?"

"I added that part myself about trusting." Her voice was apprehensive. "He remembered you were chubby. Hargrove father told the men to leave the child alone. The first good act they did that day, among the atrocity that was about to occur."

"Why did he remember me, my color, and my hair? And even care?"

"I… I don't know."

They went around to the side of the house, spotting your parents. Your daddy was naked from the waist up at the water pump; your mama's dress was pulled over her hips. They had just finished making love."

"Did they see 'em?"

"No, but he could tell."

"That what he said, making love?"

"No, I put it that way."

"You don't have to clean it up for me."

"I know. I guess over time, I cleaned it up for me."

"It ain't your story!"

Diana quietly agreed but knew there would be moments when she'd still clean it up for both. She could not explain it yet, but somehow, it had become both of their stories. "Your mother's foot was up on a log. He said her legs were as long as the day."

"A man coming to murder another man got time to look at his wife's legs! What kind of man is that?"

"I thought the same when he told me. Shame he didn't leave the looking as his only crime."

"Your daddy was pumping water and catching it for her in a big washing bowl. She was splashing water on her private parts."

"My mother still got that bowl. Well, I got it now." Her mother's face smiled in her memory, as solid as a picture, for which she had none.

Every movement her mother made was deliberate, from the stirring of a pot to climbing the mountainside for herbs. Her mother never moved her body as if it were meant to wander. "If my body has no reason to move, then it has reason to be still, daughter." She moved with deliberation on the day she died. The birds chattered incessantly at the window that morning. After three days of not feeling so well, her mother got up to wash her body with the juices of fermented apples. She stood naked for the sun to dry. Finally, she asked her daughter to rub her skin with sage oil. "Make sure you take more time with my feet, daughter. Not sure how long I will be traveling in my new journey."

"*Syshki.*"

"Your hands will do for you whatever you ask of them. They will follow. I pray you ask them to do good. In this life, daughter, your heart will ask you to follow it. Be as obedient to your heart as your hands are to you. Your spirit, not your mind, should guide both your hands and heart."

That was it, nothing more. It was her words before saying goodbye. As quietly as the sun dried her body, she let go of her life in a similar silence.

"Whose life?" Diana asked as Evening had spoken the last word of her thoughts out loud.

"Oh, I was remembering my mother. Keep going."

"Your daddy dropped the bowl and said one word to your mother in another language. What did your mother speak?"

"Choctaw."

"Your mother took off around toward the back of the house. Three of them run to the front, two chasing your mama. Your daddy had already leaped in the window of the house. He was going for his shotgun. Your mama threw an ax. She hit the shoulder of the door just as one of the men rushed in behind your daddy. It was a hard fight, your mother fighting by your daddy's side. The men were losing. One of the men ran and grabbed you from the other room to even the fight. He was holding you up, his hunting knife near your throat."

The thought of a man holding a hunting knife to her and what that sight looked like to her mother and father turned inside Evening. She felt the muscles in her face harden. Evening looked around the room and tried to imagine the violent chaos of the fight. The still peace of the room availed her of nothing but its calm.

"Did he say what I was doing?"

"Yes."

"Was I crying?"

"Yes, you were wailing in distress. He said…" Just as it had when Diana first heard this part of the story, her heart swelled with grief. She could barely think about it. Now, with the circumstances of her responsibility, she had to say it out loud. She closed her eyes and waited for her heart to speak.

"What happened?" Evening sensed the challenge for Diana, and she stiffened her body to prepare.

"Your father said something to you. This is the love story I spoke about"

"What?"

"He didn't know. I asked, though. It was the Choctaw language or African. He said you looked at your daddy, and the room quieted. He said…"

"Tell me." Evening's eyes swelled with tears. "Tell me what happened."

"He said, 'Every angry weapon, every fist hung in the air, every blade of the knife dulled at the sound of your laughter.'"

"He said that?"

"Just like that, every word."

"How could he remember that?"

"He had nearly sixty years living in that memory."

"Then what?"

"You were looking at your daddy, laughing. All danger collapsed. It was you and your daddy, that was it! Nothing in that room was as big as the moment between you and your daddy, nothing. The sound of laughter, in the face of death, most prominent was laughter. He said your father laughed right along with you."

"My daddy was laughing with me?" If no more were said, it would have been enough for Evening. Without words to tell her why it was enough, she knew. Her daddy. Without his flesh and bones and blood to hold her, he came to his wife each Sunday. One day of the week to a child who called it crazy then, now in this moment as a woman, understood the empty chair, only emptiness can offer love a place to rest. Sip…Sip…

"Evening?"

"It's okay. I am okay."

"That was it! He said your daddy looked over at your mama and nodded. The fight was over. He said your mama smiled at your daddy."

Without a thought, Evening's hand went to her face, her fingers tracing the lines that moved upward and lifted her cheeks. She thought of Lena's words and Sylvie's laughter, "You'se always smiling, Evening."

She turned her attention back to Diana.

"Your father turned to leave the room, but that wasn't good enough for one of the men. He took the butt of the gun and began beating him. Your daddy did not fight back. The man said each blow of the rifle butt, and your father bowed under it before it touched him. He palmed to the sky. He was done fighting."

"You can't break what opens itself up," Evening added gently.

"What?"

"My mama always says you can't break what opens on its own."

"He told 'em to hand his daughter to her mother, and let's get this dying over with.' They left. He said they tried to drag him off his porch, but he walked. They lifted him under his armpits. He walked on air away from his home, woman, and child."

"He walked away with love."

"Yes. Everything on him was swollen, broken, cut, raw, and bleeding to the bone by the time they got him to the woods. Most of his teeth were gone, but he was still alive."

Evening got up and walked to the table, tears streaming down her face onto the wood.

"Evening, it took me three months to hear all this, and it nearly killed me. Let me stop and start again tomorrow, but the story is almost done."

The table seemed new to her. Evening looked down at the table like her daddy had just carved it, her mother had just polished it. The sound of a hammer hitting the nails rang within her like church bells. She suddenly craved sawdust. "Daddy?" She blinked quickly at the image the sound of her voice evoked. Her daddy's smile came through the decades and reflected in her image in the tears. "Diana!" Her voice was as sudden as thunder clapping.

"He picked me up—I remember. I said *Pata,* and he picked me up and lifted me to the sky. I was walking on air. We laughed."

"Evening!" Diana's face was excited, knowing that Evening was remembering her daddy. *There are more ways to the meaning of getting sight back,* she thought. *I am getting my sight, but I do not want it to interfere with what is important—why I came! My miracle can wait.*

"Evening, you remember something?"

"Yes, I remember my daddy, hands the color of walnuts, teeth like ivory, Sister Elizabeth, Diana!"

Like the constant pecking of the bird and its singing the morning of her mother's leaving, the memory of her father, like a picture of which previously she had none, was there before her. "I look like my daddy!" Both women clapped their hands eagerly.

She did not want Diana to stop. The beauty of her father possessed her. She did not want to go to bed. She did not want to sleep or eat, die, or live outside of his memory, which rose quickly after being buried for six decades. Diana sat listening to the fire and the excitement of Evening uncovering the memories she had buried for so long. Now, she was in the story after all the days and nights of listening as his spiritual adviser. Evening stood at the table laughing and holding herself.

And Diana welcomed each moment. All she had wanted was to come and meet the child that lay stretched out on a bed, trusting the world, and now here she was. She tasted the salt of her tears running happily down her face. There seemed to be no other world but the one she lived in now. She wondered if life in the convent ever existed. She tried to picture the other sisters moving as quietly as her thoughts into the chapel to pray. Nobody in her life would understand these last weeks with the women. Nobody. It was more spiritually palatable for them to imagine the epic adventures of the Bible than to imagine a house made of wood that returned to its proper story and offered the stories of those who had run for freedom.

For a long time, Evening and Diana did not speak. Evening was leaning over the table her father and mother built, and Diana was sitting near the fire. Each woman was far into their thoughts, past and present, with no thoughts toward the future. So involved that neither Diana nor Evening noticed Robert outside the window hidden near the bush, stooping low. He wanted to make sure the light of the stars did not reveal him, but Robert could see most of the room.

He had been watching the two women since they had sat at the table, and long after, they moved to the fireplace. His legs ached something awful. Robert held back his first intention to enter the house. Robert waited and watched, thinking a man or two might be off in the rooms he couldn't see. Both women dressed in nightgowns: one Negro and the other white, he squeezed his manhood. Robert moved away from the window toward a tree to relieve himself. His pee was loud, and the stream continued for a while. He had not figured on coming upon a house on the road to Culver Tusk. This discovery changed his plans. He tilted his head back as the urine poured out of his body. A few drops of rain hit his tilted forehead. "Oh shit, rain!" he called out.

"You hear that?"

"What?" Diana whispered

"I heard something." It would not have surprised Evening if Sylvie had come to look in on them. Since coming to live at Culver Tusk, Sylvie often, alone and without visiting, took it upon herself to scout the area. She secretly hoped this was the case. Evening walked over to the door and pulled the shotgun off the wall before opening it.

The night air met her with a cold breeze. The dark offered nothing for her eyes. Even the trees had gone into darkness. She stepped onto the porch and slowed her breath to match the night air. The wind brought a faint smell of tobacco. She raised the rifle and called out. A rustling sound came to her left, and her body jerked quickly around. In the moonlight, she saw Seven large coyotes come into the light and sit back on their hind legs, looking towards the woods. She smiled. Hargrove might have come down this back way to the house. He smoked that kind of tobacco. "Hargrove?" She waited. "That you, Hargrove?"

"Evening?" Diana called out softly.

Evening's head tilted toward the woods. She slowed her breath before responding. "I think Hargrove has been around this way."

"Oh…and he didn't stop?" She sensed uncertainty in Evening's voice.

"He is probably circling to check on things or could be one of his men."

She went back through the door and bolted it. The air had pushed the warmth right out of the room. Evening put on another log. She decided that they could use a drink to warm up. She fixed one for each of them and sat down again with Diana.

"If you want to wait till morning to finish talking, I can wait, Diana. But if you can go on, so can I."

"I can go on, and I will go on." Diana took a deep breath and let it out slowly. Evening watched her face soften as her lips parted to continue and thought, "My Diana." As the story continued, she thought, *Diana, you brought me my father's laughter. This is my father's love story to me.*

# TWENTY-SEVEN

Hargrove covered the table with newspaper clippings, letters, and legal documents. Lena sat next to him and Claire on the other side. The others had gone to bed.

Nothing was between the three but the papers, the lantern's light, and their thoughts. Jed had turned over to them everything he had taken from the office, minus what he lost in his travels.

Claire broke the silence. "How much of this is true, you think?"

Hargrove looked up from the papers. Claire's eyes were red with exhaustion. He could only imagine what he looked or smelled like. "What part? The legal documents or his tales?"

"All of it." Lena picked up an official-looking piece of paper.

"What does this mean?" Hargrove took the paper from her hand, knowing already what it was.

"It's part of a signed treaty that the land under this house belonged to Evening's mother and father."

"Did your father know it?"

"Sure, he did."

"He one of the men that killed Evening's father?"

"That I can't tell you."

"But what do you think?" That's the point, Hargrove wanted to answer back to Lena. *Thinking* ain't doing nobody any good. And now that this was all coming to a head, he had to clear his mind to think.

Claire looked over several pieces of the documents very carefully. She searched every detail and felt uneasy with more disturbing documents.

"I have been matching the documents' dates with the signatures, which almost tells us the story." She picked up one fragile document. "This goes back to 1780, almost a hundred years ago. Can you believe it?" In some familiar way, the long-ago-dated documents confirmed to Claire how vital her writing was. "Look,"—she patted the table— "all of this is a history of people negotiating what was important and valued. Who gave and who took? And it was all buried in a vault, Jed said."

Claire became breathless at the very thought of what she was unfolding. She took a moment to collect herself. She had Lena and Hargrove's full attention. "These newer papers go back to just before the invasion of the troops. It talks about what happened the night H.G. was killed."

Hargrove watched Lena closely. He knew at some point very soon; he'd have to tell Lena that Thomas was the brother of the overseer of Grove Plantation. That it was he, Robert, who was one of the people coming for the land. Lena looked at Hargrove, searching his face as if she were reading his thoughts. Lena was fine with Claire sorting through the papers to make sense of it all, but her mind was still sifting back to something that happened earlier.

"Hargrove, who do you think Jed was talking about? The man that chased the boy in the water for the sack of jewels and caused the child to drown?"

Claire interrupted. "You think any of that was true?" Claire looked at both, unsure what could be counted outside the papers Jed brought. She spoke her out to Lena and Hargrove. "Jed was rambling that he killed the boy because he didn't stop it. Jed ran away when the boy's head did not come back up to the water's surface. The papers are closer to the truth than anything we'll get out of Jed. Something's wrong with him. He talks to himself and cries for no reason. What do you think, Hargrove? Does any of what he said sound right to you?" She turned to see the color leave Hargrove's face.

He hesitated. "Whatever is wrong with Jed is going on in his head!

You must know how to sort it out. But he ain't lying—they did find the body of a boy."

"What!" Lena cried out. Hargrove knew he had to come clean.

"The man that chased the boy into the water was Robert, Lena! The overseer."

"Whatcha saying, Hargrove?" She clasped her hands together but not to pray. Hargrove's eyes watered. By God, he did not want to bring the memories back to her. "You'se sure?"

"Yes, Lena, I'm sure."

Claire saw some private understanding being shared between Hargrove and Lena. She sat quietly.

"What's dis?" Lena was holding a document. Her hands matched her voice; both were trembling.

"Nothing." Hargrove got up quickly and went to Lena. Claire watched his one hand fold over Lena's hand, holding the letter as he sat down next to her; his other hand went to her back and began to rub tenderly. Claire clasped her mouth in shock. This was more than a friend's comfort. She tried to convince herself that it was just a hand, one holding and the other rubbing, but it was more than that. This Claire knew. As a writer, she felt she would be hard-pressed to think of the words to express it. The only word that came to mind, as detailed and meticulous with words as her nature allowed, was intimate. Embarrassed by the thought of Hargrove and Lena being intimate, Claire dropped her head momentarily before reconsidering and glancing up at the pair. Intimate was the word! And more.

Lovers! Hargrove leaned closer and wrapped his arm around Lena's shoulders. Not even the paper that had caused Lena to tremble could have fit in the space between them. Claire watched his face turn towards Lena, his lips brushing her cheek and coming as close to Lena's ear as he could. He was whispering. Claire realized her body had involuntarily leaned forward to listen. What was on the paper that caused Lena to tremble and Hargrove to react immediately and tenderly? What could he be whispering? Ashamed of her actions, she pulled herself upright and cleared her throat, but still, she could not help but watch. Lena sat slightly slumped in the chair, listening intently. Whatever words Hargrove whispered brought tears to Lena. It was too much for Claire to be between the brush of his lips on Lena's cheek and their hands; now, Lena was crying. Hargrove helped to turn Lena towards him and held her in his arms. "Lena, my Lena."

Claire thought it best to leave them alone. She had no idea why, but she was crying, too. She did not bother to say good night. The staircase leading to the bedrooms was chilly. Upon reaching the second floor, Claire hurried along and noticed the lantern light was lit in Isabel and Izabal's room. Claire moved past the closed door on tiptoes. She heard sounds but could not distinguish what, so she moved forward. She stopped, thinking she heard crying. She walked back and pressed her ear against the door. Claire remembered that one had difficulty walking, and both had gone to bed early. She thought the week's adventures were more than a notion to fix one's mind; there were trees in the house and children on the wall. That might be the reason for their early departure to bed. She listened. There was nothing but silence. Of course, Claire considered; the crying was coming from Lena downstairs. She left their door to move to her room. She was glad to discover someone had started a fire in the hearth and lit her lantern. Claire undressed, put on her nightgown, and sat at her desk. She picked up her journal to record the day. Everything on her body ached, and she dozed off before she could finish the second sentence.

*There is more to Lena and Hargrove than I imagined. Of course, my dear Sylvie always said there was. I wonder what or how Sylvie has come to know our most delicate secrets? Is Sylvie…*

It was late morning when Claire awakened. The inkwell remained open, and the pen's ink had bled over most of the page. She had fallen asleep on her desk. "Oh Lord, let this not be a sign!"

Jed, hungry and alone, was awakened by the sun through the window in his room. He got up and washed his face in the cold water in the bowl near the bed. He dried his face with a towel he'd used the day before. It was the first time since he'd joined the women in the big house that no one had left warm water and fresh towels.

He looked down at his new shirt in the kitchen but could not remember putting it on. He became worried about what had happened last night after meeting Hargrove. Sylvie walked into the kitchen. "Good morning, Sergeant Jed!" His failed body reacted strongly; Jed liked it when Sylvie called him a *sergeant* and soon forgot about the shirt and Hargrove. He stood as tall as his tiny body would allow and saluted her. "Good morning, Captain Sylvie. What are my duties this morning?" He snapped his salute from his forehead to his side.

"Go to da coop and get as many eggs as da chickens have laid." She handed him a basket.

"Yes, ma'am!" he responded with pride.

# TWENTY-EIGHT

Robert got to the house exhausted. He headed straight to the barn, gave his horse some water, and fell asleep in the hay nearby. Upon awakening, he got confused, unsure where he was. It was the space and the smell of hay and horse shit that reminded him he was back at the shack. Robert looked around, expecting to see more than just his horse. Then he remembered Lincoln was gone. "Dog better off than the rest of us." His stomach growled. He realized he still had the ham and bacon from days ago in his pocket. He leaned against the wall and began eating. The sour, hard-crusted bread was as dry as his mouth.

He started going over his plans. Knowing that the house was occupied by women and Hargrove was nearby, Robert wanted to go about his next moves carefully. Maybe the white woman was Hargrove's. Once the Negroes were dead and out of the way, he and Sarah would take over the house. Hargrove had to die first. Any man, he thought, that killed his daddy should've been dead! The bitter taste of that day sickened him still. For sure, that Negro woman, Lena, was probably living in the house if she had survived the beating Grove whipped on her, and to think she nearly outran Grove's horse. What the hell, he wondered, has come over the South? The dry biscuit was as hard as horse shit pellets, he thought. He threw the remaining biscuit at the horse and started getting ready.

There was not as much ammunition as he thought. The four men had said five women were living in Culver Tusk, plus the two in the house he'd seen. Robert was worried that Hargrove might have more men looking over the house and land than they had. Take them by surprise;

that would be the best way.

He packed what he needed and fed the horse before walking to the house. There was still just a faint hint of Lincoln's blood on the steps. The door was unlocked. He did not expect Sarah to be up this early or sober. "Sarah?" He was caught off guard to see her sitting at the table, not passed out.

"What da hell you up so early?"

He pulled a canteen out, half filled with booze, and threw it on the table. Sarah didn't jump or reach for it. "What's da hell da matter with you, gal?" he asked mockingly. He let his eyes roam over her, taking in her clean face, her hair pulled up on top of her head and twisted fancy-like.

Sarah had on a blue dress he had not seen in years. Robert looked at the white skin on her arms. She had scrubbed up good; it must have taken her the whole night he belched. Sarah had missed by a long shot if she wanted to please him. The thought that she had washed herself up and put on a dress brought nothing but suspicion to his mind. "Whatcha been doing while I been gone, woman? That nigga Bailey been over here! Or that nigga lover from the North?"

Sarah watched him with steady eyes. She wanted every bit of his anger this morning. It had been a long night for her. Willing herself not to blink wasn't easy. She was sober. Sarah would not take her eyes off Robert. She wanted to drink him in, not the liquor he had thrown at her. Sarah's eyes moved slowly down to his boots and back to his overgrown beard. The smell of his body had already come in and filled the house before he entered. Sarah never noticed how much he smelled worse than an outhouse. Disgusting, but his smell fitted the moment just fine. She lifted her hand intentionally, moving gently over her belly, between her breast, and to her neck; she was caressing herself, slowly and deliberately— something her husband had never done. Her hand stopped when she got to her mother's necklace. She watched for any recognition from Robert.

The rage in his eyes did not seem to be directed at the necklace, though.

He pulled his revolver out from his coat, waving it at her threateningly; unbothered by the act, Sarah blinked once and began to stare him down again. He grunted his disgust, but it was lost on Sarah. She didn't flinch at the gun or his disgust. Nothing! They remained still, watching each other, until Sarah opened her legs wide and laughed. As she threw her head back into the laugh, the pearls caught in the sun's brilliant light coming in the window. *She is crazier than a dog that got rabies,* he thought. The image of Lincoln, panting by his side, passed through his mind. It angered him.

"You dare taunt me, Sarah, huh?"

"Sure, I dare you." She did not care that Robert was walking up to her. She kept her hands on the pearls and a smile on her face. "Sure, I am, honey child. Sure, am."

Robert felt the confusion in his mind like a dog chasing its tail. He had planned to come in, get a few things, leave her some whiskey, and get out, but his plan was turned upside down. Sarah sitting there cleaned up, hair combed, and sober was not what he expected. Robert looked over at the neatly made bed in the corner and thought of tossing her on it and taking her before he took off. Robert slid his good arm down to his groin. "You'se want dis, Sarah?" Sarah made a clucking sound with her mouth. "You'se hear me, Sarah?"

"I WANT MY MOTHER'S JEWELRY, ROBERT!"

"What?" He looked at her throat and saw the pearls. "Where da hell?"

"My mother's jewelry, where is her jewelry!"

"In da goddam river with dat toothless redheaded boy!" he spat in her face. Another handful of sunlight found its way through the grimy window; Sarah chuckled inside, thinking, *It ain't snow.* "Robert, where is my mother's jewelry?" Robert cocked the gun. "I'll show you'se to ask me questions. You'se wanna blame me for dat stupid kid running his stupid self in da river and dat freak of a beast running away, woman?"

He meant to slam the gun against her cheek as he'd done before. To scare the shit out of Sarah, make her piss herself. Robert jammed the steel of the barrel right on her cheekbone. He'd given her man-made dimples a few times and watched with pleasure as they turned blue, then black. Sometimes, the swelling reached her eyes.

Sarah had her idea of where the gun should go. She turned her head slightly to the right and across her lips. The nerves in his arm twitched and started shaking from side to side. Robert tried to grab his bad arm, but it was useless. Sarah held the barrel in her mouth, letting her lips wrap around the cold surface.

"What da…" Robert's bowels loosened, and the urge to shit was nearly unbearable. He looked down the line of the gun into Sarah's eyes; her lashes were as his brother Thomas had described them, longer than the longest day of summer. Sarah's eyes were empty, as if he could have fallen into the greenish-blue pupils and never reached the bottom. Her fingers tenderly left her mother's pearls to touch his hand. His manhood pulled inward, and he felt his sack squeeze tight. *Damn it*, he thought. "*I just wanna take a shit, a damn fucking shit!*

The blast of the gun jerked his hand back and pushed his bowels out, exploding into his pants. His eyes bulged at the image of the back of Sarah's head breaking apart. Blood and scrambled-egg brain shot in the air. Parts of it claimed his forehead. "Damn, Sarah!" he shouted, as if she would or could answer.

It took a few minutes for the room to settle down and even longer for Robert to gather what had happened. Did he? Did she? He looked down at the lower half of her and gasped. She was still upright; her mother's pearls were secure on her neck. Without the baggy pants and his oversized shirt, he looked down as her body slid sideways from the chair. Sarah was pregnant. "Sarah… you got me and Thomas a baby?"

Less than a quarter of a mile away, Shelton and his men had just saddled up when they heard the gunshot. They waited, listening for the direction of the shot. What followed seemed to come from the belly of the devil: a horrid howling. They rode off in the direction of the long, unending howl towards the cabin. The howling had ceased as they arrived, and the door was open. Robert was naked from the waist down.

Shelton and his men ran up on the porch with their guns drawn but were not ready to see a half-naked man holding a bloody hunting knife, kneeling over his near-headless wife. Robert was in the final step of removing the baby. He turned, lifted, and extended its bloody form to the men. "Looka here, I'se got me a toothless boy for sure." Sheldon Wyman pulled his trigger without hesitation and shot Robert dead. He felt it was the best choice. The other choice was to hear anything coming out of the mouth of the man, Robert.

# TWENTY-NINE

Lena awakened to blue vapors with black tips rising from the Ozark Mountains; she understood it meant grief. With that understanding, she dressed herself in bright colors to negotiate with grief in some small way. Around her shoulders, she wrapped a gold lace shawl. It was during breakfast that grief began to tell its story. Izabal or Isabel came down the stairs, brushing past those at the table with barely a greeting. Whichever of the sisters, she carried a large basket out the back door and returned minutes later with it filled with large stones. She gently tossed them into the fire. The sparks of the fire flung wildly into the air. Izabal or Isabel took the hearth's shovel to retrieve them and placed each stone back in the basket. With no recognition of their gaping mouths, the one sister turned and hurried past the women up the stairs. Leaving them in shock. Lena pulled her shawl over her shoulders, and the women remained quiet for the rest of the meal. Afterward, Lena took what remained of the meal and made a plate for Hargrove. He was late this morning. She thought *of all the mornings!*

Down the road, Hargrove drove his wagon down the road to Evenings' home. Evening and Diana greeted him from the porch and welcomed him in. Hargrove was taken back. His mind told him the woman beside Evening was Sister Elizabeth, but his eyes argued it was a lie. It was the first time he'd seen her since picking her up from the train station. "Hargrove, please come in and have some coffee. Have you eaten?" By gawd, he thought, indeed, it was Sister Elizabeth. He'd spent beautiful miles in harsh weather with her voice beside him. "Sister

Elizabeth!" Diana was anxious to tell Hargrove about the miracle that had occurred. But what she saw in his face and voice caused her to whisper to Evening. "It's not time to let anyone know about my new life. Not even my sight. Somethings amiss"

Hargrove said, "I'm here to fetch yawl and take you to Culver without a fight, Evening." Evening didn't offer a fight. She put her hand under Diana's elbow to guide her to the wagon.

"Sister Elizabeth and I planned to visit the women, so you're just in time."

Once at Culver Tusk, Hargrove asked to speak with Lena alone.

"Hargrove, you see the blue mist coming off the mountains; it means grief." Hargrove knelt on one knee in front of her.

"My niece Sarah is dead."

Lena folded her arms in her lap. Her eyes moved slowly over his face. "I'm sorry, Hargrove."

"Things have come to a head; folks at the hub were close to here a week ago. I got enough men circling the property." He nodded in reassurance, taking her hand. "A family is coming in a bit. They'll be safe here with y'awl."

"Who?" Lena asked.

"Bailey, his woman, Mary, and child."

"Dat da Mary dat…?"

"Yes."

He squeezed Lena's hand. "Lena, Robert's dead."

"Dead—you sure?"

"Yes, Shelton killed him." He refused to offer the details he was still grappling with. "I've got to go take some supplies to my men. I'll be back in a few, Lena."

Sylvie was disappointed Hargrove spoke alone with Lena. Hargrove didn't serve in the war. She put back on her uniform and let Jed wear her hat. They were an odd pair, an odd and brave pair. Under the hat, Jed's face beamed. He was taller than he'd ever been or could have prayed to be. Jed had been right, after all; the Negroes had fixed what was wrong with him. They accepted him, and Sylvie needed his service. He had ordered the voices—commanded them—to leave immediately or be court-martialed. The voices left.

"Sergeant!"

"Yes, sir!" Jed returned Sylvie's salute

"Take you'se post at da window facing da pond and let me know if you'se see anything or anybody at once!"

"Yes, sir!" He walked to the window and looked at the beauty of the land, covered with the thick tops of the trees. He didn't run from his post when he heard footsteps. Claire came down the stairs. The women were gathered around the table waiting. Claire's eyes were swollen and red, and she tried to avoid their view. She sat down, thinking it best lest she collapse.

"Are the twins joining us?" Evening inquired to no one in particular, but she noticed all eyes were on Claire. She alone had been up and down the stairs, each time more nervous than before. Sitting there solemnly in her chair, she placed her napkin on her lap and her face in her hands, praying.

"Sylvie?" Her voice was barely recognizable, so low and deep inside her grief. It was enough for Claire to breathe. "Sylvie?"

"Yes, Claire."

"Come sit with me."

"Of course, dear." Sylvie went and put her arms around Claire's shoulder and kissed her cheek. From where she sat, Lena began to put the pieces together as awkwardly as they fit. If Lena had not known better, she would have taken Sylvie for a man. She had heard that some women had disguised themselves to fight in the war, but Sylvie? And what and how did it connect to Claire, who had weeks before crumpled to the ground, crying out, "It is you." Lena shook her head, more clouded than ever. She watched them closely.

"What is it, Claire? You'se been running up and down the stairs, each time carrying more sadness in your face." Lena asked this as gently as possible.

Claire shook her head, still in disbelief. She did not want to share the grief she had held all morning and break anyone else's heart as hers was broken. But it was not something for her to hold on to. There was a dead body, no longer the woman they had known, lying upstairs.

"Last night, I thought I heard crying from their room, but then you, Lena, and I thought… Oh Lord, give me strength."

Lena spoke up to relieve Claire of her burdening news: "Which sister is dead, and how is the other doing?" As firm as the words came out, Lena felt her heart breaking.

"Lena, I am not sure who died, just as we never knew how to tell them apart. I do not know whose name I should call to comfort Isabel or Izabel."

"What did she say when you'se walked in?"

"That sister died in her sleep."

"Whatcha say?"

"I asked her with as much tenderness to the circumstance…feeling the pain of my heart beginning to set in at a loss. For a while, I stood and cried. Finally, I said, 'I could never tell the two of you apart; I do not know to whom to offer comfort and who to grieve, Izabal or Isabel.'"

"What she says?"

"She told me both names to comfort and grieve both will do."

"What?"

"Yes, she looked at me sympathetically as if I held the naivety of a child unable to understand a simple lesson. I was shocked at my embarrassment. She took me in her arms to comfort me!"

"Bless her."

"As if I were a child."

"Lord has mercy."

"Yes, mercy," Claire cried, "She said both are dead, both alive. I held onto her with all my might and cried out for forgiveness. Claire broke under the weight of her own words, collapsing into Sylvie's arms. Sylvie rocked gently back and forth, side to side. The women took turns consoling one another. Evening went to the drawer near the kitchen, bringing back hankies, into which they cried and blew until finally, Lena said, "We'se got to go on up now. Come on, now."

Evening and Sister Elizabeth took each other's hands. Sylvie clasped Claire. Sylvie turned and said, "Jed, we'se got a fallen soldier. You'se got my permission to leave your post." Hargrove had walked in and heard the last of their conversation. He remembered the night of the cherry blossom story and the laughter that had shamed him then. Isabel or Izabal. Hargrove was sorry he had been ashamed of something so tender now—a simple memory of a woman feeling pleasure. He thought back to her words.

"It got so good, I pulled my own hair," one of them had recalled.

"Shut up, woman," Lena had laughed out.

"I ain't lying." Again, one of them, but which one? He didn't care.

He cleared his throat before he spoke. "Y'all go head-on up. I got Lena." Hargrove walked over to where Lena was sitting. He did what the twins had done for years for Lena: stooped down and lifted her full frame into his arms. Hargrove arched his back, pulling Lena in as tightly as he could. Her flesh had grown softer over time and yielded to his arms; Lena cradled in his arms and let her body collapse. The weight of hearing one of the twins died was heavy. The warm smell of rose oil from Lena's body filled Hargrove's nostrils. Lena rested her head on his chest. The quick beating of his heart gave her comfort. Her moans told him new grief was starting to fill the spaces in her body. Hargrove could feel her moans down to his bones.

"It's okay, Lena. I'm here, I'll always be here. Whatever it takes." Life had given Hargrove time to learn to say the words he wished he'd said long ago when she'd declared she was running from the plantation. When They reached the top landing, the front of his shirt was wet with his sweat and her tears. He adjusted his body to see her face. "Look at me, Lena."

Lena lifted her face to him. Hargrove dared himself to do it; he kissed her lips; Lena didn't pull away. Hargrove leaned against the balcony to hold them both up. He couldn't stop kissing. Lena gently pulled her lips away. "Take me in. I'm strong enough; the women need me." Hargrove said. "I love you, Lena." He meant it in more ways than one and for every reason between them. Hargrove was grateful he had the chance to say it, just sorry for the reason the chance was there; one of the women was dead.

Everyone in the room stood quietly around the bed. Hargrove walked Lena closer. Hargrove could not tell how Lena reacted to seeing Izabal and Isabel lying side by side, but the sight caught his breath. Lena's body did not respond. Between the struggle to continue holding Lena and seeing both twins lying down in cream-colored lace dresses, holding hands, Hargrove felt weakened at the stillness of both women, eyes closed. He wanted to know but was afraid to ask, *Are they both dead?* So still were the bodies before him, no sign of breathing from either body.

The window was partially open, and the cool breeze roamed the room. Hargrove found comfort in the fresh air. He finally noticed the hot stones placed under one's armpits to keep the body from getting cold. The other rose off the bed carefully as if not to awaken the other. She leaned over, kissed her sister's cheek, and then turned to them.

"Sister is gone now. We wish to be buried now. She turned to the vast window. The blue mist is lifting, da brightest of the sun is arriving. Looks like a gold halo around the mountain—a gold like you'se shawl, Lena. We'se ready."

*Ready? We'se? Are you planning on jumping in the grave with her? Hargrove thought. The steadiness of her voice confused them all, but they nodded and said, "Yes, we'se ready. "We'se don't want to smell," they nodded. Before we eat supper, we'se must be buried," they nodded. Say goodbye, Sister." They nodded.* Hargrove, get someone to help dig our grave?" Hargrove nodded.

Jed was the first to hear a wagon in the distance, so he ran to the window. "Captain Sylvie, I see people!" The speed with which he took off to his post made Sylvie proud.

Bailey, Mary, and the baby arrived. When the wheels stopped, Lena was seated on the wide porch; Sister Elizabeth, Evening, Claire, Sylvie, and Jed had gathered to meet them. Hargrove walked to his horse. He trusted that the women would handle what needed to be said about the situation better than he could, including the introduction to Bailey and Mary. Izabel or Isabel followed out the door last and walked to the steps to speak. "We'se got a burying to take care of. Ya'll see dat halo over da mountain?" Mary handed the baby to Bailey. She jumped off the wagon and ran to the edge of the porch. "Yes, ma'am, we'se watched dat halo all da way here. I'se Mary. My Bailey, he told me somebody who loved good has left us." Mary turned over her shoulder. "Dat Bailey. Bailey says God put dat halo on ya'll loved one. They spent the next minutes making acquaintances before Mary asked, "Ma'am, is it okay if I ask, ya'll, the name of da person who God granted such a lovely halo so dat, I'se can pray properly?" Everybody answered without direction, hesitation, or reason, with a burst of laughter, "We'se!"

Hargrove, his handyman, rode up to robust laughter. Hargrove thought, *Go figure, these women, none like 'em!* He glanced at Sister Elizabeth, thinking, this ain't the nun with the bellowing outfit. She was right at home. Bailey looked at the shovels and then at the women. "It be my honor to help dig in God's sweet labor." Lena took off her shawl, slowly and with deliberation, and let it rest on the chair. Grief had negotiated, allowing the women their humor on this day. She understood more than she had when she awakened to the blue mist with black tips; the mountain was wearing a halo. She said, "Women of Culver Tusk, I'se suggest we'se wash sister in da river and we'se git in with her. River holds life and death. She knows what we'se need. Sylvie, git your prayer bowl and fetch dat wagon, you'se carry the logs for me to ride in." "Da wagon wheels ain't' gonna…" "Gonna what Sylvie? Hold my big behind! If da wheels fall off, I'll crawl." Claire gasped, "Unbelievable!" Bailey nodded to the men, signaling they best get on with men's business. Izabal or Isabel said. "Lena, dat's a fine idea most fitting for us." The wagon wheels did their job. They found a good spot near the river near a field of lotus flowers. The air Sister Elizabeth said, "Smells pretty." Mary respectfully went to sit under a tree nearby with Grace. Mary took in the soothing sounds of the water splashing and the women singing and humming. She didn't know what to do with the overwhelming joy that filled her heart. So, she whispered precisely what her eyes saw to her sleeping daughter. Mary tucked as many words as possible in her memory, hoping she'd remember, thinking Bailey would like this story.

When they were done, sister was shrouded in gold cloth. They headed to the burial site, and the men followed their lead. Sister was placed in the wooden coffin Hargrove had fetched. He waited until he got the nod that it was okay, and they put her coffin.

The halo rose to the center of the sky, and the heat told them it was time. They walked away in silence. They returned to Culver Tusk—the last place Mary had been enslaved to.

Bailey watched Mary intently when they arrived at the house. It had been many years since Mary had been back to Culver Tusk. Mary was focused on their sleeping child and her new friend. "Mary, I'm stepping outside for a minute. Be right back." If she heard Bailey, Mary didn't respond. She was soaking up the attention their baby was getting.

"We'se ain't had a chance to ask girl or boy?" Lena asked. She caught herself from adding *squash* and smiled.

"Girl. She named Grace after Bailey's mother." The women gathered around as Mary lifted the blanket further off the little girl's face.

"Oh Lord, if she ain't the picture of Grace, I don't know who is," Sister Elizabeth exclaimed. "And her hair is so dark and curly." She looked over at Mary. "Who does she get her hair from, all thick, curly, and shiny?" Lena's eyes widened, replaying Sister Elizabeth's words.

"Am I losing my mind!" Lena asked, leaning back in the chair, shocked by the return of Sister Elizabeth's sight.

"Sister Elizabeth, … you'se see…how you'se…? What is…?" Lena was stumbling over her words.

Evening spoke for Sister Elizabeth. "She doesn't go by Sister Elizabeth. Her name is Diana."

"What?"

"And yes, she got her eyesight back, mostly." Diana smiled. Claire thought this was the best time to get a drink and did so for each of them. The men, including Bailey and Jed, talked on the front lawn. Jed was pointing and gesturing like he was about to fly. Lena noticed a few others had joined them. Mary asked Lena if she would like to hold the baby.

"I'se love to. Bring me little Grace." She laughed. "Lord, she is a big baby. She crawls?" Her voice was thick with longing. The smell of the child caused her to close her eyes.

Claire moved toward her. "Lena?"

"I'm okay, Claire. I'm more than okay. These happy tears." Bailey walked in and looked around. By every indication, it looked like the threat of violence was calming down. He was considering taking Mary out of Culver Tusk.

"Ma'am?" Mary was speaking to Lena. There was a plea to her tone. "I'se used to work in dis house fo' we'se freed. Ma'am I'se like go upstairs to look around?"

Bailey's body was used to hard labor, but it didn't know what to make of this rush of feeling, making him weak and helpless. Bailey walked over to Mary and shook his head. "No, Mary."

"Please, Bailey." This she said firmly, but inside her words was a desperate plea. She stood before him in her brown cotton dress, the top bottoms loose, ready for breastfeeding at any moment. Mary had plaited her hair in two thick braids and pinned them around her head like a crown. Her face was fuller since becoming a mother, and her skin was darker. Bailey loved her skin even more. It seemed like anything with light was drawn to Mary's skin, everything from candle flame to moonlight. The sunlight on her face let Bailey see where her plea awaited him to say yes. But he couldn't. She was doing all she could to hold herself in one piece; Bailey could see that.

Lena said, "You can do whatever you'se feel you got to do, Mary. Bailey, let her go and fix only what she can fix for herself."

Bailey reached out to take her hand, but Mary did not reach back. "I'se got to do dis alone, Bailey." And with that, Mary moved away and walked timidly up the staircase. Thinking back on the last time she and Miss Eloise had stood, terrified, when the gunshots rang out. How suddenly that day so long ago started with the anticipation of Master H.G.'s arrival turned into murder and grief. She listened to her footsteps, fantasizing, her feet moving back in time. *When I open the door, my child will be sitting there. The world will turn around long enough for me to grab him and run.* Her throat burned with pain, and she bit her lip and opened the door. Sunlight greeted her; the room was another world from her memory. This room felt tender. It was Claire's room now. The porcelain rose-colored kerosene lamp sat on the desk, and paper and an inkwell sat beside an open book. The bed was covered in a delicate, brightly colored quilt. The light shone on a sewing basket in the corner, the bright fabrics spilled onto the floor. Mary went to the spot where her son often stood fanning the child on the days Peter visited his mother's room. Mary glanced at the adjourning. She knelt at the center point. She put her palms together and prayed. Bailey had reluctantly stayed downstairs, but he moved away from the women. He stood pensively at the bottom of the staircase, ready to run up at the slightest sound of anguish. In the background, he heard Grace stirring and knew she'd wake up hungry. He prayed it would be so, and Grace would cry loud enough to bring her mother back down those stairs.

It took a few moments, but Grace's wails and squirming sprang forth and startled Lena. She couldn't help but laugh to herself. This is the difference between holding a squash or a baby. "Come git dis child fore she flies out my arms."

Bailey rushed over and picked up his daughter. "It's okay, little Grace." His voice was soothing.

"You want me to hold her?" Diana asked tenderly.

"No, thank you, ma'am. She hungry. Dat's what dis cry is. She wants her mama's breast." He heard the fast steps of Mary descending the staircase, and his eyes widened with fear. Bailey prepared himself for a foaming mouth or a dizzy spell over Mary. Nothing on her face called out either a spell or madness, just Grace's mother running to her baby.

"Give her to me, Bailey. Let me feed her fo' she git too frustrated." Bailey took kindly to Mary's urgent tone, letting him know she had fully surrendered to their daughter's needs. Grace was wiggling and crying, so Bailey was glad to hand her to her mama. Her body twisted side to side like a fish going upstream. Grace kicked her chubby brown legs out stiff and let out a good wail.

"Here you'se go, Mary." Mary got hold of her child, had her nipple in the baby's mouth in one swoop, and sat down at the table. She started humming.

Bailey put himself right down next to them. He kissed her neck, then took his time to gaze over her face. "You'se okay, Mary?"

Mary stopped humming; her bottom lip trembled. "I'se be awright'." Her answer didn't satisfy him; he saw her bottom lip tremble, which told Bailey Mary's heart needed an answer. He guided Mary face away from looking down at Grace with his hand. Bailey needed to see Mary's eyes. If she looked directly back into his eyes, it would be okay. Not looking at his hair or past him, He wanted Mary to look him in his eyes. Mary's eyes met his; he saw she'd been crying up those stairs. Her lashes were still wet, but she was looking directly at him.

Bailey reassured, he whispered. "It will be awright, Mary, for sho." Their eyes stayed locked while the sound of Grace's hunger was being satisfied. Bailey willed himself not to blink. He wanted Mary to believe in everything this moment had to offer. Grace, his Mary, and himself were all they needed.

"Bailey," Mary whispered.

Bailey leaned himself closer. "Yes, Mary?" Bailey was so close he could smell her sweet breast milk. "What tis it?"

"His name be Joseph."

Bailey tilted his head up just enough to look again into her eyes. She started crying. Bailey's tears came forward, and he thanked God for them. He needed Mary to know she'd never been alone in her pain for her dead son. Bailey said with the same pride and love when Gracie was named, "Mary... my, our son's name is Joseph," The tension lines that always seemed a part of Mary's face, even when she slept, softened like his words were a hand running across freshly washed sheets making the bed. "Yes, Bailey, our little Joseph and Grace's big brother...Joseph." Across the room, Lena was watching. She wanted to know what happened up the stairs, but all she could do was watch with her eyes at the sliver of space between them. And read it: A light from a single star in the space between them called God's love. Lena turned reluctantly away from the two; love like a sunrise always brought her great joy.

"What da Ozark Mountains say?" Lena directed the question to either Isabel or Izabal. Whichever one was left would know.

"We's okay." Not much else was needed; the mountains had spoken. Something out there had seemed fit for them to be safe for the time. Lena closed her eyes and prayed before asking Claire to fill the glasses.

In the end, when the group at the hub got the news of Sarah's death and how it happened, they felt partially responsible. They blamed themselves for not seeing her troubles or even seeing her, for that matter. So, when the man with the ax and two others returned after retracing their steps, the men shouted at them, "It happened again plain as the nose on my face; dat mansion disappeared, nuthing but da trees!"

"What? Culver Tusk?"

"Hell, yeah! Culver Tusk.  The ax slipped from his hands, and he didn't bother to retrieve it. The ax proved useless, along with their guns.

"What about da Indian woman y'all saw last time?"

He looked at the two men with him and then back at the group in disbelief. "Is ya'll stupid! Ya'll think we's stayed around waiting on some dam Injun!? We'se got away as soon as we saw what we saw… a plantation house disappeared." He took a deep breath, shaking his head in suspicion. "If dem Negroes can make a house disappear and put three-hundred-year-old trees in its place and back again, whatta hell da gone do to us? I'se gittin' the hell away from this cursed land." He tried to shut his mouth when he was done talking, but it gapped open the lower jaw, trembling. The man moved past the group into the distance. "Dis land is cursed."

Sam had been the first to leave, and that's exactly what many did over time: they got away from this new South but took their southern ways with them. They migrated to different parts of the new world, places like Ohio and Wisconsin, and the sisters discarded their husbands and went back to Ireland. They decided they would keep their American lives to themselves, they would go back single, and there were no children as evidence. The one sister's question rang in their head: *What about love? What about it?* Those Southerners who went to the cities felt like foreign birds, displaced. They were country folks glaring up at the tall buildings with their mouths open even in the rain. Northerners asked, noting their peculiar ways, "Where you from?"

They had packed everything they owned, including their anger. They answered defiantly, "The South!"

# EPILOGUE

Each woman left the house to die on a day that was meant for their dying, one by one, as quietly as the first sign of rain on the forehead, except for Lena. Lena rolled off the bed just as death was coming and hit the floor. "Leave me here for now. Let me listen to da wood tell me da story of trees again." Done!

Until only one was left, Claire. She put down her knitting and sewing basket for good to attend to the memories in the house. Claire did not believe in ghosts like most folks did, but in the evening, more than once, she saw the shadows of children appear on the wall as they had so many years ago. She dared not ask them, "Where are you from?" for fear they might leave sooner than later, knowing children had to grow up sometime seeking their own stories. Claire just hoped they would grow into thoughtful, kind people like the ones she had once lived with in freedom.

(An excerpt from Claire's writings, the last surviving member of the former plantation home) (B.1804–1900)

*I write each word with prayer exactly like a painter's brush on canvas. To a mother's last memory of her child, to be sold, remembering herself as a child found in her mother's cry—never forgotten. I ask myself, pen to paper in prayer: Whose imagination are we living in?*

*Dearest ones,*

*I share with much certainty our lives after enslavement and war, which we gathered up to live in this story. We were gathering pieces of ourselves in the scattered remains of our lives. We were seeking wholeness. We discovered our god self as an offering to one another. With that knowledge, I offer gratitude and thanks to each of your spirits: Lena, Isabel, Izabal, Sylvie.*

*Diana and Evening came to visit today. They are neither shy nor embarrassed in their affection toward one another. They take their fingertips to place on each other's lips to hush the secrets they only share playfully. Mr. Hargrove came along with them. His body hurts, yet he continues, letting the cane carved with each of our faces Sylvia made lead him on his journey.*

*We had a good, quiet time eating our excellent supper. I made a pot of collard greens along with the food Evening brought. Diana has learned to make the best sweet tea and put some liquor in it. We had a good time, the best we could without you all being here. Dead, gone, goodbye. The chairs you once sat in, morning and night, remind me how empty the world feels without you. Evening reminds me that only an empty chair can offer love to sit.*

*We talk very little when they visit. They try hard not to mention y'awl, but what else is there to talk about? I ask them. Nothing!*

*How else am I to show how much I love and miss each of you if not through my memories? Here is my question to only myself. I have been* enslaved and freed and have *come to know love from its four directions. What would the world want to teach me after knowing these revelations?*

*It is only death that can be my teacher now.*

*I noted that Hargrove's lip-smacking has gotten worse. What teeth he has remaining is bothering him. He eats slowly and stares at your empty chair, Lena. He lives in a memory only you and he lived.*

*One or the other asks me, "How are you feeling today, Miss Claire?"*

*"Fine," I tell them. "Just fine."*

*"And what you do today, Miss Claire?"*

*"Nothing. I am old. I have nothing else to do but wait until you come to that door, and I don't answer." We laugh at this but know it is all our truth as people. One day, someone will speak our name and knock at our door, and we won't answer. We are gone. The callers and knockers are left to find suitable memories to keep them company. Thank you for my memories. I feel both blessed and rich with company.*

*It has not rained in months, but the tulips continue to bloom without rain. It is the memory of rain, I suppose, they rise toward. Like the dark people of the earth, the flowers find ways of being magical when their roots are denied water and, even more, their thirst. The memory of thirst lives in our souls, and we stick our tongues out accordingly. There is so much more I wish I knew of your lives and you of mine.*

*Sylvie, Isabel, Izabal, and Lena, you have taught me that dying never meant we were gone but that we were here. We are like clouds that break away but never leave the sky. Love is a gift that sought us out, and we had enough sense to let it come in without trying to claim it selfishly. What I claim is your names in my writings. I claim that you were here. I claim our journeys continue in freedom and love in one breath...until the next, from our stories to God's ears:*

We'se don't belong to nobody but ourselves...and each other. We's free."

*Eternal Love,*
*Claire*